The One That Got Away

Helen Warner was born in Northern Ireland and moved to East Anglia at the age of four. She studied English at London University (Goldsmiths College) before embarking upon a career in TV. She has worked on many award-winning shows, including *This Morning*, *Loose Women*, *Come Dine with Me*, *Deal or No Deal* and *The Paul O'Grady Show*. Helen is married to her childhood sweetheart and they live in East Anglia with their two children.

Also by Helen Warner

Stay Close to Me

With or Without You

The Story of Our Lives

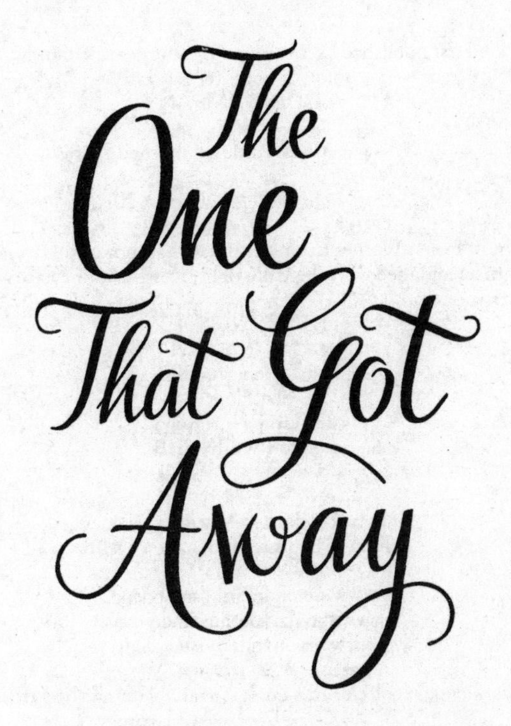

Helen Warner

SIMON &
SCHUSTER

London · New York · Sydney · Toronto · New Delhi

A CBS COMPANY

First published as *RSVP* in 2011 in Great Britain by
Simon & Schuster UK Ltd
A CBS COMPANY

This paperback edition published 2018

1 3 5 7 9 10 8 6 4 2

Simon & Schuster UK Ltd
1st Floor
222 Gray's Inn Road
London WC1X 8HB

Simon & Schuster Australia, Sydney
Simon & Schuster India, New Delhi

www.simonandschuster.co.uk
www.simonandschuster.com.au
www.simonandschuster.co.in

A CIP catalogue record for this book is available from the British Library

Paperback ISBN: 978-1-4711-7714-9
eBook ISBN: 978-0-85720-123-2

Typeset in the UK by M Rules
Printed and bound by CPI Group (UK) Ltd, Croydon, CR0 4YY

For Rob
My rock(star)

Mr & Mrs G King
request the pleasure of

Anna McKenna plus guest

at the wedding of their daughter

Rachel to Toby McKenzie

24 July 2010
2 p.m.
at
St George's Chapel,
Fulham

RSVP: 47, Evesham Mews, Cheltenham

Anna

May 2010

Even before she picks up the envelope she knows what it is. She stares at it for a moment, letting it lie amidst a sea of circulars on the floor beneath the letterbox before lifting it up and slowly turning it over in her hand. She feels the tightness in her chest, the familiar pain that she has grown so used to over the past ten years. She takes a deep, slow breath and waits for the ache to subside as she examines the envelope carefully. The paper is thick, creamy, expensive. The address has been handwritten in silver ink in a gothic style and there is a tiny, delicate silver heart on the flap at the back.

Sliding her thumbnail carefully under the seal, she opens it and removes the card within. As she does so, several filmy silver hearts flutter down and land on her bare feet. She glances down at them and wonders distractedly if she is already crying and the silver pieces of paper are, in fact, teardrops. Her vision is blurred with tears, a few words float into focus:

at the wedding of their daughter

The words swim in front of her eyes and she can't read any more. She pushes the card back into the envelope and plunges it deep into the pocket of her bathrobe, before padding into the kitchen. Feeling suddenly light-headed, she lurches towards the sink and vomits.

Then, as she gulps in great lungfuls of air and crouches shivering on the cold slate tiles, she marvels yet again at the physical manifestation of that most common of emotions – a broken heart.

January 2010

To: All year 2000 English Lit grads
From: Miranda Brown
Subject: ENGLISH LIT REUNION! TEN YEARS ON!
Date: 8 December 2009

Hey, everyone!
Can you believe it's been a whole decade since we English Lit students last darkened the doors of Trinity College? Well, you know I always was a party girl and I think this momentous milestone calls for a party! No excuses, get your dancing shoes on and join me to party like it's 1999 – again!

Where? Why, the Students' Union, of course!
When? 16 January 2010
Time? Any time after 8 p.m.
RSVP: Me!!!

Maybe she should have ignored the e-mail. She intended to at first. But every time she opened up the large, clunky, old-fashioned laptop she used to prepare lesson plans for her class of 7-year-olds, there it was. A little flicker of something approaching excitement began to dance in a corner of her brain and she couldn't help but wonder if *he* would be there. Then excitement would dissolve into pure, liquid horror at the prospect of coming face to face with him after all this time.

'Go!' Anna's flatmate, Clare, ordered in her typically brisk, no-nonsense style. 'You need closure. He'll probably be fat and bald with no teeth and then you'll wonder why you've been pining for him all this time.' They had both laughed. She and Clare had been at Cambridge together. She knew him. She knew that time would have barely breathed over his perfect face.

'Go!' laughed Matt, her laidback friend and fellow teacher. 'It'll be good to catch up with your old uni mates. I went to mine a couple of years ago and it was a laugh. I don't know why you're even hesitating,' he had added, finishing his pint with a satisfied slurp and heading for the bar again. No, Matt didn't know why because she hadn't told him.

'Go!' urged her mum when she told her during her daily phone call back home to Suffolk. 'Seriously, sweetheart, you do need to see him. To know for sure. One way or the other.'

So, having spent the Christmas holidays umming and aahing and changing her mind over and over again, she went. She took hours to decide what to pack into her battered Mulberry overnight bag, a much-loved twenty-first birthday present from her mum. Eventually, she settled on a floaty silver-grey dress and ballet pumps coupled with thick black opaque tights to avoid looking too desperate. Which is exactly how she felt.

Clare hadn't studied English and therefore wasn't invited to the reunion, so Anna was having to go on her own. Most people were staying at the same hotel in the centre of Cambridge and several of the girls from her course had been in touch to ask if she wanted to share a room, but she had declined, each time giving a different excuse. At the back of her mind, she knew there was really only one reason why she wanted to make sure she had a room to herself that night.

It was after 9 p.m. by the time she had summoned enough courage to head shakily into the night. The streetlamps gave everything a ghostly glow and she pulled her coat tightly around her, shivering with both cold and nerves as she walked the short distance along glistening cobbled streets towards the students' union, the scene of so much fun and laughter all those years ago. As she approached the building, the sound of music floated across the still night air and she smiled to herself as she recognized a U2 song from the year 2000 which had seemed to encapsulate everything back then: 'Stuck in a Moment You Can't Get Out of'. She stopped for a second to steady herself, struck by how much the words still resonated ten years later. Then she tugged open the door and plunged headlong into her past.

May 2010

Clare arrives home from work several hours later to find Anna sitting on the floor, still wearing her bathrobe and cradling her beloved cat, Scratch.

'Anna?' she says curiously, her high heels making a satisfying click on the stone floor as she walks into the kitchen.

'What's the matter? What are you doing sitting down there? And why aren't you dressed?' She unbelts her chic beige mac, shrugs it off and dumps both the coat and her sleek black Smythson briefcase on the table, then stands with her hands on her hips, frowning down at Anna as she waits for an answer.

Anna doesn't reply. She's not ready to put it into words just yet; to voice it is to make it real. Instead, she snuggles Scratch's soft nut-coloured fur and closes her eyes. Clare has brought in with her the sweet, damp smell of late spring and for a moment Anna thinks how intoxicating it is. 'Better than any perfume,' she murmurs.

'What?' says Clare, confused, the frown lines on her forehead smoothing slightly. Clare has many wonderful qualities but patience isn't one of them. 'Oh well, if you're not going to tell me . . .' she tuts irritably, scooping up her post from the scrubbed wooden table and shuffling through it as if she couldn't care less that her closest friend and flatmate for the past ten years is acting like an extra from *One Flew Over the Cuckoo's Nest*.

Anna places Scratch on the floor, where he looks at her curiously before flicking his tail and heading off in search of food. 'Bored with you now,' he seems to be saying. She reaches into the pocket of her bathrobe, where the invitation has been hiding guiltily all afternoon. Her heart bangs as her fingers close around it and she pulls out the envelope, noticing as she holds it out towards Clare that her hands are shaking.

'Invitation to Toby's wedding.' She coughs slightly as she speaks, her throat dry and constricted.

'Oh,' says Clare, glancing knowingly at her and depositing her own post back on the table. She opens the envelope and looks at the invitation. 'Well, at least he invited you,' she begins tentatively, her dark eyes flickering towards Anna again. 'And you've got a plus one – that means I can come with you and keep an eye on you.'

'No!' Anna shrieks, making them both jump. She shakes her head fiercely. 'I'm not going! How the bloody hell can I?'

Clare sighs a long, deep sigh. 'You should go, Anna,' she says, looking at her from under her long, dark lashes. 'It might help you accept the way things have worked out. To put it behind you once and for all.'

'You said that about the reunion and look what happened!' Anna shoots back triumphantly. For once, she has the last word.

January 2010

The room was remarkably unchanged. The scuffed woodblock floor had a few more stains and the dark red banquettes had a few more rips, but the smell was achingly familiar. Anna made her way through the packed room towards the bar, looking straight ahead and not making eye contact with anyone.

'Anna!' Miranda, who had organized the reunion, ran towards her, a glass of champagne held aloft in her hand, and engulfed her in a cloud of expensive perfume, drawing her into her deep, sparkly cleavage for a hug. 'I'm *so* glad you came!' she squealed.

Anna felt some of the tension leave her body as Miranda began to gabble furiously about what everyone was up to. It turned out she was married to a wealthy businessman and already had a 2-year-old daughter.

'And what about you? Are you marri—' she began.

'No,' Anna cut her off quickly. 'Still single. No kids.'

'You drama lot are all the same,' Miranda grinned, referring to the tight-knit group of students who had formed the core of the drama society back then. 'Commitment-phobes, all of you! Mind you, I heard that . . .' Miranda stopped suddenly, catching herself. 'Ooh, sorry, how rude of me – you haven't got a drink. What would you like?' she said. 'A glass of poo?'

Anna grinned at her nickname for champagne. How times had changed from the days when they would nurse a half of cider for hours, unable to afford anything else. The memory triggered another wave of nostalgia. 'I'll have a cider,' she smiled. 'For old times' sake.'

Miranda's eyes widened. 'Oh, yes! How brilliantly retro!' she cried, turning to the bar to order. She had always been this fizzing ball of energy and she had sometimes irritated Anna back then with her loud gurgling laughter and endless chatter, but watching her now, Anna felt a sudden surge of fondness for her kind, sunny disposition, so ready to see the good in everyone. She had barely aged and a quick scan of the room told Anna that the same could be said for most of the other girls too. Some even looked younger than before, while the boys generally seemed to be either balding or fat, or both.

She couldn't see him, but she knew he would be the exception.

As she sipped her cider and chatted with Miranda, a group of old friends gathered around them, chatting and reminiscing, and she felt a little grip of panic that maybe he wasn't coming. Her eyes darted as she searched for him in vain. Eventually, she couldn't stand the tension a moment longer and asked one of the girls, Sissy, if she had seen him.

'Oh! Yes, I'm sure he's here somewhere,' Sissy said, frowning as she looked around. 'Have you kept in touch? You were so close, weren't you? Oh, until . . .' She trailed off, remembering what had happened and how sensitive the subject had been.

'It was a long time ago,' Anna said quickly. 'All that's history now. But it would be nice to catch up.'

Sissy nodded vigorously, looking relieved that she hadn't blundered by bringing up the past. 'I'll tell him you're looking for him if I see him.'

Another half an hour passed and still he didn't appear. Anna looked around hopelessly, deciding that if he still wasn't there in the next fifteen minutes, she would leave.

But just as she was about to give up hope, there he was.

Time seemed to freeze and her ears were filled with a rushing sound as he appeared in front of her, wearing that slightly lopsided smile which reached all the way up to his grey-green eyes. He was dressed in a slightly crumpled white shirt which set off his olive skin, tucked into a pair of jeans that effortlessly hugged his long legs. His face looked older but even more chiselled and beautiful than she remembered.

'Hello, Anna.' He spoke softly, his gaze piercing.

'Hello, Toby,' she replied, unable to draw her eyes away from his.

'I wasn't sure you'd come,' he said, leaning forward and kissing her softly on the cheek. She closed her eyes momentarily as his lips touched her skin, instantly transported back to a happier time. A time when he was hers.

'I wasn't sure either,' she said at last, when she felt sure she could speak. 'But I'm glad I did. It's so lovely to see everyone.'

'It is,' he agreed, looking affectionately at the faces around them. Their little gang had been so close back then. It felt good that they could be so easy back in each other's company.

They stood together in silence for a moment, both drifting back in time, painful and beautiful memories surfacing then fading.

'So,' he said after the longest of pauses, 'tell me all about you ten years on, Anna. I want to know it all. Don't leave anything out.'

The years melted away as they began to talk. Toby had always had the ability to make whoever he was talking to feel like the centre of the universe and Anna could feel herself blossoming again under the spotlight of his gaze. He laughed as she told him stories about her teacher training, which she had done in Aberystwyth in Wales. She told him tales about the tiny pupils now in her care and all about her life living with Clare in London. Toby had loved Clare and she had loved him back then. Until that fateful night.

'So, neither of you have settled down then?'

Anna shook her head quickly. Lots of boyfriends had come and gone but none had lasted more than a matter of weeks for either of them. Clare was searching for something while Anna was waiting for something. Something – or someone – that was standing in front of her right now.

'So, what about you?' she asked, her heart hammering with excitement at being back in his presence again after so long.

'Oh, you found each other then!' cried Sissy, coming up to join them before Toby could answer. She was swaying slightly and Anna could tell from the alcohol fumes that she was quite drunk.

Neither Toby nor Anna replied. It was as if they were locked in their own invisible bubble. Anna wanted Sissy to go away so that she could have Toby to herself for a little longer. But she wasn't going anywhere.

'Has Toby told you his news?' Sissy said, giving Anna a conspiratorial wink and squeezing in between her and Toby.

The smile died on Toby's lips and a shadow of panic passed over his face. 'No. I . . . er, I hadn't told her,' he stuttered. 'Not yet.'

'Toby's getting married!' Sissy exclaimed, before he could stop her.

Anna's eyes, which had not left Toby's, must have asked the question because he answered it. 'Yes,' he said quietly. 'It's true.'

If the music hadn't been playing so loudly, Anna wondered if it would have been possible to hear her heart splintering into a million pieces. She forced her features into a half-smile. 'Congratulations,' she whispered.

'And, Toby,' Sissy continued, linking her arm through Anna's, blissfully unaware of the torment her words were causing, 'don't think we've forgotten the pact we all made to invite each other to our weddings! I hope you're not going to renege on a promise!'

'But that was when we thought it would be OUR wedding!' Anna wanted to scream. Instead, she gently unhooked her arm and, screwing up every ounce of dignity she could muster, turned to face them both. 'Well, I think I'd better be going,' she said carefully. 'It's been so lovely to see you all.' Her bottom lip wobbled slightly as she spoke and she knew she was going to cry if she didn't get out of there quickly.

Without waiting for an answer she spun around and headed for the door. 'See you at the wedding!' slurred Sissy to her retreating back.

May 2010

Anna's bottom is numb and her legs tingle with pins and needles. She gathers the folds of her robe together and finally gets to her feet, shaking each leg tentatively as the feeling gradually returns and seeps slowly downwards.

Clare, who towers above her in her bare feet, let alone in the four-inch spiked heels she is wearing today, reaches down and puts her arm around her. 'Come on, Anna,' she urges gently, squeezing the top of her arm. 'You can get through this.'

'I can't!' Anna wails. 'I just can't seem to get over him. The pain is still so raw. Surely, after ten bloody years, I should have moved on?' She raises her eyes up towards Clare helplessly, feeling like a toddler looking to a parent for comfort.

Clare's eyes darken to the colour of sepia ink as she tries, just as she has done so many times before, to think of something reassuring to say, but this time words seem to fail her. Instead, she loosens her grip and makes her way over to the fridge. It is a big, silver, American-style model which Clare insisted they have when they first moved into the flat, yet so far Anna has only ever seen her put white wine or champagne in it. Sure enough, she retrieves a bottle of fizz and kicks the door shut with her shoe.

'I'm really not in the mood to celebrate,' Anna protests gloomily as Clare opens the brushed steel cabinet where they keep their glasses and pulls out two champagne flutes. After opening the bottle with a practised pop, she expertly pours two glasses, the fizz racing to just below the rim before sighing back into the pale gold liquid.

'Take it,' she orders, handing one of them to Anna. 'This is an emergency.'

Anna takes the glass she proffers. She has known Clare long enough now to know that sometimes resistance is futile. Clare is a criminal lawyer – a damn good one too – and as far as Anna can tell she is able to persuade anyone to do anything.

Clare takes Anna by the hand and leads her into the sitting room, where they sink down into the comforting softness of the sofa. Anna sips the champagne in tiny mouthfuls, enjoying the tickle of the bubbles on her parched throat. Who cares if this is a sure-fire way to make her feel even worse later on. For now, it feels good.

'Right,' Clare says, gulping back her champagne and tucking her long legs up underneath her, her heels discarded on the wooden floor.

'Oh God,' Anna mutters. 'Here we go, time for some straight-talking . . .'

Clare grins. 'You know me so well. Now, before I say anything, you know that I love you, OK?'

Anna blinks back at her, mentally preparing herself for the onslaught. Clare has a surgeon's skill for taking people apart, using words as her scalpel, before building them back up again.

Clare doesn't wait for her to reply, simply nodding to

herself before continuing. 'So, here's the thing: you have GOT to get a grip, Anna!'

Anna almost flinches as the stinging slap of Clare's words hits her and tenses in preparation for the next verbal punch.

'I know you still have strong feelings for Toby but after everything that happened ...' She lets her words hang in the air like a little puff of poison between them. Anna closes her eyes. She doesn't want to think about what he did. Or what she did. 'Well, maybe now you have to accept that neither of you is going to be able to forgive and forget, so you have to move on with your life. He has. Clearly. The invitation is all the proof you need. Now you need to do the same.'

Anna inhales deeply, feeling a little winded. 'Ouch,' she says, smiling slightly.

Clare watches her for a minute, as if weighing up what to say next, before continuing: 'You immerse yourself in those dreary bloody poems and paintings of yours, as if you're some kind of tragic Pre-Raphaelite heroine, who'll one day be found floating face down in a lake with your hair festooned with flowers.'

Anna's lips twitch slightly as she waits for Clare to go on. She is getting into her stride now.

'But this is the twenty-first century, Anna! You're a grown woman with a responsible job and a life. You're not some drippy virgin, trailing the streets in her flowing gown, muttering about going to a nunnery!'

'Enough!' Anna laughs now, unable to sustain the misery a second longer.

Clare takes her hand, which looks tiny in hers. 'You are

beautiful. You are clever. And most of all, you are without doubt the loveliest person who ever lived.'

Anna shakes her head, embarrassed by her words.

'Yes, you are! Don't argue with me, young lady, because you know I am always right.'

Anna drops her head in defeat. 'But I love those poems – they're beautiful,' she murmurs weakly. Ever since her mid-teens, when her mum, also a teacher, first introduced her to the poetry of Tennyson, Keats, Donne and Shakespeare, she has adored those tales of lovers driven to despair by their passion.

'That's open to debate,' Clare cuts her off crisply. 'The truth is, Anna, you are wasting your life pining for someone who is now well and truly taken. I'm sorry if that sounds harsh, but it's a fact. What you need to do is accept the blow that this invitation undoubtedly is and turn it to your advantage.'

'And how do I do that?' she sighs, her eyelids starting to droop as the effects of the champagne on an empty stomach begin to take hold.

'I've decided,' Clare says, with a note of triumph in her voice, 'that this is going to be the start of a whole new chapter for both of us. You need to put your past behind you and I need to try and build some kind of future and stop acting like a teenager. So, not only are both you and I going to go to this wedding, we're going to have a bloody good time and then, when it's over, we're going to draw a line in the sand and say goodbye to that part of our lives once and for all. You never know, Anna, by this time next year, you might have met the love of your life.'

'I've already met him!' Anna protests, frustrated that

Clare doesn't seem to understand that even after all that's happened, there will never be anyone else but Toby for her.

Clare, who always has to have the last word, chinks her glass against Anna's. 'That's open to debate,' she says firmly. 'Conversation closed.'

Admissions Department,
Trinity College,
Cambridge,
CB2 1TQ

Anna McKenna,
Stubbs Cottage,
Church Lane,
Stebbingfield,
Suffolk,
IP18 7PQ

5 January 1997

Dear Ms McKenna,

We have now reviewed all our applications and I am glad to be able to write to offer you a place to read English at Trinity College for the BA degree from October 1997 on condition that you achieve the following examination results:

A*, A, A
at A level.

I should be grateful if you could let me know whether or not you accept our offer.

Yours sincerely,
Dr John Ashton
Tutor for Admission

October 1997

The cavernous room echoed with nervous laughter and the air of tense desperation was palpable as Anna allowed herself to be swept into the throng of excited young bodies. A wave of energy carried them all in the same direction, swirling and twisting like a human whirlpool. Her body tingled with heat and nerves as she gazed around in wonderment, marvelling that she was actually here. Outside, the biting wind brought with it the chilly reminder that winter was on its way, but inside this hall at least, it felt as though summer sweltered on.

Trestle tables laid out with the paraphernalia of dozens of different groups and societies punctuated the outer reaches of the room. After several circuits, unable to force her way out through the tide of bodies, she finally found herself spat out at a stand which grandly announced itself as the Drama Society. Anna smiled to herself – it was fate.

Behind the table stood a tall, slim girl with a severe black bob, huge dark eyes and a slash of scarlet lipstick on her sensual mouth. Anna stood watching her for a while, transfixed as she threw back her head and laughed, flashing an icy-white smile and releasing a throaty gurgle. She was the most exotic and mesmerizing girl Anna had ever seen.

As Anna gazed in awe, the girl noticed her looking and

targeted the full force of her laser-beam eyes in her direction. 'Hi,' she drawled, her voice full and resonant. 'You interested in joining us?'

Anna hesitated. The girl was watching her with an intensity that she found both unnerving and intoxicating. Her breath seemed to catch slightly as she spoke. 'Maybe,' she said shyly.

'Hideous, isn't it?' the girl said, still fixing her with that mesmeric stare. 'But let me give you a little tip . . .' She dropped her voice conspiratorially so that Anna had to lean towards her to hear. She could smell her spicy, heady scent. 'Most people spend freshers' week making as many friends as possible and joining every single society, only to spend the rest of the first year trying to dump them all. Be selective.'

'OK,' said Anna, starting to move away. They clearly didn't want her in the drama society. Probably not hip enough, she thought, suddenly feeling very aware of her brand-new Top Shop jeans and wondering if she'd inadvertently left the label on the back.

'Hey! Hang on!' the girl called after her, leaning right over the table and touching Anna's arm, giving her an electric shock. 'I didn't mean you shouldn't join us. Just that you should forget about all the others!'

Anna laughed with relief. Even from that first moment, she wanted to impress this girl.

She produced a form and a pen. 'Just fill this out and we'll do the rest. I'm Ella, by the way,' she said, proffering her hand.

Anna shook her head slightly, as if trying to clear the weird, hypnotic effect Ella was having on her.

'Anna,' she replied, noticing as she shook Ella's hand how cool her skin was. They touched for longer than seemed comfortable. 'What year are you in?' Anna stuttered as she gently extricated her hand from Ella's grasp.

'Second,' she smiled. Her teeth were so white and straight, Anna wondered if she'd ever seen a more perfect specimen of the female form. 'Reading English. And you?'

'English too.' Anna nodded, feeling strangely elated that they were reading the same subject. She filled out the form shakily, all the time aware of Ella scrutinizing her. There was something unnervingly sexual about her. 'Here, I'm done.' She handed her the form.

'Great,' said Ella, taking the page and scanning it. 'How are you getting on so far?'

'OK.' Anna wished her voice would stop quavering. 'I only arrived this morning, so I'm just finding my feet.'

'Well, enjoy the rest of freshers' week and I'll look forward to seeing you at the first meeting, *Anna*.' She said her name very deliberately, as if she was trying it out to see how it sounded on her tongue.

As Anna walked away, she could feel Ella's eyes boring into her back, as if there was some kind of magnetic force field connecting them. If only she hadn't stopped at that stand that day. If only she had never met her.

Mr & Mrs G King
request the pleasure of

Max & Ella Corbett

at the wedding of their daughter

Rachel to Toby McKenzie

24 July 2010
2 p.m.
at
St George's Chapel,
Fulham

RSVP: 47, Evesham Mews, Cheltenham

Ella

Ella pulls her Mercedes SLK onto the driveway of the house and waits for the large, black iron gate to roll shut behind her, before turning off the engine. She reaches for the pile of post she collected before she left home that morning and begins to sort through it. Several bits of junk mail, a couple of bills and a handwritten, cream-coloured envelope with a tiny heart in one corner. She turns it over in her hand with a feeling of foreboding before ripping it open, already knowing what it is.

She sits for a couple of minutes trying to compose herself before opening the car door and stepping out onto the cobbled driveway. She looks up at the beautiful whitewashed stucco mansion before her and tries to recapture the swell of pride she used to feel whenever she arrived home. Nothing. Situated on a leafy square in Notting Hill, it is one of the most desirable properties in London. And it belongs to her.

Well, that isn't strictly true. It is Max's house and because she is married to Max, it is now half hers too. But she has never quite felt that she owns it equally, mainly because it is the home Max shared with his first wife, Camilla. Camilla was the perfect wife; posh, prettily blonde and subservient, she might have been plucked straight from central casting as the ideal trophy wife for an obscenely rich City banker. Their children, Jasper, Rupert and Araminta all went to the best schools and universities in the country, before following their father into the City. All have now accumulated their own private wealth and all of them have something else in common: they hate Ella with a passion.

When she is feeling in a more reasonable mood, Ella supposes she can understand their animosity. Camilla had died of breast cancer four years previously. So far, so tragic. But what turned Max's children against her was that for the two years prior to Camilla's death, Ella had been having a very public affair with their father.

Ella had met Max a couple of years after leaving university. She had found a job at a major investment bank mainly to get some money to go travelling and found herself working as his PA. She could tell from the second he clapped eyes on her that he fancied her, but that was nothing new to Ella. From her early teens, when she experienced the first stirrings of sexual awareness, Ella found that she was able to cast a spell over any man she wanted. Gradually, however, she found herself attracted to Max too. He was tall, slim and boyishly handsome, despite the fact that he was fifty-five – easily old enough to be her father.

They started working together later and later into the evenings, their conversation becoming more and more sexually charged, until one night, as she leaned over his desk to hand him a document, he pulled her to him and kissed her hard. Ella had often scoffed at the idea that people justified things they shouldn't be doing by saying they couldn't help themselves, but in that instant she understood just how bewitching and powerful pure lust could be.

After that first night, Max and Ella progressed from having sex in his office (once they were sure everyone else had gone home) to booking hotels. They would change the hotel each time so as to avoid suspicion and very soon they had run out of places to go. 'I'll buy us a flat,' Max said simply.

Any misgivings Ella may have had were pushed to the back of her mind once she and Max had their own place. She moved in permanently and enjoyed making a home for them. She tried to ignore the niggling feeling that, instead of rent, she paid Max with sex. She reassured herself with the thought that she was in love with him, so it wasn't the same as prostituting herself. The trouble was, she wasn't really in love with *him*, she was in love with the situation.

They pretended to themselves that no one at work knew their guilty secret but of course everyone did. And before long his wife did too. She called the office one day and asked to speak to Max. Ella was about to put her through when she suddenly added, 'And I know what's going on, Ella, so you don't need to act the innocent around me any more. Here's how it's going to work: you stay out of my way and I'll stay out of yours. Don't *ever* come to my house and don't speak to my children. OK?'

Her face burning with embarrassment, Ella had nodded and gulped, 'OK.'

'Good, now do you think you could put me through to *my* husband, please?'

A year later, Camilla died. And from then on everything changed. To begin with, Max was devastated. He was consumed with guilt and avoided Ella completely, asking for her to be transferred to a different department. He lost weight and looked as though he hadn't slept for months.

At work, Ella became Public Enemy Number One, seen as the evil mistress who had been screwing Camilla's husband while she was dying. No one spoke to her, except to issue basic instructions. Eventually, the head of HR said what everyone else was thinking: 'Wouldn't it be better if you just left – you can't be happy with things as they are?'

Ella wasn't, so she did. Nobody said goodbye. She went home to the empty flat which wasn't even hers and wondered where her life was going now that her meal ticket had deserted her. She was twenty-four with no job, no relationship and no friends.

Of course, she knew the reason why she had no friends. Ever since she first became aware of the effect her looks had on the opposite sex, she had used her powers of seduction to get any man she wanted. The trouble was, the men she wanted always seemed to be attached to other women.

Even Ella had to admit that there was a pattern to her treachery. She would make friends with someone, usually a sweet, trusting, caring girl who would welcome her into her life and her circle of friends with great generosity, only to find that Ella developed an all-consuming passion for her boyfriend and would stop at nothing until she had stolen him away.

Time and again, Ella had wreaked havoc on the lives of good people and she didn't seem able to break the habit. Any amateur psychologist could have pointed to the reasons why she behaved like she did – her parents were emotionally stunted and slow to give either praise or affection. Her father, a successful businessman who travelled often, was so distant towards both her and her mother that it made little difference to Ella whether he was physically present or not. Her mother was positively cold towards her daughter, preferring the company of a vodka bottle instead. They had both made it quite clear that Ella, their only child, had failed to live up to their expectations and always had a vague air of disappointment about them whenever they spoke to her.

Ella was sent to boarding school at the age of five, where she learnt very quickly that she had to grab whatever she could for herself whenever the chances presented themselves. She craved both attention and affection and realized at a very young age that she could use her looks and charm to get both. If she sensed that the spotlight had wandered away from her for too long, she would invent a drama to ensure that it swung firmly back in her direction. Lying became second nature and Ella often found that she had convinced herself something was true, so adept was she at the art of fabrication.

So while other girls forged numerous lifelong alliances on the sports fields or in the dorms at night, Ella would choose her friends cautiously, always targeting the ones that she was most jealous of, the ones who were most popular. She would reel them in, only to stitch them up a few months later, usually by spreading rumours or lies and poisoning everyone else against them. Occasionally, she would go one step further and actually frame them for something like stealing or taking drugs, but usually she could just let her malicious tongue do all the work, leaving them wrung out and damaged – just like her. Then she wasn't jealous of them any more. Easy.

Except Ella soon ran out of options as the other girls became wise to her antics. By the time she moved on to university, she might have been friendless but now she had a whole new pool of victims to choose from and this time it wasn't friendships she would break up, it was relationships.

Time and again, she would befriend someone with the sole intention of seducing their boyfriend. Once she had got what she wanted, she lost interest in both him and her and dropped them abruptly. Because there were so many people moving in and out of university all the time, there was always some fresh prey. But her treachery finally caught up with her when she picked on the wrong person. When she picked on Anna.

Rachel

May 2010

Rachel wakes up early and stretches. She lifts her head so that she can see past Toby's still-sleeping body to the clock on his bedside table. 6.27 a.m. She slumps back down on her pillow and stares at the ceiling. She has been waking up earlier and earlier recently, even at the weekends, as the wedding inches closer. She reassures herself that it is perfectly normal to be nervous – isn't every bride the same?

She lifts the duvet and creeps out into the cool of the room, which is only dimly lit by the dawn light. She pulls on her robe and opens the door as quietly as she can, glancing towards Toby to make sure she hasn't woken him. She doesn't want him to be disturbed just yet. She pulls the door until it is almost closed behind her and walks down the hallway where she scoops up her giant, lime-green, soft leather holdall and rummages through it, her heart quickening as the need for nicotine intensifies.

Finally, she locates her cigarettes and exhales with relief as she makes her way to the french doors leading from the kitchen. She undoes the pretty wrought-iron latch and walks out onto the roof terrace, already flicking her lighter impatiently. She draws heavily on the cigarette and perches cross-legged on the blue painted wooden bench that she and Toby had taken hours to haul up the stairs, only to find it was far too big for the space they had available. 'Fuck it,' she had laughed, lying down on it. 'I'm not moving it again.'

Sitting on it now, looking out over the topsy-turvy rooftops of North London, she is glad they kept it where it was, slap bang in the middle of the small paved oasis. She breathes in deeply, enjoying the solitude and the calm. The sun is a melon-coloured semicircle, emerging from its slumber and winking over the city in the late spring air, heralding the imminent arrival of summer.

Rachel loves the summer more than any other time of year – she cherishes the change in mood the warmth brings with it, as skin turns from almost blue to golden brown and frowns melt into smiles. She loves swimming in the open-air lido on Hampstead Heath and lolling in the vast expanse of the city's parks, engrossed in a trashy magazine or tabloid newspaper, Toby at her side with his infinitely more high-brow reading matter.

Toby, who in just eight weeks would become her husband.

Rachel finishes her cigarette and wonders idly if by the following summer he would also have become father to her first child. No more cigarettes then, she smiles to herself. Baby hunger is a strange expression, she thinks, but it is a perfect description of what she has been experiencing for some years now. It had started to rumble gently when she turned thirty but now, at thirty-four, it is raging so fiercely that she sometimes feels that she can actually picture her child's face and smell its sweet, musky baby smell. With Toby as the father, there was no doubt the baby would be inheriting amazing genes and Rachel is sure that Toby would be a great dad.

So why is there this horrible gnawing feeling within her that she can't shake off? She is getting married to the man she loves in a matter of weeks, yet she isn't excited or even happy. Instead, she is wracked with anxiety and tension and she can't help the niggling feeling that her nerves are different to those of other brides. She isn't worried whether the cars will turn up or the flowers will be delivered in time. No, her worries are all about the groom.

She loves Toby. It would be impossible not to. He is gorgeous. He is kind, generous, funny and clever. And he is devoted. But Rachel has long suspected that it isn't her that he is devoted to.

Anna

October 1997

Over the next week, Anna took Ella's advice and was careful not to dive too quickly into friendships. She was staying in a hall of residence, where she watched the other students all scrambling to accumulate as many new names to add to their address books as possible. The only friend she made was one who would be with her for the rest of her life.

Clare Stanton had knocked on Anna's door that first night. 'I'm Clare, who are you?' she smiled, waving.

Anna laughed at her directness. 'Anna,' she said and mirrored her jokey wave.

'Can I come in and have a nose?' Clare was already nudging past her and into the room. 'Ooh, this is a bloody sight better than mine!' she squealed, running straight over to the window and peering out. 'You've got a view!'

'Hardly!' Anna joined her at the window and motioned towards the railway line where a couple of saplings attempted to provide scenery.

'Yeah, well all I've got is the bloody gas tank. What are you doing?'

'Standing here talking to you,' Anna replied.

'No, you silly cow, what are you READING?'

Anna laughed again. She instinctively liked this girl and was glad she was going to be living opposite her. 'Oh! English.'

Clare pulled a face. 'Hope you're not too wanky. There're some right prats in your department.'

Anna raised an eyebrow. 'Well, I can't promise, obviously. What about you, then?'

'History,' Clare sighed. 'But I'm not a completely boring bastard, that I *can* promise! Anyway, I'm making supper. Come and find me in the kitchen when you're ready.' With that she bounced back out of the room and disappeared.

Anna felt lucky meeting Clare when she did. Later Clare told her that she was feeling uncharacteristically shy and slightly lost that first evening. Not that she had shown it, of course. Everyone assumed she was uber-confident, which Anna soon learnt wasn't the case. Sure, she had no trouble meeting people and she had loads of friends that she hung out with, but she confessed she had never really got close to anyone – until she met Anna.

Anna knew immediately that she and Clare were going to get on. They were total opposites in both looks and personality but somehow they were a perfect fit. While Anna was small and blonde with curves, Clare was tall, slim and athletic, with large brown eyes and olive skin. Anna thought Clare was gorgeous but she would always dismiss any compliments about her appearance, saying she thought she looked like a teenage boy.

Clare was easily the most popular person in their year at university – and that was despite studying history. Normally populated by posh geeks, she said she added a certain 'common touch' to the course. She got on well with her tutors because she worked hard and was bright but she partied hard too and knew how to let her hair down.

Over their first few weeks, Clare and Anna went to every party going. They made a pact early on never to leave the other on their own and to always go home together. Anna found herself carried along in the slipstream of Clare's energy and enthusiasm. She was fun, sociable and in demand and Anna soon realized that teaming up with her could only have a positive effect on her reputation.

It had been a long and difficult journey for Anna to get this far. Unlike many of her fellow Cambridge students, she didn't come from a well-to-do family. Her mum had brought up her and her brother, Tim, alone after breaking up with their father.

Anna was only nine years old when they separated but the effects of their split had stayed with her. Her dad, a TV cameraman, had been her hero. He often used to take her and Tim on shoots with him. He had two mini director's chairs with their names printed on the back that he would set up beside his camera and he'd make them giggle with his antics between takes.

Sometimes, they even got to stay overnight with him, in an interconnecting hotel room, if he was filming too far from home to get back each night. Which is how Anna came to walk in on him having sex with the costume designer, Milly, who had been so friendly and accommodating towards her and Tim during the day. Having woken from a nightmare and still half asleep, Anna didn't immediately understand what she was seeing. But she certainly understood her dad leaping off Milly's naked body and yelling at her to get back to bed.

She lay awake shaking with fear and worry for the whole night, already aware that what had happened was going to change her life forever. The next morning, her dad took Anna for a walk and told her that he had just been comforting Milly because she was upset and that there was no need to tell Mummy about what she'd seen.

Anna knew he was lying but she loved both her parents and didn't want to cause trouble, so for the first time ever, she kept a secret from her mum and didn't mention it. As time went on, she began to wonder if she had dreamt the whole thing and gradually started to relax. Then one day she came home from school to find her mum screaming at her dad, tears pouring down her face. She had popped home during the day and walked in on him in bed with her best friend. She stopped yelling as soon as Tim and Anna came through the door but they had already heard enough to know what had happened.

Her dad had begged and pleaded with her mum to forgive him, swearing on his kids' lives that it was a one-off and that he would never betray her again. Despite being shocked to her core, her mum had looked into his tear-filled eyes and agreed that she would give him one more chance. As she told Anna later, she was terrified of how she would cope without him, so felt she had little choice but to forgive him. Two days later they came home from school to find him gone. Which is when Anna finally told her what she had seen months earlier. She would never forget the look of horror that crossed her mum's face, but from that moment on, she became as protective of Anna as a lioness and they developed the closest bond a mother and daughter could have. None of them heard from him again.

'How are you doing, love?' Anna's mum, Cassie, asked anxiously when she called her on her second evening. 'I'm missing you so much already.'

Anna's stomach flipped with homesickness as she pictured her mum sitting on their battered old leather sofa, her legs curled up under her the way she always sat. She was alone now that Anna had gone. Her brother had moved to Australia the previous year and she had always known it would hit her mum hard when she went.

'I'm doing fine,' Anna assured her. 'I've made one really lovely friend already and she lives right opposite to me. I think it's going to work out, Mum.'

Anna knew by Cassie's voice that she was choking up. 'That's great, darling,' she managed.

'You'll have to meet someone new, you know, Mum,' Anna said, the lump in her own throat changing her voice into a higher-pitched squeak. She couldn't bear to think of her being lonely.

Cassie laughed gently. 'Yes, maybe. But you know what I'm like, sweetheart – it's all about The One.'

Anna groaned. They were both hopeless romantics who were addicted to the idea that everyone has only one true love in their lives, an idea fed by a relentless diet of romantic poetry, movies and books.

'Shame your One and Only was such a shit, then,' Anna said bitterly, then immediately regretted it. She was supposed to be making her mum feel better, not worse.

To her relief, Cassie laughed. 'Yes, it is. But it doesn't have to be that way for you. Have you met any potential One and Onlys yet?'

Now it was Anna's turn to laugh. 'No, only Not on Your Lifes so far! But it's early days.'

As it turned out, she didn't have long to wait.

Clare

May 2010

Anna and Clare sit at the small, round silver table on their tiny patio. Anna is calmer now, although the invitation is still sitting like an unexploded bomb on the table between them. The dusk is drawing in, cooling the air and licking the evening with a fine layer of damp. Clare shivers slightly as she reaches for the bottle of champagne they have almost finished between them and pours the last dregs into her glass. Anna has changed out of her grungy bathrobe into a pair of grey tracksuit pants and a slim-fit, pale pink t-shirt. Her silky, blonde hair is scrunched carelessly into a messy ponytail and her tiny, heart-shaped face is make-up free, but as Clare looks at her, she is struck by how breathtakingly pretty she looks.

Clare is still wearing the tailored trousers and fitted white shirt which have become her signature outfit for her work as a lawyer. Beside Anna, she feels masculine and brittle but she has never been jealous of her friend. Instead, she has always felt protective and maternal towards her. Anna has that effect on people. They want to take care of her. Which is why Clare is worried about Anna's reaction to this invitation and feels so guilty that she was so adamant that Anna should go to the reunion. Clare had been convinced that Anna would either return home with Toby in tow, or would have finally consigned him to the past, along with the rest of her university memories.

Clare has never felt the same yearning for the past that Anna has. Yes, she loved her time at university, but because she always knew what she wanted to do, studying was more of a means to an end. Whereas Anna was passionate about the books and poetry she studied – too passionate as far as Clare was concerned – Clare simply wanted to pass exams so that she could get started on the career she had always wanted.

And while Anna met Toby and fell madly in love, Clare only ever had an endless stream of short-lived dalliances. She has never been short of offers from the opposite sex but she gets bored quickly and doesn't want anything to interfere with her job. It's a philosophy drummed into her by her mother, who was a successful career woman long before it became the norm, relying heavily on nannies to care for her daughter. Now Clare has dutifully followed her mother into a high-profile profession, her warnings never to be dependent on any man ringing in her ears.

After her father died when she was fifteen, Clare gradually came to recognize that her mother only stayed with him because she fell pregnant and was trapped into getting married. As a result, she was adamant the same fate shouldn't befall her daughter.

'Shall I open another?' Clare realizes that she's slurring slightly as she gets to her feet and grabs the empty champagne bottle. She is really cold now and thinks longingly of the cosy cashmere cardy hanging in her wardrobe.

Anna shakes her head, releasing the scrunchie holding her ponytail and letting her hair fall in golden rivulets around her shoulders. 'Better not. I've got work tomorrow.'

'Pah!' snorts Clare, smoothing down her charcoal grey trousers. 'I should think so too! You bloody teachers have it easy. What was it today? Another study day?'

Anna grins back at her. 'Yes, but I think you'll find, my dear friend, that my salary is on a par with your expenses for one month, so I'd say we're pretty even!'

Clare raises a finger and wags it jokily at her. 'When you put it like that,' she laughs. 'So, are you going to be OK? You're not—'

'Going to do anything silly?' Anna says, reading her friend's mind. 'No.'

Clare's eyes soften. She understands Anna's pain better than anyone else. 'We'll get through it together, Anna. We'll go to the wedding, dazzle everyone with our gorgeousness and then we'll start again from scratch. How does that sound?'

Anna smiles slightly as she gets up and turns towards the door leading back into the kitchen of the flat. 'Impossible,' she says. 'That's how it sounds.'

Clare stands for a while longer, listening as the sounds of nature from their postage-stamp garden fight to be heard over the cacophony of life screeching from the South London street behind her. As the air starts to cool even more, her limbs stiffen and she follows Anna back inside, deciding to run herself a hot, oily bath.

She turns both taps on full blast and stirs the soothingly

scalding water with her hand, watching in fascination as the bath oil swirls into abstract shapes on top of the water. *Oil and water*, she thinks distractedly, *they never mix*. A bit like Ella and Anna. And how she wishes they had never mixed.

Anna

June 2010

Anna sits on a bench beside the Thames, across the road from the Tate Britain, watching the world clatter on around her. Buses jostle for position and cab drivers furiously beep their horns as they attempt to negotiate a passage along the busy Embankment. Tourists stroll hand in hand, workers scurry irritably, their frowns heavy and hostile. Beside her, a party of Japanese schoolchildren jump up and down, posing for each other as they snap away on their phones, their chatter incessant and incomprehensible but nonetheless soothing to her ears.

She watches them distractedly, enjoying the warmth of sunshine on her face and the sound of the Thames behind her. She wonders when she last laughed with the carefree spirit of those children. She was once happy but it seems a very long time ago now. Looking back is like looking down through a very deep pool of water. Through the ripples, memories float to the surface, then sink away into nothingness.

She often comes to the gallery, whenever she feels low and needs the sustenance of the timeless beauty hanging on those many walls. She could have spent whole days staring at Waterhouse's *The Lady of Shalott* in that building. Clare is right – she is obsessed with the tragic, lovelorn heroines of the past, trapped forever in oil or prose.

Anna has searched for the same connection that she had with Toby in other relationships but it has never been there. Every time she meets someone new, she wonders if this might be the one who will take Toby's place but it's as if there is an invisible force field around her heart that no one can break through. And she has a stubborn streak which means that once she's decided that whoever she's dating isn't The One, that's it.

Inevitably, it has only ever been a matter of weeks before she's ended it and although some of them have been upset, she never seems to feel anything herself, other than a vague sense that she's just passing time. She didn't fully realize until the university reunion exactly what it was she was waiting for but it became crystal clear that night. She was waiting for him.

October 1997

Lectures and seminars began in earnest at the beginning of the second week. This was one of Anna's first outings alone since meeting Clare and she suddenly felt vulnerable and clueless. As she approached the venue for her first lecture, she noticed someone leaning casually against the wall outside the lecture theatre. She ran her hand through her hair in the way that she always did when she felt self-conscious. He turned as she approached and fixed his bright green-grey eyes on her. 'Hi, I'm Toby,' he smiled, his voice deep, melodious and unmistakably upper class.

He was tall and gangly with a dishevelled mop of dark hair and a face so chiselled that his cheekbones looked like they'd been hewn out of granite, and Anna almost did a double-take at the sight of him. He took her breath away. She tried to smile back but her face felt frozen. 'Hi,' she murmured, rifling in her bag to try to distract him from the furious blush that had exploded on her cheeks, right down to her neck. 'I'm Anna.'

'Anna,' he said, nodding slowly.

She stopped searching through her bag and looked up, ready to say something witty and clever. She was too late. At that moment another girl ambled up. 'Hey, guys!' she drawled. 'Am I in the right place for the intro to English Lit?' Toby and Anna both nodded. Again, no words would come out of Anna's mouth.

'I'm Toby,' he said, smiling at her with that slightly lop-sided smile. Anna watched as the full force of his lovely eyes turned away from her and towards this new arrival.

'Jess,' the girl replied brightly, dropping down cross-legged onto the floor and resting her back on the same wall he was leaning against. *Oh, to have that easy confidence*, Anna thought miserably.

While Anna tried desperately to think of something to say, Jess and Toby started chatting easily, discussing which school they'd come from and trying to think of friends they might have in common. Those two struck gold straight away.

'Oh, you went to Ixworth? You must know Ella de Bourg! She's here, you know, in the second year.'

'Oh, really! What a coincidence! I must try to find her.'

On and on they went, as more students joined the group.

Soon Anna could no longer see Toby on the other side of the crowd but snippets of his conversation kept floating towards her. It was as though she was trying to tune a radio and his voice was all she could hear clearly through the hum of other people's words.

'Yeah, tomorrow night, at my halls . . .'

'I'd love to. Yeah, that'd be great. Cool.'

Finally, the heavy wooden door opened and they all filed into the echoey lecture theatre and took their seats where historical figures of learning had sat for centuries before them. An awed hush descended as the head of English, a quietly spoken, charismatic man called Robert Lee, introduced himself, then explained that they were going to be divided into a number of smaller groups for the first year of the course. He handed out sheets of paper printed with their names and the details of which group they would be in. Anna scanned the page eagerly and almost whooped with joy. There were four others in the group but she only saw one name on the list. Sitting neatly below Anna McKenna was Toby McKenzie. Anna mentally said a prayer of thanks to her dad – wherever the stupid shit was living these days.

They filed silently out of the lecture theatre, still shrouded in that veil of awe which had dulled and quietened them all, and headed for the room they had been allocated. Anna's sense of direction had always been poor and soon she was totally disorientated. Looking around her in confusion, with a rising sense of panic in her throat, she heard a voice behind her and spun round. 'Are you lost?' asked Toby, looking amused.

'I am,' she admitted. *He must think I'm such an idiot*, she thought hopelessly, cross with herself.

'Me too,' he said, smiling now and fixing her with a stare which seemed to look right into her soul. 'Let's get lost together.'

June 2010

'Let's get lost together.' Over the years that have passed since that day, Anna has so often thought about those words and the effect they had on her, the chain of events they set in motion. As soon as Toby spoke, it was as if something shifted in her, never to return.

Standing now in front of her own class of students, she looks down at their shiny, innocent faces, so full of hope and devoid of complication, and wonders how different her life might have been if she hadn't met Toby. She wonders what would have happened if their paths had never crossed. Would she be happily married by now? Maybe she would even have had a child of her own.

She loves her tiny pupils with their scuffed shoes and their dirty faces and, on a good day, she loves her job. The children make her laugh with their honesty and lack of guile and she never tires of seeing the joy in their eyes when they first conquer the alphabet or learn how to count. She would have felt out of her depth dealing with stroppy teenagers struggling to control their raging hormones. The little ones did not make huge demands on her and gave their trust and love so willingly. If only all relationships could be so uncomplicated.

The school she teaches at is in Wandsworth, a leafy suburb of South West London nicknamed 'nappy valley' because of the number of young families living in the area. It's a small private school but yet there are enough 'ordinary' children to keep her interested and inspired. She has been there nearly two years now but it feels like longer because she feels so at home. The school she was at before was a large, tough, inner-city school and it broke her heart on a daily basis to see so many young lives already heading in a downward direction by the age of seven.

This school, Heathlands, is an oasis of tranquillity by comparison and she feels lucky to have landed a job there. There is a small staff of six teachers, several of whom are in their forties and fifties, leaving Anna and her friend Matt as the only 'youngsters'. Having settled down happily with his wife, who is pregnant with their first child, Matt despairs of Anna's inability to hold down a relationship and has fixed her up with several of his friends, only for her to ditch them when she realizes they're not The One. 'How the hell do you know he's not The One?' he tutted when she told him that another embryonic romance had hit the buffers. 'You haven't given it enough of a chance.' But she did know.

During the summer months when it is too hot to sit in the canteen with everyone else, she often takes herself off at lunchtimes to a quiet corner of the orchard, where she can sit under the breathy blossom of an apple or cherry tree to indulge her passion for poetry. She ignores the teasing she gets from Matt, who is as dismissive about her choice of literature as Clare.

Today, as she sits reading, Anna notices a little girl in her regulation blue gingham dress hovering nearby. Anna looks up and smiles. It is Tilly Taylor, who only joined her class recently, her mum having remarried and moved into the area. Tilly smiles back, her big pale eyes widening with curiosity. 'That looks good,' she says, nodding towards Anna's book of Tennyson's poetry. 'What's it about?' She hops from foot to foot as she speaks, her blonde plaits bobbing up and down.

Anna carefully replaces her bookmark. 'Well,' she begins, unsure how to explain such complex themes to such a young child. 'One of the poems is about a lady who falls in love with a man . . .'

'Oh,' she says, still hopping sporadically. There is a short pause, broken only by the sound of bees humming gently as they buzz around the orchard. 'That's nice, isn't it?' she says eventually, after much thought.

'Well, yes, it is nice. But in the end it's quite sad,' Anna replies, thinking how Tennyson would baulk at such a bland description.

Tilly's eyes flicker with uncertainty. 'Oh dear,' she says. 'What happens to her?'

Now it's Anna's turn to hesitate. 'Well, she eventually dies of a broken heart,' she says. 'See, I told you it was sad.'

Tilly shrugs philosophically. 'That's a bit silly really,' she says, gesturing with her hands. 'Why didn't she just get another boyfriend? That's what my mum did.'

Anna laughs then. 'You know what, Tilly? You're absolutely right.'

She nods, satisfied, and half-hops, half-skips back through the orchard to join her friends, whose squeals of delight are carried and amplified by the summer air.

Out of the mouths of babes, Anna thinks. Why is she wasting her life pining for Toby? And Clare is right about her unhealthy obsession with tragic heroines. She closes the book firmly and tucks it into the embroidered cloth bag she brought back from a holiday in Thailand with Toby and tilts her face towards the sun. It's time she moved on.

October 1997

Toby was confident and popular – and after Anna met him, so was she. She basked in his reflection and blossomed. The other female students adored him and would make futile attempts to attract his attention, but for those three years, he never seemed to waver in his devotion to her. They spent endless nights curled up together in her single bed, talking, laughing and sharing their thoughts with each other. From early on in their relationship, there was a sense of solidity, of permanence. Without ever actually saying it, it was obvious they were for keeps, the real deal.

They were lovers but also great friends. They shared the same passion for poetry, for drama and for music. Their circle of friends centred around the drama group they had both joined in the first week but Toby also played guitar in a band he had formed with three other students from his hall of residence. Anna would help him to load up his ancient Morris Minor and travel to gigs with her legs squeezed close to her chest to accommodate all his gear. At the end of the night, she would wait for them to pack up before returning home and repeating the exercise all over again the next night. The other guys in the group, Ben, Pete and the lead singer, Daniel, became used to her presence and even though Daniel began to refer to her as 'Yoko' – which Toby reckoned was only because he secretly had the hots for her – they accepted that wherever Toby was, Anna would be there too. They came as a package.

At university, it could have been awkward that they were in the same tutor group but Anna loved that they would have heated debates about the texts they were studying. Toby was easily the cleverest in the group but he never patronized or talked down to her, always listening eagerly to whatever she had to say and making her feel interesting and intelligent. Anna worked harder and performed better because of him.

At the end of that first term, Toby went home with Anna to meet her mum and spend the few days before Christmas with her. They boarded the intercity train and headed out to Suffolk. Anna watched him proudly as he made his way unsteadily back down the train carriage towards her, clutching two Styrofoam cups and grinning broadly. Every female head turned in his direction as he passed but he was oblivious, his eyes fixed only on her. His hair had grown since they had been together and it now fell in front of his eyes, giving him a slightly hippy look. His jeans hung sexily from his hips and his t-shirt rode up as he steadied himself, revealing a tiny glimpse of his toned stomach.

'I think you've lost weight,' Anna said as he flung himself into the seat beside her, pushing his long legs out into the aisle.

'It's all that exercise,' he grinned, leaning towards her and kissing her on the lips.

Anna's whole body crackled with electricity. 'Don't say things like that in front of my mum, will you?' she chided half-heartedly.

'I meant football, tennis, basketball . . .' he protested innocently. 'Actually, I'm a bit nervous.'

She took a sip of scalding coffee and looked at him in surprise. 'Really?'

As Anna spoke, a middle-aged woman approached and Toby pulled his legs in under the seat in front to let her past. 'Thanks!' she said, a little too enthusiastically. 'No problem,' he replied, giving her the benefit of his killer smile.

'Flirt,' Anna said, nudging him playfully. 'She's old enough to be your mum! So come on, why are you nervous?'

'Meeting the mother-in-law,' he said, sending a little thrill of delight through her. 'What if she hates me?'

She raised her eyebrows at him. 'She won't. Trust me.'

As they emerged, blinking, onto the little country station platform, which was glittering with frost in the pre-Christmas cold, Anna heard a yelp of delight from her mum, who was waiting for them, bundled up against the elements. 'Anna!' she cried, running towards them and wrapping her arms around her daughter.

'Hi, Mum!' she said, her voice muffled as her face pressed into the padding of Cassie's coat. They hugged for a moment before standing back and looking at each other delightedly. 'This is Toby,' Anna said shyly, looking up at him, her heart swelling with pride.

The lamps on the platform cast an eerie glow in the icy mist but Anna could see Cassie's eyes shining as she shook Toby's hand. 'At last I get to meet the famous Toby!' she smiled.

He laughed and bowed slightly. 'And I get to meet the famous Mrs M!'

Cassie giggled and winked at Anna. 'Oh, he's good, isn't he?'

Anna beamed back. 'Oh yes, he certainly is! Now let's go before we freeze to death.'

They trudged towards Cassie's ancient little red Clio, their feet crunching on the icy ground as Cassie and Anna, arms linked, chattered away, while Toby lugged the bags along, looking at them both with an air of amusement.

They drove along the country lane leading to the cottage. 'Wow,' breathed Toby as Cassie pulled into the short gravel driveway. 'It's like the little house from Hansel and Gretel.'

For the first time, Anna became self-conscious about the differences in their backgrounds. Toby's parents – a lawyer and an artist – lived in Georgian splendour in the Cotswolds, while her single mother's cottage wasn't much bigger than Toby's parents' garden shed. As Anna looked up at it, she felt a prickle of unease at the peeling paint and general run-down appearance. She hated the thought of her mum here all alone night after night.

'It's not quite in the same league as your mum and dad's pad,' she muttered, yanking open the boot and lifting out the bags.

Shielded by the tailgate, their faces inches apart, Toby looked at her and tilted her chin towards him. 'No – you're right,' he said softly. 'It's much prettier.'

They followed Cassie through the peculiar inky blackness that you only ever get in the countryside, towards the front door, Toby ducking as he passed under the low timber frame. Immediately, the herby smell of roasting chicken filled the air and Anna was transported back to her childhood, feeling safe and happy to be home again.

'What do you think then?' she whispered to her mum as they cleared away the dinner dishes later, Cassie having vigorously declined Toby's offer to wash up. She stopped scraping the plate she was holding and looked at Anna with her thoughtful blue-grey eyes, now permanently crinkled at the sides by the years. 'I think . . .' she began slowly and Anna realized that she was holding her breath waiting for her verdict. 'I think he's lovely,' she ended simply.

Anna exhaled, trying to quell the bubble of happiness within her that seemed ready to pop. 'I think so too.'

Cassie raised her eyebrows mischievously. 'So, is he a contender for your One and Only then?'

But he wasn't a contender. In Anna's eyes, he was the only candidate for the role.

'I can't believe your dad walked out on her like he did,' Toby said as they travelled back to Cambridge on the train nearly two weeks later. 'What an absolute wanker.'

The dark, sulky skies of early January flashed past outside the train window. Anna linked her arm through his and laid her head on his shoulder. 'I know. She really loved him too.'

'His loss,' said Toby, kissing the top of her head.

Anna closed her eyes for a few moments. The trouble was that it was also her mum's loss. She had never recovered from his departure and despite what he did, Anna knew she still missed him.

She felt slightly nervous to be going back to real life, having spent an idyllic Christmas with Toby and her mum. It could have been awkward, just the three of them in such a confined space when Cassie and Toby had only just met, but instead it was pretty much perfect. The plan had been for Toby to leave on Christmas Eve to go to his parents' house for the festivities but the gods had intervened and they woke to find they were well and truly snowed in. 'So, it looks like you're stuck with us then!' her mum had laughed to Toby who, having tried to get out of the front door, was greeted by a four-foot wall of snow.

'Suits me just fine!' Toby had laughed back, putting his arm around Anna and squeezing her excitedly. 'I've never been snowed in before!' So, having made an apologetic call to Toby's parents, they spent the ten days that followed watching endless films on TV, reading, talking and playing ancient board games like Scrabble and Monopoly, which suddenly took on a whole new energy and excitement now that Anna was playing them with Toby. For Christmas, he bought her a beautiful silver key ring in the shape of a cat, saying he thought it might stop her missing her own beloved pet, Ophelia, who she'd had to leave at home with her mum, quite so much. She adored it and knew that she would treasure it forever.

Anna could tell that her mum loved having Toby around too, helping her to fill the void that had been left by her brother's absence, now that he was living in Australia.

As Cassie had waved Toby and Anna off that morning, laden down with various goodies, carefully wrapped in individual parcels, Anna could almost feel the loneliness enveloping her once more and wished they could all just stay holed up there forever.

As the train rumbled through the Cambridgeshire countryside, the picturesque snow now melted to a sludgy, battered, brown landscape, she looked up at Toby searchingly. 'Toby, tell me you'd never cheat on me. It would kill me if you did. And after my dad . . . well, it's the one thing I could never forgive.'

'I know,' he said, gently stroking her face. 'You don't need to worry, because it's never going to happen.'

Ella

January 1999

Anna fitted the profile of one of Ella's victims perfectly. She was pretty, bordering on beautiful; she was sweet-natured and gentle; but most of all, she was popular. No one seemed to be able to find anything to dislike about her, which inflamed Ella's jealousy a little more every time she saw her. Then, to add to Ella's annoyance, Anna got together with Toby McKenzie, who Ella had known all her life, as their families were friends.

Having never shown the slightest interest in him before – after all, he was younger than her and had always seemed like nothing more than a gawky annoyance – Ella now found herself becoming obsessed with him. He had turned up in Cambridge looking like an old-fashioned matinee idol and had apparently fallen head over heels in love with Little Miss Perfect. As time went on, she found herself wanting to wipe that annoying smile off Anna's face and show her how it felt to be rejected.

Over the first year, as they were both members of the drama society, they saw each other regularly. Gradually, Ella began to invite Anna to join her for lunch or a drink after lectures and rehearsals. She took things slowly, mainly because it was so difficult to get Anna alone, to find a time when she wasn't mooning around with Toby. But her patience paid off. Like most people, Anna was in thrall to Ella and it wasn't long before she considered her a friend.

Anna used to compliment her all the time about her looks, always comparing herself unfavourably. Ella, of course, would compliment her in return, reassuring Anna that she too was utterly gorgeous, drawing her further and further into her confidence.

Once she had gained Anna's trust, Ella started to make a point of being wherever Anna had told her that she and Toby were going to be and would conveniently 'bump into' them. Toby, who had known her for so long, and Anna, being the sweet-natured type, were always quick to invite her to join them for dinner, the cinema, or one of Toby's gigs. Neither of them appeared to be threatened or irritated by her presence.

The same couldn't be said for Anna's friend Clare, who seemed to see straight through Ella from the moment they met. Ella could tell by the way Clare narrowed her eyes when she spoke to her that she would be poisoning Anna against her if she wasn't careful.

She grabbed the opportunity to make a move on Toby one night in the January of his second year, after they had all been to the pictures. As so often happened, she had conveniently met them on the way into the cinema and they had invited her to join them. Afterwards, Toby and Ella had dropped Anna home first because Toby had an early lecture, and he had decided to spend the night at his own place. As he and Ella walked home together, Ella began to get more flirtatious with him, alternating between coyness and outrageousness.

'I wish I could find some of what you and Anna have got,' she sighed, the tears welling up in her eyes on demand.

'You will,' he replied cheerfully, striding purposefully along, apparently not noticing her distress.

'No one wants me!' Ella wailed suddenly, allowing the tears to fall and her voice to crack.

Toby stopped and looked at her in shock. 'What? Hey, Ells belles, don't cry, of course they want you!' He reached out and hugged her to him, and she allowed herself to sob into his overcoat.

They stood entwined for a few minutes until Ella stopped crying and looked up at him, knowing that no man so far had ever resisted her at this point. She tilted her face towards his and waited for the inevitable kiss to come. Instead, Toby let go of her like he had been burned and jumped backwards. 'What are you doing?' he asked, puzzled.

'Nothing!' she retorted, feeling herself cringe. This was not going to plan.

Toby frowned. 'Listen, Ella, I like you, you know that. But you're like an older sister to me . . .'

Ouch.

'You're a good friend, but I love Anna,' he continued.

Ella nodded. 'I don't know what came over me. Sorry!' She tried to laugh.

To her relief, Toby smiled. 'Forget it. Pretend it never happened. C'mon, let's get you home. I'm cold and tired.'

Forget it? thought Ella later. There was no way she would

forget it. In fact, after that night, Ella's passion for Toby intensified a thousandfold. She was determined to get him. She had never failed yet and she wasn't going to start with Toby.

Anna

Anna thought Ella was amazing. She was poised and confident with a magnetic quality that drew people to her. 'She's so beautiful,' Anna said to Toby as they walked home after a drama rehearsal one night. 'How come you and she never . . .?'

Toby pulled a face. 'I've known her most of my life. It would be weird. Anyway, she's not my type,' he added simply.

'And what *is* your type, exactly?' Anna giggled, twirling her hair around her finger and gazing up at him suggestively.

He smiled that slow smile and kissed her. 'You are,' he grinned.

But although Toby made it clear he wasn't interested in Ella, after several months, Anna started to wonder if Ella might be interested in *him*. Whenever Anna found herself alone with her, Ella would try to wheedle out as many details about their relationship as she could. She would casually enquire which restaurants they were going to, which films they planned on seeing and how they would be spending the weekend. Then, surprise, surprise, more often than not she would appear 'by coincidence' and they would invariably ask her to join them. Anna wasn't worried about her, despite the way she looked, because Toby never gave her any cause for concern. And she enjoyed Ella's company – she was clever and fun, plus she seemed to genuinely like Anna.

But alarm bells really began to ring when Anna introduced Ella to Clare. 'Isn't she lovely?' Anna said as they walked home after a night at the pub.

'Hmm,' replied Clare noncommittally.

'What?' Anna spun round to look at her. Clare rarely disliked anyone.

'Just watch her,' Clare said ominously.

Anna didn't say anything for a few minutes as they walked along the road.

'Especially with Toby,' Clare added, meeting Anna's eye meaningfully.

Clare adored Toby. She loved the fact that even though Anna had met him early on, he was always happy to have her around and never made her feel excluded. If she was ever at a loose end, which admittedly wasn't often, he was always happy for her to join them, which only made Anna love him even more. 'You two will have such good-looking kids,' Clare used to tease them. Anna and Toby would laugh but no one who knew them could imagine them ever breaking up.

'Just watch her,' repeated Clare.

Anna felt her insides clench at Clare's words but she casually laughed off any suggestions of impropriety on Ella's part. She pointed to the fact that their families had known each other since they were both kids and said it was unthinkable that they could be anything other than friends.

'She's trouble,' said Clare, her mouth set in a line of grim determination. 'She might turn heads wherever she goes, but she is *so* insincere. And don't you think it's a bit suspicious that she doesn't have any female friends?'

Anna shrugged. 'She's friends with me.'

'Is she?' asked Clare archly, scuffing her foot on the ground as she walked along, the noise seeming to echo her irritation. 'Is she *really*? She latched onto you pretty damn quickly and I just can't help thinking that she's using you to get to Toby.'

This time Anna laughed. 'Now that is totally ridiculous. She doesn't need to use me to get to Toby. She's known him forever.'

At this, Clare seemed to soften slightly. 'Yes, that's true, I suppose. I'm sorry, Anna. I don't know why but for some reason I just don't trust her.'

It was dark and Anna was glad Clare couldn't see the flush that had spread over her cheeks. She felt a little chill creep into her belly and realized that Clare had voiced something that had started to niggle away at the back of her mind. It was a culmination of things: like the way Ella would drop into the conversation that Toby was bombarding her with e-mails all day, stopping her from getting on with her studies. When Anna told Toby about it, he had looked puzzled. 'More like the other way around,' he had shrugged. Or she would call him on his mobile and as soon as Toby mentioned he was with Anna, she would ring off.

At the end of the second year, Anna moved out of the halls of residence and into a flat with Clare. It was above a wool shop on a busy main road and was freezing cold in the winter and boiling hot in the summer. But she loved it. Clare was a social butterfly, always out at parties or the pub, leaving plenty of evenings for Toby and Anna to have the flat to themselves.

Anna was so completely happy, so totally secure that whenever she contemplated the future that snaked out ahead of them, it was always about the two of them. Never once did she consider that Toby might not be with her on the journey ahead. To Anna, they were unbreakable. Anything else was unthinkable.

Ella

May 2010

Ella lets herself into the house and listens for signs of life. 'Hello?' she calls out, automatically tensing in case Max is home.

'Hi, darling!' comes his voice from the kitchen. 'In here!'

Ella's shoulders sag with disappointment as she makes her way down the beautiful flagstoned hallway in the direction of her husband's voice. As she rounds the corner, he jumps out and startles her. 'Surprise!' he grins, gesturing towards the table, which is laid out for two, a single-stem red rose in the middle.

Ella grits her teeth in annoyance. She has been looking forward to taking a bottle of Malbec upstairs and drinking herself into oblivion to try to forget about the invitation she is still clutching in her hand. Instead, she will have to sit opposite Max's sagging, ageing face and make stilted conversation about the excruciating details of his day.

As if reading her mind, Max frowns sympathetically. 'Are you OK, darling?' he asks, his voice gentle and full of concern.

God, she could be such a bitch sometimes, she thinks,

softening. 'Yes, I'm fine,' she sighs, kissing him chastely on the cheek. 'Just a bit tired, that's all.'

'Well, you probably need a good meal!' he smiles. For reasons she doesn't understand, Ella feels an urge to punch him square in the face, but resists. 'Sit down and let me look after you.'

Much later, she makes her escape, clutching the bottle of Malbec she has so been looking forward to. Max seems to disapprove of her drinking, so she stops at two glasses in front of him. But when she is alone she will polish off the rest and sometimes launch into a second. *Tonight is an emergency*, she thinks as she locks her bathroom door and turns on the taps, already pouring herself a large glass. As she watches the water line rise, she takes a long gulp and finally allows herself to think about the invitation she has received to the wedding of the man she still loves. She wonders for the hundredth time if she could have done anything differently which would have made him love her back.

December 1999

By the next year, when Ella was studying for her master's and Toby was in his third year, Ella was beginning to boil over with frustration. Her passion for him was undiminished but it was impossible to get through to him. He and Anna were inseparable, which only intensified Ella's jealousy and determination to get him. Her next opportunity came at a house party someone was having just before Christmas.

Ella had been upstairs using the bathroom and as she came out, she saw Toby staggering into one of the bedrooms. He was either very drunk or very stoned – Ella couldn't be sure which. She followed him into the room, closing the door carefully behind her. He looked around him with a dazed expression on his face and collapsed onto the bed.

'Hey, Tobes,' she said gently, kneeling beside the bed and reaching for his hand.

Toby gazed at her with unfocused eyes and laughed. 'Hey, babe,' he said, reaching out and stroking her hair.

She leaned forward and kissed him. He didn't respond but he didn't push her away either, so Ella took it as a gesture of encouragement and climbed on top of him, her heart pounding with lust and excitement. This was her moment and she was going to seize it. He mumbled something which she couldn't hear but she suspected he was hallucinating. She lifted his t-shirt and began to plant small kisses all over his chest, before pulling it over his head and throwing it onto the floor.

He was still mumbling to himself as Ella reached down and pulled off his jeans, followed by his boxers. She then ripped off her own sheer dress and half-managed to get her leggings off before straddling him. It was an entirely new sensation for Ella to feel a man anything less than erect as she sat astride him but Toby was resolutely limp. She laughed gently as she began to writhe back and forward as sensually as she could, knowing she would never get another opportunity like this, but he remained totally unresponsive.

Just as she was about to give up, she heard a gasp then a scream behind her. She looked around in surprise; Anna stood in the open doorway looking as though she might faint with shock. For a split second Ella felt a surge of elation, followed by triumph. 'Anna!' she called out half-heartedly but Anna had already turned and fled down the stairs. Ella spun back round to look at Toby. He had passed out cold.

All these years later, as Ella luxuriates in her Jo Malone-scented bath and pours herself another huge glass of wine, she can still feel the hair on the back of her neck tingle with embarrassment and shame. Any sense of triumph Ella had fleetingly felt was quickly replaced by mortification that she had stooped so low. It might have done the trick in wiping the smile off Anna's face but it certainly hadn't made Toby want Ella instead. Quite the opposite, in fact.

Anna

The crash, when it came, was cataclysmic. It wasn't as though there were any signs either. They had spent the whole day in bed together, skipping lectures but 'studying biology in great depth' as Toby put it. At about eight in the evening, they got up, had a bath and headed out to a Christmas party at someone's house. As they stood on the doorstep, mistletoe above their heads and their breath freezing on the cold night air, Toby leaned down and kissed Anna. 'I love you,' he whispered.

'You too,' she smiled, before the door was flung open and they descended headlong into the musky, sweaty heat of too many bodies crammed together in a warren of tiny rooms. Anna made her way to the kitchen and helped herself to a can of cider. Toby had already been collared by a couple of his bandmates and had disappeared upstairs. She suspected they were going to do some kind of drugs, so she ambled through to the sitting room, which had been transformed into a makeshift nightclub. The rhythm of the music was trancelike and several dazed-looking people with a vacant look in their eyes were pulsating in time to the beat.

Anna sat down on a sofa, sipping her cider and enjoying

the cold fizz as it hit the back of her throat. 'Hey, Anna!' said a voice. Through the gloom and smoke she could just about make out Clare, pushing her way past the dancers and slumping down on the sofa next to her. 'You should have told me you were going to be here – you could have come with my lot rather than on your own.'

'Thanks, honey, but I'm fine – Toby's here somewhere,' she replied, patting Clare's leg. Clare nodded and grabbed Anna's cider, which she gulped down greedily. 'Hey! Get your own!' Anna laughed, snatching it back.

'Oh, all right,' Clare said, reluctantly getting up. 'Want another one?'

Anna shook her head. 'I'm good, thanks.'

'Well,' Clare replied cheerfully, 'my lectures have finished for the term so I'm intending to get totally shit-faced.' With that she headed off.

Anna watched the dancers for a long time, enjoying the feeling of total relaxation, before deciding that she needed to use the bathroom. She picked her way up the stairs, which were covered with a hideous, swirly, brown and orange carpet, which in turn was littered with empty cans, bottles and cigarette stubs. At the top of the stairs, she turned right and opened the first door she came to. It wasn't the bathroom but a tiny box room.

The bare red light bulb gave off enough light to make out a couple on the bed. The girl was sitting astride the man, with only one leg out of her leggings. She was still wearing her G-string but she was naked from the waist up and was laughing as she writhed on top of him. The man was completely naked, his clothes strewn carelessly across the floor.

'Oh! Sorry . . .' Anna stammered, reversing quickly back out of the room, reddening with embarrassment, despite the fact that neither of them had noticed her.

She was just about to close the door when her heart froze. Slowly, she opened the door again. The t-shirt, lying discarded on the floor, was unmistakably Toby's. Just in case there was any room for doubt, his jeans and Mickey Mouse boxer shorts were on the mattress close to his feet.

She must have screamed because the girl stopped writhing and turned to look at her. Ella. Her eyes narrowed for a fraction of a second and a look of triumph crossed her face momentarily, before the beautiful mask returned.

Anna staggered backwards, her hand over her mouth. She wondered briefly if it was possible to die of shock. Toby still hadn't moved. Feeling her way blindly back down the stairs, she was dimly aware of Ella calling her name and people turning to look. 'Clare!' she yelled.

Clare emerged from the kitchen clutching a can of Strongbow. She looked up at Anna through the gloom and, seeing that something was very wrong, she dropped her can and grabbed Anna's hand, dragging her towards the front door. As they lurched out into the cold, Anna bent over and retched noisily. Clare stood holding her hair and rubbing her back until she'd finished. 'What happened?' she asked gently, her eyes darting nervously towards the house, where the party was noisily continuing.

Anna shook her head as tears filled her eyes. 'Home! I want to go home!' she wailed.

'Of course,' said Clare, quickly steering her towards the road and hauling her into the first taxi she managed to hail.

Clare slept on the floor of Anna's room that night. She

didn't ask any more questions but seemed to know instinct-ively what had happened.

Anna woke up feeling as though she had emerged from a general anaesthetic, like the time she had had her appendix removed when she was twelve. Her throat was dry, she felt sick and groggy. She still couldn't take in the enormity of what Toby had done. She felt for her phone and switched it back on. She had turned it off deliberately in the cab home, knowing that he would try to call. There were twenty-four missed calls. Reluctantly, with her heart pounding, she pressed the voicemail button. Toby's voice filled her head. 'Anna! Where are you!' he yelled, his words slurring as he spoke. 'You left without me – what happened?'

Anna snapped her phone shut in fury. What happened? He screwed someone else! How dare he act the innocent! She deleted all the other messages from him and switched the phone back off.

On the floor, Clare was waking up slowly. 'Hi,' she mur-mured croakily. 'How are you doing?'

Anna was trembling and pulled the duvet more tightly around her. 'Not great,' she said, her eyes already welling up.

'Oh, poor you . . .' Clare climbed onto the bed beside her and hugged Anna to her. They sat for a few moments in silence.

'I just can't believe he'd do that to me,' Anna whispered. 'I thought we were so happy.'

'You were,' insisted Clare. 'Something must have hap-pened to make him behave like that. It's just not like him.'

'Yeah, I know what happened,' Anna hissed murderously. 'Bloody Ella de Bourg, that's what happened.'

Anna felt Clare stiffen. 'Ella?'

Anna nodded miserably.

'Fucking cow!' Clare fumed. 'I told you to watch her! She's been trying to break you up for ages.'

'Well, now she's succeeded,' Anna said, giving in to the tears once again.

Clare reached for the box of tissues and pulled out three or four, then thrust them towards Anna. 'No!' she snapped. 'Don't let her get away with it! If you dump him now she's won!'

Anna considered the thought. Despite what Toby had done, she was still in love with him. But after seeing how her dad's infidelity had screwed up so many lives, she knew there was no way back for them. How could she ever trust him again? She would always be worrying that the same thing might happen again. And what's more, she had told him enough times that if he ever betrayed her it was over.

At around nine, Toby arrived at the flat. Clare opened the door scowling and grudgingly allowed him to squeeze past her and up the stairs. Anna was sitting on the sofa, clutching a cup of fresh coffee that Clare had gone out to get from the nearest coffee shop. 'It's an emergency,' she had insisted when Anna had protested that it was too much trouble.

'Hi,' he muttered sheepishly as he came into the room and stood awkwardly, unsure whether to sit down. Anna lifted her eyes towards him and her stomach immediately flipped at the sight of him. His eyes were hollow, his face was covered in stubble and his hair was matted.

She looked away again as she felt her eyes burn.

'About last night . . .' he started, running his hand through his hair distractedly.

She snorted and looked at him accusingly.

'Oh God, Anna, don't look at me like that,' he pleaded. 'I don't know what the hell happened. I really don't!' he added, seeing her look of disbelief.

'You had sex with Ella, that's what happened,' Anna said flatly, a numbness beginning to swirl its way through her. She couldn't believe this was happening to her. To them.

'What? No, I didn't!' Toby stormed. 'The last thing I remember is going up to a bedroom with Ben – we did a couple of lines each and I must have blacked out. There's no way I could have had sex with anyone, I was out cold.'

Anna wanted to believe him. She really did. But she'd seen it with her own eyes and the image was now indelibly etched onto her memory.

Toby seemed to sense that she was softening and came over to sit beside her. 'Please, Anna, you KNOW me. I didn't have sex with her, I promise you.'

Anna shook her head sadly. 'Toby, I saw you with my own eyes.'

Toby struggled to hold back his tears. 'Baby, please believe me, I was unconscious – I wasn't capable. I don't know what you saw but it wasn't what you think.'

'I think you'd better go,' she said, a physical stabbing pain shooting through her heart in a way that would become her constant companion over the years ahead.

'No! Anna, for fuck's sake!' yelled Toby, roughly wiping the tears from his cheeks. 'Don't do this! You can't let go of what we've got!'

'YOU did,' she snapped coldly. 'You let go of it! Get out, Toby.'

He threw his head back and covered his face with his hands. 'Anna, don't do this . . .'

'Just go,' she said, getting up and marching towards her bedroom, where she slammed the door loudly and flung herself onto the bed.

June 2010

Anna looks down at her hands, which are scrunched into tight fists as the memories of that awful night wash over her afresh, the horror of it still leaving her feeling faint a decade later. Should she have forgiven him? She couldn't accept that nothing sexual had happened between them; the picture of Ella sitting astride his naked body was burned into her brain as indelibly as the image of her dad in bed with Milly all those years before. She simply couldn't let history repeat itself.

'Here you go, darling,' says her mum, emerging from her kitchen into the sunshine of her little cottage garden with two mugs of tea. Anna takes the chipped, flowery mug from her and blows gently before sipping the scalding liquid. She comes home to Suffolk as often as she can, partly because she wants to make sure her mum is OK but mostly because she is feeling increasingly lost and lonely herself. 'So. What's upset you?' Cassie says, settling herself beside her on the weathered wooden bench.

Anna pauses and takes a deep breath. 'Toby's invited me to his wedding.'

Without speaking, Cassie reaches out and takes her hand. They sit in silence for a while, both lost in their own thoughts.

'Tell me what I should do,' Anna says at last, looking at her mum now. Cassie is staring into the distance, her tired eyes brimming with unshed tears.

'I'm so sorry,' she says, turning towards Anna as a tear escapes and winds its way through the creases of her freckled skin.

'What for?'

She composes herself before continuing. 'For everything. For making you *feel* everything so deeply. All that romantic nonsense about the One and Only. It's all rubbish! You should be enjoying your life, having lots of boyfriends, having *fun*.'

She looks furious now. 'It's all my bloody fault for encouraging you. If I hadn't, you wouldn't be so . . .'

'Screwed up?' Anna finishes, smiling.

Cassie sighs and her face softens. 'Well . . . yes, I suppose so.'

Anna squeezes her hand and takes a sip of her tea. 'You're not to blame, Mum. I was never going to be a good-time girl. I was always going to be looking for The One, no matter what you said or did. It's in my DNA. And despite everything, I still don't think it's rubbish. I still believe in it.'

Cassie doesn't answer and they sit quietly for a few more moments, drinking their tea and watching a couple of sparrows fighting in the grey stone birdbath, their splashes in the water looking like dozens of tiny diamonds in the sunlight. The garden is idyllic at this time of year, with everything bursting into flower and the strong smell of honeysuckle and clematis hanging heavy in the air.

'So, are you going to go?' says Cassie, breaking into Anna's reverie.

'I can't decide. Clare says it will give me closure. But then, she said that about the reunion.'

Cassie grimaces slightly. Like Clare, she feels guilty for persuading Anna to go to the reunion in the first place.

'But if I don't go,' Anna continues, 'I can't see how I will ever move on.'

'Then I think you just answered your own question.'

Ella

Ella saw Toby the following day when he arrived at her flat looking like a train wreck. 'You fucking bitch!' he yelled, barging through the door and slamming her up against the wall. Ella's stomach spasmed with fear. He looked like a madman and for an instant it occurred to her that he might kill her.

'Toby! You're hurting me!' she yelled back, pushing his chest with all the force she could muster before managing to free herself.

Toby slumped against the wall, panting. 'OK,' he rasped, 'here's what you're going to do. You're going to phone Anna and you're going to tell her that we did NOT have sex last night and that you're sorry that you're such a fucking saddo that you would even try to do anything with someone who was unconscious but that's exactly what you did. OK?'

Ella started to protest her innocence but the murderous glint returned to his eye and as he moved towards her, she put her hands up in a gesture of surrender. 'OK!' she shouted. 'OK! Just bloody well calm down.'

'Right,' he hissed, 'where's your phone?'

It was the worst phone call Ella had ever had to make. Anna sounded utterly broken. For the very first time, it hit her that her behaviour could inflict so much pain. With

Toby glaring at her, Ella told Anna repeatedly that they hadn't had sex. She even admitted that although she had given it her best shot, he just wasn't interested. Or conscious, for that matter. But Anna just kept repeating the words, 'I saw you, I saw you with my own eyes,' over and over again. Finally, Anna hung up while Ella was mid-sentence.

Toby stormed out of the flat and refused to speak to Ella after that. Strangely though, even the acute embarrassment of that whole incident didn't dim her infatuation with him. She found that her desire to find new victims had dissipated. She had room in her head now for only one object of her affections.

Anna

Over the next few weeks, during the holidays, Toby called Anna an average of five times a day. Each time he'd say the same thing: 'Babe, please. You can't just end it like this.'

Each time Anna would let it go to voicemail and delete the message as soon as she had listened to it. Gradually, she started to delete the messages without even listening to them.

When Ella called after the party, she had insisted that Toby was telling the truth. But there was a slight hesitation in her delivery which told Anna she was almost reading from a script. She didn't believe her.

'Don't ever call me again,' Anna had replied coldly, hanging up as she started to speak again. Something inside her had turned to stone and she couldn't – or wouldn't – countenance the idea that maybe she had made a mistake. Memories of her mum accepting her dad's lies only increased her determination not to be taken for a fool the way she was.

When January came, Clare was constantly asking her to go out with her to try to take her mind off the break-up and to stop her sitting at home brooding. For weeks, she refused point-blank, until one night when she couldn't stand staring at the four walls of the flat any longer. 'Oh, all right then,' she sighed, getting up.

Clare looked at her in surprise. 'Seriously? Oh, Anna, that's great. C'mon, let's get plastered and have some fun.'

And it was fun, to begin with. They went to a bar that Anna had been to many times in the past when Toby's band had played there. It was a spit and sawdust type of place, with terrible toilets and beer spilt everywhere but it was always packed and the music was usually great.

Ironically, despite the fact that she had felt so wretched for weeks, she was looking better than ever. She had lost weight, revealing cheekbones she never knew she had, her skin was clear and her hair was shining. The heartbreak diet was certainly more effective than any other. After just two halves of cider, her head was spinning. After four, she was tipsy and after six, well and truly drunk. As the band struck up with 'I Feel Good', they all piled onto the dance floor and she lost sight of Clare. Flinging her head around to the beat of the music, letting her hair down after so long feeling miserable, she started to feel an intoxicating buzz of energy and excitement.

As she spun around in one particularly ambitious dance move, she stumbled and started to fall, only to find herself caught by a pair of strong male arms. 'Whoa! Steady!' laughed a voice as she regained her balance and turned to see who the arms belonged to. It was Daniel, the lead singer of Toby's band. He looked as surprised to see her as she was to see him. 'Oh, it's you, Yoko,' he laughed.

Anna narrowed her eyes at him. He had given her the nickname because she had always accompanied Toby to their gigs. Then, through her drunken haze, she remembered Toby telling her that he thought it was because Daniel secretly fancied her. Now, with Daniel standing before her and with enough cider inside her, she suddenly thought how attractive he looked. Whether it was because she also subconsciously knew there was probably nothing more guaranteed to hurt Toby than her getting together with Daniel, she still doesn't know.

'Are you OK?' he said, his arms still loosely on her waist, sending a little thrill of delight through her.

'Yes – thank you for rescuing me.' She smiled what she hoped was a flirtatious smile, grateful that he had saved her from the embarrassment of a drunken tumble. She tried to stop her words from slurring as she spoke but seemed unable to help it.

Daniel raised his eyebrows in surprise. Anna had always been quite reserved with him before. 'So, you dumped Mac then?' he ventured, taking her hand and pulling her to him as they began to sway in time to the music.

She nodded, trying hard to focus as the room swam around her.

'About time too,' he grinned mischievously, his hands moving more tightly around her waist as he pulled her closer to him. 'And good news for the rest of us . . .'

Anna smiled back woozily, slightly giddy and enjoying the feeling of being in a man's arms again. 'I don't know about that,' she said, trying to sound coy, an effect somewhat ruined by a mistimed hiccough.

Suddenly, without warning, Daniel was kissing her hard on the lips. She tried to push him off but his grip was strong and it was several seconds before she was able to lean away from him. 'What are you doing?' she asked, looking at him in confusion.

'Oh, come on, Anna,' he soothed, using her real name for the first time as he pulled her to him again and stroked her hair. 'You're a free agent now . . . and it's not as if Mac was whiter than white.'

'What do you mean by that?' Anna demanded, holding him at arm's length and wishing her head would clear so that she could digest what he was saying.

'I mean,' he continued, still holding onto her, 'that we all know Toby was knocking off Ella de Bourg. And I doubt very much she was his only little bit on the side. So, what's to stop you having a bit of fun? As I said, you're a free agent.'

Indignation rose within Anna like a wave. As if her humiliation wasn't already bad enough, it now sounded as though Toby had been cheating on her all along. What a bloody fool she'd been to think he was being faithful.

If she had been sober enough to stop and think, she would have realized that they had spent every free moment together. Toby wouldn't have had the time or the opportunity to have an affair with anyone else.

But at that moment, Anna looked into Daniel's dark, brooding eyes and decided there and then, that she would sleep with him that night. She would show Toby and everyone else that she was over him.

'Let's go,' she said, taking Daniel's hand and leading him from the bar.

The next morning, Anna awoke with a start. Her head was hammering and her stomach was churning ominously. She lifted the duvet and gingerly swung her legs over the edge of the bed. Beside her, she felt Daniel stir so she jumped up and raced from the room, hoping to make it out before he saw her nakedness. In the hallway, she stood panting for a second before she felt the bile rise and ran to the bathroom where she threw up. She grabbed Clare's dressing gown from the back of the door and wrapped it around her, before making her way back down the hall to Clare's room. She knocked quietly on her door, praying inwardly that she was alone.

'Come in,' Clare called groggily.

Anna went in and sat down on the bed beside her. 'Oh God, Clare,' she sobbed, crying with fear and helplessness. 'I've just made the biggest mistake of my life.'

Clare sat up in surprise. 'What? What's happened?' she said, putting a comforting arm around her shoulders.

Anna hesitated, shame enveloping her like a thick blanket. 'Well, I was having a great time last night . . .'

Clare nodded and rubbed her sleepy eyes with her one free hand. 'Well, that was the idea, wasn't it?'

Anna dropped her head miserably. 'Yes . . . but then Daniel – you know, from Toby's band? He told me that everyone knows about Toby . . . and Ella.' She could hardly say her name without flinching.

'Oh, honey,' said Clare, giving her a squeeze. 'The trouble is, there were so many people at that party . . .'

'I know!' Anna wailed. 'But then he said it had been going on for ages and that she wasn't his only bit on the side . . .'

Clare frowned. 'That's bollocks,' she said crossly. 'Surely you didn't believe him?'

Anna blew her nose and shrugged. 'I don't know. I just wanted to die, thinking about everyone laughing at me and thinking how stupid I was.'

'Honestly, Anna, the only thing anyone would have felt for you is sympathy.'

'They won't feel sympathetic any more,' Anna cried, her face burning with shame.

Clare looked at her curiously. 'Why?'

'Because I just spent the night with Daniel!' she blurted out, hoping somehow that by speaking the words it would make it all go away.

Clare opened her mouth to say something and then closed it again. She knew, as Anna did, that any hope of a reconciliation with Toby would be impossible if he found out that she had slept with Daniel. Although it had always been unspoken, Toby shared his biggest rivalry with Daniel.

Anna shook her head helplessly. 'I thought it would make me feel better. To prove that I'm over Toby once and for all.'

Clare nodded slowly. 'And has it?' she asked at last.

Anna looked up and met her eye, desperate for comfort. 'No,' she whispered. 'It's just made me feel a million times worse.'

They sat in silence for a few minutes, until Anna heard movement from her bedroom. 'Oh my God!' she hissed, clutching at Clare's arm in panic. 'It's him. What the hell am I going to do?'

Clare looked uncharacteristically flustered. 'Oh shit!' she snapped, climbing out of bed and going towards the door. 'Are you sure you don't want to see him?' she asked, her hand on the doorknob.

Anna shook her head violently, terrified at the prospect of having to face him.

'OK,' Clare sighed wearily. 'I'll get rid of him. I'll say you had some sort of an emergency.'

As she waited for Clare to return, Anna's heart was thumping so hard she could actually hear it.

When Clare finally came back into the bedroom, she was carrying two cups of tea. 'He's gone,' she said, putting one of the mugs down on top of the stack of history books on her bedside table.

'Thank you so much!' Anna exclaimed, grabbing her tea and gulping it gratefully. 'Was he all right about it?' she asked nervously.

Clare nodded dismissively. 'Yeah, yeah – he was fine. Mind you, he's probably more used to doing a runner himself the next morning, instead of being thrown out by someone's flatmate.'

Anna closed her eyes as the night's events returned in flashback. 'Oh my God, what have I done?' she groaned.

Clare sat down beside her and sipped her tea. 'Try to forget about it,' she said quietly. 'No one need ever know.'

Relief flooded through Anna. Clare was right. She would blank the whole hideous experience from her mind and pretend it had never happened. Daniel was a well-known womanizer who probably wouldn't give it a second thought and Anna knew for certain that Clare would never tell anyone. For the first time since waking up that morning, she started to breathe easily again.

Looking back, she should have known that nothing in life is ever that simple.

Rachel

June 2010

RSVP

Anna McKenna and her guest, Clare Stanton,
will be delighted to attend the wedding
of Rachel and Toby.

Thank you for the invitation.

Rachel turns the card over in her hand and looks at the picture on the front. It's a print of a Waterhouse painting, *Troilus and the Nymphs. A bit naff*, she thinks with satisfaction, before realizing that it's exactly the sort of thing Toby would love. The RSVP has shaken her. She had hoped and prayed that Anna wouldn't come to the wedding. She hadn't wanted Toby to invite her, but he had been adamant that he had to invite everyone from his old gang at university. It was part of some stupid pact they'd made years ago and, despite Rachel telling him she didn't think they would hold him to it, Toby said he had promised to invite them and couldn't go back on his word. *That's the trouble with Toby*, she thinks glumly. *He's too bloody decent.* It's one of the things she loves about him but at this moment, she also wishes he would put his old life behind him, once and for all. And if he did that, then maybe he could forget about Anna too.

Rachel knows that Toby and Anna were together at university but she didn't hear it from him because he never talks about it. She only found out from his sister, Helen, after they had been together a year. They were at his parents' house for Toby's dad's sixtieth birthday party and Rachel got chatting with Helen. She had always liked Helen – she was bossy and direct and, maybe because they were quite similar, they had always got on.

'I'm so glad you and Toby seem to be working out,' Helen began.

'Me too,' Rachel nodded and smiled, watching Toby as he listened politely to some chinless man's chatter about golf. She found it hard to concentrate on anything else when Toby was in the room.

'I think you were just what he needed after Anna,' Helen continued.

Rachel felt a frown crease her forehead before she could stop it. 'Anna?' she said quizzically. She had never heard Toby mention the name.

Now it was Helen's turn to frown. 'Yes, Anna . . .' she trailed off, looking embarrassed. 'Oh God, you do know about her, don't you?'

Rachel shook her head slowly. 'What about her?' she asked, already wondering if she wanted to know the answer.

Helen's eyes clouded slightly. 'Oh, bloody hell, I think I

might have put my foot in it. I can't believe Toby's never mentioned her.'

'Never,' confirmed Rachel. 'So . . . what about her?'

Helen sighed. 'Well, they met in their first week at university and were inseparable for most of the three years they were there. Everyone was so shocked when they split up – we all thought they'd be together for good.'

'But they must have been so young,' Rachel said, trying to shake off the unease that had settled over her. 'It would be more surprising if they had stayed together, surely?'

Helen hesitated, as if unsure whether to continue with such a delicate conversation. 'Yes, I know what you mean, young love usually burns out quickly. But it was different with them.'

'Really? So, why did they split up?' asked Rachel in a level voice, belying the punch of jealousy which had just fired through her.

Helen shrugged. 'No one knows. All I know is that it was very sudden and very unexpected.'

Rachel felt her face grow hot and a little ball of tension knot tightly inside her stomach. In all the time that has passed since that day, the knot has never left her.

Later that night, as she and Toby lay in his childhood room, decorated with the film posters he had thought so cool when he had last lived there, aged eighteen, and crammed with his books and guitars, she raised the subject of Anna. As soon as she mentioned her name, Rachel felt Toby's whole body stiffen. 'She's history,' was all he'd say. 'I don't want to talk about something that's in the past.'

After that, Rachel found herself becoming fixated with Anna, obsessing about her with a mixture of hatred and fascination. She needed to know what she looked like, to put a face to this creature who had so captivated Toby. As soon as she had the opportunity, she took herself off to Toby's old room and rummaged through the box of photos she had noticed he kept in the bottom of one of his cupboards. She felt deceitful and guilty doing it but the urge to see her rival was overwhelming.

Many were of his schooldays and there were several packs of family photos. But, buried right at the bottom – whether intentionally or not, she couldn't tell – she discovered six photo envelopes labelled simply 'Anna'. With shaking hands and a dry mouth, she began to sift through them. With slightly ghoulish rapture and the fervour of someone on a binge, Rachel stared at the face of her nemesis. Some of the photos were of the two of them together: a close-up shot of Anna giggling at something Toby had said, his lips almost pressed to her ear; Toby towering over Anna from behind and enveloping her tiny frame with his arms, his chin resting on her shoulder; Toby and Anna embracing each other on a white sandy beach with an indigo ocean behind them, both looking young, tanned and sickeningly (to Rachel) beautiful.

But by far the majority of the pictures were just of Anna, taken by Toby when she was unawares. As Rachel sat cross-legged on the wooden floor, working her way through the packs, she felt a fresh wave of misery with each new shot. Compared to Anna, she began to feel like the biggest, ugliest girl in the world. Even minus her make-up, often with her shiny blonde hair scraped up into a messy scrunchie and usually in the least glamorous locations and poses, Anna still looked perfect. And worse: *they* looked perfect together. The story of Toby and Anna's relationship and the depth of their love was almost tangible through the small glossy prints scattered all around her.

Rachel gets up and puts Anna's RSVP on top of the pile with all the others her mum has forwarded to her. Then, for reasons she doesn't quite understand, she thinks twice and quickly buries it in the middle of the pile, not wanting Toby to see it. At least not yet anyway. Then she scoops up her packet of cigarettes and darts out onto the roof terrace to fit in a quick smoke before Toby arrives home from work.

Over the seven years she has been with Toby, Rachel has built Anna up in her mind until she thinks of her as the most beautiful creature she has ever seen and curses her bad luck that Toby knew her first. And now, sitting here looking out over the early evening haze hanging over London, just weeks before she is due to get married, she also curses her bad luck that Toby ever went to that damned reunion. If he hadn't gone, he wouldn't have seen Anna again and he wouldn't have invited her to their wedding. The thought of coming face to face with her is almost more than Rachel can stand.

Ella

June 2002

The thaw in Ella's relationship with Toby finally came at Ella's parents' annual garden party two years after they left university. Toby's parents, Martha and Graham, were invited as usual, and to Ella's surprise, they turned up with Toby and his sister, Helen, in tow. Naturally, neither of them had mentioned their falling-out to their parents and they smiled stiffly as they greeted one another. Toby kissed Ella perfunctorily on both cheeks and turned quickly away before he could be drawn into any conversation.

Ella grabbed a glass of champagne from a passing tray and linked arms with Helen, steering her down towards the lake and away from the crowds. 'How have you been?' she began.

Helen took a sip of her champagne and smiled. 'Good. Really good, actually.' Ella listened enviously as Helen told her how she'd landed a fabulous job with one of London's biggest advertising agencies and how she was always being sent off around the world at a moment's notice. Her life sounded glamorous and fun – the complete opposite of Ella's, in other words.

'How about you?' Helen asked Ella, smiling. 'Still planning on becoming an Oscar-winning actress?'

Ella felt her cheeks flush with embarrassment. Had she ever really said that? 'Er, maybe,' she replied lamely. 'I'd better get a proper job first. I'm still working as an assistant in the City.'

'Well, that's fine as a stopgap,' said Helen briskly. 'But you do need to get yourself on the ladder, or you'll find the next lot of graduates flooding the market and you'll be left behind.'

'Too late,' said Ella grimly. She had done nothing for the past couple of years and sure enough, she was being leapfrogged by younger graduates. 'So, what's Toby up to these days?' she asked, keen to change the subject.

Helen looked surprised. 'I thought you two were friends. Surely you've kept in contact since you left uni?'

Ella shrugged. 'Yes, of course, but you know how it is. Busy lives get in the way . . .'

'Well, he's hoping to get into TV. He's been doing work experience with one of the big production companies and I think they're going to offer him a job. He's really thrown himself into it – at least it seems to have finally taken his mind off the break-up with Anna. That hit him very hard.'

Ella looked around nonchalantly, hoping Helen wouldn't notice her hands shaking slightly or the sudden flush in her cheeks. 'It was probably for the best,' she muttered.

Helen frowned. 'Do you think so? I'm not so sure. I thought those two were made for each other. And it was all so sudden. He won't talk about it but I wish he would. Do you know what happened? You were still at uni then, weren't you?'

Ella nodded, trying to compose her features. 'Yes, doing my master's. But I didn't really hang out with their group. All I know is that it was quick.'

Helen sighed. 'Yes, must have been someone else involved, I suppose. I'm sure he'll find a girlfriend and maybe it's just as well for him to have no distractions while he's at the beginning of his career. I'm certainly glad I haven't got to try and keep a relationship going while doing my job – it would be a disaster!'

Ella nodded her agreement. She watched Toby chatting to an older lady who was doing her best to flirt with him, despite the fact that she was probably old enough to be his grandmother. Toby must have felt Ella watching because he looked up and met her eye. After a moment's hesitation, he excused himself to the lady. He strolled down the lawn towards Ella and Helen, his angular limbs lending a natural elegance to his walk. *He really is beautiful*, thought Ella, still mesmerized by him, even after all this time.

'So, Ella, long time no see,' he said, his words charged with meaning.

'Yes, Ella's been telling me that you've hardly seen each other since uni – you really should keep in touch,' Helen said bossily.

Toby's eyes narrowed slightly. 'Yes, well, things are never that easy, are they?'

'No,' Ella agreed, looking at him directly. 'Yet another regret to add to the list.'

'Ooh, look, there's Peter. I must go and say hello,' said Helen, waving at a tall, horse-faced man up on the terrace. 'See you later, Ella. Let's do lunch!' she added, leaving Toby and Ella alone.

'So,' said Toby.

'So,' Ella laughed nervously.

They looked at each other in silence for a few seconds before Ella couldn't stand it any longer and broke the silence. 'I'm sorry,' she said quietly, looking down at her shoes.

Toby shrugged. 'Yes. So am I. But Anna should have known me better than that. She should have known I wouldn't ever be interested in you.'

God, it hurt when he talked like that. 'Do you ever hear from her?' asked Ella quickly, aching for him to be kind to her even if he didn't want her.

'No. But I still think about her. Sometimes.' He half-grinned, half-grimaced as he spoke. Ella could see that even now, more than two years since they broke up, Toby was still far from over Anna.

'Why don't you get back together then?' she asked, hoping the answer would be that he didn't want to.

'Where do I start? Too much water under the bridge. Both too bloody stubborn. Neither of us willing to forgive the other.'

Ella wondered what Anna had done that Toby couldn't forgive her for. As far as she knew, Anna was the wronged party.

'But you still love her, don't you?' Ella pressed, despite dreading the answer.

Toby thought for a moment before replying. 'I'm not sure. I'm not sure I can even remember how we were.'

Ella felt a small surge of hope. Maybe there was a chance for her after all.

Then Toby smiled shyly. 'And I've been seeing someone else for a couple of months.'

Maybe not.

'Oh?' croaked Ella, trying not to look crestfallen.

'Yeah, it's early days. But she works for the TV company where I've been doing work experience. She took me under her wing when I started and we've been out a few times. She's nice.'

'Well,' Ella said, trying to sound upbeat and recover her composure. 'I hope it works out. And I'm glad we're on speaking terms again – I'd have hated to lose you as a friend.'

'You deserved to, after what you did,' he said gruffly. 'But I know you were drunk,' he added in a slightly more conciliatory tone. 'Let's let bygones be bygones.'

Ella flinched with shame. She hadn't been drunk, she had known exactly what she was doing that night. But there was no harm in Toby believing that she was under the influence. Yet another little white lie wouldn't hurt. 'Yes, let's move on,' she muttered. 'Anyway, I'd better circulate or Mummy will give me one of her trademark death stares. Let's keep in touch, eh?'

Toby clinked his glass with Ella's. 'Sure,' he smiled. 'See you soon.'

Anna

March 2000

Anna tried to take Clare's advice and forget all about spending the night with Daniel but it simply wasn't possible, mainly because Daniel wouldn't leave her alone. He called and texted incessantly and began to follow her around, making her feel as though she was being stalked.

'C'mon, Anna,' he said as he followed her home from a lecture late one afternoon. 'It was good, wasn't it? We're perfect together, you and me. I've even stopped shagging around, if that's what's stopping you?'

Anna sighed and kept walking, her head down against the spring drizzle. Toby had been at the lecture and she always felt shaky and sick after seeing him, even though they barely looked at each other. She just wanted to get home and close the door to the outside world behind her.

'Anna!' Daniel called, running slightly to keep up. 'Let me take you for a drink, at least – think of it as my way of saying thank you!'

Anna stopped walking and looked at him in horror. 'What do you mean by that?' She looked at his boyishly handsome face, so appealing to many of her fellow students but so repellent to her now, and wondered yet again how she could have been so stupid.

'For a great time . . .' Daniel leered suggestively. The rain had flattened his hair and his good looks turned to something darker.

She took a deep breath. 'Listen, Daniel,' she began gently, 'you're a really nice guy . . .' His face lit up and she quickly realized being nice to him would only encourage him. 'But,' she continued firmly, 'I'm not interested in doing it again. Please leave me alone.'

His face hardened and a little pulse of fear torpedoed through her. She couldn't win in this situation.

'I'm sorry,' she said, trying to smile through the rain, which was now pelting down, plastering her hair to her face and stinging her cheeks.

Daniel smiled back but it was a nasty, menacing smile. 'You will be,' he growled, before stalking off, leaving her shivering.

After that, she studied for her finals on autopilot and stopped socializing altogether. Clare tried hard to get her to join her on nights out but she had lost any enthusiasm for enjoying herself after what had happened the last time. She didn't tell Clare how she was feeling and Clare thought she had forgotten all about Daniel. If only she could.

Reluctantly, Clare gave up asking Anna to join them but she never gave up listening to her. Late at night, they'd sit on their sofa, armed with large glasses of wine, and talk long into the early hours. Or, to put it more accurately, Anna would talk about Toby and Clare would listen. She would nod patiently, knowing Anna didn't really want her to say anything, she just wanted to talk.

On the night before Anna's first exam, Clare finally made

a suggestion. 'Look, Anna, if you feel like this, why don't you call him?'

Anna shook her head. 'I can't!' she cried. 'I've left it too long.'

'Call him, Anna.' Clare sounded so certain, so sure that it was the right thing to do.

Anna felt the faintest glimmer of hope start to ignite within her. 'Do you honestly think he'd speak to me?' she asked hopefully.

Clare got up and grabbed Anna's mobile from the table. 'Do it now,' she ordered, before leaving the room.

Anna's fingers shook as she dialled the number. He picked up after two rings. 'Anna?'

'Hi, Toby,' she whispered, feeling both bereft and hopeful as she heard his voice. 'How are you doing?'

He paused for the longest time. 'OK,' he said in a measured voice. 'I'm doing OK. How about you?'

Anna nodded, tears streaming down her cheeks. 'Great,' she sobbed.

He laughed. 'You don't sound it. What's up?'

'I miss you!' she blurted out, hiccoughing between sobs.

Another pause.

'Well, you know what? I miss you too.'

Anna's spirits soared so much at those words that she thought she might just lift off the sofa and fly. 'I need to see you!' she cried, suddenly overwhelmed by the urge to hold him and touch him.

Toby sighed loudly and she knew he was rubbing his face. 'I'm not sure that's a good idea, Anna,' he said quietly.

She stopped in her tracks and looked at the phone in disbelief. 'What?'

'You hurt me,' he said simply.

She reeled with shock. 'I HURT YOU?' she cried. 'What about how YOU hurt ME?'

'You hurt me,' Toby continued, as if she hadn't spoken, 'because even though I didn't have sex with Ella, I don't think the same can be said about you and Daniel. Jesus, Anna, of all the people, you couldn't have picked anyone worse.'

Anna was so stunned she couldn't speak. The little bubble of unease which had been lurking since that night with Daniel suddenly popped. 'How did you find out?' she whispered eventually.

'Oh, Daniel was only too keen to break it to me,' he sighed, sounding more pissed off than she had ever heard him. 'You *knew* what he was like and how much he would love getting one over on me. Why did it have to be him?'

'It was a mistake,' she sobbed, tears coursing down her cheeks. 'Please, Toby, you've got to know how sorry I am.'

'Why? You didn't listen when I tried to tell you how sorry I was. You wouldn't give me a chance.' His voice was cold and hard and he sounded a world away from the man she loved.

Anna slumped down into the sofa, trying to calm herself. 'So, you won't see me then?' she asked, her voice sounding high-pitched and childlike.

'I don't think I can,' he said after a long pause. 'Too much damage has been done. It's over, Anna.'

She nodded, even though he couldn't see her. She'd blown it. For good.

Ella

September 2005

Dear Max,

I presume it will be you who finds me. I imagine you will be relieved. One less problem to deal with. That's all I am – a problem. It's all I've ever been. I'm sorry for the trouble I have caused you. Please tell my parents I'm sorry too – although they will probably be expecting it. I so badly wanted to be a different person to the one I am but it's too late now.

I hope you go on to have a happy life. You can move on now that I am gone. It's for the best.

Ella

Ella carefully folded the note and left it propped up on the coffee table. Her life was worthless, everyone hated her and, worst of all, she hated herself. Even though she didn't love Max, she did care for him. Now that he no longer cared for her, and now she had lost her job, what was the point in continuing? Who would miss her? She honestly couldn't think of a single person who would care if she died.

She went to the bathroom cabinet and peered at its contents. Loads of Nurofen, quite a few aspirin and a couple of packets of paracetamol. She couldn't decide which to take so she grabbed the lot and skulked back through to her open-plan kitchen/living room. She retrieved a bottle of Max's favourite whiskey from the drinks cabinet and poured herself a large glass.

She gulped down the entire tumbler and immediately refilled it, gagging as the burning amber liquid trickled down her throat and hit her stomach. God, she hated whiskey. Quickly she gulped down the second glass, shuddering as she tried not to taste it.

With an increasingly unsteady hand, she refilled the glass again. She picked up the packets of paracetamol and started popping them out one by one until there was a little mound of pills on the coffee table, beside her note. Shaking violently with a mixture of fear and drunkenness, she sat for a long time staring at the innocent-looking white pile that would put an end to her life. Outside, the sun was setting and the flat was growing gloomier and darker. *How appropriate*, she thought bitterly.

With tears streaming down her face she picked up the first tablet and placed it gingerly on her tongue. She swallowed it down with a gulp of whiskey and picked up another. Then another and another, until she had swallowed fifteen in total. *That should do it*, she thought, curling up on the sofa, waiting.

Ella woke up in hospital. Her throat felt raw and dry and she hurt all over. As she opened her eyes she gagged but nothing came up and she knew immediately what had happened – she had had her stomach pumped. But how had she got here? Who had brought her here? No one knew what she was planning to do and as far as she was concerned, no one cared.

The answer was sitting beside the bed. Max leapt out of his seat as soon as she stirred and came over to her. 'Oh, you poor baby!' he sobbed, stroking her forehead with one hand and holding her hand with the other. She closed her eyes for a moment and enjoyed the feeling of Max's fingers rubbing away her pain. 'Why, Ella? Why did you do that?' he cried in an agonized voice.

Ella's eyes filled with tears and, exhausted, she let them spill out onto her cheeks. 'No one cared,' she whispered, wincing with pain at the effort.

'Oh God, Ella. What if I hadn't found you?' he cried. She opened her eyes again to see him roughly wiping the tears from his face.

'You'd be better off without me,' she whispered.

He shook his head vehemently. 'How can you even think that?'

He perched on the bed and stroked her hair. She felt tired and closed her eyes, just wanting to sleep. Suddenly a thought occurred to her. 'How did you find me?' she croaked.

Max sighed heavily. 'I heard from Jane Lewis in HR that you'd been persuaded to quit. I think she thought I'd be pleased. And I was – for about ten minutes. Then I thought about it and remembered that you weren't the one in the wrong – I was. I was the one who was married.'

Ella tried to concentrate on what he was saying.

'Anyway, I realized that whatever the rights and wrongs of the situation, I still love you. I had to see you, so I went to the flat . . .' He trailed off, breaking into gruff sobs once again. Once he'd composed himself, he continued, 'I thought you were dead and I felt as though I'd lost my wife all over again.'

He squeezed her hand and she squeezed his back.

'I'm sorry,' she whispered. 'I hate myself.'

Max put his fingers to her lips. 'Shh, darling, don't. When you get out of here, I'm going to get you some help.'

'A shrink,' she said flatly.

Max nodded. 'Yes, but it'll help. You need to find out why you feel so bad about yourself. And you need to learn to love yourself – like I love you,' he finished.

Ella turned her face away. She had been such a fool. She had come so close to killing herself and yet this kind man was prepared to risk the wrath of everyone he knew by declaring his love for her.

Max gently turned her face back towards him and looked deep into her eyes. 'Will you marry me, Ella?' he said, his voice charged with emotion.

She looked into Max's gentle blue eyes and finally saw a tiny glimmer of hope that she might have a future after all. 'Yes,' she whispered back.

May 2010

Ella's bath is getting cold and she runs some more hot water. The bottle of Malbec is empty now and her head is blissfully fuzzy. Remembering how Max saved her life all those years ago makes her feel warm towards him again and yet sad for him that he has married someone who can never truly love him.

She thinks about the invitation to Toby's wedding and

wonders if Toby feels the same as she did when she married Max – that there was someone else who couldn't be forgotten, no matter how hard he tried. Even though she rarely sees Toby these days, she somehow suspects that that is the case. She instinctively feels that, just as she hasn't been able to get over Toby, he in turn is still in love with Anna. They were the real thing and she is in no doubt that if it hadn't been for her, they would still be together today.

She shakes her head slightly to dismiss the thought and stands up. She reaches for a white, fluffy towel from the warm rail, which she expertly ties into a turban on top of her head. Then she wraps another, sarong-style around her body, enjoying the sensation of warmth as it seeps through to her bones. As she stands, swaying slightly from too much red wine, there is a knock at the door. 'Darling?' enquires Max softly. 'Are you OK? You've been in there an awfully long time.'

Ella looks at herself in the steamy bathroom mirror, her face illuminated by the dressing room lights, giving her a slightly ghoulish appearance. 'I'm fine,' she calls back before opening the door. They stand face to face in silence for a few seconds, Max's eyes sad and uncomprehending, until Ella lets her towel drop. Max takes her hand and leads her naked to the bed. Little does Ella know this is to be the last time.

Rachel

May 2010

Rachel has watched Toby carefully for signs that he still has feelings for Anna but has never seen any. And now that she thinks about it, maybe that's the problem. She doesn't remember ever hearing him talk about Anna or even mentioning her name. He has never said so, but Rachel also senses that Toby thinks his university friends would be too intellectual for her, which irritates her, even though he is probably right. Rachel trained as a journalist straight from school and she has an inverted sense of snobbery about university.

She first met Toby when he started doing work experience at the TV company she was working for as a producer on a daily magazine show. He was assigned to shadow her and she liked him immediately. He was different from most of the young men who started at the company, who took one look at Rachel and promptly decided that they should be doing her job, rather than acting as her lackey. Toby had no such airs and graces. He was genuinely interested in what she was doing and would listen with rapt attention whenever she explained how her job worked. The show was a mix of current affairs and features, so the subject matter was wide-ranging and interesting. No two days were ever the same, as the teams worked tirelessly to come up with the best ideas and produce the most filmed inserts. There was intense rivalry between the five day teams, so Rachel was thrilled to find she had landed a work-experience intern who might actually be of some benefit to her.

Rachel was a talented producer; she had a good instinct for the stories that would make great TV and her scripts were the only ones the editor rarely changed. Toby was happy to get involved in whatever needed doing, whether it was making cups of tea, delivering packages or typing up research notes and she quickly found herself becoming reliant on him. Some of the other researchers on the show were lazy and disinterested, which only made Toby stand out even more.

The hours were long and tough and, despite being unpaid, Toby never tried to slope off early. By his fifth week, Rachel had suggested to the editor that they take him on as a full-time researcher the next time a vacancy became available. They didn't have long to wait; Karl, one of the longest-serving researchers on her team, was offered a job on a huge reality show and decided to leave the following week.

Rachel took Toby out for a drink to celebrate. She knew she was interested in him in more than a professional sense when she started to avoid inviting any of the rest of the team to join them. And that was it. From the start, it was Rachel who did all the running. Toby always seemed happy to go along with whatever she suggested but he never instigated anything. She told herself that this was only natural; she was three years older than him so was bound to take the lead in their relationship. Occasionally she would worry that she was keener on him than he was on her but she had fallen for him so hard that she just pushed any worries to the back of her mind.

When, about six months into their relationship, Toby's landlord put his studio flat up for sale, Rachel suggested that they move in together. She tried not to be disappointed when Toby agreed that it would be a practical thing to do. He was endlessly sweet and considerate towards her. He cooked for her, ran her baths and gave her foot rubs on demand, but although he was thoughtful and affectionate, he always stopped short of declaring his undying love for her and she couldn't shake the nagging sense that he was holding something back.

In many ways they were opposites. Rachel was loud and gregarious while Toby was quieter and more thoughtful; she devoured the *Sun*, *Mail* and *Mirror* every day, while he gravitated towards the broadsheets and serious literature. She needed to be surrounded by other people while Toby was happy to spend time alone. But they were very happy together. They rarely argued, had the same sense of humour and enjoyed each other's company. As well as a shared passion for TV, they also loved the cinema and going to gigs and concerts with their wide circle of friends. They had great sex and laughed a lot.

Toby, predictably, soon leapfrogged her at work. He was a wunderkind and quickly got noticed by the bosses. Rachel wasn't jealous of his success – she felt proud. She had 'discovered' him and taught him a lot of what he knew. Most of all, she was proud that she was his girlfriend.

She was pretty certain that Toby would never cheat on

her. He simply wasn't that type of person. He was loyal and honest and she didn't think he could have coped with the deception involved in having an affair. Anyway, he was too busy forging ahead in his career. They both worked long hours but Toby was mentally driven in a way that Rachel wasn't. She loved her job, but as soon as she hit thirty, her biological clock began to tick and she tentatively raised the prospect of kids with Toby. He nodded distractedly and agreed that he would like to have kids 'someday'. But as the months and years passed, she became increasingly desperate. Toby was now bringing in enough money to support them both and she was more than happy to take a back seat career-wise now that hers had stalled at producer level.

It was her dad who suggested they get married. They had spent the weekend with Rachel's parents in Cheltenham and as they were leaving, her dad opened his diary and peered at it comically. 'What are you doing?' she laughed.

'I'm checking when I'd be available for your wedding,' her dad replied, still scanning the pages. 'About time you made an honest woman of my daughter, young man,' he grinned at Toby. 'After, what is it? Seven years now?'

Toby laughed. 'Anything you say, George. I just do what I'm told.'

In the car home, Rachel jokingly mentioned her dad's comments and Toby laughed. 'He's a funny guy, your dad.'

She inwardly fumed all the way home and for the rest of the evening, until finally Toby asked her what was wrong. 'I'm upset that you think it would be a joke marrying me,' she said, trying to keep her voice steady.

Toby frowned. 'When did I say that?'

'In the car on the way home. You said you thought my

dad was a funny guy because he suggested we get married.'

Toby sighed and rubbed his face. 'I didn't mean that it would be a joke marrying you. I just thought it was funny the way he got out his diary, that's all.'

Rachel looked at Toby and steeled herself. 'Well, in that case, how about it?' she said, her heart pounding.

The colour drained slightly from Toby's face. 'What?' he croaked, clearly trying to buy some time while he collected his thoughts. 'How about what?'

'Toby, will you marry me?' she persisted, knowing that it was now or never.

Toby hesitated, suddenly looking as though he'd rather be anywhere else than where he was now. 'I don't know,' he whispered eventually.

Rachel got up and walked into their bedroom, the tears already starting to pour down her face. If he didn't want to marry her, that was it. They would have to break up. *Oh, why the hell did I have to open my big mouth?* she thought. *And why did my stupid dad have to bring the subject up? We were perfectly happy as we were.* She climbed into bed and hid under the duvet, crying uncontrollably.

After a couple of minutes, she felt Toby's weight as he sat down on the bed beside her. He waited a moment more before he pulled back the duvet. 'OK,' he said gently.

She shook her head and carried on sobbing. 'It's too late!' she cried. 'I know you don't really want to marry me or you'd have said yes straight away!'

Toby pulled her over so that she was facing him and stroked her face. 'I was just a bit shocked, that's all,' he said softly. 'Really, Rachel. Come on, baby, don't cry.'

She sat up and allowed herself to be cradled in his arms

as he kissed away her tears. She took a deep, shuddery breath and smiled a watery smile at him. 'Thank you,' she whispered.

Sitting out on her terrace now, watching the sun sink into the distant horizon, Rachel lifts her face towards it, closing her eyes, trying to enjoy the last rays of warmth before it disappears altogether. Behind her, she hears Toby emerge onto the roof terrace and wander over to join her on the bench. 'Your childish dependence on nicotine is quite endearing,' he drawls, picking up the full ashtray and putting it on the ground, before sinking down beside her and kissing her gently on the top of her head.

Without looking at him and with her face still tilted upwards, Rachel flicks a V sign at him and is gratified to hear him chuckle.

'What are you doing sitting out here anyway?' he says, ruffling her short dark hair affectionately. 'Something on your mind?'

Rachel looks at him now. Even stubble and the bags under his eyes can't detract from his beauty. If anything, they add to it. She wants to tell him that she feels like she has only ever had him on loan and that she can't bear the thought that she might have to give him back someday soon. Instead she quietly says, 'No. I'm absolutely fine.'

Anna

July 2010

Anna looks at herself in the changing room mirror. She is wearing a knee-length, petrol-coloured chiffon backless dress. 'What do you think?' she asks Clare, who is sitting on the floor of the cubicle.

'I hate you,' Clare replies cheerfully.

Anna smiles at her reflection and twists from side to side. They have been shopping for hours now, hunting for something to wear to the wedding. Clare knows how important it is for Anna to look sensational. She has taken a lot of persuading to go and has only just sent the RSVP, but Clare has convinced her that seeing Toby get married will help her to finally get over him. Anna feels physically sick at the prospect but at the same time she hopes that Clare is right. She usually is.

She turns 180 degrees so that she can see herself from behind. The dress is beautiful. Her back is brown and toned, thanks to the hours she spends running each week, trying to shake off her depression. With a pair of killer heels and her hair up, she will look as good as she possibly can. 'I'll buy it,' she says decisively, trying not to think of the price tag and her credit card bill.

'Yay!' Clare cheers, clapping her hands and gathering her bags as she scrambles to her feet. 'At bloody last.'

Anna swipes her affectionately across the top of the head. 'Shut up, you! You took just as long as me to find something and you have a lot less reason than me to want to look drop-dead gorgeous.'

Clare looks indignant. 'I've got just as much reason as you! I'm hoping to meet some tall, dark, handsome stranger there so I need a bloody good outfit too.'

She'd got one – it was a fitted white trouser suit which, thanks to her distinct lack of lumps and bumps, only she could have got away with. Teamed with a pair of strappy skyscraper heels, she would look like a supermodel.

Anna is so glad Clare is going to be with her on the day. She would never have even contemplated going alone. Clare has become like a protective sister to her. She is the only person who knows everything about her and her patience has been extraordinary.

With just a month to go until the wedding, Anna has given up hoping that Rachel and Toby might both have a change of heart and call it off at the last minute. She knows Toby well enough to know that he wouldn't hurt Rachel like that. But that doesn't stop her wondering every day if there is a tiny part of him that still loves her.

It isn't just Toby and Rachel she is dreading seeing at the wedding. It is Ella too. Anna has spent many nights over the past ten years imagining all sorts of vicious ways to exact her revenge on Ella for what she did; she is slightly worried that as soon as she sees Ella, all that pent-up rage will come out and she will end up throttling her there and then in front of all the other guests. Anna did wonder if she would even have been invited but then remembered that her parents and Toby's are great friends and they would think it strange if she wasn't on the guest list.

She's decided that the best revenge would be if Ella looked haggard and old. Hopefully, her glossy black hair is now grey and her skin is shrivelled and wrinkled. Unlikely, she has to concede; Ella would only be thirty-two now, not sixty-five.

From: Rachel.King@mail.com
To: Undisclosed recipients
Date: 1 July 2010
Subject: Hen & Stag night!

Hi all,

We weren't going to bother with all that stag and hen business (Toby thinks it's naff!) but I have persuaded him that we should have a get together before the big day with all the 'young 'uns' who'll be coming. So, hope to see you there for a glass or two of fizz.

Rachel & Toby
xxx

Toby & Rachel would like you to join them
for a celebration of their forthcoming marriage
at Bar Bastille,
72 Hockley Street,
London,
W1
on 17 July 2010

RSVP: rachel.king@mail.com

Anna stares in horror at the e-mail which has just pinged into her inbox, reading and rereading it several times. She has steeled herself for the wedding day but hasn't even considered having to face them as a couple any sooner. The thought gives her goosebumps. But once she has made herself a cup of tea and calmed down a bit, she begins to think that it may be better to get it out of the way, so that she is not such a bag of nerves on the day. She wonders if Rachel has organized the party for the same reason, then mentally chastises herself for being so arrogant. She probably hasn't given Anna a second thought. It's Rachel that Toby is marrying.

Anna persuades Clare to come with her for moral support, which she is all too happy to do. 'I can assess the men ahead of the big day,' Clare laughs.

The party is being held in a trendy basement club in Soho and it is already in full swing by the time they arrive. Toby and Rachel are greeting guests as they reach the bottom of the stairs and Anna feels her heart pounding with jealousy, fascination and fear as she approaches them. She has imagined so many times what Rachel looks like and now that she is about to come face to face with her, she suddenly wants to turn and run back up the stairs, to get away from her. And him.

'Hi!' they beam in unison at Clare and Anna as they reach the bottom of the steps.

Anna doesn't look at Toby but focuses instead on Rachel, the woman Toby has chosen to marry. 'You look lovely,' she tells her, meaning it, her eyes drawn to Rachel like a magnet. She is so different from her that Anna can't stop staring. She is tall and dark with short, spiky hair. She towers over Anna in a simple black shift dress with strappy sandals and a pretty flower clip in her hair. But her face looks strained, creases of anxiety around her eyes.

'So do you,' she smiles tightly as they kiss awkwardly on both cheeks. 'Have a lovely evening.'

With a monumental effort, Anna pulls her eyes away from Rachel and looks at Toby, who is watching her with an unreadable expression. 'Hi,' he says, suddenly snapping on a polite smile as he kisses her. Anna is so aware of his proximity, the smell and the feel of him that her legs wobble slightly. He grips her arm and their eyes meet for a split second. 'Steady,' he says.

'Thank you,' she smiles, feeling her equilibrium return. The worst part is over. 'Enjoy your evening,' she adds, moving away from him. From them.

'Blimey, she looks a bit uptight,' whispers Clare as they walk off. 'Maybe she's having second thoughts.'

Anna's stomach creases with a mixture of hope and terror. 'Oh God, please don't say things like that!' she hisses back.

Clare looks at Anna with a sheepish expression. 'Sorry, hon. That was insensitive of me. Are you OK?'

She nods. 'I'm just focusing on the fact that it'll all be over in a week's time.'

'Come on, let's get some champagne and mingle,' orders Clare, already grabbing two glasses from a passing tray. She smiles easily and confidently, pulling Anna with her to join a group of three people who are talking nearby. 'I'm Clare and this is Anna, we're friends of Toby.'

The two guys in the group smile and step outwards so that Clare and Anna can join the circle. The girl stays where she is. 'I'm Marco,' one of them introduces himself. 'I work with Toby and Rachel. I'm the best man.' Anna feels a stab of shock at the realization that she has never met Toby's best friend – he must have become friends with Toby after he left uni. 'And this is James, another of Toby and Rachel's colleagues,' he continues, pointing towards a tall blond man with a handsome, mischievous face. 'And this is Vanessa, our boss.' Anna smiles at the attractive but hard-looking girl, who does not smile but rather grimaces in return.

'Wow, so you all work in TV? That must be exciting,' Clare says pleasantly, picking up the conversation after a slightly awkward pause.

Vanessa snorts derisively. 'Hardly. And what do you two do?' she asks, her birdlike eyes narrowing, looking straight at Anna.

'Oh! I'm a teacher,' Anna replies, trying not to sound too apologetic.

Vanessa's eyes glaze over immediately. 'Oh, right,' she mumbles, looking bored.

'And I'm a lawyer,' interjects Clare. 'Which really *is* exciting!' The rest of the group laugh.

Vanessa just nods. 'How very funny,' she drawls without humour. 'Do excuse me.' With that, she turns on her heel and walks off to find someone more interesting to talk to.

'Nice,' says Clare sarcastically, with one eyebrow raised.

James and Marco look at each other and laugh. 'She's nothing compared to some of them,' says James. 'Our boss before her actually punched a producer and pushed her off a chair!'

As Clare and Anna both gape in disbelief, Marco picks up the story. 'Yes, but only after she'd slapped a VT editor because he wasn't pressing the buttons fast enough!'

Both Clare and Anna laugh. Having felt so tense, Anna

is surprised to find herself relaxing. Before she knows it an hour has gone by and she is actually enjoying herself.

She looks around her and notices with a slight start that James and Clare and Marco and she have gradually moved into two couples and that Marco seems to be chatting her up. Physically, he wouldn't normally be her type at all. He is only about five foot eight and quite stocky, with lots of hair and a dark complexion. But he has beautiful dark eyes that twinkle with laughter and intelligence and he seems like a lovely guy, asking lots of questions about her job and seeming interested in her answers. Finally, the inevitable question comes: 'So, how do you know Toby and Rachel then?'

Anna reddens slightly but feels reassured that he won't be able to tell because it is so dimly lit in the club. 'I knew Toby at university,' she says, trying to keep her voice light.

Marco nods. 'And it's Anna, you said your name was?'

'Yes,' she says slowly.

'I know all about you, Anna,' he grins mischievously. 'You made quite an impact on him, didn't you?'

She shrugs and sips her drink, unable to meet his eye. 'It was a long time ago.'

'Some things are hard to forget,' he says meaningfully. 'And I can see why you were hard to forget.'

Anna has had several glasses of wine and is starting to feel woozy. She leans against a wall and can feel the warmth from Marco's body as he inches closer and closer. 'I'd better find Clare,' she whispers, their eyes still locked.

'I doubt she's at a loose end,' he smiles, still holding her gaze. 'Stay here. With me.'

'I see you two have already met,' says a voice, making

Anna jump and jolting both her and Marco out of the moment. Toby is smiling but the smile doesn't quite reach his eyes, which are blazing.

'Oh, all right, mate?' says Marco, slapping Toby on the back. 'Having a good time?'

Toby looks around the room. 'Yeah. But not as good as you, I see.'

Marco reads Toby's meaning straight away. 'I was just about to get some more drinks,' he says quickly. 'Want one?' Toby nods curtly and Marco walks off, leaving Anna and Toby alone together.

'You two seem to be getting on well,' Toby says archly.

'I've only just met him, but yes, he seems nice,' Anna replies carefully. She can see a nerve in Toby's cheek twitching and it gives her a strange sense of satisfaction. Maybe she hasn't been the only one pining for these past ten years, after all. 'He seems to know all about me,' she adds softly.

'He's my best man,' he replies, glancing at her defensively. 'He knows everything about my past.'

They stand enveloped in a heavy silence for a few minutes before she can't stand it any longer. 'Well, enjoy the rest of your evening,' she says, already moving off. 'I'll see you next week.'

Toby stays where he is and Anna glances back to see him leaning his head against the wall where she has been standing. And then she knows. He might be about to go off and marry someone else but he still loves her.

Anna looks around for Clare and spots her wrapped around James in a corner alcove. She thinks about finding Marco at the bar but decides she would be better off leaving. He is a nice guy but he's too close to Toby for comfort. She can't be entirely sure that this isn't part of the reason she finds him attractive.

She climbs the steel stairs to street level and pulls open the door. As she walks into the road, she notices a figure leaning against the wall, smoking. Rachel. 'Hey,' she waves awkwardly, her eyes half on the road on the lookout for a cab. Rachel nods and attempts to smile. Anna hesitates, before walking over to her. 'Are you OK?' she asks, her heart heavy because she already knows the answer.

'No,' Rachel says softly.

'Last-minute nerves?'

Rachel sighs and takes a long drag of her cigarette before looking directly at Anna with her knowing brown eyes. 'Maybe. Anna, can I ask you something? I'd really like you to give me an honest answer.'

Anna's stomach clenches as she nods and waits for the question she has dreaded anyone asking her for years.

'Do you still love Toby?'

Anna holds her gaze for a long time, knowing that how she replies could impact her life for years to come. Rachel hasn't done anything wrong apart from fall in love with someone who has a history. 'I did,' she whispers eventually. 'But we're different people now. I don't really know him any more.'

'Neither do I,' Rachel replies bitterly. 'He never talks about you, you know.' Her eyes flicker with something like triumph as she speaks.

'Why would he?' Anna says at last, her mind whirring. 'He's getting married to you and we broke up a long time ago. It's you he loves.'

A tiny glimmer of hope ignites in Rachel's eyes. 'Do you

really think that?' she says, her voice and her expression demanding honesty. 'Do you really believe that he loves me?'

'Yes,' Anna replies quickly – and honestly. 'I do. Toby was never deceitful, he wouldn't be with you and be getting married to you if he didn't love you.'

Rachel takes another drag on her cigarette and Anna can see a small smile playing around her lips. Finally, she looks up and meets her eye. 'Thank you,' she says, touching her arm fleetingly.

Anna nods, turns on her heel and walks quickly down the street, hunting desperately for a cab, her eyes blurred, even though the pavement beneath her feet is bone dry.

Clare

Clare set out with Anna expecting Toby and Rachel's pre-wedding party to be a bit of a chore but it turns out to be a lot more successful than she could ever have imagined.

It is immediately obvious that Marco, Toby's best man, is transfixed by Anna. As usual, she looks beautiful in a simple pale green shift dress and delicate silver high heels. Her blonde hair is loose and she looks toned and tanned. Beside her Clare feels like a human tower block: tall, straight up and down and grey. Her job as a lawyer doesn't allow her to spend much time outside enjoying the sunshine, whereas Anna's long holidays give her ample opportunity to perfect a honey-coloured hue.

Clare waits for James' tongue to start hanging out in Anna's direction too but to her great delight he seems interested in her. He laughs at her jokes, buys her drinks and regales her with plenty of funny anecdotes of his own. He knocks back quite a bit of alcohol but he doesn't appear drunk and Clare thinks he is very handsome, with his short blond hair and pale piercing blue eyes that crinkle as he laughs.

They share lots of common interests, mainly sports-related. Clare loves football, motor racing and tennis. 'You look like the sporty type,' says James, looking her up and down appreciatively. Clare flushes with delight. There is something different about this guy, he is not like the many others she has dated in the past. She is never short of male attention but she can't remember feeling the same sort of tingle she is feeling now. She somehow knows that James won't just be a one-night stand.

Without knowing how they built up to it, they are soon snogging like teenagers in the corner of the club. By the time the party ends, they are both practically ripping each other's clothes off. 'Can I come back to yours?' James whispers as they climb the steps out of the club. Clare hesitates. She senses that there is something special about him and she doesn't want to ruin any potential relationship by sleeping with him on the first date. Second, maybe. First, no.

'You haven't even bought me dinner yet!' she laughs, tucking a strand of hair behind her ear.

He smiles. 'That's true, but I've bought you lots of expensive cocktails with fruit in them . . . that's practically dessert. Does that count?' Clare looks into his bright, clear eyes and decides to throw caution to the wind. 'Why not?' she grins, hailing a taxi.

Clare can tell that Anna is already in bed by the time they get back to the flat. Her door is closed but she has left the hall light on and Clare feels a pang of guilt. She had only gone along tonight to give Anna moral support and what had she done? Dumped her at the earliest opportunity and gone off with the groom's mate. But, she reasons, when she last remembers seeing Anna, she seemed to be getting along rather well with the best man.

She is about to offer James coffee but he is already making his way towards her bedroom, holding her hand as he pulls her along with him. He kicks her door shut with one foot as though he has lived there all his life and she can't help giggling at his cheek as he throws her onto the bed. 'Right,' he growls comically, 'me Tarzan, you Jane,' before diving on top of her and planting tiny kisses all over her body.

Clare screams with laughter as he pulls her clothes off and swings them above his head before depositing them on the floor. 'What about YOUR clothes?' she cries indignantly once she is naked beneath him.

'What about them?' he mutters, moving up to her breasts, licking and biting them teasingly. Clare has never experienced a feeling like it before. Finally, when she feels like she can't stand it any longer, she reaches for his buttons and rips his jeans open, before unceremoniously yanking them down and off, closely following them with his boxer shorts. His body is tanned and smooth, with muscles in all the right places. She feels like she is melting at the sight of him.

Even though she is more than a little drunk, it seems like her senses are heightened and every nerve is responding to his touch, which is somehow delicate yet fierce at the same time. 'Have you got any condoms?' he whispers, having kissed every single part of her body and brought her to an almost agonizing state of ecstasy. She is aching to feel him inside her.

Without pausing from kissing him, she reaches over and opens her bedside drawer. James grins and delves in, laughing as he rummages around among old bottles of nail varnish, books, cards and scraps of paper until his fingers close around a small box of condoms. He opens the box and takes one out. 'Only two left,' he says, raising an eyebrow, as he rolls it on.

'Think you'll need more than that, do you?' teases Clare, pulling him down to kiss her again as he slides inside her.

Both of them moan with pleasure as he moves in and out of her, gently at first, then more urgently. 'I don't *think* so . . .' he groans, as he is about to come for the first time, 'I *know* so!'

By the next morning they are both utterly exhausted. They have barely slept, alternating between bouts of energetic and amazing sex, trying every single position possible and a few Clare hadn't thought possible, interspersed with brief periods when they would doze with their bodies entwined together, before waking up and starting all over again. It is like nothing Clare has ever known before. His body seems to fit hers so perfectly. Every time he touches her, it is with the practised skill of someone who has spent years getting to know every part of her. She is totally uninhibited with him and feels an overwhelming sense of belonging that shocks her in its intensity.

As the morning sun peeps through the top of her blind, Clare lifts her head up and rests her chin on one elbow, looking down at James, who is now sleeping soundly. His long eyelashes brush his cheek and his breathing is deep and rhythmic. She knows as she watches him that he is The One. Before now, she had never believed in all Anna's romantic rubbish about soulmates and The One and Only. But just when she is least expecting it, her soulmate has walked into her life and she knows it will never be the same again.

*

Smiling dreamily to herself, Clare walks into the kitchen. Anna is sitting at the kitchen table, cradling her cat on her lap as she reads some dreary tome that Clare would have used as a doorstop. In front of her is a mug of coffee which has a slight film on the surface, suggesting that it went cold some time ago. The sight of her tiny frame pulls Clare up sharply and she feels a swirl of remorse. She hadn't given Anna a second thought last night.

'Hi,' she murmurs gently, pulling out a chair and sitting down opposite her.

Anna raises one eyebrow and looks back at Clare knowingly. 'Good night?' she asks, carefully replacing the bookmark and closing her book. There is no malice in her voice and her eyes are mischievous.

Clare blushes furiously. 'Mmm. Yeah. Quite good. How about you? Are you OK? I'm so sorry I didn't look after you properly last night.'

Anna waves her hand dismissively. 'Forget it. You're not my babysitter and I'm really glad you had a good time. He seems nice,' she adds, nodding in the direction of Clare's bedroom.

Clare smiles, the butterflies of excitement making her unable to help herself gushing, 'Oh, he is! He's so funny and so clever and so—'

'Good in bed?' interrupts Anna, grinning as she strokes Scratch's fur. 'Sounded like it.'

Clare nods sheepishly. 'Yeah, that too. Oh, Anna, he's perfect.'

Anna's eyebrow shoots up again. 'Wow! Praise indeed. Well, you did say you were looking for a man at this wedding, didn't you?'

'You know what, Anna?' Clare replies, her eyes shining. 'I really think he might be the one.'

'It's been one night!' laughs Anna. 'I don't think I'll be buying my wedding hat just yet. You know what you're like – you start off like this and then get bored two weeks down the line.'

Clare shakes her head fiercely. 'No, this is different,' she insists. 'I can't explain it but I know he's special.'

Anna smiles and reaches for her book again, before gesturing towards Clare's room. 'Well, in that case, don't leave him waiting too long.'

Walking back into her bedroom with two mugs of coffee, which she places on the bedside table, Clare takes off her robe and snuggles back into bed beside James. Automatically, he wraps his arms around her and she lies cradled in his embrace for another few minutes before reluctantly nudging him awake.

'Come on, sleepyhead,' she murmurs, 'time to get up.'

James strokes her back and kisses her. 'No, I want to stay here with you forever.'

Clare almost cries with happiness. How could her life turn around in such a short space of time? This time yesterday she was trundling along with no sign of a decent man in sight. Now here she is in bed with someone she already feels is her soulmate.

As if reading her thoughts, James suddenly tenses beside her.

'What's wrong?' she asks, twisting around to look at him, feeling a little sting of alarm. She's getting carried away.

'There's something you need to know,' he says ominously, unhooking his arm and sitting up, unable to meet her eye.

Oh my God, thinks Clare. *He's married, or* . . . but she can't think of anything else.

'I'm emigrating – to Australia,' he says, dropping his eyes shamefacedly.

Yes, how quickly her life had turned around. This time yesterday she was trundling along quite happily, without any man to screw things up. Now here she is, crushed because the man of her dreams, her soulmate, is moving to the other side of the world.

'When?' she asks, her voice trembling, terrified of the answer.

'Next week,' he replies. 'After the wedding. I've got a big new job with a TV network there. It's the sort of opportunity you only get once in a lifetime.'

Talk about a crash-landing. Clare's mouth drops open in horror at James' words as she digests the full meaning of what he has just said.

'I'm sorry,' he says, gazing at her beseechingly with those lovely eyes. 'I should have told you.'

'Yes,' Clare says, her chin wobbling with the effort of not crying. 'You should.' He reaches out and pulls her to him but she shakes him off angrily. 'No,' she snaps defiantly. 'Don't touch me!' She suddenly feels exposed and raw, sitting naked beside him. She gets up and snatches her robe from the hook. Pulling it around her defensively, she sniffs away the tears that are threatening.

'Would it have made any difference?' he asks gently, pulling the duvet around himself.

'Of course it bloody well would! I wouldn't have . . . I wouldn't have . . .' For once, she can't find the words to finish what she is trying to say.

'Wouldn't have slept with me?' he prompts, running his hand through his mussed-up hair.

Clare shakes her head miserably. 'No, that's not what I was going to say.'

'Well, what then?' he asks, looking puzzled.

God, men were so bloody stupid sometimes. 'I wouldn't have . . . let myself LIKE you!' she cries eventually.

His face softens and his eyes flicker with amusement. 'Oh, right,' he nods. 'Yeah I get it. You would have been introduced to me, found out I was emigrating next week, made your excuses and left. Is that it?'

Clare smiles, despite herself. 'Yes,' she says sulkily.

James gets off the bed and pulls on his boxers and jeans.

'Are you leaving?' she asks, alarmed.

'No,' he replies, coming to sit beside her on the bed. 'But I don't want to have an important discussion with no clothes on. I can't concentrate . . .' He leans towards her and kisses her deeply.

'Don't,' she says, pulling away. 'It's not fair.'

He sighs heavily. 'Listen, Clare, if it makes you feel any better, I feel the same as you. Last night was amazing. You're amazing. I didn't plan on meeting Miss Right a week before I left to start a new life in Australia, you know.'

Clare's heart leaps suddenly. 'Do you think I'm Miss Right?' she can't stop herself from asking.

He stares into her eyes, as if he is searching for something. 'I don't know,' he says. 'But I think you could be. Do you think I'm Mr Right?'

'I don't know,' she whispers back. 'But I think you could be.'

*

Later that evening, James has gone back to his own flat and Clare is drowning her sorrows with Anna. 'Why does it have to happen to me?' she mopes. 'Why did I have to meet him now? He could have gone off to Australia next week and our paths would never have crossed. I'd be carrying on as happy as Larry, instead of wallowing in this misery!'

'And would you honestly prefer it to be that way?' asks Anna gently.

Clare nods furiously. 'Yes! No! Oh, I don't bloody know!'

Anna smiles sympathetically. 'Who was it who once said, "It's better to have loved and lost than never to have loved at all"?'

'Someone who's never loved and lost!' Clare wails back. 'Oh, what am I going to do, Anna?'

Anna rubs Clare's back and takes a sip of wine. 'Well,' she says thoughtfully, 'I think you should definitely make the most of your time together this week. You never know, by the time he goes, you might have gone right off him and you'll be glad to see the back of him. You know what your track record's like.'

Clare's spirits lift again suddenly. Maybe Anna is right. Maybe if she spends the whole week with James and totally indulges her lust for him, by the time he's due to go, she might have had enough. 'You know,' she smiles at Anna, 'I think you may have hit on something. I'll call him now,' she adds, getting up and grabbing her phone.

Clare can still hear Anna laughing as she looks up James' mobile number which she had hastily added to her phone that afternoon when he left.

'Hi, you,' he says as he answers the phone. Clare can tell

by his voice that he is smiling. 'I only just got back. Missing me already?'

'No,' lies Clare, her insides churning at hearing his voice again. 'I just wanted to say that I had a great time last night but I really don't think we've got a future together, so I think it's best if we call it a day right now.'

'Me too,' he says slowly. 'Shall I come round now?'

'I'll leave the door on the latch,' Clare replies, beaming.

James has already left his job, so is free to spend the whole week that follows with Clare. She calls in sick, telling work that she is incapacitated by a sudden debilitating and mysterious sick bug that is refusing to go away. 'Well,' she tells Anna earnestly, 'it's not a complete lie.'

'Yeah, yeah,' laughs Anna. 'Tell it to the jury.'

Since meeting James, Clare has felt like a giddy teenage girl, in a way that she never did as a teenager. James has unlocked something in her that she's never experienced before. Like anything and everything is possible, there are no longer any limits.

Every day they get out of bed late, after eating croissants and drinking coffee, while sitting up in bed chatting. 'You'll get crumbs on my sheets!' Clare protests lamely one morning as James stuffs down his third croissant, flakes cascading from his lips.

'Good!' he laughs, planting buttery kisses down her back. 'Then I'll have fun clearing them up, won't I?'

Both of them seem to want to devour every last morsel of each other before their enforced separation. Each time it feels better and better and, instead of going off him as she had hoped, Clare falls for him that little bit more.

'Your plan isn't working,' she whispers to Anna as they pass in the hallway one evening.

Anna hugs Clare close to her and sighs. 'I know,' she says simply.

The day before the wedding, Clare picks up James in her little MG sports car and they head for Brighton. Driving along with the top down, the sun beaming and the breeze blowing through her hair, Clare feels like this is her perfect moment. She glances across at James and can see that he is feeling the same way. He catches her looking and smiles back, squeezing her bare knee. 'I love you,' he mouths.

Clare screeches the car to a halt at the side of the road. 'What?' she gasps, unsure she has heard him correctly. 'What did you say?'

'I said "I love you",' he repeats, looking her straight in the eye.

'I love you too,' Clare replies, her eyes filling with tears. 'I don't want you to go.'

James reaches over and pulls her to him, stroking her hair gently as she sobs. 'Listen,' he says eventually, 'let's not spoil our last full day together. Let's make the most of it and pack everything into it that we can. What do you think?'

Clare nods and wipes her eyes. 'You're right,' she agrees. 'I don't want to spoil it either, it's just—'

'I know,' he interrupts her. 'I know.'

So they make the most of their precious short time together. They eat ice creams on the beach and go swimming in the sea, giggling as their feet stumble over sharp stones. They eat fish and chips and drink cold beer in a little place overlooking the harbour. They wander hand in hand over the shingle, talking, laughing and learning as much about each other as they possibly can. Clare tells him all about her childhood as the daughter of an alpha mum, making him laugh as she describes her mother's insistence that she should never let a man come between her and her career.

In turn, he tells her all about his hippy father who didn't want to be 'tied down' by a family so left his mum to go travelling and would pitch up every year or so, armed with ridiculous presents, before disappearing again in the dead of night to some other far-flung corner of the world.

'That must be where I get my wanderlust from,' he smiles, sinking onto the pebbles and pulling Clare down beside him.

'As long as you didn't inherit anything else from him,' Clare laughs, shivering slightly as the sun begins to set in a flamingo-coloured sky.

'Well, I've certainly never had any money out of him, if that's what you mean,' laughs James as they lie down side by side and gaze up into the sky, their hands entwined.

'So, what's your greatest ambition then?' he says, turning his head to look at her, making her stomach swirl with love and desire. 'Let me guess . . . to represent some obscenely rich client and make your fortune?' he grins cheekily.

Clare slaps him playfully. 'I'm not that mercenary!' she says indignantly.

'Tell me,' he prompts, squeezing her hand. 'I won't tell anyone, I'll be on the other side of the world.'

Clare's heart flips at the very thought. She doesn't need reminding of where he is going the day after tomorrow.

'My greatest ambition is just to be happy,' she says, feeling a lump forming in her throat as tears threaten. 'And I think I might have achieved it today.'

James props himself up on one elbow and looks down at her. 'Me too,' he says sadly.

Neither of them speaks very much on the journey home, both of them engrossed in their own thoughts. Every song that comes on the radio seems to puncture Clare's bubble that little bit more and as they reach the outskirts of London all she can see is litter, dust, dirt and decay, the city seeming to sum up her mood perfectly. She feels a blanket of depression envelop her. The day after tomorrow he will be gone.

Ella

November 2005

TELEGRAPH WEDDING
ANNOUNCEMENTS

Mr M Corbett & Miss E de Bourg
The marriage between Max and Ella
took place at Marylebone Registry Office, London
on Friday, 19 November 2005.

Ella's wedding to Max was a quiet affair, with only her mother and father present. Her father acted as best man as well as giving her away, while her mother was her maid of honour. Neither of them could understand why no one else was there. 'We want it that way,' was all Ella would say. She suspected that both of her parents were delighted to get her off their hands. They liked and trusted Max and seemed grateful to offload Ella and her problems onto him.

They honeymooned on the island of Capri and for that brief period Ella finally found a tiny bit of the happiness that had always eluded her. Max was loving and attentive, giving her everything she wanted before she even knew she wanted it. He seemed so proud to be seen with her and enjoyed the envious looks he got from men of a similar age to him.

For Ella's part, every time they went out together, she lived in terror of someone mistaking him for her father. And while the men did indeed shoot envious glances in Max's direction, their wives were giving her looks of an entirely different nature. She could see in their eyes that they thought she was nothing better than a whore, using Max for material gain, while repaying him with the oldest currency in the world.

But, despite her fears, Ella was the closest she had ever been to happy in that two-week period. She enjoyed Max's company; he made her laugh and he made her feel cherished. While she wasn't sure if she could ever really love him, he left her in no doubt about his feelings for her. And he had saved her life. She knew that, because of Max, every single day was a gift she wouldn't otherwise have had.

Once they returned from their honeymoon, she moved into the beautiful mansion he had shared with Camilla and set about transforming it. For six months, she project-managed the renovations and thrived under the pressure. She loved flirting with the builders, who melted every time she walked into the room and she finally made her first genuine friend in the form of a designer she had recruited called Fabien. Well, his real name was John but he refused to answer to that, describing it as 'outrageously dull'. For the first time ever, she had no other agenda. She just liked him and felt as though she had found a kindred spirit.

It was once the renovations were over that the problems

in their marriage really began. Ella was bored and listless and spent her days wandering from one perfect room to another, wondering why it all felt so empty. 'You need a job, you lazy cow,' Fabien said bluntly when she moaned to him one night.

Ella knew he was right but Max insisted he didn't think it was the right thing for her to do. 'You've got all the money you could possibly want,' he reasoned. 'Enjoy it.'

But there were only so many handbags she could buy and only so much time she could spend browsing the designer boutiques on Sloane Street. The sales assistants made a beeline for her the second she stepped into the shop now, mindful of their commission and knowing that she was in the habit of spending an obscene amount of money. But she would get the bags of designer goods home and wonder why they no longer brought her the high she was craving.

She suspected that Max didn't want her to get a job because he was worried that she would meet another man; after all, she had met him at work. Even though he seemed happy, she knew he was deeply insecure about his age and his appearance. She also knew that having alienated his entire family and his work colleagues for her, he couldn't bear the humiliation if she ever left him.

So they limped on for a couple of years, with Ella becoming more and more resentful of him and him becoming clingier by the day. He started to check up on her movements, calling her from work and demanding to know where she was and who she was with. The answer to the second question was always the same: she was with no one – she was always on her own. Fabien was great company when he was around but he had a job that took him all over the world, at the beck and call of rich clients like them, so he wasn't around much.

It was out of desperation that she started to write. At first she just kept a diary of her days, which were repetitive and dull. Once she realized that every entry was the same, the only variation in the food, she decided to abandon the diary and use the overactive imagination she had employed so well over the years instead. She began to create a world for herself that was everything her real life wasn't.

In her stories, she was popular, funny, clever and kind. Naturally, she kept the bit about her being beautiful too. One day as she sat at her computer typing furiously, she suddenly realized that the character she was creating for herself was actually that of Anna.

She hadn't seen Anna since they had left university but she had left an indelible impression on Ella, mainly because everyone seemed to love her in a way that Ella could only dream of. More importantly, Toby had loved her. Ella didn't know what Anna was doing now but she had a pretty good idea. She imagined that she was married to a perfect man who adored her, with two perfect children, living an idyllic life in the countryside. She had no doubt that Anna would be happy. Ella told herself that she probably did her a favour breaking her and Toby up and that if they met now, Anna would probably thank her.

It took her a surprisingly short time to write her first book. Once it was finished, she gave it to Fabien to read, feeling nervous about his reaction. 'You're not the target market,' she warned him, already prepared for his searingly honest critique. But she needn't have worried. The next morning, he called her before she had even got out of bed. 'I love it!'

he yelled. 'You are a genius! And you're going to be rich! Oh, I forgot, you already are rich, you bitch!'

Ella laughed, feeling light-headed with relief. 'Do you really think so?'

'I do,' he replied solemnly. 'You must get it published.'

Ella hadn't got a clue how to go about getting something published. As if reading her thoughts, Fabien added, 'One of my clients is a big fish in publishing, I'll tell him to publish it.'

'And how are you going to do that?' she laughed. 'You're only responsible for his wallpaper, not his business.'

'Oh, ye of little faith!' sighed Fabien. 'I can assure you that his wallpaper is not the only thing that's well hung in his house.'

'Ew!' she cried. 'Too much information. OK, OK, give it to him. And let me know as soon as you hear anything.'

For the next couple of days, Ella was fidgety and tense as she waited for news. She hadn't mentioned anything about her writing to Max, although she didn't know why. Maybe she was worried that he would scoff at it and tell her not to be so silly. All he knew was that she was irritable and even moodier than usual.

Finally the call came. 'Will you give me half of your advance?' wheedled Fabien mischievously.

Ella's heart literally leapt inside her body. 'Does he like it?' she asked breathlessly.

'No,' said Fabien, flatly.

'Oh.' She slumped down on the sofa, deflated.

'He LOVES it!' screamed Fabien.

'What?' she shrieked back. She couldn't believe it had been so easy. What about all those tortured writers slaving for years before anyone took an interest in their books? Clearly she was a genius.

Fabien organized a meeting with Bruce Martin, the publisher in question, who failed to offer her millions of pounds there and then but told her she needed an agent. 'It won't be hard to get one now that you've already got a publisher interested,' he told her, while playing footsie with Fabien under the table.

The agent he put her in touch with was Monica Walker. Ella went to meet her at her central London offices. As she waited in reception, she watched girls like her clicking prettily away at their keyboards – posh and stinking rich, they were using Daddy's money to tide them over until they met a husband who could take over and keep them in handbags. She figured that she and Monica would get along just fine if they came from the same background.

Ella couldn't have been more wrong. As she was ushered into Monica's office, she could hear her chatting on the phone in a rough cockney accent, while smoking a cigarette and pushing her hands through her bleached-blonde, spiky hair. She waved at Ella to take a seat on a sofa that was piled high with books and magazines. 'No,' she was saying gruffly, 'tell him it's three hundred or he can fuck off, OK?' Finally, she hung up and grinned in Ella's direction.

'So, Ella de Bourg,' she started, 'you've done pretty well, haven't you?'

'Have I?' replied Ella, bemused.

Monica nodded. 'Yeah, not only have you finished the book, but you've got a publisher interested. How the fuck did you manage that? Contact of Daddy's, is he?' She had a mischievous glint in her eye that made what she said sound less offensive than it probably was.

'Not quite, no,' smiled Ella. 'Friend of a friend. I will admit that I think Bruce was more interested in my friend than my book, but hey, I'll take it!'

Monica nodded. 'Too fucking right,' she agreed enthusiastically. 'But the book's not bad. Don't be too hard on yourself. You're the one who had to write it.'

Ella felt herself flush with pride. No one had ever complimented her like that before. Usually it was her looks or her body that got her attention but this time it was something she had actually done. The feeling of achievement was overwhelming.

'So, tell me a bit about yourself, Ella,' said Monica, cocking her head to one side and looking at her intently.

'I'm not sure where to begin,' Ella said. She really didn't want Monica to know too much about her. Once she found out what a bitch she was and that she was married to a rich man old enough to be her father, she was scared that she would decide not to represent her after all.

'Well, how about your home life?' she persisted. 'Single, married, gay, straight?'

Ella laughed. 'Definitely straight.'

Monica stuck out her bottom lip in a pretend sulk. 'The gorgeous ones always are,' she said ruefully.

'And married,' added Ella.

Monica nodded. 'I bet your husband is one hot young thing.'

Ella flushed. 'Not young, no. But he is hot. At least I think so.'

Monica's eyes glittered. 'Not young, eh? Not poor either, I imagine?'

Ella couldn't help giggling. 'Stop it!'

She spent the rest of the afternoon in Monica's office, getting to know her and talking tactics. She liked her a lot. As she got up to leave, it seemed natural to kiss her on both cheeks, rather than shake hands.

'So . . .' Ella ventured carefully, 'you'll represent me then?'

'Yup,' replied Monica in a matter-of-fact tone. 'You, young lady, have got yourself an agent.'

On the way out of the building Ella called Fabien. 'Hey, baby, I'm just leaving my new agent's office. Fancy helping me celebrate?'

'I'm on my way!' he yelled.

They stayed out until 3 a.m. drinking cocktails and dancing. For the first time in years Ella felt young and alive. This is what she had been missing out on ever since she got together with Max and she intended on making the most of it.

It was the early hours of the next morning before Fabien dropped her off in a cab. She staggered up the steps to the front door and fumbled in her Prada bag for her keys. 'Shit,' she muttered to herself, swaying drunkenly as she failed to find them. Suddenly the door swung open and Ella looked up in surprise to see Max standing over her in his dressing gown, his arms folded and a furious scowl on his face.

'Where the fuck have you been?' he snapped.

Ella walked into the house, pushing past him roughly. He slammed the door and marched after her. 'I said, where the fuck have you been?' he repeated, quietly this time, but with a sinister edge to his voice. 'I was worried sick.'

Ella slumped drunkenly down onto the sofa. 'Celebrating,' she slurred.

'Celebrating what?'

'I've got myself an agent,' smiled Ella, closing her eyes and suddenly feeling an overwhelming urge to go to sleep.

Max stalked over and shook her roughly. 'What do you mean, you've got yourself an agent? Answer me!'

Ella's eyes blinked open in shock. She had never seen Max get angry like this. 'For my book,' she replied, her head in a daze.

'What?' Max looked as though she had slapped him. 'You've written a book? Why didn't you tell me?'

'I thought you'd try to put me off like you always do when I mention getting a job.' God, she was tired.

Max slumped onto the sofa beside her. 'So, let me get this straight – you've written a whole book and you never mentioned a word to me?'

'I didn't think anything would come of it. I just did it for myself and then Fabien suggested—'

'I might have known that bloody faggot had something to do with it!' he stormed.

'Max! Don't you dare speak about him like that! He's been a good friend to me. And the fact that he's gay suits you very well, seeing as I'm not allowed to mix with any other men in case they might find me attractive.'

Max looked puzzled. 'When did I say you couldn't mix with other men?'

'You say it every day with your bloody possessiveness. Refusing to let me get a job. Calling me every hour wanting to know who I'm with and checking up on me all the time.'

Max went to the window where he stood looking out over the garden. 'God, have I really been that bad?' he asked, stunned.

Ella gazed at him, wishing she could return the love he

so obviously felt for her. 'No . . . well, yes,' she shrugged. She didn't want to hurt his feelings. 'It's just that it gets really lonely rattling around in this house. I started writing as a way of taking myself out of this life and into another, more exciting one.'

'But your life IS exciting,' Max protested. 'You have all the money you could possibly want, you can buy whatever you—'

'For God's sake!' she snapped. 'Don't you get it, Max? Money does not buy you happiness.'

'Or love,' he said sadly.

Ella got up and walked over to him, wrapping herself around his body. They stood for a long time without saying anything. Eventually, she broke the silence. 'Let's go to bed,' she whispered, pushing their problems to one side yet again, to be dealt with another day.

May 2010

By the time she gets the invitation to Toby's wedding, Ella is a published author, with two books under her belt. Monica had negotiated her a great two-book deal to start with and is now talking about her signing a four-book deal. 'Do you think you're up to it, Your Ladyship?' she asks, glancing at Ella slyly, as she sits in her office drinking coffee one afternoon.

'Piece of piss!' Ella laughs back. In all honesty, she loves writing and doesn't find it a chore at all. She has finally found a respectable outlet for her lies and deceit, which also makes the most of her fertile imagination. She feels as though a ten-book deal wouldn't be a problem. And at the back of her mind is the thought that the last time she saw

Toby, she was a dismal failure with no proper job and no future. Now she can go to his wedding with her head held high, knowing that she has earned the respect of her peers. Whether they'll like her any better is a separate issue but they couldn't dispute her achievements.

'What's on your mind?' Monica interrupts her thoughts, watching her carefully.

Ella shrugs. 'Got a wedding to go to next week. Old flame.'

'Really!' cries Monica, her eyes blazing with curiosity. 'Tell me more,' she orders, lighting up yet another cigarette. Ella loves the fact that Monica has absolutely no regard for the law and has continued to smoke in her office despite the smoking ban.

'Well, I've known him all my life,' Ella begins. 'Our parents are friends.'

Monica nods and signals to her to continue.

'But we didn't get together until we were at university.'

'What was he like?' Monica's dark eyes are beady through the clouds of smoke swirling around her face.

'Handsome, funny, clever . . . I could go on,' smiles Ella. 'We were together for the three years we were at university.'

'Wow,' breathes Monica. 'So why did it end?'

'He slept with someone else,' says Ella, allowing herself to feel genuinely anguished at the betrayal.

'Bastard,' says Monica. 'Typical man. That's why I stick to women. So he's getting married – is he marrying the one he slept with?'

Ella shakes her head. 'No. It didn't last. She was a complete bitch anyway.' She can see the sympathy in Monica's eyes and laps it up.

'You poor baby. That must have been tough.'

'It was,' agrees Ella solemnly.

'And will she be at the wedding?'

'God, no!' says Ella indignantly. 'I doubt he's even given her a second thought since their one-night stand.'

'Well, that's good,' muses Monica. 'It would have been hard to see her and him in the same room again.'

'Yeah,' agrees Ella, loving the feeling of being the wronged party for once. 'It really would.'

Rachel

July 2010

Rachel wakes up at dawn on her wedding day. It is the most important day of her life and she lies still for a while, not opening her eyes, remembering Toby's kiss as he left her yesterday. He loves her, she is sure of it. She just wishes he would tell her more often. 'Actions speak louder than words,' he says irritably if she ever brings up the subject. But the truth is, sometimes she needs to hear the words too.

Toby has spent the night before the wedding at Marco and James' flat, while her sister, Becs, and her mum, Mary, are staying with Rachel. They had a great night together, painting each other's nails and applying fake tan, while knocking back champagne and giggling over various childhood memories. 'Remember when you made a pretend wedding dress out of that old net curtain?' laughed Becs. 'You thought you looked the bee's knees.'

'I was only five!' protested Rachel. 'I thought I did a bloody good job.'

'You did, darling,' soothed Mary, hugging her daughter tightly. 'But even so, I'm glad you didn't decide to make the real thing yourself!'

'The funny thing is,' Rachel giggled, 'I keep having the weirdest dream. I keep dreaming that I get up on my wedding day and I've forgotten to buy the dress. So I pull down a dirty old net curtain and wrap that round me instead.'

'You obviously remember your first effort better than I thought!' Becs interrupted.

'Shut up, you!' Rachel scolded cheerfully. 'Anyway, on the way to the church, we have to stop to get petrol and I get oil all over this bloody net curtain so that by the time I'm walking up the aisle, I'm trailing a puddle of grease behind me and the dress is practically black. Toby takes one look at me and does a runner!'

'Can't say I'd blame him!' laughed Becs.

'No,' Rachel agreed, suddenly turning serious. 'But I hope it's not an omen.'

'Of course it's not!' Mary reassured her. 'It's perfectly natural. I had weird dreams before my wedding to your father and I know loads of other women who've said the same.'

'Really?' Rachel felt comforted by her mum's words. Even though she was laughing, the dreams had unsettled her more than she could admit and they kept playing on her mind.

By the time they got to bed, it was nearly midnight. 'C'mon, Cinderella – bedtime!' Mary had ordered. 'Can't have you looking like death warmed up on your wedding day. You need your beauty sleep.'

'Yes, sir!' Rachel gave her a small salute. 'Are you sure you don't want to sleep in my bed?'

'Well . . .' Becs began.

'No, we don't!' insisted her mum, nudging Becs furiously.

'We'll be absolutely fine on the sofa bed, won't we, darling?'

'Suppose so,' agreed Becs grudgingly.

Now, Rachel opens her eyes and smiles. She told herself that if it was sunny when she woke up, then everything was going to be OK. Despite the earliness of the hour, she can already see blue sky and sunshine peeping through the curtains. It is all going to be fine.

Her mum and Becs are still asleep when Rachel glances into the sitting room on her way to the kitchen. She pours herself some water and puts the kettle on before picking up her mobile from the kitchen worktop and scanning it for messages from Toby. She had texted him before she went to bed saying, *C U 2morrow, gorgeous boy. Can't wait to be your wife.* She was desperately hoping for a loving reply. But there is nothing. She tries not to feel too disappointed.

'Morning, the soon-to-be Mrs McKenzie!' says Mary brightly from behind her, interrupting her thoughts.

'Morning, Mum,' Rachel replies, quickly shoving her phone into her dressing gown pocket. 'Did you sleep OK?'

'Fine,' Mary says, wrapping her arms around Rachel and hugging her tightly. 'But you're not to worry about anyone else today except yourself. This is your day and you're going to love every minute.'

Rachel relaxes into the warmth of her mum's embrace. She used to be able to bury her face in her chest but now she towers over her, so has to content herself with resting her head on her shoulder.

'Are you OK, love?' Mary asks, releasing her grasp and holding Rachel at arm's length so that she can look at her properly.

'Yes, fine!' Rachel says gaily, aware that her voice sounds shrill.

'I know my little girl better than that,' Mary replies wisely. 'Don't worry, darling, whatever you're feeling, it's completely natural. It's just wedding day jitters, it would be weird if you didn't feel nervous.'

Rachel nods and smiles. 'I know, I know. I just can't shake this feeling that something's going to go wrong.'

'Completely normal,' Mary dismisses her with a wave of her hand. 'Just don't let it spoil your day. Nothing is going to go wrong.'

After cooking a breakfast of bacon and scrambled eggs, Mary runs her a bath and fills it with some lovely Molton Brown bubble bath. 'Take as long as you like!' she says, shutting the door behind Rachel.

'Oi!' shouts Becs from the kitchen. 'Don't take too bloody long or there won't be enough time for me to tart myself up and I won't be able to pull that mate of Toby's.'

'Which one?' Rachel shouts back, curious.

'Which one do you think? The best man, Marco. He's cute.'

Rachel laughs and sinks down into the bath thinking about what Becs has just said. Actually, it would be rather fun if Becs got together with Marco. They could go out on joint dates, if married couples still had dates, that is. But then, what would happen if it all went wrong? That would be a disaster. Then they would have to make sure their paths never crossed. And what about the christening of their first child? What about . . .

She shakes her head crossly, telling herself to banish all such negative thoughts. *Typical me though*, she thinks. She can't help looking beyond the moment to worry about what will happen next. Anyway, Marco seemed quite taken with Anna at their pre-wedding party. Now THAT would be a disaster. She would spend the whole time worrying that whenever they spent time with them, Toby was secretly wishing he was with Anna instead.

Mind you, having a pre-wedding party had been one of her better ideas. She had been dreading meeting Anna for so long that when she actually came face to face with her, the reality was nothing like as bad as she feared and it was one less thing to worry about on the big day. Plus, Anna had scarpered early, which Rachel had convinced herself meant she was boring. Although, thinking about it now, Toby had acted very strangely for the rest of the evening, as if he was on edge and jittery about something. Maybe seeing Anna had stirred up his old feelings for her, Rachel thinks now in a sudden panic.

Oh God, she isn't doing very well with this positive-thinking lark. Why is she on such a downer on her wedding day? She should be leaping around with ecstasy and excitement. Instead, she sinks further under the water until her whole face and head are submerged. It feels comforting to block out the outside world for a few seconds, just to enjoy the swoosh and gurgle of the underwater sounds. She wants to stay there forever. Instead, she hauls herself up and, with a Herculean effort, out of the bath.

'Becs!' she calls, pulling out the plug and rinsing the bath with the shower attachment. 'Bath's free!'

'God, that was quick!' Becs opens the door and, munching on a piece of toast, gazes at her sister curiously. 'You OK?'

'Yup,' Rachel replies briskly, concentrating on applying body lotion to every part of her body that she can reach.

'Here, let me do your back,' says Becs, taking the bottle and shaking some cream out into the palm of her hand. 'Rach,' she begins tentatively as she massages the lotion into her skin, 'it's not too late to back out if you're having doubts, you know.'

Rachel's stomach swirls at Becs' words. It was easy for her to say but Rachel could just picture the scene at the packed church if she didn't turn up. All those people gasping in horror as they realized that she had jilted poor Toby at the altar. And what about afterwards? She and Toby would have to split up, so he would have to move out of the flat and Rachel would be back to square one. How the hell would she have a baby then? She was thirty-four. There was no time to meet someone else. She would be dried up and left on the shelf.

'No,' she replies decisively. 'I don't want to back out. I love Toby. I'm just nervous, that's all.'

Becs put the lid back onto the bottle. 'It would be more worrying if you were overconfident.'

'Why? In case *he* jilts *me*, you mean?' Rachel wishes she could stop being so cranky, so defensive.

Becs swirls her round to face her. 'No! That's not what I meant at all! Why would you think for one second that Toby would jilt you? He's the most adorable man on the planet. He would never do anything to hurt you.'

'I know,' Rachel sighs. 'But . . . Becs, I'm going to tell you something that I've never told anyone. Because if I don't talk to someone about how I feel I think I might just explode.'

'OK.' Becs waits patiently.

'I think Toby might still be in love with his ex-girlfriend.'

Becs nods and frowns at the same time. 'And what makes

you think that? It must have been so long ago. Has he been talking about her a lot?'

'No, just the opposite. He's always refused to talk about her.'

Becs nods again, understanding immediately why this is so significant. 'Right. And do you have any suspicions that they've been seeing each other behind your back?'

'Oh, no! Not at all. I don't think he'd ever do that to me.'

Becs perches on the edge of the bath and scratches her chin as she thinks. 'Well, it's you he's marrying, isn't it? And it's you he's spent the last seven years with. I bet he doesn't even remember her after all this time. If he was still in love with her, then surely he'd be marrying her?'

'Yes, it's me he's marrying,' Rachel agrees. 'But I'm worried that I forced his hand. It was after Dad had prompted us and it was me who proposed, not him. His first answer was "I don't know".' Her voice is a whisper as she trails off miserably.

'You took him by surprise, that's all,' says Becs firmly. 'He needed time to think about it. Listen, Rach, Toby is not a clueless toddler. He's a grown man with a mind of his own. Knowing him like I do, I don't think he would ever have agreed to get married if he didn't want to. And he loves you. I'm sure of it.'

Rachel nods slowly. 'Yes, he does love me. I'm sure of it too – but is he *in love* with me? He hardly ever tells me, you know.'

'Lots of men don't like telling someone they love them,' says Becs briskly. 'They prefer to let their actions do the talking.'

'That's what he always says,' Rachel sighs.

'Well then. Look, honey, I know you're nervous but it's

just you being a worryguts as usual. You are going to have an amazing day and you are going to marry the man you love. It's all going to work out fine, I promise.'

Rachel leans forward and hugs her sister tightly. Becs is four years younger than her and they haven't always got on that well, but she loves and trusts her. And, especially today, she is glad of her reassurance.

She makes her way back into the bedroom and perches on the bed, gazing up at the gorgeous Vera Wang dress hanging on her wardrobe door. She feels better now that she has talked to Becs. It just helps to have told someone how she was feeling. She has been bottling it up for too long. Becs is right. It is going to be fine. Rachel should be enjoying herself instead of worrying over something that probably isn't even true.

Just at that moment the doorbell rings, making her jump. She leaps up and runs to the front door. 'That'll be the hair and make-up girl,' she calls back to her mum and Becs. But it isn't. As she flings open the door, she is met with a dozen red roses and a man with a grin so wide it seems to wrap right around his head. 'Oh!' she exclaims, so shocked that she jumps back slightly.

'Delivery for Rachel King,' the beaming man announces.

Rachel takes the bouquet from him and closes the door in a daze. With shaking hands she opens the card. *To my bride, see you at the church, love from your groom xxx.* Tears fill her eyes. How thoughtful of him. She loves him so much, how could she have doubted him?

'Aah!' sighs her mum, emerging from the kitchen. 'What a good boy he is, doing what he's told!'

Rachel frowns. 'You told him to send them?'

Mary flushes. 'No! No, not at all, I just assumed you had,' she blusters.

Rachel knows she is fibbing and the elation she felt seconds ago melts clean away. She wanders into the kitchen and dumps the roses onto the worktop where she stares at them accusingly.

'He didn't have to though, Rachel,' says Mary, coming up behind her and putting her arm around her shoulders, reading her daughter's thoughts.

Rachel nods. Perhaps her mum was right. Surely he wouldn't have sent them if he was having doubts?

'Wow!' breathes Becs, coming into the kitchen and spotting the roses. 'What a sweetheart sending those on the morning of your wedding! *See!*' she adds in an exaggerated stage whisper.

Rachel smiles weakly before rallying herself. *Right*, she tells herself firmly, as she arranges the flowers in a vase, *pull yourself together and get on with it. You've got a wedding to get to.*

Anna

Anna gazes at herself in the bathroom mirror, thinking how much her face has changed in the ten years since she left university. Since Toby. In many ways, she looks better now than she did back then. Her face is thinner, her cheekbones more defined and her skin is taut and tanned. But, she realizes with a start as her reflection stares mournfully back at her, she has lost her bloom. *Happiness and being in love are the best beauty products on the market*, she thinks to herself, *it's just a shame you can't buy either of them*.

She desperately wants today to be over but she doesn't want it to begin either. She picks up a large, soft brush and sweeps some rose-coloured blusher over her cheekbones, wondering as she does so if Rachel is doing the same. She wonders how she is feeling, now she is about to marry the man Anna loves and wonders if she is as happy as Anna knows she would be in her position. The yearning to swap places with her is almost overwhelming.

'You look gorgeous,' says Clare admiringly as Anna emerges from her bedroom an hour later.

'Do you really think so?' She is already shaking with nerves about what lies ahead but she is determined to be strong and not to make a scene of any kind, not that she has ever been given to making scenes – especially at someone else's wedding.

'I do,' Clare replies solemnly. It isn't the last time today that Anna is going to hear those words and she is dreading hearing them again. She still can't imagine hearing Toby say them to someone other than her. Yet it has been ten long years since they broke up and she knows that it is time for her to move on and start living her life again. She hopes that today will be the first step towards her doing that.

She looks at Clare, resplendent in her white trouser suit and looking truly beautiful. Anna can't believe how much Clare has changed in the one short week she has spent with James. Her eyes are brighter than ever, her skin is glowing with health and her hair is shining like silk – she has blossomed before Anna's eyes. Today is going to be hard on her too. It is the last full day she will spend with James before he sets off for his new life in Australia. They may have only been together for one week but Anna knows that Clare's pain will be every bit as raw as hers. 'You look gorgeous too,' she tells her truthfully, giving her a quick hug.

Deep down, Anna is sure Clare would probably have preferred to go to the wedding with James, making the most of every precious second they have left. But Clare knows how hard this day is going to be for Anna and she would never leave her in the lurch. 'I wouldn't mind,' Anna had lied unconvincingly.

'Yes you would,' Clare had replied. 'And more to the point, the only reason I'm going is to be your moral support. What sort of a friend would I be if I left you to go on your own?'

And even though Anna would have understood, she has to admit she is relieved that Clare is coming with her. 'Right,' she says, looking at her watch, 'we'd better get going.'

Walking out onto the street, they hail a taxi and head for the church. Travelling through the streets of London in a black cab, Anna gazes out of the window, watching as other people go about their happy, summer lives. It is a perfect July day with the kind of azure sky that doesn't often appear through the smog and fumes of the capital. Somehow, it seems like some kind of omen but she's not sure why.

ORDER OF SERVICE

The marriage of

Rachel King
to

Toby McKenzie
at
St George's Chapel,
Fulham

The church is a pretty little building tucked away at the back of a busy main road in the centre of Fulham. 'Wow,' Anna breathes as they walk through the doors. The church is packed and the scent of roses hangs sensually in the air. She looks around her, feeling dizzy with jealousy and pain. This should have been *her* wedding. Her smiling friends and family. Her white roses, nestling tastefully in a bed of dark green leaves. Her order of service, tied prettily with a delicate white ribbon. The happiest day of *her* life.

'You OK?' asks Clare, turning to look back at her with a concerned expression.

Anna takes a deep breath in through her nose and lets the air escape through her mouth, trying to calm her palpitations. She nods quickly and follows Clare to the top of the aisle.

'Bride or groom?' asks James, smiling as he greets them both with a kiss, lingering slightly longer on Clare. Clare flushes at his touch and gazes at him with undisguised longing. 'You both look stunning,' he adds, dragging his eyes from her.

'So do you,' they reply in unison. It's true, he does. He is wearing a black morning suit with white shirt and tie, which he carries off beautifully. He stands in between them and bends his arms out to the side theatrically, inviting them to take one each. Anna links her arm through his gratefully as he walks them to a pew. She stares at her feet and, concentrating on walking in her impossibly high heels, she doesn't look up until they are safely seated. When she does look up, the smile dies instantly on her lips. She is sitting next to Ella de Bourg.

'Oh my God!' Anna mutters and Clare looks round in alarm.

'What's wrong?' she asks anxiously, trailing off as she spots Ella. 'Oh, I see,' she hisses, her eyes narrowing. 'Want to sit somewhere else?'

Anna nods gratefully and stands up to move. But before she can escape, she feels Ella's cool hand on her arm. 'Don't, Anna,' she says pleadingly in that deep voice Anna remembers so well.

Anna looks at Ella properly for the first time in nearly ten years. She is still beautiful. Her sleek bob is still shiny and dark, her angular limbs are as slim as they always were and her eyes are still impossibly huge, but for some reason Anna can't put her finger on, she looks jaded. Her bloom has gone and in its place is a bitter expression.

Clare tugs at the back of Anna's dress. 'Do you want to move or not?' she whispers.

Anna hesitates. 'Too late anyway,' she snaps, sitting back down. 'There's nowhere else to sit.' Anna glances at Clare apologetically, who pats her leg to show that she isn't really annoyed, while simultaneously shooting Ella a vicious stare.

'Anna, you look amazing,' Ella smiles confidently.

God, the bloody cheek of the woman, thinking she can smarm her way back into her good books after what she did.

'Thanks,' Anna mumbles, staring fixedly ahead. An older man is sitting to Ella's right and he leans round to see who she is talking to.

'Oh, Anna, can I introduce you to my husband, Max,' Ella says, still smiling.

Despite herself, Anna's head jerks round to look at him in astonishment. 'Your HUSBAND?' she blurts.

Now it is Ella's turn to look uncomfortable. 'Yes. We've been married for four and a half years now.'

Anna makes a concerted effort to shut her gaping mouth as she shakes hands with the man. 'Er, pleased to meet you, Max,' she stutters. Max looks expectantly towards Clare, who is deliberately scowling in the opposite direction.

'Clare,' Anna says, tapping her on the back. 'This is Max, Ella's HUSBAND,' she emphasizes the word meaningfully.

Clare spins round immediately. 'Her WHAT?' she gapes rudely, before finally shaking his outstretched hand with an undisguised smirk on her face.

'And how do you girls know each other?' asks Max pleasantly, apparently oblivious to the strained atmosphere between the three of them. 'Old university buddies?'

Clare snorts rudely.

'Um, yes, something like that,' Anna cuts in quickly before Clare can say any more.

'And what are you doing now, Anna?' asks Ella, clearly wanting to move the conversation on. 'Married, single? Kids, dogs? Big house in the country?' she laughs.

Anna frowns. 'Single. No kids. No dogs. I'm a teacher,' she replies matter-of-factly. She is determined not to ask what Ella is doing. She knows it will be something good. She has obviously married Max for his money so maybe she doesn't work at all. Probably spends her days trotting up and down the King's Road buying stuff she doesn't need.

'And you still keep in touch with Toby?' Ella probes, one eyebrow raised, clearly surprised that Anna should have been invited to his wedding.

The realization triggers a spike of fresh malice in Anna towards her. 'Yes, that's generally what friends do,' she replies chippily. 'I didn't see *you* at the pre-wedding party,' she adds craftily. 'I guess that was just for the younger guests?' It's not like Anna to be so bitchy but it's just a tiny act of revenge against the woman who caused her so much pain.

Anna turns away from Ella as she glimpses Toby walking down the aisle towards the front pew. Her stomach knots at the sight of him, striding along, looking like a cross between Daniel Day-Lewis and Hugh Grant in his beautifully cut morning suit. She had, in the deep, dark recesses of her warped mind, half-hoped that he wouldn't turn up. But she knows him better than that. He isn't the type to jilt a girl at the altar, humiliating her in front of all her friends and family.

As if he feels Anna staring at him, Toby stops walking, turns in what seems like slow motion and their eyes lock. And, like in a film, everything else melts away; it is as though it is just the two of them standing alone in the church, staring at each other. Every fibre of Anna's being wants to tell Toby how much she still loves him and wants him but she can't breathe, let alone speak.

The moment is broken as Marco comes up behind him and whispers something in his ear. Toby nods and, with one quick glance back at Anna, he walks towards the front of the church. Marco turns to see what Toby has been looking at and waves as he spots Anna. She waves back self-consciously, shaking from the intensity of her exchange with Toby.

Clare grasps her hand. 'You going to be OK?' she whispers.

Anna nods, keeping her head low as the tears begin to fall into her lap. She bites her lip, desperately trying to stop the flow but it is impossible.

'Do you want to go?' Clare asks, grabbing her bag and fishing in it for a tissue.

Anna nods, still too choked to speak. They stand up and, ducking their heads in an attempt to escape unnoticed, make their way back up the aisle. Just as they reach the door, it opens and they are stood face to face with Rachel, looking radiant in a stunning but simple ivory gown, clutching a perfect bouquet of white roses and holding the arm of an older man who looks like the proudest man in the world.

Anna and Rachel stare at each other in shock.

'What's going on?' Rachel's dad asks, gaping in confusion

at Anna's teary face and her and Clare's guilty expressions. Behind them there is a commotion in the church as everyone turns to see what the hold-up is.

Mistaking the congregation turning towards the door as a sign that the bride is ready to walk down the aisle, the organist launches into the 'Wedding March', before someone hastily shushes him and an eerie hush descends over the whole church.

Rachel's delicately made-up face crumples, now a mirror of Anna's. 'I knew it,' she whispers, almost to herself.

One of the bridesmaids pushes her way forward and looks at Anna accusingly. 'Who are you?' she demands angrily. 'And what the hell are you doing?'

'I . . . I'm Anna,' she gulps, trying to wipe the tears from her eyes. 'And I'm just leaving.' She looks desperately for an escape route but the bridal party are blocking every available exit.

'She's his ex-girlfriend,' sobs Rachel to her bridesmaid, who continues to glare at Anna.

'Well, there's Toby,' says the bridesmaid after a pause, gesturing towards the front of the church. 'And he's not leaving. So why don't you let her go and get on with getting married? Come on, Rachel, she doesn't matter.'

The silence that follows is broken by the sound of echoing footsteps. Anna turns and sees Toby walking towards them. Finally, he reaches them and looks from Anna to Rachel. 'What's wrong?' he asks quietly.

'This is,' says Rachel, weeping silently as she speaks.

Instinctively, Toby moves towards her and wraps his arms around her. 'Hey, don't cry,' he soothes gently, stroking her back and kissing the top of her head.

Rachel allows herself to be held for a few minutes while they all stand watching them awkwardly. Finally, she pulls away. 'Toby, I want you to answer me something and I want you to tell me the truth.'

Anna feels as though she might faint and staggers slightly. Thankfully, Clare catches her arm and she leans against her gratefully.

'Do you . . .' Rachel continues, taking a deep breath to compose herself, 'do you love me?'

'You know I do,' he replies quickly. Too quickly.

She nods slowly and pauses. 'And do you still love Anna?'

There is a gasp from the congregation as everyone spins round to look at Anna. Time seems to be suspended as Toby turns slowly and for the second time in less than ten minutes, their eyes lock. They hold each other's gaze for what seems like an eternity before he finally speaks.

'I do,' he says.

Clare

The church erupts in shock. Rachel whimpers like a wounded animal before dropping her bouquet and pushing through the wedding party to escape down the steps of the church. Toby races after her, calling her name. The chief bridesmaid pushes forward and starts yelling at Anna.

'It's not her fault!' storms Clare, putting her arm around her friend defensively. 'She's been broken-hearted about Toby for years and she's never said a word to anyone about it!'

'Well, if they were so in love, why did they break up?' demands the bridesmaid, her eyes blazing with fury.

Clare looks around the church. 'Because of that bitch there!' she says, pointing towards Ella.

Then all eyes turn in Ella's direction, and in the midst of the commotion, Clare grabs Anna's arm and pulls her through a side door, before jumping into the road and hailing the first cab she can find. Anna seems to be in a state of suspended shock and Clare is pretty shaken up herself. She can't believe what has just happened. The look on Rachel's face has imprinted itself on Clare's brain and despite her loyalty to Anna she feels devastated for her. She can't imagine how she must be feeling.

They arrive home within minutes and Clare has to

practically carry Anna into the flat. She deposits her on the sofa and heads back to the kitchen, where she leans against the worktop, her mind whirling as she wonders what to do next. James would have had to stay behind and try to sort things out along with Marco so she can't call him, although she desperately wants to speak to him. Their time together now is so short that she can't bear the thought of wasting a single precious minute of it.

She makes coffee and takes some in to Anna, who is still sitting on the sofa staring into space. She hands her a mug and sits facing her. Anna's hands shake as she puts the scalding coffee to her lips and Clare winces as she spills some onto her beautiful dress.

'Hey, careful,' she says, taking the mug off her and putting it on the floor. Anna's mascara is running in rivulets down her face as her tears continue to fall. She doesn't even seem to notice that she is crying. 'Tell me how you're feeling,' Clare says at last.

Anna shakes her head fiercely. 'I don't know . . . I'm feeling that I should never have gone to the wedding in the first place. What the bloody hell was I thinking of? I've ruined that poor girl's life!'

Clare says nothing. She is thinking pretty much the same thing herself. She really hadn't expected Anna to react like that. She had thought that seeing Toby get married might give her some closure, help her to move on. Instead it had just unlocked all the emotion she had been bottling up for years.

'He said he still loves you,' Clare says, almost to herself.

Anna waves her hand as if trying to swat away a fly. 'Don't!' she cries. 'I can't bear it.'

'Why?'

'Because . . . because I've wasted all these years.'

'So has he.'

'Yes, but that doesn't make it any better. In fact, it makes it worse. We were both so stubborn. And that poor girl!' she wails.

Again, Clare says nothing. Rachel must be in agony. But while she feels desperately sorry for her, she also feels a little tinge of hope that Anna and Toby might finally get together again.

They sit in silence for several moments, both deep in thought, until Clare's phone rings, cutting through the atmosphere and making them both jump. She presses answer.

'Hi, it's me,' shouts James over the hubbub of people talking loudly close by.

'Hi,' Clare says, getting up and walking into her bedroom so that she can speak privately. In the background, she can hear music and laughter. 'What's all the racket?'

'I'm at the reception. Rachel's mum and dad went straight home but George insisted everyone else should go ahead and enjoy themselves – seeing as he'd paid for it. They didn't take long to get over the shock,' James adds wryly. 'Probably glad not to have sit through a boring service first – it means more drinking time.'

'Poor Rachel,' says Clare.

He sighs, 'I know. Marco's gone to see her. She's a great girl, she didn't deserve that.' Clare is about to agree when James continues, 'Your stupid bloody friend should have stayed at home!'

Clare feels the indignation rise within her like a volcano spewing out lava. 'What? It wasn't Anna's fault!' she snaps. 'Toby was more to blame – he was the one getting married!'

'Yeah, but he'd have gone through with it if she hadn't turned up and started weeping and wailing all over the place.'

Clare can't believe what she is hearing. 'She didn't just turn up! She was invited! And anyway, you think that would have been better, do you? Going through with a wedding to someone he doesn't really love?'

'He DOES love Rachel. It's just that that silly cow threw him with her histrionics.'

There is a tense silence. Clare doesn't want to argue with James on their last day together but she can't let him get away with slagging off Anna either. 'I think she's been incredibly dignified, actually,' she manages tersely.

'Yeah, right,' James replies sarcastically.

'Look, I don't want to speak to you if you're going to be horrible about Anna,' says Clare hotly.

'Fine,' he says. 'Then I guess we're finished speaking.'

Clare's mouth drops open. She can't believe their brief, perfect relationship is ending so brusquely.

'Is this goodbye then?' she asks quietly, feeling suddenly sick with fear.

'It looks like it,' James says coldly. 'Goodbye, Clare.' The line goes dead.

Clare stares at the phone in shock. He's gone.

Several minutes pass before Clare can bring herself to return to the sitting room, where Anna is still sobbing quietly on the sofa. She sits down beside her, trying to quell the little bubbles of resentment that are welling up inside her. It isn't Anna's fault, she knows that. And yet . . . if it wasn't for her, the wedding would have happened, Rachel's heart wouldn't be broken and she and James wouldn't have quarrelled on their last day together.

Anna looks up in surprise and blows her nose inelegantly. 'That was James, I take it?'

Clare nods.

'Is he coming round?'

Clare shakes her head, unable to speak and willing herself not to cry.

Anna frowns. 'So you're going to meet him then?'

Clare shakes her head again, this time more roughly.

'What's happened?'

Suddenly, Clare can't hold back any longer and the misery pours out of her in a torrent. Anna gasps in shock. Despite the fact that Anna has spent so much time crying in all the years that she and Clare have known each other, she has very rarely seen Clare break down. Anna wraps her arms around her and rocks her back and forward, as though she is comforting a small child in her class.

'What a total and utter bloody mess!' Clare shouts to no one in particular.

Anna leans back and sighs as she realizes. 'You've broken up with James haven't you?'

Clare nods miserably.

'It was because of me, wasn't it?' Anna says, looking aghast.

Clare sniffs loudly and looks away. She doesn't want to blame Anna but she can't help it. Because of her, she has just lost the only man she ever loved.

Ella

The shock of seeing Anna again is greater than Ella had imagined. Her small heart-shaped face has slimmed down even more and her golden hair now drapes over impossibly high cheekbones. She looks toned and tanned in a deep blue-green chiffon dress that shows off her shapely legs. Beside her, Ella suddenly feels old and ugly. She had hoped that Anna would have grown fat and be settled living in the country with lots of kids and dogs running around because it would have assuaged the guilt she still feels about breaking up her and Toby. But she was so wrong. The pain is still written loud and clear in Anna's eyes.

The look on Anna's face when Ella introduced her to Max was one of genuine horror and Ella could see that she had mistaken him for her father. Ella wanted to come to this wedding basking in the glory of being a published author with a rich, handsome husband. Instead, no one is interested in what she is doing and they clearly think she has married Max for his money.

She steals a glance at him beside her, looking around in a slightly bewildered fashion. He does look old enough to be her father, especially today amongst all the handsome young men at the wedding. When had his skin become so thin and wrinkly? Why has she never noticed the hairs protruding from his ears or the fact that his nose is becoming ever more bulbous?

Ella sighs deeply. Their relationship is faltering badly. She does care for him but she no longer desires him and has started to make excuses not to have sex with him. The last time was the night she received the invitation to this wedding and she hasn't been able to bear him touching her since. His conversation bores her and they have nothing in common. But how can she ever leave him now? He has saved her life in more ways than one. And she is in no doubt that he truly loves her. She feels trapped.

Just then a commotion at the back of the church distracts everyone and they turn eagerly to see Toby's bride make her entrance. Ella is desperate to see how Rachel compares to her. And to Anna.

But, although the organist has struck up the first few bars of the 'Wedding March', the bride doesn't appear down the aisle. Ella cranes her neck further and sees that the wedding party has congregated at the door, along with Anna and Clare.

The conversation of the group by the door is initially drowned out by the organ but once the organist has been hastily silenced, their voices echo clearly around the eerily quiet church. Ella watches as Toby locks eyes with Anna and admits that he still loves his ex-girlfriend. A gasp of shock echoes around the church and the congregation gapes in horror as Rachel bursts into a fresh bout of tears, before turning on her heel and fleeing back down the steps. Ella can only hear snatches of the conversation: 'This is YOUR bloody fault!' . . . 'I didn't mean for this to happen.' . . . 'It's not her fault.' . . . 'Well, if they were so in love, why did they break up?' And then, as she sees Clare look furiously round the church, Ella knows what is coming. 'Because of that bitch there!' Clare hisses, shaking with rage as she points to Ella.

All eyes turn towards Ella and she feels her cheeks burn with shame as her insides turn to liquid. This day definitely isn't working out the way she had hoped. All she can see are accusatory faces staring at her from all angles. Her parents, sitting up near the front, are wearing a look of confusion, coupled with the look of anger and disappointment that they have perfected so well over the years. Toby's sister Helen's puzzled expression quickly morphs into one of fury, as the realization dawns that Ella is implicated in the break-up of Toby and Anna's relationship.

'It's not my fault,' Ella mutters weakly, her eyes searching desperately for a sympathetic face.

'Well, what do we all do now?' asks Rachel's dad, looking bewildered and upset. Rachel's sister walks over and hugs him. They are joined by her mum, whose heels click on the cold stone floor as she runs to the back of the church, trying but failing to keep her composure. 'Let's just go,' she gulps. 'I just want to get to Rachel and make sure she's OK.'

Rachel's dad nods before straightening his back and looking around the church. 'Well,' he begins, clearing his throat nervously. 'This isn't quite how I envisaged making a speech, but there obviously isn't going to be a wedding now . . .' His voice catches and his wife puts her hand on his arm. 'Anyway,' he continues gruffly, 'you all know where the reception is being held . . . it's all paid for so you might as well go and enjoy it. I'm sure you'll forgive my wife and me for not joining you.'

With that, he puts his arm around his wife and they walk out of the door and down the steps.

There is dead silence in the church. No one knows what to do or say. Finally, the best man speaks. 'Right, well, you heard what George said. If you'd all like to make your way to the reception, we'll see if we can make the best of what's left of today. I'll see you all there.'

Ella turns to look at Max. He has a strange expression on his face. 'What?' she asks, feeling slightly alarmed.

'Do you want to go to the reception?' he asks, his tone clipped.

'No,' she replies quickly. There was only one person Ella was interested in seeing and he isn't going to be there. Everyone else will be baying for her blood. 'Let's just go home.'

'I think we should go somewhere and talk,' says Max in a way that brooks no argument. Ella has never heard him speak so forcefully.

'Oh,' she stutters, thrown. 'OK then.'

The rest of the congregation is making its way towards the reception, led by the best man and the chief usher, and Ella allows Max to take her by the arm and lead her out of the church. The atmosphere is one of stunned excitement. While some are clearly feeling guilty at the prospect of enjoying themselves at someone else's expense, others seem glad not to have to sit through the boring formalities before being able to drink themselves stupid and dance the night away.

As the throng turns right, towards the buses that will carry them to the reception venue, Max and Ella turn left, heading towards the busy Fulham Road. After a few minutes walking in silence, they arrive at a small bistro and, without either of them discussing it, they open the door and go inside.

A waiter leads them to their table and they sit down and study their menus in silence.

When the waiter returns to explain that day's specials, Max interrupts him. 'We'll just have some olives, thank you,' he says stiffly. 'Followed by two steaks, rare,' ordering for them both, as he has always done. Ella hadn't realized until now just how much she resents it.

'There's something I need to tell you,' she says as the waiter takes their menus and disappears.

Max looks up and sighs. 'Go on then. Any more ex-lovers I should know about?'

'Toby and I were never lovers,' she says, ignoring Max's barbed tone. 'That was an unfortunate mix-up.'

Max nods. 'You've had a lot of those in your life, haven't you? Funny the way unfortunate mix-ups seem to follow you around.'

'It's not my fault!' snaps Ella, flushing with irritation.

'No, it never is.' Max is now sounding, as well as looking, like her father. 'So, what did you do to make them all dislike you so much?'

'Like I said,' she replies grimly, 'it was just a misunderstanding. Anyway, that's not what I wanted to tell you,' she continues, keen to change the subject.

Max says nothing, only gestures for her to continue.

'I don't like my steak rare.'

His forehead creases in confusion. 'Since when?'

'Since always. But you never bothered to find out how I liked it.'

'And you never complained before,' he shoots back.

'Well, I'm complaining now,' Ella says firmly.

'And why's that?' Max looks and sounds tired. Defeated.

'Because this relationship isn't working and I think the steak sums up why. You don't really know me at all.'

'But I love you,' he says wearily, without passion.

'I'm not sure you do,' she replies, more thoughtfully than aggressively. 'I think you love the idea of having a beautiful young woman on your arm . . .' Max opens his mouth to protest, then shuts it again quickly as she continues. 'But, Max, I won't be young and beautiful forever and then what's left between us? We don't really know what makes the other tick. I feel as though my life is passing by in front of my eyes – like a film at the cinema – and I'm just sitting in the front row watching it. I've felt like an outsider all my life and being married to you is no different. I'm an outsider to your work, your family, your friends—'

'What's left of them,' Max mutters.

'Exactly. You've given up everything for me. And yet you don't really know me at all. And I don't really know you. I'm grateful to you,' she sees the flicker of annoyance pass across his features as she continues, 'but I want more out of my life. I'm just existing, rather than living.'

'You've got your writing,' he says.

She nods. 'Yes, I do have my writing and I love it. But it's not enough. I create the person I want to be and the life I want to live in my writing, but as soon as I switch off the computer, I'm right back to being the bored, shallow bitch that I've always been. I want to put things right before it's too late.'

'Don't leave me, Ella!' Max gasps suddenly. 'I couldn't cope without you.'

Ella's insides tighten with a mixture of fear and sympathy. She feels so trapped. How can she possibly leave Max when he hasn't done anything wrong, and loved her when no one else did? But she can't bear the thought of spending the rest of her life with him either. She might as well die now.

'I have to, Max,' she says gently but firmly. 'I can't go on like this.'

By now both of them are crying. The waiter arrives with their drinks and, seeing their faces, his smile promptly dies on his lips.

'Your drinks,' he says, depositing them as quickly as he can in front of them. 'Your food won't be long.'

'Cancel the order,' says Max, wiping his face roughly as he stands up and throws a twenty-pound note onto the table. 'We're finished,' he says, looking straight at Ella.

Rachel

The strange thing is: because Rachel almost expected it, she isn't nearly as shocked as everyone else around her. She is embarrassed, of course. And humiliated. But apart from that, she feels strangely calm. She had never been able to shake the niggling feeling that she had only ever had Toby on loan. He was younger than her, better looking than her and there was the small fact that deep down she had always known that he was still in love with Anna.

Rachel wants to hate Anna. She has ruined her wedding and wrecked her life. But it is hard to feel hate towards her. Even in the midst of her own despair, Rachel could see that Anna's emotions were just as raw as hers.

And what would have happened if Anna had managed to keep herself in check and Toby had gone through with the wedding, as Rachel knows he would have done? Would she have been happy knowing that she was married to a man whose heart belonged to someone else? Would she have been happy to spend the rest of her life being second best? *Maybe*, she thinks sadly as she sits in her bedroom, removing the delicate tiara from her hair.

There is a tentative knock at the door. She sighs at her tear-stained reflection. 'Come in,' she says.

Becs opens the door and puts her head through the gap. Rachel looks at her sister in the mirror and realizes with a start that she looks even worse than her. 'Are you up to having a cup of tea?' Becs asks shakily, her dark eyes darting nervously as she comes into the room, clutching a mug of steaming liquid.

Rachel nods and pats the bed, motioning for Becs to sit down. Becs puts the mug on Rachel's dressing table and sits, carefully rearranging her strapless pale pink silk dress. Finally she looks up and meets Rachel's eye. 'I'm so sorry,' she cries, clutching her sister's hand.

'What for?' Rachel asks in surprise.

'I feel so awful. You knew this morning that something was up and I talked you into going ahead with it. It's my fault you ended up walking into that bloody church!' Becs hangs her head miserably, twisting her hands together.

'No, no, don't be daft!' Rachel chides her gently. 'It wasn't your fault at all. I would have gone to the church anyway. I love Toby, I really do.' Becs' face contorts with anger and disbelief as Rachel continues. 'I wanted to marry him. But you're right, I did know something was up. I've always known. But there's no way I would have jilted him.'

'Shame he didn't have the same scruples!' snaps Becs and Rachel is touched by how much pain she can see in her sister's eyes on her behalf.

Rachel looks down and strokes her hand. 'He didn't jilt me, Becs. He was there. He would have gone through with it if—'

'If that fucking bitch hadn't turned up!' finishes Becs furiously.

Rachel nods. 'Well, yes. But I've been thinking about it,

Becs. What would it have been like to be married to a man I knew was in love with someone else? And I did know. I've always known. I would have married him because I love him, but you know what? Maybe I'm better than that.'

'You are!' Becs cries. 'You *are* better than that! I just feel so bad for you that you had to be humiliated like that in front of all those people! And poor Mum and Dad . . .'

Rachel feels a lump in her throat at the thought of her lovely parents, both dying inside for their broken-hearted daughter. 'How are they doing?' she asks, choked.

'They're devastated for you. And worried sick.'

Rachel nods. 'I'll go and talk to them,' she says, getting up. 'Just help me out of this bloody dress, will you?'

Her mum leaps up as she hears Rachel coming into the sitting room. 'Oh, sweetheart, are you OK?' she asks, her face crumpled with worry. Rachel walks into her mum's open arms and allows herself to be hugged for a few seconds before she becomes aware that there is someone else in the room. Over her mum's shoulder she sees Marco sitting awkwardly on the edge of the sofa clutching a mug of tea, which he is holding away from his morning suit. He looks so incongruous in his surroundings that Rachel can't help smiling. 'Hey, Marco,' she says, walking over and sitting down beside him. 'What are you doing here?'

Marco flushes and drops his eyes. 'I just wanted to make sure you were OK. I feel so bad for you about what happened . . .' he trails off miserably, staring down into his tea.

'I'm OK,' she says, surprising herself as much as her parents and Marco. 'I really am.'

Marco shakes his head. 'The stupid fucker!' he hisses

angrily, before clapping his hand over his mouth. 'Sorry,' he says, looking from her dad to her mum.

'Don't apologize,' her dad says gruffly. 'I feel much the same way myself, son.'

A sob escapes from her mum and she dashes from the room, leaving the three of them looking helplessly at one another. Eventually her dad stands up. 'I'd, er, better go and see if your mother's all right,' he says, patting Rachel on the head in his attempt at a comforting gesture. She nods as he leaves the room, suddenly feeling desperately awkward alone with Marco.

'So,' she says finally, unable to bear the silence any longer.

'So,' he agrees and they both laugh, breaking the tension.

'What do I do now, Marco?'

'I don't know,' he sighs, shaking his head. 'It's a mess.'

'We live together, we work together. How the hell am I going to pick up the pieces?'

'Well, he can move in with me for a while, although I'm so bloody angry with him . . .'

'Don't be. Honestly, Marco. Toby's a good guy.' As she speaks, Rachel suddenly feels so tired she can barely form a sentence. 'He just didn't love me enough,' she says, her eyelids drooping. 'I need to sleep now,' she continues drowsily, getting up. 'Thanks for coming round, Marco but I'll be OK. Don't worry.'

She awakes with a start the following evening. She looks at the clock on her – their – bedside table. It reads 19.03. Her mouth feels dry and her back hurts like hell. In the dusky light she can see her wedding dress hanging on the front of the wardrobe.

Rubbing her sore eyes, she sits up tentatively and stretches, listening out for sounds of life in the flat. She can hear voices and the noise of cutlery scraping on plates. She walks over to her dressing table and picks up the pair of scissors she had used the previous morning to trim her fringe. Very calmly she lifts her dress from the hanger and starts to cut. At first, she cuts delicately, making small snips in the pale ivory silk. Then, as she gets into her stride, the cuts become bigger and more savage until she is literally sweating with the effort. By the time she has finished, her beautiful dress is a pile of rags, lying forlornly on the bed. Finally, she buries her face in the scraps of fabric and allows herself to scream as loudly as she can.

Ella

Max and Ella don't speak in the taxi home but it isn't an awkward silence. Instead, a sense of relief hangs in the air as they both retreat into their own private reflections on a marriage that is now ending. For Ella's part she doesn't regret marrying Max. He saved her life and has given her the love and affection she craves so much. He chose her over his family and friends and made her feel special. He gave her the confidence to live her life and she knows she will always be grateful to him for that.

Whether he feels any gratitude towards her, she doesn't know, but she doubts it very much. She has caused him nothing but trouble and she wonders, looking at him now, with his grey pallor and world-weary expression, whether he regrets marrying her.

As Max pays the driver, Ella walks up the steps to their house and fishes in her handbag for the keys. Just as she finds them, she hears a noise from the pavement. Her heart lurches as she looks around and sees Max slump to the ground, groaning and clutching his chest.

The next thing she knows, she is kneeling beside him, cradling his head in her lap and stroking his face. The taxi driver leaps out of his side of the cab and runs to help, hauling Max off her lap and giving him the kiss of life. As he pumps furiously up and down on his chest, he screams at Ella to call an ambulance. She looks at him dumbly, unable to take in what he is saying.

'Call an ambulance – NOW!' he yells, the perspiration dripping from his forehead and onto Max's cornflower blue shirt, leaving an almost symmetrical pattern. Suddenly, Ella comes to and runs for her bag, which she had dropped on the steps, scrabbling furiously for her phone and punching in 999 with shaking fingers.

'It's my husband,' she screams when the operator puts her through, 'I think he's having a heart attack.'

It seems like an eternity before the ambulance arrives and Ella sits shivering on the pavement beside Max and the taxi driver, who is still administering first aid. A crowd has gathered and someone puts a coat around her shoulders. 'He'll be OK,' says a woman, crouching down and putting her arm around Ella.

As she speaks, the taxi driver suddenly stops what he is doing, his shoulders sagging in a gesture of defeat. 'No,' he says, trying to catch his breath. 'He won't. He's gone. I'm so sorry.'

There is a gasp from the crowd and someone screams. It is a few seconds before Ella realizes that that someone is her.

Back home from the hospital much later that day, she knows that she will have to tell Max's children – who else is going to make that call? But it is the worst thing she has ever had to do. Even though they are all in their late twenties and early thirties, they have already lost their mother and, despite the fact that they have more or less refused to speak to their father for the past few years, Ella knows that they still love him and will take his death very hard.

She decides to call Jasper, his elder son, first. She can't face calling either Araminta who, at twenty-eight, is only four years younger than her, or Rupert, who is the same age as her. At thirty-six, Jasper is not just the eldest, he has always been the most reasonable. He hates her every bit as much as the other two, he is just better at hiding his emotions.

She retrieves his number from Max's mobile and waits as it rings. After six rings, it clicks into the answerphone message: 'Hi, this is Jasper, leave your number and I'll call you back,' he drawls. Ella shivers at the sound of his voice and hangs up. She hadn't expected him not to pick up. Then it dawns on her. Of course, he isn't speaking to his father. He will have seen Max's number come up and refused to answer.

Still shaking, she picks up her own phone and taps out the number. This time Jasper answers immediately. 'Hello?' he asks quizzically.

'Jasper?' she says, her voice strained and alien.

'Yes,' he replies, sounding irritated. 'Who is this?'

'It's Ella,' she says quickly. 'Ella de Bourg.'

Silence.

'Your father's wife . . .' she continues awkwardly.

'I know only too well who you are,' he cuts in coldly. 'What do you want?'

Ella gulps. 'It's about Max . . .' she begins, suddenly wanting to cry. What she is about to say will devastate him and change his life forever. 'He's dead.'

There is silence on the other end of the line. Tears course noiselessly down Ella's cheeks.

'How?' Jasper says at last, his voice tight with emotion.

'Heart attack,' Ella sobs. 'I'm so sorry, Jasper.'

She can hear a strange sound, like the keening of an animal, as Jasper tries to reply. 'OK,' he croaks, before hanging up.

The next call she makes is to her parents. She doubts that they will have gone to the wedding reception for Toby and Rachel's non-wedding. They have probably gone home with Toby's parents and maybe Toby himself. Sure enough, when her mother, Annabel, answers her phone, Ella can hear muted voices in the background, not the raucous sounds of a party. 'Hello?' her mother says in her clipped, upper-class tones.

'It's me – Ella,' she manages to say, before bursting into noisy tears.

Annabel sighs loudly. 'Unfortunate business, back there at the church,' she begins and Ella can picture her raising her eyebrows in exasperation at her father. 'Really, Ella, your father and I were most embarra—'

'Max is dead!' Ella cries, cutting her mother off before she can launch into a lecture.

There is a stunned silence. 'What?' Annabel splutters eventually. 'What did you say?'

'Max is dead. He died this afternoon – of a heart attack.'

Immediately Annabel's tone softens. 'Oh dear! Oh, Ella, I'm so sorry. What a dreadful shock!' Again, she lapses into silence while Ella tries to compose herself at the other end of the line. 'Here's your father,' her mother says, trailing off helplessly.

'Ella!' her dad says gruffly. 'What's happened now?'

Ella blows her nose and wipes her eyes before replying. How typical of her father to assume she is to blame. 'It's

Max,' she says, speaking more clearly now. 'He died this afternoon of a heart attack.'

'What?' he gasps, thrown. 'Oh, bloody hell. Where are you?'

'At home,' she sighs.

'Alone?'

'Of course I'm alone. Who else would be with me?'

'Right,' he says briskly. 'Your mother and I will be there in an hour or so,' he adds, hanging up. Despite their coldness towards her, Ella is grateful and surprised that her parents are coming. They might not be of much comfort to her but at least her father will know how to deal with the practicalities of the situation.

She sits down on the oak floor with her back against the wall of the huge kitchen and watches the sun at the back end of the garden as it begins to set on the horizon. She tries to analyse how she feels, apart from the overwhelming sense of numbness. She is shocked and saddened that Max has gone but there is also a tiny part of her that feels relieved. There aren't many 32-year-old widows and it is an altogether more comfortable title than either mistress or gold-digger, both of which she has been called many times before.

True to their word, her parents arrive about an hour and a half later. Her mother kisses her on both cheeks, which strikes Ella as a peculiarly cold way to comfort your bereaved daughter, but as they have never had a tactile relationship, it is too difficult for her to start playing the earth mother now. Her father, Patrick, looks flustered and gives her a perfunctory pat on the back, before getting straight down to practicalities. 'Who's organizing the funeral?' he asks bluntly.

'I don't know,' Ella begins. 'I spoke to Jasper earlier to

break the news but we didn't discuss arrangements. He was too upset,' she adds.

Her father nods. 'I'll speak to him. Give me his number and I'll sort it out.'

Ella feels a sudden outpouring of gratitude towards her dad for dealing with everything so matter-of-factly. It occurs to her even now that Max was more of a father figure to her than a husband and, now that he is gone, there is a vacancy. Maybe Max's death will help her and her father establish the relationship that has eluded them so far.

She leaves her father in the sitting room, and goes to find her mother, who is in the kitchen busying herself making tea. 'Where were you?' Ella asks, sitting down at the kitchen table. 'When I called you?'

'At Martha and Graham's,' her mother replies, setting a cup of tea on the table in front of her. 'They were terribly upset, after what happened.'

Ella nods and sips the tea gratefully. 'Was Toby there?' she asks.

'No,' Annabel replies quickly. 'I didn't realize you and he were . . . well, involved.' Her cheeks redden slightly as she speaks.

Ella shrugs. *Let them think what they like*, she thinks. She can't be bothered to correct her. Not now.

'Anyway,' her mother continues, 'very poor form, him dumping that poor girl like that. Martha and Graham are livid with him. They were very fond of Rachel. I suppose he must still be in love with that other one.'

Despite the fact that Ella's husband has dropped dead in front of her that afternoon, her mother carries on chattering about the non-wedding, oblivious to the great churn of emotions that are cascading through her daughter's head. 'I don't care about their stupid bloody wedding!' Ella wants to shout. 'My husband's just died!'

Suddenly, a memory of Max, standing where her mother is standing, telling her a funny story about losing his swimming trunks when he dived into a pool in Barbados, punches through Ella so hard that she drops her teacup, unable to hold off the torrent of gulps and sobs that wrack her whole body. 'He's dead,' she cries in a voice that doesn't sound like her own. 'He's dead.'

Rachel

Dear Rachel,

I fully understand why you won't answer my calls but I really, really need to see you or, at the very least, speak to you. When you feel ready, please call me. I am more sorry than you could ever know.

Toby

Rachel rereads the note she has received in the post that morning. She lifts the paper to her nose and inhales deeply, trying to absorb some of Toby's scent. Her tears trickle onto the paper, smudging the deep blue ink into angry blobs. She gulps back a sob and folds the note carefully. She then slowly bends double, letting the blood rush to her head to try to distract her from the pain. She can't call him. Not yet. It is still too soon. She thought she was coping so well but now she realizes with a jolt that she must have been numb with shock. The reality of what happened is only now sinking in.

The next couple of weeks pass by in blur. She should have been relaxing on a palm-fringed beach, drinking cocktails and enjoying her new husband's company. Instead of which she is cooped up in her flat, with either her mum or her sister standing guard like something out of *Prisoner Cell Block H* in case Toby should try to visit. Rachel knows they will have to meet, will have to discuss where the hell to go from here but while she is just about coping, she doesn't want anything to set her back.

'I'm worried that if I see him, I'll suddenly fall apart,' she tells Becs one evening.

Becs nods sagely. 'I agree. If I were you I'd never want to see the stupid bastard ever again.'

'Don't, Becs,' Rachel pleads. 'Don't hate Toby. I don't.'

'I don't know how you can be so understanding after what he did to you.'

'I don't know either but I'm not faking it. I genuinely feel sorry for him. He must be going through hell too. And I'm going to have to see him sometime. We need to talk about what to do with the flat. Plus, there's the small issue of us working together.'

'That's not a problem – Marco said he's quit.'

'What?' Rachel gasps in shock. 'What did he say? When did he tell you this?'

Becs looks sheepish. 'Well, I've seen him a few times actually, since the wed— I mean, since the day.'

Rachel feels a rushing sensation sweep through her. Toby quitting his job was one thing. But Becs seeing Marco – that was quite another.

'How?' she manages to ask, bemused.

'Oh, we've just met for a couple of drinks. He's really worried about you. We all are,' she adds, taking Rachel's hand in hers.

'Oh,' is all Rachel can say. Her emotions are tumbling over one another as she tries to work out why she feels so wrong-footed. She doesn't want Toby to have left the job that he loved. She knows he will easily get another one, it was just that she supposed she had counted on at least seeing him at work, if they weren't going to be living together any more. But then again, seeing him every day might have rubbed salt into her already seriously wounded heart.

And why is she so perturbed about Becs seeing Marco? They are two of her favourite people in the whole world, wouldn't it be brilliant if they got it together? Then it clicks. She feels pissed off that, out of her misery, they have potentially found happiness.

'There's nothing going on between us, if that's what you're wondering,' says Becs quickly, as if reading her thoughts.

Rachel nods.

'Really!' Becs insists.

'Whatever,' says Rachel huffily, getting up and retreating back into the cocoon of her bedroom, where she is spending an increasing amount of her time.

At the end of the two weeks, when she should have gone back to work, she calls in sick, still unable to face the humiliation. Her mum comes in and sits on her bed. 'What are we going to do with you?' she smiles, pushing back the hair from Rachel's face.

Rachel shakes her head. 'I don't know, Mum. I can't face them all. Sooner or later I know I'll have to. But I just can't do it today. It's too soon.'

'I know, darling. Which is why I'm taking you away for a holiday.'

'No!' cries Rachel in panic. 'I can't! What about ...' She looks around her for reasons why she can't go. 'What about ... everything!' she says lamely.

'Everything can wait,' Mary replies firmly. 'You need some sun, some relaxation and some time away from this flat. You've had a big shock and you're stressed. I don't want to get antidepressants for you, I think you need a break.'

Rachel sighs heavily. She has run out of excuses. 'OK,' she agrees. 'When are we going?'

'Tonight,' smiles Mary. 'Get packing.'

The holiday is exactly what Rachel needs. They go to a small village in southern Spain where they stay in a tiny, family-run hotel where no one takes any notice of them and they are free to spend their days lying by the pool talking, reading and thinking. At her mum's insistence, they both leave their mobiles at home. Over the week, Rachel gradually feels her head starting to clear.

She still thinks about Toby constantly but she knows that is only natural. He has been such a big part of her life for so long now, she isn't going to be able to forget him overnight. And of course she still loves him. The problem with her family and close friends is that they expect her to hate him for what he's done and although she can understand why they might feel that way, she knows that it isn't possible to love someone one day and hate them the next – emotions are so much more complex than that.

'I wonder how he is,' she muses aloud to her mum one afternoon as they lie by the pool.

Mary puts down the Joanna Trollope novel she is reading and rolls over so that she is facing Rachel. 'How do you think he is?'

Rachel thinks for a moment. 'Terrible,' she says. 'Worse than me, probably.'

'What makes you say that?' Mary asks, frowning.

'Because he loves me and the guilt will be killing him.'

Her mum tuts slightly. 'It didn't have to be like this though, it's his own bloody fault!'

'I know,' sighs Rachel. 'But even though I'm feeling bad right now, I think that at some point in the future I will realize that he did the right thing.'

Mary looks dumbfounded.

'Oh, I know it should never have gone that far,' Rachel continues. 'I know that he should have called the wedding off long before we got to the church, but I genuinely don't think it hit him that he was doing the wrong thing until he was actually there.'

'Well, you're a lot more understanding than I'd be in your shoes, darling,' Mary says, looking at Rachel with a concerned expression. 'But what about going forward? How do you think you would feel if he now gets together with . . . her?'

'Anna?' Rachel can't help smiling slightly at her mum's refusal to say Anna's name out of loyalty to her daughter. This whole situation has really brought home to Rachel how much she is loved. 'Well, I think it would be better if he jilted me because he couldn't live without Anna, rather than if he jilted me because he couldn't stand the thought of being married to me.'

'You really feel that way?' says Mary, still looking bemused.

Rachel shrugs. 'Obviously I'd prefer for us to be living happily ever after but if that wasn't to be then yes, I think I'd prefer him to have gone back to Anna. At least it would give me some closure, instead of always wondering and hoping that he would eventually come back to me.'

Mary lies back down and they both spend the next few minutes lost in their own thoughts. Her mum, Rachel suspects, is plotting ways to have Toby murdered.

'I'm going to need to see him when we get back,' Rachel says, breaking the silence eventually. 'I just need to get up a bit more courage.'

Mary reaches across and clasps her hand. 'You've already been braver than I ever imagined possible,' she says, her voice breaking. 'You take your time. He can bloody well wait.'

But patience has never been Rachel's strong point. As soon as she closes the door to her flat on returning home a week later, she races to find her mobile and switches it on. There are several messages from Toby, each one sounding more and more tortured with guilt. 'Please call me back, Rachel,' he would say. 'I need to know that you're OK.'

She walks out onto her lovely terrace and sits on her bench, noticing afresh how big it looks in the tiny space. Taking a deep breath and feeling unusually calm and controlled, she dials his number.

'Rachel!' he cries, answering on the second ring. She can hear shouting and laughing in the background. He is obviously in a pub somewhere, enjoying himself. So much for him being wracked with angst and guilt, she thinks bitterly. 'Hang on, I'll just go outside,' he says.

She waits a few moments until he comes back on the line. 'Sorry about that,' he puffs, sounding out of breath. 'I'm in a pub.'

'So I gathered,' she replies, trying to keep her voice neutral but only succeeding in sounding clipped and cross. She cups the phone in the crook of her neck as she lights a cigarette. 'Bit early for celebrating, isn't it?'

Toby gives a small, nervous laugh. 'Not as bad as it sounds. I'm meeting someone about a possible job.'

'I heard that you quit. You didn't have to do that, Toby.' The air is chilly after the heat of Spain and she shivers involuntarily.

'Well I sort of did,' he says. 'It was the least I could do. So, anyway, how are you doing?' he asks, quickly changing the subject.

'I'm doing fine, considering I was jilted at the altar just a few weeks ago.' Despite her best intentions, she can't help sounding bitter. She takes a long drag on her cigarette and tucks her legs up underneath her.

'We need to talk,' Toby says in a small voice. 'Can I come and see you?'

Rachel's stomach lurches. How will she cope with seeing him face to face? She has been managing well so far but what if she crumbles completely when she sees him? 'I don't know,' she falters.

'Please, Rachel,' he pleads. 'We need to see each other sooner or later. Let's make it sooner.'

She sighs deeply. 'OK, you can come over.'

'Now?'

'Shouldn't you have your job interview first?' she says, trying not to sound exasperated.

'Oh! Yes, I suppose I should. I'll be there as soon as I can.'

Rachel finishes her cigarette and then spends the next hour and a half making herself look as good as possible. She might not have Toby but she still has her pride. She supposes she is wanting him to regret what he's done, although she already knows that for Toby it has always been about more than how she looks. Nevertheless, she is glad of her golden tan and the pounds that have fallen off her in the past weeks.

When the doorbell finally rings, she nearly jumps out of her skin. She opens it with shaking hands and there, looking more heart-stoppingly beautiful than ever, is Toby. For a moment she thinks she might actually throw up, so she doesn't move until she has regained her composure.

'Hi,' he says shyly, looking unsure of whether to come in or stay on the doorstep.

'Hi,' she murmurs back, stepping aside so that he can get past her into the flat. 'You could have used your key.'

'It just didn't seem right somehow.'

'No,' she agrees. Would it always be like this between them now? Tiptoeing politely around each other, not saying what they really felt?

'So,' he begins, following her up the stairs and into the kitchen where she automatically puts the kettle on, busying herself making coffee. 'How are you really? You look fantastic.'

Rachel smiles to herself, glad she has made the effort and hasn't just crumpled into a make-up-free, greasy-haired wreck. It makes her feel more confident. 'I've been away, with Mum.'

The colour drains from his face. 'Oh God, your parents must hate me,' Toby groans.

'Parents' prerogative,' she smiles, enjoying his discomfort and feeling proud of the dignified way she is coping with such an awkward situation. She hands him a mug and they walk out onto the roof terrace, where the weak afternoon sunshine is beginning to peep through the clouds. They sit down at either end of the bench and look out together over the city, which seems to be buzzing with life. Neither of them speaks for several long minutes, each lost in contemplation. 'I always loved this view,' says Toby finally.

'Me too,' says Rachel, feeling sad that it was yet another thing they wouldn't be sharing again. She is desperate for another cigarette but knows that Toby disapproves, so she sits on her hands and tries to ignore the urge. Then suddenly she remembers that she doesn't have to care what he thinks any more and she stands up decisively.

'Where are you going?' Toby asks in alarm, grabbing her arm as she passes by him.

She shakes him off gently. 'Don't worry, I'm just going to get my cigarettes.'

She goes back into the flat and retrieves them from her bag. She is just about to walk back out onto the terrace when she looks up and sees Toby watching her. She stops and blinks hard. *Don't cry, Rachel*, she tells herself firmly before stepping over the threshold and rejoining him. She smokes quietly for a moment, closing her eyes as the nicotine hit kicks in. Toby takes her free hand and clasps it between his own. She looks away, watching the trail of smoke evaporate into the warm air as she exhales.

'Rachel, I'm so, so sorry,' he says quietly. 'I never wanted to hurt you.'

Once again, she feels her composure slipping. She takes a deep breath and wills herself not to cry. After a few seconds the urge passes and she is calm again. 'I know,' she says, looking at him now. 'But the fact is, you did.'

'I'd give anything to turn back the clock,' he says, stroking the top of her hand with his thumb.

For an instant, her heart leaps. Is he saying he wishes he

had married her after all? As if sensing what she is thinking, he continues quickly. 'We should never have got married in the first place.'

She laughs bitterly. 'We didn't!'

He smiles back. 'No, but you know what I mean.'

She nods. She knows what he means all right.

'The thing is, I always knew,' she says, almost to herself, drawing hard on her cigarette, before stubbing it out altogether.

Toby looks surprised. 'How could you have known? I didn't know myself until . . . well, you know.'

'I always knew you were still in love with her,' she continues. She takes her hand away from him and folds it with the other in her lap.

'But how?' Toby frowns. 'I never talked about her . . . never even mentioned her name.'

'Exactly,' says Rachel. 'That's how I knew.'

Toby closes his eyes and throws back his head. 'Oh God, I've made such a balls-up, haven't I? You don't deserve this.'

'No,' she agrees, 'I don't. But I don't regret you either, Toby. I've been happy with you and, despite the small fact of you standing me up on our wedding day, I will always love you.'

She can see a wave of guilt and misery pass over his face. 'Oh, Rachel . . .' he whispers, opening his eyes and gazing at her.

A single tear trickles down her cheek and she brushes it away crossly. She vows there and then that that will be the last tear she will ever cry over Toby.

'So, have you seen her?' Rachel asks, dreading the answer. 'Since that day?'

Toby shakes his head fiercely. 'No, of course not,' he says and she knows he is telling the truth.

'Why not?'

Toby looks puzzled. 'Well, how could I, after what we did to you?'

Rachel looks at him intently. 'Toby, you should see her. You need to work it out.'

He shakes his head. 'I don't know how you can be so generous about both of us—'

'I'm not being generous,' she snaps. 'Far from it. But it would make me feel better if you and Anna made a go of it.'

'How? That doesn't make any sense.' Toby rubs his forehead, suddenly looking tired.

'It makes sense to me. If you didn't go through with our wedding because you're in love with someone else, that's something I can deal with because there's nothing I can do about it.'

Toby nods slowly.

'But if you didn't go through with it because you just didn't want to be married to me, I'd find that much harder to cope with. So you getting together with Anna would, however strange it sounds, make me feel better about what happened.'

Immediately, Toby's eyes fill with tears and he reaches across to hug her. As she leans into his chest and smells that familiar soapy smell of him that she adores, sitting in the sunshine on their special bench, he says the words she knows she will never hear from him again. 'I love you, Rachel.'

Anna

Days turn into weeks and the summer begins to pass. It has been hot and humid in the city this year, with a cloying atmosphere that seems to stick to Anna's skin, matching her misery. She wants to talk to Clare. She wants to tell her that she's sorry that she and James quarrelled because of her and he left for Australia without making things up with her. But she can't talk about it. Not yet. She is still in shock herself and doesn't know how to break through the invisible wall of resentment Clare has erected around her. Her lips are permanently set in a grim line and her smooth, olive skin has lost its glow, replaced by a greyish pallor. Their eyes stop meeting and Anna begins to watch her silently and furtively as they exchange polite enquiries as to whether they need to stock up on washing-up liquid or loo roll.

Eventually, unable to bear the tense atmosphere at home, Anna takes the coward's way out and buries herself in her work, trying hard to avoid seeing Clare as much as possible. Normally, she would have gone to see her mum for at least a few weeks of the summer holidays, but not this year. She doesn't want to have to explain what has happened, she is too ashamed of her part in it all. She has told Cassie that the wedding didn't go ahead but didn't go into details, saying simply that they'd had a change of heart. She tried to ignore the excitement in Cassie's voice as she asked if Anna had made contact with him since, answering honestly that she hadn't seen or heard from him.

To the obvious surprise and delight of Anna's headmistress, Mrs Kennard, she goes into school almost every day – planning lessons, working out how to structure the year ahead and thinking up new ways to make her class of 7- and 8-year-olds interested in learning. Mrs Kennard, thrilled by her new-found dedication to duty, wastes no time in giving her plenty of other tasks to do while she is there. Sensibly, all the other teachers are off enjoying their breaks and won't reappear until the last possible moment, so Anna gets landed with most of their stuff as well as her own. In reality, she is hiding from the outside world and all her problems, but for now at least, she is grateful for the focus and distraction that work gives her.

Things at home continue to be strained, with everything that Anna and Clare are thinking left unsaid. Nights are spent holed up in their separate rooms, engrossed in their own private grief, and rooms that used to reverberate with laughter and chatter, now sit silent and accusing.

Now, several weeks after the wedding-that-never-was, Anna is walking down their dusty Battersea street, returning home to the flat in the sticky heat of a late summer evening, when she spots a figure sitting on a wall in the distance. It is the wall outside the flat and her heart quickens along with her pace as she squints into the harsh glare of the angrily setting sun, wondering if she is hallucinating. The closer she gets, the clearer his outline becomes until she can make out that he is watching her with an unblinking stare.

The street is busy, the sounds from the city evening continuing around them rudely. But as she comes to a halt just a few metres away from him, the scenery around them seems to fall away, until there is just him and her, cocooned in a silence so deep that she can hear her breath coming in short, sharp bursts.

'It's you,' she says, her heart pounding with the sudden burst of adrenaline.

'It's me,' he agrees, looking at her in the way that he always did, which makes her feel that he can see right into her soul.

'I ruined your wedding,' she says, and it feels like her voice is travelling slowly from her mouth in her trance-like state.

'You didn't ruin my wedding,' he says, still holding her eyes with his own. 'I did.'

'Well, I suppose, strictly speaking, we both did.'

'I suppose,' he says quietly. 'Strictly speaking.'

A siren screeches somewhere in the distance. Anna looks around the scruffy street, where other city dwellers are living their lives – coming and going, hoping to make the most of the late-summer sunshine. 'So, what now?' she says, wanting to be away from the bustle.

'Shall we start with you inviting me in?' he says, jumping off the wall and dusting himself off as he looks down at her.

Anna holds his look for a few seconds more, while the movie of their relationship seems to play in fast-forward in her mind. *How will it end?* she wonders. 'Yes, that's a good idea,' she says slowly, struggling to focus.

Still, neither of them moves until finally a strangled, embarrassed laugh escapes from Anna's throat, pulling her back to the present. She fumbles in her bag, trying to locate the fat bunch of keys hanging from the silver cat-shaped key ring that Toby bought her for their first Christmas together. She is acutely conscious of his presence, leaning over her as her fingers close around it at last.

'I can't believe you kept that,' he says, reaching forward and touching the cat as she unlocks the door. Their hands whisper past each other and the surge of electricity is so intense as they make contact that she feels a physical crackle.

'I never managed to lose it,' she smiles, looking lovingly at the little silver moggy.

'I'm glad,' he says, following her into the flat. 'So, this is where you live,' he says, looking around him as he speaks. 'It's nice. Really nice.' He emphasizes the word 'really' in a way that makes it sound as though he is paying her a personal compliment.

Anna puts her bag on the floor and follows his gaze, seeing the flat through fresh eyes. 'It's only because I share with Clare,' she admits, even the mention of her name causing her to wince with shame and guilt. 'I could never afford it on my teacher's pittance.'

'But the job's reward enough, right?' smiles Toby.

'Something like that,' Anna laughs, heading for the kitchen.

Toby follows, still looking all around him in awe. 'It seems weird that I've never been here.'

Anna puts the kettle on as he arranges his long limbs onto a chair at the kitchen table. 'Why?' she says, not looking at him, all the time aware of a powerful atmosphere between them. It's as if they both know why he is here but neither of them is ready to say it. Not yet.

'It just feels weird that we've both got these whole other lives that we've lived in between.'

She shivers involuntarily and turns to look at him. He has hardly changed at all in the time they have been apart. He is still tall and angular with that perfectly chiselled face. Looking at him now, she is once again suffused with a mixture of love and lust that has never really gone away in all those years.

'We wasted so much time,' she says, almost to herself.

'It wasn't a waste.'

She daren't speak again, suddenly terrified of what he is going to say.

'Rachel wasn't a waste,' he says, slightly aggressively, struggling to keep his composure. 'I love her, she's a great girl.'

Disappointment crashes through Anna like a speeding train. 'No, of course not . . . I didn't mean . . .' She starts to speak but can't find the words, so busies herself making coffee instead. She puts the mug in front of Toby and sits down, looking across at him, waiting for him to continue.

Finally, having regained his composure, he speaks again. 'I do love her, but it's not the same.'

Anna stares down at her coffee, hardly daring to breathe. 'Not the same as what?'

'Not the same as how I felt about you,' he says, fixing her with his intense eyes and this time she is unable to look away.

'Past tense,' she murmurs. 'You used the past tense.'

'The past is all I know about you and all you know about me,' Toby replies gently. 'We don't know about the future – yet. We got lost along the way.'

'"Let's get lost together." That's what you said to me the first time I met you,' she murmurs, drowning in his gaze. It is as if the years have just melted away and all the emotion she has suppressed has come bubbling back to the surface. She feels like she is twenty again and just as hopelessly in love with him as she was back then.

'Well, we certainly did that,' he smiles back at her.

'We messed it up, didn't we?'

'But we can put it right.'

'Can we?' she whispers as he stands up and comes round to her side of the table.

Toby holds out his hand and Anna takes it, allowing him to pull her to her feet. They stand looking at each other for a few seconds before he bends his head and kisses her, tentatively at first, then more fiercely. Immediately, her whole body ignites with the passion that has lain dormant for so many years. She knows that they aren't lost any more.

Clare

Clare tries hard not to blame Anna but it is impossible not to feel that she is at least partly responsible. James has gone to Australia for good and they parted on bad terms because of Anna. Clare can see that Anna is wracked with guilt because she is obviously trying to avoid her as much as possible in the weeks after the non-wedding. She seems to spend most of her days at school, which is unprecedented during the long summer holiday.

For Clare's part, she too throws herself into work. It helps to focus her attention on anything other than the fact that she has lost the only man she has ever loved. They might have only spent a week together, but it was long enough for Clare to know that she wouldn't ever feel that way about anyone again.

For the first time, Clare begins to truly understand what Anna must have gone through in the years since she had split from Toby. Clare has always been sympathetic, but she has never really understood it. Until now. She marvels at the physical symptoms of her mental anguish. She feels so tired all the time that she can barely drag her bones out of bed in the morning and has actually been physically sick on some occasions. Clare remembers the same thing happening to Anna and feels a pang of remorse that she has often felt that Anna should pull herself together.

She contemplates calling James or getting his e-mail address from . . . who? She isn't sure who would give it to her. She doubts that Marco would entertain a conversation with either her or Anna after what happened. She has gone over their last conversation again and again in her head. Why did James turn so suddenly? It really didn't make sense after he had been so loving. Clare desperately wants to talk to someone about it but with her and Anna avoiding each other, she has to keep her thoughts to herself, which only makes things worse.

About six weeks after the wedding, Clare comes home from work early to find Toby sitting in the kitchen. 'Oh!' she shrieks, making him jump. 'What the hell are you doing here?'

'Nice to see you too, Clare,' Toby laughs, coming over and giving her a hug. 'I didn't expect you to be home this early.'

'I wasn't feeling too good,' Clare frowns. 'But, seriously, what *are* you doing here? Does Anna know you're here?'

'Course she does,' he says, slightly indignantly. 'Who do you think gave me a key to get in?'

'A key?' Clare gulps. 'I didn't even know she'd seen you since the wedding . . . er, I mean, the day you were supposed to be getting married . . .'

'I know things haven't been great between you and Anna since that day and I'm really sorry. She feels so bad about James. She thinks it's all her fault.'

Clare shrugs and sits down, dumping her bag on the table. 'Well it is, sort of,' she sighs heavily, feeling tired and nauseous as usual at the mention of James' name.

'Do you want to tell me what happened?' Toby says gently.

As soon as he speaks, Clare bursts into floods of noisy tears. The kindness in his eyes and the relief of finally being able to talk to someone is overwhelming. Without saying anything, he gets up and pulls several tissues from a box on the window sill, before coming round to her side of the table. He hands her the tissues and sits down with one arm around her heaving shoulders.

After a while, she manages to compose herself and gives him a watery smile. 'Sorry, Toby, it's just that I've been desperate to talk to someone about it and with Anna and me not speaking . . .'

'I know,' Toby says, giving Clare's shoulder a squeeze. 'Don't worry, it's fine. Take your time and tell me what happened with James.'

'Well,' she begins, still hiccoughing, 'we spent the week after your stag party together and I know it sounds ridiculous but we really fell for each other – or at least I really fell for him.'

'No, it wasn't just you,' Toby cuts in. 'He was crazy about you too.'

Clare's heart leaps at his words. 'Thank you,' she smiles, 'that helps a lot. I'd begun to wonder if I'd read more into it than there really was.'

'No, I don't think so,' says Toby firmly. 'Both Marco and I said how different he was with you to anyone else he's ever gone out with. It seemed . . . serious.'

'Yes!' cries Clare, gratitude sweeping through her. 'That's exactly how it was . . . it was serious. Even though it was quick, we just totally connected. I've never felt that way about anyone.'

Toby nods and she can see that he understands completely. 'So, how come you left on such bad terms then? Anna said he called you from the reception . . .?'

'He did,' says Clare, the tears welling up again. 'And he was fine at first but then he started slagging off Anna. He called her some horrible names and said that you'd have gone through with the wedding if it wasn't for her.'

Toby closes his eyes for a second. 'Oh God,' he sighs, clearly struggling with the memory of that day.

'Well, obviously I couldn't let him get away with that,' Clare continues, her voice breaking. 'So I told him that I didn't want to speak to him any more unless he stopped being so horrible. He said, "Fine," and hung up. That was the last time I spoke to him,' she wails, tears cascading down her cheeks once more.

Toby rubs her back until she stops crying.

'I just don't understand why he turned so suddenly, Toby. What the hell was that all about?'

Toby looks away, deep in thought for a few moments.

Clare takes the opportunity to dry her eyes and blow her nose as delicately as she can into the thickening silence.

'Maybe he deliberately picked a fight with you,' Toby says at last.

Clare frowns. 'Why would he do that?'

'Maybe he was making it easier for you – and for him – to say goodbye.'

Clare thinks about it for a while. It does make a certain sense. They were both struggling with the idea of him going away for good and perhaps the only way he could handle it was by instigating an argument, so that they didn't have to have a long, agonizing farewell.

'I'd never considered that possibility,' she says aloud.

'And does it make you feel better or worse?' Toby probes gently.

'Better, definitely,' Clare replies, nodding slightly. 'And it means I can stop blaming Anna . . .'

Toby smiles. 'Don't beat yourself up about that – you're only human. But she loves you to bits, you know, she'd never do anything to upset you.'

Clare nods. 'I know. I love her too. I've missed her so much.'

As if on cue, they hear Anna's key in the door, followed by her footsteps echoing on the wooden hall floor. 'Hi!' she calls brightly, bounding into the kitchen. Immediately, the smile dies on her lips when she sees Clare sitting next to Toby at the table.

'Oh! Clare! God, I didn't expect you to be home,' she stammers.

'Obviously not,' smiles Clare, standing up. 'But look who I found lurking in our flat.'

Anna's cheeks flush. 'I wanted to tell you, but with everything that's happened . . .' She trails off miserably.

Clare walks over to her and hugs her tightly. 'I know. Let's forget about it and be friends again. And I am SO happy for you.'

Anna's eyes fill with tears.

'Oh God, don't you start!' laughs Toby. 'There aren't enough tissues left.'

Anna wipes her eyes briskly and grins. 'Sorry,' she says, walking over to Toby and kissing him.

'So, are you going to tell me what's going on then?' asks Clare, feigning indignation as she sits back down again.

Anna and Toby look at each other and beam. Watching

them, Clare feels more cheerful than she has in weeks. They look so right together, so in love that it is impossible not to be caught up in their happiness. Maybe there is hope for her after all.

Once Clare knows about Toby and Anna's rekindled relationship, Toby moves in with them. Although Marco has said Toby could replace James as his flatmate, Toby knows Marco is still furious with him so he is glad not to have to take him up on the offer. Marco has always been close to Rachel and can't believe that Toby jilted her. Clare has never said it to Toby but she also suspects that Marco fancied his chances with Anna and is pissed off that she is now with Toby.

Once they are reunited, Anna and Toby's relationship seems to pick up exactly where they left off a decade ago, with such a strong aura of love surrounding them that Clare can always tell as soon as she walks into the flat whether they are there. It is as if there is an invisible bubble around them, holding them in their own private world. Toby has started a new, more high-profile, high-pressure job as editor of a breakfast show and Anna's teaching brings with it a different type of stress, so they aren't the social butterflies they used to be; anyway, they seem to find all the entertainment they need in each other's company.

The transformation in Anna is staggering. She has blossomed overnight and seems to have lost all the angst and misery she has carried on her narrow shoulders for years, making her look about ten years younger than she is. It's like the sun shining on a flower after years of darkness. Her confidence, humour and bubbly personality have resurfaced and she seems to exude joy from every pore. 'It's so good to have you back,' Clare tells her one night as they cook supper in the kitchen, Anna making her laugh with stories about the kids from school.

'It's good to be back,' Anna grins, her eyes shining. 'I don't know how you've put up with me being such a miserable old cow all these years but I'm so grateful that you did.'

'I don't know how I put up with you either,' laughs Clare, dodging out of the way as Anna flicks her with a tea towel.

Suddenly, Clare is overcome by a wave of emotion and slumps at the table. Anna looks at her in concern. 'Are you feeling OK, hon?' she asks, frowning. 'You know, you don't look great.'

Clare fights the nausea that is sweeping through her. 'I'm fine,' she lies. 'I think I'm just overtired. Or maybe lovesick.'

Anna smiles sympathetically. 'Well, I know how that feels.'

'But it passes, right?' asks Clare hopefully, knowing she can't go on feeling this bad indefinitely.

Anna nods slowly. 'Yes, it passes.'

What she doesn't say, but what they both know, is that her lovesickness only passed when she and Toby got back together. Seeing as Clare has not heard from James since he went to live on the other side of the world, she feels that this is unlikely to be the remedy in her case.

The next evening when she gets home from work, Clare finds Anna waiting for her clutching a small plastic bag. 'What's that?' she asks, dumping her handbag on the table and frowning.

'Have a look,' says Anna, handing the bag to her.

Clare takes it from her and opens it, curious. Inside is a

small rectangular box. She pulls it out and looks at Anna quizzically, still not understanding.

'It's a pregnancy test,' Anna says gently.

Clare gasps and clasps her hand over her mouth. 'Oh God! No! I can't,' she stammers, her head beginning to swim. 'Oh Jesus, Anna, what if it's positive?'

Anna comes over and wraps her arms around her. Clare is shaking. 'If it's positive, we'll deal with it,' Anna says calmly. 'If it's not, at least that's one less thing to worry about.'

'How did you know?' asks Clare, disentangling herself from Anna's embrace and sitting down on the nearest chair.

'Our theme for this term is babies,' says Anna wryly, sitting down opposite her. 'It just suddenly clicked, today, why you might have been feeling so rough these past few weeks.'

'I can't be pregnant,' says Clare, shaking her head. 'I just can't be.'

'Did you use protection?' Anna sounds slightly embarrassed as she speaks.

'Yes!' cries Clare indignantly, before pausing to think for a second. 'Well, at least, most of the time,' she adds, suddenly remembering their first night together when they ran out of condoms.

'Then I think you should do the test,' Anna replies firmly.

Clare's shoulders sag. 'I don't need to,' she says miserably, feeling the tears and panic threatening to engulf her. 'I already know the result.'

Ella

DEATH NOTICE

Max Corbett
Born 16.05.49
Died 24.07.10
Devoted husband of the late Camilla,
loving father of Jasper, Rupert & Araminta.
Funeral to be held at
Our Lady Queen of Heaven Church,
Chiswick, London,
31.07.10 at 1 p.m.
Family flowers only.

Max's funeral is a strange experience for Ella. At most funerals the widow is treated with sympathy and respect but there is precious little of either shown towards her. Max's three children have made it abundantly clear that they blame her for their father's untimely death and spend much of the service shooting her looks of pure venom. The younger two, Rupert and Araminta, both have partners who have clearly been briefed about her and follow suit, while

Jasper manages to produce enough vitriol for two, despite being on his own.

Max's former work colleagues aren't much better and nobody offers her their condolences. Ella's mother, father, her friend Fabien and Monica her agent are the only people who have come to support her. Ella can tell that all of them are shocked at the level of hatred that is spewing out in her direction.

'Jesus,' Monica whispers. 'Anyone would think you were on a par with Hitler the way they're carrying on!'

Ella shrugs. 'No one forgave me for taking over where his first wife left off.'

Monica looks at her with a sympathetic expression. Ella hasn't been entirely honest with Monica about the circumstances surrounding her getting together with Max. She hasn't actually said so, but she has certainly led Monica to believe that there was no overlap. Come to think of it, she has also led her mother and father to believe the same thing. Fabien is the only one who knows the truth.

'Well, really,' her mother splutters as they file out of the church, dodging the mutterings. 'I do think that they could behave with a little more decorum at a funeral, for God's sake!'

Ella links her arm through her mother's, glad of her support for once. Her mother is not given to displays of emotion or declarations of love but Ella is nonetheless grateful for her presence today. Likewise her father, who seems oblivious to the toxic atmosphere and is busy offering his condolences to Max's children. Ella can see them weighing up whether to shake his hand or not, but he isn't the sort of man you can refuse.

Jasper had spoken about his father beautifully at the service. He had described him as a devoted and hands-on father who had given them all a very happy childhood. He had spoken of his generosity of spirit, his devotion to his family and his loyalty to his many friends. As he spoke, Ella's throat constricted and she felt the tears starting to roll down her face. She wasn't sure if it was because she was mourning Max's loss or because Jasper had totally eradicated her from the story of Max's life. He spoke only of Camilla and their happy family life together.

Whatever the reason for her tears, Ella feels better for having let them out. And, she has to admit, she wants to at least look like a widow in mourning, even if no one actually treats her like one.

As her father speaks to Jasper outside the church, Ella senses his gaze wander until his eyes alight on her. She looks away quickly, but not before she has seen the look of contempt mixed with triumph in his eyes. She can tell he feels that by omitting any mention of her from his speech and from the death notice he placed, he has exacted a tiny revenge for what she did to his family. 'You don't matter,' he seems to be saying, 'and you never did.'

'Well, what now?' asks her mother as their tiny group congregates at the church gates.

'I don't think we'd be very welcome at the after-show party,' snipes Fabien, already puffing hard on a cigarette. Monica, also lighting up, nods her agreement.

Ella's father comes over to join them, having 'done the right thing' by speaking to all of Max's children. 'I think we should go home, Annabel,' he says to her mother, in his usual 'brook-no-argument' voice.

Ella's mother looks at her quizzically. 'Will you be all right?' she asks, clearly wanting her to respond in the affirmative.

Ella nods. 'I'll be fine – Monica and Fabien will keep an eye on me.'

Her mother looks at them and gives a tight smile that doesn't reach her eyes. 'OK, well, if you're sure . . . we'll be off then. Take care,' she adds, kissing Ella stiffly on both cheeks.

'Not the most affectionate parents, are they?' Monica sniffs as they watch them walk off.

'No,' Ella agrees, taking Monica's cigarette and drawing hard on it. 'But they're the only ones I've got.'

'Well, I think we should go out and paaaarrrrty!' cries Fabien, clapping his hands together and drawing more looks of disgust from the assembled mourners.

'Shh!' Ella hisses, giggling slightly despite herself.

'So do I,' agrees Monica. 'Fuck the lot of them!' she snaps, shooting a murderous glare at the crowd.

Ella turns and catches Jasper's eye one more time as they start to move off. He is shaking his head, but there is a sadness in his expression that discomfits her. She can tolerate the anger and vitriol, but she is much less comfortable with grief.

'Yeah,' she agrees in a whisper, 'fuck the lot of them.'

From the church, they take a cab to the King's Road and find a cocktail bar. 'Well?' says Fabien as they find a booth and sit down. 'What are you having?'

Ella thinks for a moment. If ever there was a time to drink herself into a stupor, it was now. 'I'll have several tequila slammers and the most alcoholic cocktail you can get, please. I intend to get totally shit-faced.'

*

Ella is as good as her word. Waking up the next day, she becomes aware that she is in bed – with a man. For a split second, Ella thinks it must be Max and then she remembers. With her head feeling as though it has been thumped repeatedly with a blunt instrument and her mouth as dry as cotton wool, she turns over.

'Oh, thank God!' she sighs with relief as she recognizes Fabien's tattooed back. 'It's you!'

Fabien groans loudly. 'Yes, it's me. But I wish it wasn't.'

'What happened?' she murmurs, tentatively checking if she is still wearing her underwear. Fabien might be gay but she still doesn't fancy the idea of him seeing her in all her glory. Thankfully, she is still pretty much fully clothed.

'Don't you remember any of it?' he asks incredulously, rolling onto his back and placing the palms of his hands over his eyes.

Ella screws up her face in an effort to remember. 'No. The last thing I can remember is going to a bar with you and Monica.'

'Well, it got a lot more fun after that, girlfriend!' he giggles. 'If I hadn't been there you would have found yourself in bed with one of four different guys you picked up! I hope you appreciate how much abuse I had to take to protect you.'

'Four!' gasps Ella. 'Seriously? I picked up four different guys?'

'Yup,' Fabien nods slowly. 'One of them was really hot too – wouldn't have minded having a go myself!'

'Oh God!' she groans, clamping her hands over her face. 'How did you extricate me from them?'

'Well,' he says, swinging his legs over the side of the bed and sitting up, reaching for his cigarettes and lighting one, 'when I told them you had only just buried your husband earlier in the day, they seemed to lose interest pretty quickly.'

'Oh, you little shit!' Ella squeals, reaching over and slapping his naked back.

'Sorry, darling, but drastic action was required . . . so drastic action is what I took.' He exhales a thin trail of smoke as he stands up and takes another heavy drag. 'Now, I need hangover food – I'm going to have a look at what you've got in those obscenely expensive cupboards of yours – fuck all, I bet. I'll make you some coffee, shall I?' he adds pointedly before shuffling off in his boxer shorts, clutching his packet of cigarettes and his lighter.

Ella sighs deeply and lies back down. Even by her standards, picking up four different men on the day of her husband's funeral is pretty bad. But then, she reasons, hasn't she been living the life of a virtual nun for the past six years with Max? Maybe she deserves a little fun.

Returning with a mug of coffee several minutes later, Fabien sits on the bed beside Ella and looks down at her. 'Listen, honeybun, don't beat yourself up. You haven't been happy for a long time. Maybe Max popping his clogs is the best thing that could have happened. It's a lot neater than divorce, that's for sure.'

'Fabien!' she shrieks, shocked at his honesty.

'Don't tell me that thought hasn't crossed your naughty little mind over the past week, because I wouldn't believe you.'

God, she hates that Fabien knows her so well. He is right, of course. She wouldn't say that she had wanted Max to die – even she isn't that callous. But the fact that he is no longer around certainly makes life much easier. She is now free to have some no-strings fun with other men. And she needs to make up for lost time. Seeing Toby at the non-wedding showed her once and for all that he is never going to be interested in her, so now she needs to find someone who is.

Over the next few weeks, Ella makes the most of her new-found freedom. She goes out every night, phoning Fabien and insisting he comes with her, not that he ever needs much persuading. He is delighted to discover this new wild side to his friend, who had previously been too worried about what Max would think to really let her hair down. And she has stamina too – she would emerge blinking into the sunlight after an all-night clubbing session, looking as though she was stepping flawlessly out onto a catwalk. Fabien adores beautiful women and they don't come much more beautiful than Ella.

For Ella's part, she is loving the sensation of feeling young again. She has quickly rediscovered her ability to flirt with any man under the age of ninety – and a few above that age too. She can be as provocative as she likes, safe in the knowledge that Fabien will bat away any unwanted admirers who get too close.

But eventually Fabien has to go abroad for work and, after a couple of nights at home watching TV on her own, Ella decides to go it alone. She dresses as tartily as she dares in a black crochet minidress, with just a tiny pair of knickers and a push-up bra underneath. She digs out her most towering pair of heels and gazes at herself in the bedroom mirror. *Still got it*, she thinks, turning around to admire her long, toned legs and pert bum. She has always had a great bum – Max used to say it was his favourite bit of her. She shakes her head irritably, trying to banish all thoughts of Max from her mind. She doesn't want guilt over her dead husband to stop her from having a good time.

Walking into a club alone is a strangely exhilarating experience. Every head seems to turn towards her as she makes her way to the bar. She perches on a bar stool and opens her mouth to order a drink, but before she can speak, a smooth, upper-class voice behind her says, 'Glass of your finest champagne for the lady.'

Ella spins round to find herself staring into a pair of dark, dangerously sexy eyes.

The man smiles. 'Hi, I'm Charles. My friends call me Charlie.'

'Thank you, Charlie,' Ella smiles back.

'May I join you?' he asks, raising an eyebrow.

Ella nods and gestures towards the empty stool next to her. Her heart is thumping. This is new territory without Fabien to look out for her but Charlie looks charming and handsome. And she is reassured that in a crowded bar, she is perfectly safe.

'Let's make that a bottle,' Charlie says to the barman, slickly handing over his credit card.

Ella begins to relax as they chat, knocking back the champagne, until she needs to use the bathroom. 'I'll be right back,' she giggles, realizing as she slides off the stool that she is already feeling very tipsy.

'I'll be right here,' Charlie laughs back, waving playfully.

Negotiating the spiral cast-iron staircase in almost pitch blackness seems impossible but Ella manages to grip the rail to stop herself from falling. Once inside the cubicle, she tries to focus on her reflection in the mirror but it keeps blurring like those funfair mirrors that distort your features. She fumbles in her bag for a lip gloss, smears some onto her lips and then makes her way back up the staircase and into the club. Charlie is still sitting at the bar, beaming at her as she sways slightly on her way over to join him. She thinks woozily how handsome he is – and how different from Max. Charlie is about the same age as her, wearing a stunning dark suit and a crisp white shirt which shows off his tan.

'Drink up,' he says as she reaches him. 'I'll take you somewhere a bit more lively.'

Obediently, Ella drains the remaining champagne in her glass and follows him out of the bar.

The last thing she remembers is the cold air hitting her face and Charlie taking her by the hand.

The next morning, Ella wakes up in a strange room. Without moving her head, which she already knows would be a mistake, she looks around, trying to get her bearings. She is in a bedroom. A beautiful bedroom with flock wallpaper and a stunning glass chandelier. She is lying in a four-poster bed. Gingerly, she moves her head slightly to one side. As she does so, it feels like it is splintering into a thousand pieces and she cries out in pain. After closing her eyes for a few more minutes, she tentatively opens them again and tries to get a sense of whether she is alone or not.

She listens carefully. She can't hear any sounds of life, except in the corridor outside where she can hear a vacuum cleaner droning and the loud, foreign chatter of the cleaners. She reaches down under the covers, knowing already that she is naked. She can also tell, without seeing the evidence, that she is covered in bruises. Every part of her seems to be throbbing with pain. Unable to move, she lies completely still, as a creeping feeling of dread seeps through her.

Anna

The blue line is strong and clear, just as Clare knew it would be. She is pregnant.

'Oh my God, what am I going to do, Anna?' she sobs, her voice tremulous with fear, perched on the closed lid of the lavatory, clutching the positive test in her shaking hands.

Anna sinks down onto the floor with her back against the bath and looks up at her helplessly. Pregnant by a man she hardly knows who has emigrated to the other side of the world and is no longer speaking to her. It is a hopeless situation. Anna shakes her head, unable to speak to reassure Clare.

There is a knock on the bathroom door; Toby. 'Can I come in?' he says. Anna looks to Clare for affirmation, before getting up and unlocking the door. Toby looks first at Clare, then at Anna and finally back to the white stick she is still clutching in her hand. 'Is it . . .?' he says, his eyes huge, making him look as terrified as Anna feels.

Anna nods. 'She's pregnant.'

Anna's words fall into a chasm of shocked silence and they all look at each other in horror. Clare, who always has a quick solution to every problem, who laughs her way through life and is never lost for words, bursts into a fresh bout of tears and runs from the room, leaving Toby and Anna gaping after her. As they hear the door to her room slam, it seems to break the trance they are both in. 'Jesus,' whispers Toby. 'What a mess.'

After about an hour, Clare emerges from her room and joins Toby and Anna in the kitchen. Her eyes look blotchy but she is calmer now, more controlled. 'Sorry about earlier,' she says, slumping down beside Anna. 'It's just such a shock.'

Anna rubs her hand, which feels hot to the touch. 'I know. We totally understand.' She watches Clare for a few minutes to see if she wants to talk. But Clare picks up a magazine and begins to flick through it.

Toby is cooking dinner while Anna continues with her marking. Music is playing from Toby's iPod dock and he is moving in time with it as he chops, stirs and shakes the contents of a wok. No one speaks for several long minutes, each of them engrossed in what they are doing.

Toby sets out three plates and starts to serve but Clare stops him before he can put any food on hers. 'Not for me,' she says abruptly. 'I can't keep anything down.'

Toby looks at her curiously. 'You've got to eat, Clare. Especially now that—'

'I'm not keeping it,' she interrupts brusquely. 'So there'll be no eating for two necessary.'

Toby glances at Anna as she struggles with a strange sensation in her stomach. He puts a plate in front of her and sits down opposite. Anna picks up her fork but immediately puts it down again, her appetite suddenly gone.

'I can't keep it,' Clare repeats, her voice small. Then she looks at Anna, who knows she has reddened, which frustrates her because she wants to hide her unease. 'Will you help me, Anna? You know, to get it all sorted out? Will you come with me?'

Anna nods quickly, unable to speak. However much she doesn't want to be in this situation, Clare definitely doesn't want to be in it either and it is so much worse for her.

'Are you going to tell James?' Toby voices what Anna suspects they have all been thinking ever since Clare did the test.

Clare shakes her head. 'What's the point? I don't even know how to get hold of him and judging by the way we left things the last time I spoke to him, I doubt he'd want to hear from me again.'

'I could get you his new contact details,' Toby says, as if she hasn't spoken.

Clare frowns and stands up. 'What's the point?' she says, opening the fridge and taking out a bottle of white wine. Again, Toby and Anna exchange uneasy glances as she unscrews the lid and pours herself a large, tumbler-sized glass, which she sips defiantly. 'By the time I get hold of him I'll have got rid of it anyway.'

'You seemed to be shocked that Clare is going to get rid of the baby,' Anna says as she and Toby lie in bed later that evening. What she really means is that she is shocked but she can't quite put that into words. It feels like a betrayal.

'I'm not against it,' Toby says slowly, propping himself up on one elbow so that he can look at her. He reaches down and strokes her hair distractedly as he speaks. 'I just don't think she should go ahead without telling James. He has a right to know.'

Anna rolls onto her side so that they are facing each other. The soft glow from the bedside light makes the skin on his chest look smooth and tanned. 'But they parted on such bad terms. Don't you think it's best for her to get it sorted out and move on with her life? He doesn't have to be any the wiser.'

'But if she tells James that she is pregnant and he decides that he wants to be involved with her and the baby and make a go of it, don't you think she'd love to keep it?'

Anna imagines the scenario for a minute and thinks how happy Clare would be to have James back in her life. 'I do think that if circumstances were different, she would keep the baby,' she says. 'But that's the whole point, isn't it? Circumstances aren't different. James now lives on the other side of the world and before he left they had a huge row. They only knew each other for a week. The signs don't look promising, do they?'

'I still think he has a right to know.' A muscle starts to pulse in the side of his cheek as he becomes more heated. 'He should be given the chance to do the right thing.'

Anna hesitates before responding, unsure whether to let it drop rather than have a disagreement with Toby, when they have only just resolved things between them. She decides to continue with her point. 'And do you think he would? After the way he spoke to her before he left?'

Toby lies down on his back and stares at the ceiling. 'I've got a theory about that,' he says, stifling a yawn. 'I think he might have instigated a row so that it would make it easier for them to say goodbye. He did seem as if he was crazy about her. If he knew that she was pregnant with his baby, maybe he'd rethink things and come back here to live. I know it sounds dramatic but he should at least be given the chance before it's too late.'

The words 'too late' seem to reverberate through Anna's mind. Later, as Toby drifts off, she lies in the darkness listening to the steady rhythm of his breathing and thinking about what he has said. He is right. James needs to be given the chance to do the right thing. 'Will you get me James' new e-mail address?' she asks urgently, suddenly switching the light back on and shaking him awake.

The next evening, Anna is watching TV on her own with Scratch curled up on her lap when Toby comes in from work looking upset and distracted. 'Hi,' she says, getting up to kiss him. 'You OK? You don't look great. Work problems?' Toby loves his new job but it has been stressful and he's still finding it hard to adjust.

'I'm fine,' he mutters irritably, dumping his crash helmet, bag and coat disconsolately on the floor before scooping up Scratch, who is now hovering at his feet. He strokes him for a few minutes before sinking down onto the sofa.

'You're not fine,' Anna persists, sitting down beside him and resting her arm on his shoulder. 'Tell me what's up?' she asks, twiddling a strand of his hair.

Without moving, Toby seems to shrug her off. 'I spoke to Marco today – to get James' new details.'

'Oh.' Now she understands the reason for his dark mood. 'I take it he wasn't very friendly?'

He shakes his head. 'He still seems to be angry about everything.' He strokes Scratch's fur rhythmically as he speaks and his shoulders start to lower as the tension leaves him.

'Well, it hasn't been that long, has it? He's just being loyal to Rachel. He's her friend too.' Somehow Anna knows without Toby saying so, that this is to do with Rachel.

Toby raises one eyebrow slightly. 'You didn't hear what he said about you – and Clare.'

Anna's insides plunge. 'What did he say?' She holds her breath as she waits for him to reply.

Toby shakes his head. 'It doesn't matter. Forget about it.'

An uneasy silence fills the space between them. Anna can hear the sounds of the street outside and suddenly feels claustrophobic.

'I think he might fancy Rachel,' Toby says, taking Anna by surprise.

She stands up and walks across to the window, feeling overheated and needing to put some distance between them.

'And how do you feel about that?' she asks, her back turned so that he can't see her face. And so she can't see his.

There is a long pause. 'A bit weird actually,' he says at last.

The silence thickens as Anna digests what he has just said. She is glad he can't see her expression, which she knows to be one of annoyance.

'Sorry, baby, I'm just trying to be honest,' Toby says quietly. 'It's not that I want to get back with her or anything.'

'Good!' Anna laughs without mirth. She can feel her world shifting back onto uneasy ground, as she imagines the prospect of losing Toby again. She knows for certain that it would finish her off for good.

'I guess it's just that I was with her a long time and I don't like the thought of her and Marco getting together. Does that sound strange?'

When Anna doesn't answer immediately, Toby puts down

the cat, before getting up and joining her at the window.

'Anna?' he says, putting his hands on her shoulders and turning her round to face him.

She blows out her cheeks in a stalling tactic until she can speak without anger. 'It sounds like you're being a dog in the manger,' she says finally. The thought of Marco and Rachel being together is quite appealing to her; it might help to ease some of the enormous guilt she still feels about Rachel. But Toby's reaction has unnerved her. She doesn't want him to care who Rachel's with or what she's doing. She doesn't want him to give her any thought at all. The fact doesn't escape her that now she knows what it was like for Rachel, having Anna in the background all those years.

'Yes, maybe I am being a selfish git,' he says, a sheepish look in his eyes, encouraging Anna to soften towards him. 'Anyway, let's not dwell on that,' he says briskly. 'I've got James' new e-mail address. What do you think we should do? I think we should tell him.'

This is a difficult decision. Anna is unsure whether they should give it to Clare and let her choose whether to make contact with James herself or whether they should contact him themselves. Having only just got their precious friendship back, Anna is reluctant to risk screwing it up again. 'I think we should give it to her and let her make the decision herself.' Suddenly, her mind is made up and she knows it is the right decision.

'But if we do that, she might just go ahead with the termination without telling him.'

'That's true, but it has to be her choice.' Anna looks up at Toby beseechingly, feeling torn between her loyalty to Clare and her desperation to avoid any more conflict with Toby.

'And he has the right to know,' he persists. They look at each other in silence for a few tense moments until finally Toby speaks. 'OK, we'll do it your way,' he says, pulling Anna to him and talking over the top of her head, as he strokes her hair. 'She can decide whether or not to tell him. And I suppose at least then she won't blame us if he still doesn't want to know.'

'Exactly.' Anna looks up at him and stands on tiptoes to kiss him gently. 'Give me the address and I'll write it out and put it under her door. She can think about it overnight.'

The next morning dawns crisp and clear with a definite autumn chill in the air, as Anna awakes to the sounds of someone moving about in the kitchen. A little ripple of worry reminds her that she pushed James' details under Clare's door last night and she hurries out of bed, whisking her robe off the floor and closing the door gently behind her.

Clare is making tea, her dark hair lank in a half-hearted ponytail and her face suggesting a sleepless, tear-filled night. Anna wants to hug her but something about her demeanour stops her.

'How are you feeling?' Anna asks, just as she does every morning.

'Sick,' Clare replies, just as she does every morning. 'Tea?'

Anna shakes her head. 'Coffee, please.'

'Sorry, if you want coffee, you'll have to make it yourself. The smell of it alone makes me heave.'

'Tea's fine,' Anna says quickly, putting a teabag into a mug. 'So, did you see the note I pushed under your door?'

'Uh huh.'

'So . . . what do you think?'

'I think I wish you hadn't got the address,' Clare whispers and Anna's insides plummet.

Mentally, she thanks God that she hasn't actually contacted James already. If this is Clare's reaction to Anna getting his e-mail address, she can just imagine how she would have been if Anna had gone ahead and told him her news.

'Then I wouldn't have had a choice,' Clare continues.

'You still have a choice, Clare, even if you tell him,' Anna says, as kindly as she can. 'It's your decision and if you still want to go through with a termination, there's nothing he can do to stop you. But what if he's really pleased? How would you feel then?'

A flush spreads across Clare's pale cheeks. Then she seems to sag again. 'That's not exactly likely, is it?'

'You don't know until you try,' Anna says more urgently, desperate for her to make contact, certain now that it is the right thing to do.

'I'll think about it,' Clare says, getting up quickly. 'If you'll excuse me, right now I need to throw up.'

With the sound of Clare's retching ringing in her ears, Anna makes Toby some tea and takes it into the bedroom where he is still asleep in bed. 'Wake up, sleepyhead,' she calls, sitting down and shaking him. She watches him tentatively open his eyes and then sees his expression light up as he looks at her.

'Morning, gorgeous,' he grins, pulling her into bed with him. 'Come back to bed, it's too early.'

Anna half-heartedly protests before dissolving into him as he kisses her neck in that way he knows is always guaranteed to fire her up. She has never once managed to resist and today is no exception. It feels so right to be back in Toby's arms. She hasn't felt anything approaching the same sexual attraction towards another man and even though she sometimes shivers with jealousy at the thought of Toby sleeping with Rachel, she tries to remember that she had sex with other people too and it was totally forgettable. She knows, without Toby telling her, that what their bodies achieve together is on a different plane to what either of them has experienced with anyone else.

Lying with her head on his chest afterwards, Anna lets out a sigh of pleasure.

'What?' asks Toby, stroking her hair tenderly.

'Just thinking how much I love you and how happy I am,' she replies.

'Same here,' he grins, bending his head to kiss her. They lie there for a few more minutes of contented silence before the sounds of Clare throwing up echo through the flat once more.

'Nice,' chuckles Toby, stroking her arm.

'Poor Clare.'

'Do you think she'll contact James?'

'I honestly don't know. At least she's said she'll think about it.'

'Good. I'd want to know if I was him.'

Anna nods. 'I know you would. Toby, can I ask you something?'

'Sure,' he replies, looking at her quizzically.

'Did you want to have kids with Rachel?'

Toby exhales loudly. 'Phew. Where did that come from?'

She shrugs. 'Maybe it's Clare being pregnant ... I just wondered how you felt about it?'

'Well, the truth is,' he says slowly, 'I do want kids. But . . .' There is a short pause before he continues. 'I just couldn't visualize it with Rachel. Not like I can visualize it with us.'

A fizz of excitement bubbles up inside Anna. 'Can you really? Can you imagine us having a baby together?'

Toby squeezes her shoulder. 'I always could.'

Contentment floods through her as she drinks in his words. 'Thank you, Toby, that means so much.'

Toby suddenly slides his arm out from underneath her and sits bolt upright.

'What's wrong?' Anna looks up at him in alarm.

Toby moves so he is kneeling up on the bed beside her. 'I've got something to ask you,' he says, shifting position slightly and looking incongruous in his white cotton boxers.

'What?' she giggles, perplexed.

'Will you marry me?' Toby says.

There is a loud gasp and Anna realizes that it has come from her. 'Is this a joke?' she asks, knowing already by the look on Toby's face that it isn't.

'No, it's not a joke.' Toby's face is serious and his expression intense. 'I don't want to lose you again, Anna. Will you marry me?'

Anna's heart swells with joy on hearing the words she has yearned to hear all these years. She's not going to mess it up this time. 'Yes, Toby, I will marry you.'

Rachel

Having Marco around has helped Rachel cope better than she ever thought she would. Going back to work for the first time was desperately hard, especially bumping into people who didn't know what had happened and who cheerfully commented on her lovely honeymoon tan, saying they hoped the wedding had gone well. For those first days, Marco hovered around her as much as possible, trying to head off any difficult encounters and quietly taking those who offered their congratulations aside and explaining that Rachel and Toby had had a change of heart.

Because she had started to take a back seat at work as Toby's career took off, Rachel now decided to throw herself back into it to regain some of the ground she had lost. She put herself forward to be the series producer of a huge celebrity entertainment show that she knew would involve working every waking hour and quite a few sleeping hours too. When she got the job, she was delighted that her bosses hadn't completely forgotten that she had talent.

Marco was the editor of a political programme made by the same company and enjoyed ribbing Rachel about the 'tacky' show she was doing, but he also helped her out a lot. They would pore over DVDs of various celebrities, trying to get the casting absolutely right. Marco's journalistic leaning, which she hadn't thought would be much use on an ice-dancing show, proved remarkably useful in dissecting the characters of the potential candidates, assessing whether they could handle the pressure of the commitment they were about to undertake.

With a job that is fun, engaging and all consuming, Rachel no longer bursts into fits of uncontrollable tears or slams out of rooms. She is calm, measured and reasonable. That is, she was, until the night she found out about Clare being pregnant with James' baby.

She and Marco had gone for a pizza after work and Marco mentioned that Toby had called him that day, asking to see him. Rachel's heart still skipped at the mention of his name but she swallowed hard and nodded. 'What did he want?'

Marco put down his fork and took a sip of red wine. 'He wanted James' new contact details in Australia.'

They sat in silence for a few minutes while Rachel summoned up the nerve to ask. 'So, why did he suddenly want James' contact details? Did he just want to make up with him?'

Marco shook his head. 'No, it was more than that . . .'

'What?' asked Rachel, perplexed.

'Well, I'm really probably not supposed to tell you any of this . . .'

'Oh, for God's sake, Marco!' snapped Rachel. 'Who am I going to blab to?'

'Yes, yes, you're right. Well, apparently Clare is pregnant with James' baby,' Marco babbled. 'She was going to have a termination but Toby persuaded her that she should let James know first, which is why he needed his contact details.'

Suddenly the pizza Rachel was eating tasted like cardboard and she thought she might actually throw up. Her eyes clouded with fat tears, blurring her vision.

'Rachel!' Marco cried in alarm, touching her arm. 'Oh God, what's wrong? I'm such an idiot, I shouldn't have mentioned Toby, not so soon after . . .'

Rachel shook her head roughly and swiped at her tears with her napkin. 'No, it's not that,' she gulped, struggling to speak.

'Then what? Oh God, I'm so sorry,' Marco said helplessly as Rachel sobbed openly. Around them, other diners started to look round curiously.

Rachel shook her head, unable to say anything as she convulsed with grief. All the emotion that she had kept a lid on so well came pouring out in a torrent. She wanted a baby so badly. But, at thirty-four years old, with no boyfriend or husband and none within sight, it was too late for her. She was probably never going to be a mother now and the realization hit her like a bereavement.

Any man she met now would run a mile when he saw the desperation in her eyes and they'd be right to be concerned. She wouldn't just be looking for someone to date – she would be sizing up every available man as a potential father for her baby.

Rachel stood up and grabbed her coat. 'Rachel!' Marco was calling as she stumbled out of the restaurant. 'Wait! I'll come with you . . . just let me get the bill.'

His words were lost as Rachel let the door fall shut behind her and felt the cold night air cool her flaming cheeks. She raised her hand as a taxi with its light on approached. If the driver thought it was strange that his passenger howled like a baby for the entire journey home, he didn't say anything, assuming that she was drunk. In a funny way she *was* drunk, but it had nothing to do with alcohol. She was drunk with grief.

Clare

Nothing could have prepared Clare for how ill she feels. She knows all about morning sickness of course, but she hadn't expected the sickness to last all day, every day. And if the sickness is bad, the exhaustion is worse. Every step she takes feels like she is wading through water. If this is how she feels at ten weeks, how the hell would she feel by the end of the pregnancy? It doesn't bear thinking about.

But she has made her decision. She is definitely having a termination. However much she wants to be a mother, Clare simply doesn't think she could cope with either the pregnancy or the baby all by herself. She tells herself that she doesn't have any choice, which makes her decision easier.

She thinks about James constantly and aches to make contact with him, but her pride won't let her. She was so stunned by his aggression towards her before he left that she can't bear the thought of another row or, worse still, him totally ignoring her. Anna and Toby have made it clear that they think she should contact him, but now that they have found their own happy ending, Clare feels sure that they are seeing everything through rose-tinted glasses. Even if Toby's theory that James deliberately provoked a row was right, she can't forget how truly horrible he had been.

Toby and Anna getting engaged hasn't helped either. Although they have been incredibly sensitive about announcing it, being careful not to do it with any kind of fanfare, forgoing a celebratory party, Clare still can't help feeling jealous of their happiness. Their families and close friends are all so thrilled for them – even Toby's parents seem to have forgiven him for jilting Rachel – that Clare can't help contrasting their situation with her own. On more than one occasion she has watched them gazing adoringly at one another and wished fervently that it was Anna who was pregnant and not her. Why did things have to work out so awkwardly in this life?

She has scanned the Internet for help and advice on how to go about having a termination, feeling slightly sickened by the experience and terribly lonely. It seems straightforward enough in theory, as long as you have the money, but it is far from simple in practice. With shaking hands, she phones the clinic to make an appointment.

'It's eighty pounds for an appointment,' the receptionist tells her, and although the way she says it isn't unkind, her words cause Clare to flinch. It isn't that she doesn't have the money. It's the coldness of it all that seems so shocking. Clare makes the appointment in a voice that sounds so detached and robotic to her own ears, as though it belongs to someone else, wishing for the millionth time that this wasn't happening to her.

Then she goes to find Anna, who is sitting at the kitchen table, marking. Toby is still at work.

'Hi, hon, how are you doing?' Anna asks, getting up and making her way towards the kettle. 'Tea?'

Clare shakes her head. 'No, thanks. Anna, I've made the

appointment at the clinic,' she blurts. 'Will you come with me?' Anna blanches as soon as Clare speaks, and Clare, in her hormonal and fragile state, snaps, 'Don't look at me like that!'

Anna's eyes widen in shock. 'I wasn't looking at you like anything!' she protests.

'Yes you were. I can see what you're bloody well thinking!' Clare cries, knowing she is being unreasonable but unable to stop herself.

'Honestly, honey, I'm not thinking anything,' says Anna, shaking her head, a nervous rash spreading up her neck and across her cheeks.

'Well, why did you look so . . . disgusted!' Clare spits.

Anna shakes her head vehemently. 'I'm not disgusted! Don't be so defensive. You have to do whatever you think is best and if you think this best . . .' She trails off, unable to continue.

'There you go again!' Clare yells, now out of control and aware that she is being ridiculous.

'What the hell are you talking about?' Anna yells back. 'I think you know damn well that this isn't the right thing to do but you won't admit it because you're too bloody stubborn.'

'You can talk!' screeches Clare. 'You wasted ten years of your life because you were so bloody stubborn. Don't you dare lecture me! Christ, I was there for you all that time, putting up with your weeping and wailing and endless moaning and yet the one time I need your support, all you can do is judge me!' She storms off towards her bedroom, with Anna following close behind.

'I'm not judging you,' says Anna, more softly this time.

'Really, Clare, I'm not. I love you like a sister and I'll do anything I can to help you get out of this mess. But once you've had a termination, there is no way back. I just don't want you to make a decision that you'll regret for the rest of your life.'

Clare slumps onto her bed, exhausted. 'Why did this have to happen to me?' she wails. 'I just don't know what the hell to do. Help me, Anna! Tell me what to do.'

'You should keep the appointment,' says Anna as calmly as she can. 'And of course I'll come with you. You can talk it through with the doctor and make a decision once you know all the facts.'

Clare takes a deep breath to steady her nerves and nods.

'But in the meantime,' Anna continues, 'you should e-mail James and tell him.'

Clare groans. 'I can't! What if he just ignores me?'

'Then you'll know that it's really over between you and you can make your decision. At least you will have given him the chance to do the right thing. And face it, Clare, you're not going to be any worse off than you are now, are you?'

Clare knows Anna is right. 'No, I suppose not,' she agrees at last.

'So?' Anna says, standing in the doorway with her hands on her hips. 'You'll do it?'

'I'll do it,' says Clare, her voice muffled as she buries her face in her duvet. 'Now leave me alone to be miserable.'

Anna comes over and pats Clare on the back. 'You're doing the right thing,' she says, before leaving the room, closing the door gently behind her.

Dear James,

I know how much of a shock it's going to be for you to hear from me.

Anyway, I wish I was e-mailing just to see how you're enjoying your new life and to exchange pleasantries but unfortunately I'm not. I have agonized over whether to even tell you what I'm about to do, mainly because we parted on such bad terms. But I have been persuaded by Toby and Anna that you have a right to know, so here goes: James, I am pregnant with your baby.

I am ten weeks gone now and have decided that it would be best all round if I had a termination. I simply don't feel like I can cope with a baby on my own. Obviously, I will need to do this very soon and although I am certain you will feel the same way, I can't afford to wait too long to hear your verdict. So if you are happy for me to go ahead with the procedure, just let me know and I will carry on as before, with no hard feelings. If, however, you want to discuss it further, you need to call me. Soon.

I am so sorry that this has happened and I wish more than anything that it hadn't, but I need to deal with it and get on with the rest of my life.

Clare

Composing the e-mail was tough. Clare started it again and again, only to furiously press the backspace button to delete what she had written. She knew that it would be a shock for James just to hear from her, let alone for him to digest what she had to tell him. She had to find the right wording but it was so hard to think what that would be.

Clare reads and rereads the e-mail a dozen times before she takes a deep breath and clicks 'send'. Then she lies down on her bed and allows her emotions to overwhelm her as she cries herself to sleep.

The next morning she wakes early and immediately opens her laptop. She watches the little daisy icon spinning as the computer scans for new e-mails. Silently, a red circle appears, with a number two in the middle. Clare realizes that she has been holding her breath as she clicks on it. The next second, disappointment crashes through her as the two title boxes reveal nothing more exciting than junk mail.

Clare slouches into the kitchen feeling even more miserable than usual. Anna is at the kitchen table eating a bowl of muesli. 'Hi . . . oh, honey, you look terrible!' she cries, leaping up. 'What can I get you?'

Clare shakes her head. 'I can't eat anything. Maybe just a cup of tea.'

'Sure,' smiles Anna sympathetically, getting up and putting the kettle on. 'God, this morning sickness is a killer, isn't it.'

Clare nods gloomily. 'I sent James an e-mail last night but he didn't reply,' she says flatly.

'Oh!' replies Anna, sitting back down and looking at Clare intently. 'Well you only sent it last night – give him a chance. There's the time difference, don't forget. He may not have seen it yet.'

Clare can't bear the bright optimism in Anna's voice. 'Well, he's had a full day – doesn't everyone check their e-mails all the time during the day?'

'It depends,' says Anna. 'He might not have been near a computer.'

Clare shakes her head. 'No, I bet he's seen it all right. He's just going to ignore it.'

Anna bites her lip. 'Well, let's not give up hope just yet,' she says nervously, although Clare can tell she is also thinking that it was pretty unlikely that James wouldn't have seen the e-mail. 'So, when's the consultation?' she says briskly.

'Tomorrow at five,' replies Clare, her voice catching. She knows this is the only thing to do but it is just so hard.

'OK, well I'll be there, obviously,' says Anna, taking Clare's hand in hers. 'Perhaps you'll feel a bit better once you've talked it through properly.'

Clare nods and a fat tear rolls down her cheek. 'The trouble is, I don't feel that I have a choice.'

Anna strokes her hand. 'I've been thinking about that,' she says slowly. 'I know your biggest worry is having the baby by yourself but you wouldn't be by yourself. Toby and I will be there for you. I will do everything a male partner would have done for you. I'll come to all your antenatal classes with you. I'll rub your back and make you weird concoctions when you get cravings. I'll help you get everything ready and I'll be there with you at the birth. Apart from having sex with you, I'll do everything!'

Despite herself, Clare laughs. She squeezes Anna's hand. 'Thank you. But I don't think it's quite that easy. You've got your own life . . . your wedding. You won't want to be stuck with me and a baby in tow.' Anna opens her mouth to protest but Clare continues: 'I really, really appreciate the offer but I've got to be realistic about the practicalities. And it's not just a baby we're talking about – it's a child who will grow up, go to school, become a teenager. Think about it, Anna, you and Toby will be having children of your own in the not-too-distant future, I know you will. You'll want a place of your own . . . and then where will I be? I can't come and live with you guys forever, like some kind of weirdo hanger-on in the attic!'

'I guess when you put it like that . . .' Anna says, smiling. 'I just want you to feel like you have choices. Remember that lots of people have babies on their own and they cope just fine. And maybe you could move nearer your mum so that she could help you out a bit . . .'

Clare snorts. 'As if! My mother's got her own career and life. She's always made it abundantly clear that if I get into trouble, I'm on my own.'

She knows that if she turned up at home and announced that she was pregnant, her mother would immediately suggest a termination. So why bother consulting her? She will get on and do it anyway. Clare looks at Anna enviously and imagines how different her mum's reaction would be. Having brought Anna and her brother up on her own after her bastard of a husband walked out on them, she would give her daughter all the support she could. There would never be any question of ending the pregnancy.

'Nope,' says Clare, sipping the tea Anna has put in front of her, 'in a week's time this will all be over and I can get on with the rest of my life.'

Ella

Somehow Ella manages to get herself home. Her dress is torn and she couldn't find her underwear but luckily her coat is long enough to cover her modesty. She just wants to get out of the hotel as quickly as possible. She staggers through reception and out into the busy street, trying to ignore the searing pain that shoots through her with every step she takes. Her head is pounding and her vision is still blurred. 'Heavy night was it?' chuckles the cab driver as she lolls in agony on the back seat. Ella ignores him and throws far too much money at him as he pulls up outside her house, she is so desperate not to have to speak.

She limps up the steps and flings herself through the front door. Once inside, she bangs the door shut behind her, falls gratefully onto the floor and curls up in a ball.

She doesn't know how many hours she spends lying there. She is totally and utterly numb. It is getting dark by the time she finally manages to get up. She flicks the light switch and flinches as the brightness hits her sore eyes.

She walks into the kitchen and stands staring around her, still feeling as though she is having an out-of-body experience. *He must have drugged my drink*, she thinks. She can't remember anything. Judging by the state of her body, she knows that this is a good thing.

She needs to talk to someone but doesn't know who to call. She doesn't want to tell her parents, Fabien would just get hysterical, while Monica would personally go out and hunt him down, swearing blind that she wouldn't rest until she had collected his balls in a jar.

Everyone would tell her to go to the police and of course that's what she should do, but she just can't face the humiliation and interrogation that would follow. The shame is already overwhelming. Her eyes rest on a photo of her and Max on their honeymoon. They are both wearing stupid hats and beaming at a camera that Max must have been holding in front of them. Suddenly, Ella wants to talk to him so badly and she instinctively reaches for her phone to call him. Then she remembers. He's gone.

It is like hearing the news for the first time and the realization that he is never coming back hits her with such force that she actually staggers backwards. She grips the back of the nearest chair and howls into the empty room, which howls back at her with equal force.

Still crying, Ella climbs the stairs, wincing in pain with every step. She rips what is left of her dress off and climbs into the huge stone bath, turning the taps on and ignoring first the freezing cold, then the scalding hot water. She doesn't care if it burns her, she just wants to be able to feel something other than the physical hurt he has inflicted. She lets the water run so high that it starts to overflow. She needs to be submerged totally to get rid of any trace of him. Picking up the soap and a pumice stone, she scrubs away at her skin, leaving it raw under the ugly bruises that now cover her torso and legs.

Once she has scoured every visible part of herself, Ella lies back, feeling shaky and sick, until the water covers her head and face. Under the water she feels better. The world is shut out and she feels safe. Time and again she comes up for air, only to submerge herself again, for longer and longer each time, wondering if it would be easier not to come up for air at all. Maybe in that strangely gurgling world she could wait until she stopped breathing. But she can't do it, the urge to breathe is too great and each time she comes close, she then breaks the surface, gulping great lungfuls of air.

All around her the water cools and when she finally starts to shiver uncontrollably, she hauls herself out. She wraps her soft, fluffy robe around her and curls up on the bed. She tries to remember something – anything – from the previous night, but it is all gone and in its place is a black hole. Even now, Ella feels like she is looking through a frosted window. Nothing is clear.

After a while she falls into a fitful sleep and wakes up to the sound of her phone ringing. It takes her a moment to realize where she is and she shakes her head groggily.

'Hello?' she hears herself saying as she picks up the receiver.

'It's Jasper,' says a clipped, cold voice.

Ella's heart plummets. She desperately needs to hear a friendly voice right now, not more recriminations and anger. 'Hello,' she says, clearing her throat.

'I'll get straight to the point. I need to talk to you – about my father's will.'

'Oh.' Ella hasn't even given a thought to Max's will. She just assumed he would have left everything to her.

'I'll come round to discuss it. Are you in this evening? I

could be there in half an hour.' Like her father, Jasper has a way of speaking that is so assertive it is almost impossible to say no to him.

'Um, well it's not really convenient right now,' says Ella hoarsely, trying to turn over and wincing in pain as she does so.

'I see,' Jasper says coldly. Ella can tell that he thinks she has someone with her.

'It's just . . . I'm not feeling gr—'

'Fine,' he cuts her off before she can explain any further. 'I'll come tomorrow evening. Do you think you might be available then?' His voice is laced with sarcasm and even though Ella is used to this type of reaction from Max's children, in her current state his words cut through her viciously. She so desperately wants someone to be nice to her after what has happened that she bursts into tears.

Jasper, apparently unmoved, tuts at the other end of the line. 'I said, are you going to be in tomorrow evening?' He enunciates each word very slowly, as if he is having trouble controlling his temper.

'Yes,' whispers Ella, tears cascading down her face.

'Fine. I'll see you then,' he says curtly, before hanging up.

Ella reaches across to replace the handset and pulls a batch of tissues from the box on her bedside table. Then she crawls under the duvet and pulls it over her head.

The next morning Ella wakes up feeling slightly better. Her head is starting to clear and the physical pain is less acute. Even so, she quickly downs a couple of Nurofen from the packet in her bedside drawer. She lies there for about an hour, trying to summon the energy to get up.

Eventually, she crawls out of bed and heads for the shower, where she stands under the stinging jets of water, almost enjoying the painful sensation. Once again, she scrubs herself inside and out with an aggression that shocks even her. She wonders if she will ever feel truly clean again.

She stumbles around the house, feeling disorientated. She drinks as much water as she can stomach to try to flush out of her system whatever he has used to drug her.

At about four o'clock, Fabien calls from New York. 'Hey, babe!' he drawls. 'How you doing? Hope you're not getting up to anything you shouldn't while I'm over here.'

Despite the fact that he can't see her, Ella flushes bright red. She feels so ashamed and immediately wishes she could turn the clock back and stay home that fateful night.

'Ella?' bellows Fabien. 'Can you hear me OK?'

'Yes!' she manages to croak. 'But I'm a bit tied up at the moment. Can I give you a call back later?'

'I bet you are, you filthy minx!' he giggles, cheerfully oblivious to the horror with which each of his words is filling her.

Ella can't say anything else and hangs up as his laugh reverberates across the Atlantic.

Listlessly, she eats some toast and makes herself a cup of tea. As she sits at the table nursing the hot mug, she realizes with a start that being alone in such a huge house is suddenly very uncomfortable and she feels horribly lonely.

She wracks her brains to think who she could call but there is no one. Now she's learning what it means to have no real friends. For some reason, Ella keeps thinking about Anna and how, if she were in the same situation, she would have so many people to turn to. But of course Anna would never find herself in that situation. She would never go out dressed like a tart with the sole intention of picking up a man to have sex with. Well, Ella had certainly got what she wanted and look at the mess she is in now.

She spends the rest of the day prowling from room to room, thinking about Jasper's impending visit. She has a bad feeling about it. His voice had sounded ominous – although when she thought about it, Jasper's voice never sounded anything other than ominous.

Ella hadn't thought about the will at all. Maybe they are going to contest it. Her heart sinks at the thought of having to go to court and argue over who'll get the family silver. She has already decided that they can have whatever they want. She is doing well enough with her writing to support herself whatever happens. Her parents aren't exactly on their uppers and Ella knows that however distant they are, they wouldn't see her out on the streets.

Jasper arrives promptly at seven. Ella tries not to hunch too much as she walks towards the door but it is the only way she can move without hurting. She opens the door and looks into his clear, cold, blue eyes. *Icy*, she thinks as she stands aside so that he can get past. He stands in the hallway looking around him in wonder and for a second Ella feels like an intruder in her own home.

'It feels strange,' he says, more to himself than to Ella, 'being back.'

Ella nods. This was the house he had grown up in. Before her.

'Tea?' she asks, wincing as she shuffles into the kitchen.

'What have you done?' he asks coldly as he follows her down the hallway.

'I had a fall,' Ella mutters, filling the kettle. The strain of leaning over the sink is agony and she cries out.

'You should get yourself checked out,' he says awkwardly. 'You might have cracked a rib . . .'

'Or two,' she agrees, holding her stomach.

'Drunk, were you?' The edge has returned to Jasper's voice.

Ella reddens but doesn't say anything.

Jasper shoots her a look of disgust and sits down. 'Right, I might as well get straight to the point,' he says, opening his briefcase and pulling out some papers. 'My father's will leaves everything to us. You're not even mentioned.'

'What?' Ella gasps, clutching the worktop for support. She had assumed it would be the other way round, that Max would have left everything to her. 'That can't be right.'

'It is,' he smiles triumphantly, nodding towards the papers on the table. 'He obviously never changed it. It's as if you never existed.'

'Which is exactly what you wanted,' Ella says wearily, in too much pain and too tired to argue.

'I can't deny that,' he says. 'You caused a lot of distress to our family when you stole my father. It suits all of us if you're written out of existence.'

'It takes two to have a relationship, Jasper,' whispers Ella. 'You can't just steal someone – they have to want to leave.'

Jasper's eyes flicker slightly. 'You used every trick in the book to get him – including that pathetic suicide attempt.'

'I didn't know you knew about that.'

'Of course I knew,' he spits. 'He was my father, you know. Before you came along, we were incredibly close. I loved him very much.'

His voice catches as he speaks and Ella feels a wave of

guilt sweep over her. She hadn't cared how his children felt about Max and her being together. She had imagined that as they were older, they were too busy with their own lives to bother what their father was up to.

'I loved him too,' she says, tears springing into her eyes.

Jasper snorts. 'You seem to have recovered from his death remarkably quickly!'

'What do you mean by that?' Ella snaps back.

'Well, going out and getting so drunk that you can't stand up for a start,' he snarls contemptuously.

'You don't know anything about me,' Ella yells, suddenly consumed by a rage that is greater than her pain. 'Don't you *dare* judge me when you have no idea what I've been through!'

Jasper stands up and packs the papers back into his briefcase. 'My heart bleeds,' he says sarcastically. 'Anyway, we're going to sell this house so I'm giving you notice to get out as soon as possible. You'll be entitled to something – your gold-digging won't have been entirely in vain. But we'll make sure it's as little as possible. If you want any more, you'll have to fight us for it.'

Ella watches in horror as he picks up his bag and stalks out of the house, leaving her slumped on the kitchen floor, crying in agony, consumed by self-pity. Here she was again – right back at square one.

Anna

It has been three days since Clare sent James the e-mail and she hasn't heard anything.

'Did we do the right thing?' Anna asks Toby for the tenth time as they sit watching TV one evening.

Toby sighs. 'I don't know. I think so but I can't believe he isn't going to reply. What kind of arsehole does that? Even if it was to say yes, fine, get rid of it, you'd think he'd at least have responded in some way.'

'I know,' Anna agrees. She is desperately worried about Clare. Having plucked up the courage to contact James, she is devastated that he hasn't replied. Anna has watched her endlessly checking her e-mails, seeming to shrink a little more every time there is nothing there.

They went to the consultation about a termination and Clare is due to go ahead with the procedure the following day. They were kind and helpful at the clinic and emphasized how important it was that she do it quickly, so that she is still within the twelve-week limit. Anna can see the sense in doing it as soon as possible, but she is absolutely dreading it. She has to keep telling herself that if she feels bad, Clare undoubtedly feels much, much worse.

Anna is also worried that Clare blames her and Toby for

persuading her to tell James. She has been short-tempered and has started avoiding Anna again. She sits in her room for hours, listening to gloomy music and staring into space.

'Maybe you should try to contact him, Toby,' Anna says suddenly. 'By phone. Find out what the hell's going on. There's always a chance he didn't get the e-mail . . .'

'Oh God,' Toby sighs. 'I don't know about that. It's not really any of my business.'

'It's all our business!' Anna protests. 'Seriously, Toby, we made it our business by persuading her to contact him. Maybe you could get his new number from Marco and give him a call.'

'What would I say?'

'Well . . . ask him if he got the e-mail and if he's OK? Just find out why he hasn't replied.'

'I suppose I could,' he says reluctantly, clearly not relishing the idea.

'Go on, Tobes. Call Marco and get the number.'

Toby looks at Anna strangely before tutting irritably. 'OK, OK! I'll go and see Marco.' With that he stands up and stalks out of the room, leaving Anna with her mouth gaping open. Toby has never been irritable with her before. They aren't one of those couples who thrive on rows and they rarely argue. She sits chewing her thumbnail as she listens to the slam of the front door.

A few moments later, Clare pokes her head around the door. 'Oh! I thought I heard you going out,' she mutters, about to retreat back to her room.

'Clare! Don't go,' Anna says, anxious not to lose this chance to speak to her. 'It was just Toby going out. Come and have a chat.'

Clare slouches reluctantly back into the room and slumps down onto the sofa beside Anna. She looks truly awful. Her skin has broken out in spots and her hair is lank and greasy. So much for women glowing during pregnancy – Anna has never seen anyone look worse. 'How are you doing?' she asks, slightly unnecessarily.

Clare shrugs and Anna can sense the hostility coming from her. 'Not great. Still, it'll all be over soon.'

Anna feels heartbroken at the sight of Clare. 'Still no word from James?' she asks, also unnecessarily.

Clare shakes her head slowly. 'Nope. Wish I hadn't told him now. I feel about a million times worse.'

'Oh, Clare, I'm so sorry!' Anna blurts out, rubbing her back. 'It's all my fault for making you send that bloody e-mail. I didn't think for one minute that he wouldn't reply.'

'Yeah, well that's James for you, isn't it?' she shoots back angrily. 'And it's not like it's the first time he's let me down.'

Anna says nothing.

'At least you and Toby are happy,' she says after a few minutes' silence. There is more than a trace of bitterness in her voice and Anna flinches, aware of how hard it must be for Clare that Toby and she decided to get engaged. They have tried to do it with as little fuss as possible but she can see that it must still hurt.

'Sorry,' Clare says quickly, her eyes flickering towards Anna as she notices her reaction. 'I'm pleased for you. I am, really. It's just that the comparison between our situations is so stark. I wish it was you who was pregnant. It would make everything so much easier.'

Anna nods because Clare is right. She wishes there was something she could do or say that would help but there isn't anything and she feels so helpless in the face of what Clare is going through.

'Where's Toby gone?' Clare asks, changing the subject.

Anna shakes her head slightly. 'He's gone to see Marco.'

'That's good,' she says. 'Are they getting on better now?'

Anna shrugs. 'Not exactly, but they're working on it. Marco's been spending a lot of time with Rachel, apparently. I'm not sure Toby's very comfortable with it.' She reddens as she speaks, hating how the words sound when they are spoken aloud.

Clare looks at her closely and pulls a face. 'I'm not sure Toby's in any position to comment. So, are Marco and Rachel seeing each other, do you suppose?'

Anna shakes her head. 'I don't think so. I think they're just friends. But Toby's been a bit taken aback that Marco has completely sided with Rachel.'

'I don't think it's that surprising after what happened,' Clare says.

'Maybe not,' Anna agrees, biting her lip and tasting coppery blood as she does so. 'But I have to admit I'm not that comfortable with Rachel being in the background either.'

Clare's expression softens and she grins at her with a raised eyebrow. 'Anna . . .' she chides gently.

'I know!' Anna raises her arms in a gesture of self-defence. 'I have no right to feel any such thing!'

'No, you have no right,' Clare agrees. 'But that doesn't mean you can help yourself. At least you're being honest. Have you told Toby how you feel?'

'Yes, but I'm not sure I should have done. I think maybe we're both being too honest. It might be better if we kept our feelings to ourselves.'

'No,' Clare says firmly. 'You two have already spent too much time keeping your feelings under wraps. It's definitely better to get them out in the open, even if you do have some difficult conversations. What you need to remember, Anna, is that all couples have rows. It doesn't have to mean the end of the relationship – it's healthy.'

'Thank you,' Anna says, looking at her gratefully. 'You're very wise.'

Clare laughs. 'Yeah, and look where it's got me! And it's not like I take my own advice either – one row with James and that was it. Anyway, I'm knackered, I'm going to bed. G'night.' She rises gingerly from the sofa and gives Anna a jokey salute before leaving the room.

Anna sits up watching TV, waiting for Toby to come home, but by midnight her eyelids are drooping and she can't stay up any longer. She gets into bed and falls into a deep yet uneasy sleep, crowded with unsettling dreams which make her heart beat too fast.

The next morning Anna wakes with a start and immediately looks over at Toby's side of the bed. She sighs in relief at his long, brown back, exposed from the folds of the white cotton duvet, which is bunched around his waist. She is still staring at him when he wakes up and turns blearily to face her. 'What?' he smiles lazily. 'What are you staring at?'

'I wasn't sure you'd be here,' she says, reaching out and touching his face, as if to make sure. 'I'm glad you are.'

Toby lifts his arm so that she can lay her head on his chest. 'Come here, you mad woman! Why did you think I wouldn't be here?'

'Because of us having a row before you went round to Marco's last night.'

Toby kisses the top of her head. 'I'm sorry, baby.'

She laughs. 'I'm sorry too.'

He squeezes her shoulder and they lie together in a happy silence for a few minutes.

'So how did you get on?' she asks at last. 'Was Marco still pissed off with you?'

'Not so much,' says Toby. 'He seems to be a bit calmer. I'm really glad I went to see him. I've missed him.'

Anna strokes his chest affectionately. She's glad if they can salvage their friendship. Toby seems much happier and lighter already. Maybe it has been playing on his mind more than he has let on.

'It's weird but it's almost as if he's glad I'm not with Rachel now. I'm sure I'm right about him fancying her.'

Anna's insides lurch violently. *Here we go again*, she thinks. 'And are you still freaked out by that idea?' she asks tentatively, not sure she can handle hearing the answer right now.

'Less so than I was,' he says, ruffling her hair.

'Good!' she laughs and kisses his bare chest. 'So . . . at the risk of starting another row, are you going to call James?'

'No need,' he smiles cryptically.

'What do you mean?' Anna sits up and looks down at him.

'He's on his way here,' says Toby triumphantly. 'He called Marco as soon as he got Clare's e-mail and said he'd be on the first flight he could get. Marco says he should be here this morning.'

'Oh my God!' Anna shrieks, wanting to leap for joy. 'But that's fantastic! I KNEW he wouldn't just ignore her.'

Toby beams. 'He's not so bad after all.'

'Oh my God, we have to warn Clare!' Anna clambers out of bed and starts to rummage around for something to put on, snatching up one of Toby's t-shirts.

'No!' Toby shouts, grabbing her arm and pulling her back. 'He wants to surprise her. Marco made me promise I wouldn't tell her.'

'Oh!' Anna says, stopping in her tracks. 'But she looks such a bloody mess. Can't I at least persuade her to wash her hair?'

Toby laughs. 'Girls are so funny sometimes. You can tell her to wash her hair and put some make-up on if you like but find some other excuse. Really, babe, he's a bloke. He wouldn't notice if she'd had a face transplant, let alone whether or not she's wearing make-up.'

'OK, you're probably right,' Anna agrees reluctantly. 'But I'm definitely going to get her to tart herself up a bit more – I know I'd want to look my best if you were travelling across the world to see me.'

Anna pulls Toby's t-shirt on over her head and makes her way purposefully towards Clare's bedroom, leaving Toby still chuckling to himself in bed.

She knocks on Clare's door. No answer. She knocks again, then hears the familiar sound of throwing up coming from the bathroom. Anna goes to the kitchen and fills a glass with cold water before returning and tentatively opening the bathroom door. 'Hey,' she says. 'I've brought you some water.'

Clare is kneeling on the floor in front of the bowl holding her hair back while she retches. Finally she finishes and slumps back, leaning against the bath, exhausted. 'Thank you,' she whispers.

'Why don't I run you a lovely bath?' Anna asks hopefully. 'You can wash your hair and put some make-up on. Honestly, Clare, it'll make you feel so much better.'

'You reckon?' Clare says doubtfully. 'Nah, I just don't have the energy.'

'Don't worry!' Anna insists brightly. 'Budge out of the way and I'll do it all – I'll even apply your make-up.'

Luckily Clare doesn't have the energy to argue. Anna runs the bath very deep, finds her a couple of clean towels from the airing cupboard and waits outside the door while she bathes. Once she is done, Anna follows her into her room and insists on drying her hair and putting on her make-up. Once again, the fight has left her.

'There!' Anna says proudly once she's finished, standing back to admire her handiwork. 'Doesn't that feel better?'

Clare smiles at herself in the mirror. 'You know what? It does. Thanks, Anna. I really appreciate it.' Then the smile slips and she adds, 'At least I'll look nice for my appointment with the abortion clinic.'

Anna meets her eye in the mirror and looks away quickly. She opens her mouth to speak, desperate to relieve Clare's misery but closes it again. She can't risk letting her know that she won't be keeping the appointment after all. 'You'll be OK,' she says, turning away to hide her guilty expression. 'Now, come on, get dressed. Slouching round in that dirty old dressing gown isn't good for you either!'

'Jesus, when did you get so bossy!' Clare laughs huffily.

'I think Toby would say exactly the same thing,' Anna says without thinking.

'How come? What have you been bossing him around for?'

Bloody lawyers, thinks Anna, *nothing gets past them*.

'Oh, er, I was telling him he shouldn't eat such crap food,' Anna mumbles unconvincingly, reddening. She is easily the world's worst liar.

Clare's eyes narrow suspiciously. 'You're up to something,' she says accusingly.

'Don't be daft!' Anna protests weakly. 'Anyway, get dressed and I'll make you some breakfast.'

Clare comes into the kitchen looking like a completely different person. Her hair is thick and glossy again and her olive skin is back to glowing.

'You look so much better!' Anna says, putting a plate of buttered toast in front of her. 'Do you think you could manage some toast?'

Clare takes a deep breath. 'I think so ... if I eat slowly.'

Anna watches with satisfaction as she munches her way through the two slices, suddenly realizing that she is starving after being unable to keep anything down for so long.

'Right,' she says, wiping her mouth with a napkin as she finishes. 'I'd better get my sorry arse off to work. I've already missed so many days ... It'll be nice to get back to normal, you know, after this afternoon.'

Anna looks round at her in alarm. 'But you can't! You can't go to work today!'

'It'll be the best thing,' Clare frowns, stacking her plate in the dishwasher. 'It'll help to take my mind off ... it.'

'But if you've got to leave early anyway ...' Anna pleads, desperate for Clare not to leave the flat. James will be arriving any minute, she is sure of it.

'All the more reason to show them that I'm prepared to make an effort. I don't think they've believed my food poisoning stories over the past few weeks. Thanks for your concern, Anna, but I'm definitely going into the office.'

Anna watches helplessly as Clare busies herself loading up her bag and putting on her coat. 'I still think you should stay at home . . .' she mutters, but knows she is defeated.

'You teachers are such bloody skivers. Just because *you* would!' Clare kisses her on the cheek. 'Thanks again, Anna. I'll see you at the clinic at 4.30 – OK? Don't worry!' she adds, seeing the look on her face, 'everything is going to be OK.'

Anna nods, frantically trying to think of a way to stop her going. She can't think of anything plausible and has to stand and watch as she grabs her things and lets herself out of the flat.

Toby emerges from their room. 'Who was that going out?' he asks in surprise.

'Clare,' Anna mutters miserably.

'Oh. Where's she gone?'

'To work – my makeover did the trick, unfortunately,' she grumbles.

'Oh well, it's good that she's feeling better,' Toby says, picking up the kettle and filling it with water.

'But what about James arriving here this morning? He's got to see her before she has the termination. Otherwise she'll go through with it.' Anna can't believe Toby is being so laid-back.

'Don't worry!' he says. 'He'll see her – whether it's here, at her work or at the clinic. And if the worst comes to the worst . . . well, you can tell her that he's on his way.'

'I suppose.' She's not convinced and has a sneaking feeling this could all go horribly wrong.

Just at that moment, the doorbell rings and Anna leaps out of her seat. 'Oh my God!' she shouts. 'It's him, it's him! Quick, Tobes, get the door!'

Toby smiles and heads towards the door, where someone is pressing repeatedly on the doorbell. 'See?' he says, walking down the hallway. 'I told you it would be all right. There's plenty of time to get it all sorted out . . . Oh!' he cries out in shock as he opens the door and Clare bursts past him en route to the bathroom, her hand clamped over her mouth.

Toby and Anna look at each other in surprise. 'Well, at least she's here,' Anna says, to the sound of Clare's retching.

The doorbell rings again and Toby turns on his heel, heading back in the direction he has just come. He opens the door. This time it really is James, standing on the doorstep looking tanned, dishevelled and unshaven. Anna hurls herself towards him. 'Oh, thank God you're here!' she cries, hugging him as tightly as his huge rucksack will allow.

James staggers into the hallway, half-dragged by Anna. He hugs Toby. 'Well?' he says, his voice tight with emotion. 'Where is she?'

Toby grimaces and cups his hand to his ear, as the noise of Clare throwing up echoes through the flat. 'Clutching the nearest toilet bowl for dear life, I'm afraid,' he says, nodding towards the bathroom.

James drops his backpack and puts his hands on his hips. 'Right, well I'd better go and rescue her then,' he says, before heading off down the hallway.

Rachel

The next day at work, Marco comes to find Rachel, looking concerned. 'Sorry for upsetting you last night,' he says, sitting down on the saggy old sofa in her office.

'You didn't!' she protests, trying to focus on the screen in front of her. Her eyes are bleary and sore from crying all night but she is calm now.

Marco laughs. 'Erm, usually when a woman runs out of a restaurant bawling her eyes out, that means she's upset.'

'I'm not denying I was upset,' Rachel says, smiling back. 'I'm just saying that it wasn't you who upset me.'

'Women are so bloody complicated!' Marco cries, throwing his hands up in the air. 'So what was it then?'

'It's hard to explain – and I'm not sure you'd understand,' Rachel says, not really wanting to go over everything she had felt last night. After leaving the restaurant she had gone home to bed and had experienced what could only be described as a dark night of the soul. During the long hours before dawn, she had finally reconciled herself to the idea that she would never be a mother. Today she feels wrung out and exhausted but her mind is peaceful.

'Why don't you try me?'

'What?' she looks at Marco curiously, having totally forgotten what he was talking about.

'Why don't you try to explain what was wrong last night? Otherwise I might get paranoid that it's me.'

Rachel sighs and rests her elbows on the desk, cupping her face in her hands. 'It was hearing that Clare is pregnant that did it.'

'Why? Because you feel sorry for her?' Marco's forehead crumples as he tries hard to understand.

'No – because I'm jealous of her,' she says flatly, flushing slightly at her own admission, which sounds silly when she speaks the words out loud.

'Oh!' Marco looks surprised and momentarily stumped. 'But that's mad. She's pregnant with the baby of someone she knew for a week who's now living on the other side of the world – it's hardly a situation to be envious of.'

'I know,' Rachel agrees. She knew he wouldn't understand. *It's so different for men*, she thinks. *They don't have to worry about time running out. They can take all the time in the world to decide whether or not they want to become fathers*. 'Anyway, what are you up to tonight?' she asks, changing the subject. 'Want to go for a drink after work?'

Marco shakes his head. 'Can't – I'm seeing Becs,' he says, before noticing Rachel's disappointed expression. 'Why don't you come too? We're going out for dinner.'

'Marco!' she laughs, touched that he should have asked her. 'You can't drag me along to your romantic meal! Becs would go nuts.'

'No she wouldn't!' he says. 'Number one, it's not a romantic meal and number two, you're her sister. She'd love to see you and see how well you're doing. She always asks about you, you know.'

Rachel feels a pang of guilt. She has deliberately been avoiding her family as much as possible since the wedding day. She isn't quite sure why. Maybe it is embarrassment at what happened. Maybe it is shame that her father spent so much money for nothing. Or maybe she is worried that her strength and resolve will disappear the moment she is back in the bosom of the people who love her most in the world. She knows it is unfair on them but she can't help it.

'How are you and Becs getting on, anyway?' she asks Marco, keen to steer the conversation away from herself. 'It's nearly three months now – must be getting serious!'

Marco laughs. 'Not exactly. We hardly ever see each other, what with her working such long hours. She's lovely but we haven't . . . well, you know.'

'Really?' Rachel cries, fascinated. 'Why not?'

He shrugs. 'It's not that sort of a relationship. We're just friends.'

'Oh.' Rachel doesn't know why but this piece of information has cheered her up enormously. It isn't that she fancies Marco. But she does enjoy his company and has been secretly hoping that he won't get serious with anyone while she still needs him so much.

'Come on, Rach, come with us tonight. Becs would be so pleased.' Marco stands up and looks down at her with an unreadable expression.

She hesitates. 'I don't know, Marco. I've got a lot of work to do . . .'

'No you haven't! You just asked me to go for a drink a minute ago.'

'Oh yeah, I did, didn't I?' she giggles, shaking her head at her own stupidity. 'Oh, bugger it, all right then.'

'Great!' Marco looks chuffed as he opens her office door. 'I've always fancied the idea of two sisters . . .'

Rachel picks up a book from her desk and throws it at him. He ducks and it hits the wall. 'In your dreams!' she calls after him as he walks out grinning.

'So, why have you been avoiding us?' Becs asks accusingly as Rachel sits down at the table with her and Marco.

Rachel glances at Marco, who is studying the menu intently. 'I haven't!' she replies as indignantly as she can.

'Yes, you have. Mum and Dad are worried sick. It's really selfish of you, Rach.' Becs has a look in her eye that Rachel recognizes as one that says she isn't about to be fobbed off.

'Nice to see you too, Becs,' she mutters, picking up a menu and looking at it. Becs has always been direct and it's something people either love or hate about her. Right now, Rachel hates it but if she's honest she knows it's because Becs is right. Her parents are the most loving parents she could have asked for and it is selfish of her to shut them out.

'I'm sorry to have a go at you but you know how worried they are.' Becs' tone becomes more conciliatory. 'The least you could do is just give them a call every now and then to let them know you're OK.'

'All right!' snaps Rachel. 'You've made your point, now shut up!'

'Girls! Girls!' cries Marco, raising both hands in an attempt to calm them down. 'Behave yourselves. Now let's just order some food, have a few glasses of wine and have a good night.'

Becs looks at Rachel sheepishly. 'Sorry for having a go at you,' she mumbles. 'It's great to see you.'

'I'm sorry for snapping at you,' Rachel replies, reaching across the table and giving her sister's hand a squeeze. 'And you're right, I'll give them a call in the morning. It's just really hard.'

'I know,' says Becs softly. 'I do understand. But we're all here for you if you need us.'

'Thanks,' whispers Rachel, swallowing hard to stop herself choking up. 'Let's order before I start blubbing.'

In the end, they have a great evening. It's lovely for Rachel to see Becs again and both she and Marco are fabulous company. As he goes off to the loo, Rachel leans across the table conspiratorially. 'So, how's it going with you two then?' she asks eagerly.

Becs smiles. 'He's a really cool bloke and I like him a lot but we're just friends.'

'Yeah, right!' giggles Rachel. 'There must be more to it than that.'

'Honestly,' says Becs, 'there just isn't that kind of spark. I don't fancy him and he doesn't fancy me.'

'How do you know?' Rachel presses her, intrigued.

'Because we've never even snogged. And anyway, I think his interest lies elsewhere . . .' she adds meaningfully.

'Really?' asks Rachel, her interest suddenly piqued. If there is someone else on the scene, she wants to know about it. She is becoming quite possessive of her friendship with Marco.

'Yup. He spends most of the time we're together asking all about her and talking about her non-stop.'

'Why? Is it someone you know?' Rachel asks, frowning.

Becs nods. 'Uh huh . . .'

'Do I know her?' Rachel wracks her brains to think who else Marco has shown an interest in recently.

'Uh huh,' Becs replies again.

'Oh! Well, who is it then? I can't think of anyone he's mentioned lately.'

Becs raises her eyebrows in frustration. 'Honestly, Rachel, sometimes you are so dumb!'

'What?' Rachel replies, still mystified.

'It's you, you silly cow,' Becs answers bluntly.

At that moment, Marco rejoins them at the table. Rachel is glad of the dim lighting as her cheeks flame and she suddenly feels overcome with shyness and embarrassment. Could Becs be right? Has Marco been giving out signals that he wants more than just friendship? She doesn't think so but she suddenly feels awkward in his presence. It is far too soon for her to be even thinking of having any kind of relationship, especially with someone who has been Toby's best friend for so long. It would seem as if she was doing it just to get back at Toby.

'I'd better get going,' Rachel says, looking at her watch and yawning broadly. 'Early start tomorrow.'

Marco jumps up. 'OK, I'll share a cab with you.'

'No! No, it's fine,' she replies quickly, suddenly desperate to be out of his company. 'You two finish your drinks. I'll see you tomorrow.' She gives Becs a quick kiss on the cheek and flees the restaurant as quickly as she can.

'That's the second time in as many days you've done that,' says Marco, marching into Rachel's office the next morning and slumping down on her sofa.

'Good morning to you too, Marco,' Rachel laughs. 'Second time I've done what?'

'Second time you've dashed out of a restaurant. Something going on with your bowels that you want to share?'

Rachel laughs, glad that the awkwardness she felt last night has evaporated. 'Euughhh! No, I just needed to get to bed, that's all.'

'That's all right then – I was going to offer you some of my special medicine.'

'Enough!' she shouts, giggling. She knows then that Becs is wrong about Marco fancying her. No man who had the hots for her would be suggesting that she share his diarrhoea medicine. Nothing could be less romantic.

'I'm glad you came last night,' says Marco. 'Becs has been so worried. Now that she's seen for herself that you're still the same bolshy cow, she feels so much better.'

'Gee, thanks!' Rachel replies sarcastically. 'But I'm glad too – I had been avoiding them and it isn't fair. Actually, I'm going to call my mum now, so if you don't mind?' She gestures towards the door.

Marco stands up with a salute. 'Yes, sir! Have a good day deciding which spangles to put on Daisy Rowe's dancing outfit. I'm just off to make some proper telly.'

Rachel sticks out her tongue at his departing back and picks up the phone. 'Hi, Mum! It's me. I'm back in the land of the living.'

Clare

When there is a knock on the bathroom door, Clare assumes it is Anna, checking to see if she is all right. 'I'll be out in a minute,' she calls, gulping as much air as she can between retches. She is only vaguely aware that the door has opened and someone is standing there. She flushes the chain and reaches for her toothbrush to brush her teeth. She scrubs as hard as she can, before rinsing her mouth and standing up. As she does so, she looks in the mirror at her reflection, now grey again after being ill, before focusing on the figure standing in the doorway behind her. She blinks hard, sure that she is seeing things. 'James?' she whispers, hardly daring to turn around in case he disappears.

James' expression is a mixture of love and sympathy. He looks tanned and handsome, despite the beard and scruffy blond hair that is sticking up in every direction. 'Hello, Clare,' he says softly.

'Oh my God!' she murmurs. 'I can't believe it's really you!'

James walks slowly towards her and opens his arms. Clare hesitates before going to him. He envelops her, as though he will never let her go and they stand entwined for several long minutes. Finally, he releases his grip and holds her at arm's length. 'You look so . . .' he begins, shaking his head.

'So shit?' she laughs, running her hand through her hair, suddenly self-conscious.

'God, no,' he replies. 'You look so beautiful. I'd forgotten how lovely you are.'

Clare feels herself glow with pleasure under his gaze. 'You look pretty lovely yourself,' she grins shyly. James tilts her face up towards him and kisses her hard on the lips. She is shaking all over with shock.

'Hey, you two,' laughs Anna from behind them, 'get a room!'

'Isn't that how they got into this mess in the first place?' says Toby.

Clare takes James by the hand and leads him towards her room. Thank God Anna had made her get dressed and wash her hair, she thinks, before stopping suddenly and turning on her heel.

'What's wrong?' asks James in alarm.

Clare stalks back to where Anna and Toby are still standing watching them. 'You knew, didn't you?' she says to Anna, her smile showing that she isn't angry.

Anna shrugs. 'Knew what?' she asks innocently.

'Well, I wish you'd told me. But I'm glad that at least you didn't let me slob around in my old dressing gown,' grins Clare.

'I don't think you'd have forgiven me if I had.'

Clare smiles her agreement before heading off down the hallway to join James who has now slumped down onto her bed. 'You must be exhausted,' she says, joining him and leaning her head on his chest.

'I am,' he nods, kissing the top of her head. 'But so must you be.'

'You have no idea,' she replies, remembering just how bad she had felt only a few short hours ago. They lapse into a contented silence for a few moments.

'So, what do we do now?' Clare asks at last. 'I'm booked in to have the . . . to have a . . . you know, later today.' She can't even say the word.

James sits up and looks at her earnestly. 'What do you want to do?'

'I didn't think I had any choice.'

'But I'm here now,' he replies, his voice heavy with intent. 'So you do have a choice.'

Clare feels her heart swell with hope. She had assumed that even though James was here, he was only here to support her through the abortion. She hadn't dared hope that he might actually want her to consider keeping the baby. 'I don't know what to do,' she mumbles. 'I had just about got my head around, well, you know, getting rid of it.' She looks up at him, feeling her face flush.

His eyes soften. 'But is that what you want to do?'

Clare looks away. 'Of course it's not what I want to do. But, James, it's such a huge commitment – the biggest commitment there is – if I keep it.' She glances back and sees him blanch as she speaks. 'You see, it's all very well you reappearing back here like some sort of superhero,' she continues, 'but you have to be sure. It's no good saying you'll support me, only to get cold feet in a couple of months' time when you realize what's involved.'

James nods slowly but she can tell that it has only just registered with him what he is letting himself in for. Her spirits, which a few seconds earlier had been soaring, begin to plummet once more. She loves him. She really does. They have only known each other for a short time but it is the real thing for her, of that she is sure. But he has let her down once before. How does she know he won't do it again?

As if he can tell what she is thinking, James seems to snap to his senses. 'I won't change my mind,' he says firmly. 'If you decide to keep this baby – our baby – I will be there for you.'

Clare squeaks with a combination of surprise and joy. 'Are you sure?' she presses him. 'Are you really sure?'

James nods and kisses her tenderly on the lips. 'I'm positive,' he whispers.

The next few weeks are easily the happiest of Clare's life. Her terrible morning, noon and night sickness stops abruptly at twelve weeks, as if a switch has been pulled. Immediately, she feels more human and able to get some of her life back. And she and James seem to just fall into being a couple again. They have lapsed back into the easygoing yet passionate relationship they had before he went away, with no arguments or recriminations over what happened.

They discussed it once, calmly, without any kind of rancour. 'I think I just flipped a bit,' James admitted. 'I had never felt like that about anyone and it freaked me out. I had everything lined up in Australia – my dream job, somewhere great to live – it would have felt ridiculous to throw it all away for someone I'd only known a week.'

'I can see that now,' Clare said, marvelling at her own maturity. 'So did you deliberately start the row so that it would be easier for you to leave me?'

James reddened. 'Was it that obvious?'

'Not to me it wasn't,' she smiled. 'But it was to Toby.'

'I suppose he would have recognized the signs,' James said wryly. 'Considering he had been living a lie for years.'

'Maybe,' replied Clare. 'So why the change of heart?'

'Do you really have to ask?' James laughed, ruffling her hair affectionately. 'There was the small matter of an e-mail that pinged into my inbox, telling me that the girl I loved was pregnant with my baby. It was a no-brainer. I booked myself on the first flight I could to get back.'

'And what if I hadn't been pregnant?' she couldn't help asking. 'Do you think you'd have come back eventually anyway?'

'I don't know,' he scratched his chin thoughtfully as he spoke. 'But it gave me the excuse I'd been looking for.'

Clare beamed with happiness. 'So, you missed me then?' she giggled, nuzzling up to him.

'Just a bit,' he replied, pulling her down onto the bed beside him.

The twelve-week scan is both scary and exciting in equal measure. Although Clare has done several positive pregnancy tests and thrown up all day, every day for weeks, she still expects the sonographer to tell her that she has made a mistake and that there is no baby there. 'Probably just a nasty bout of gastroenteritis,' Clare imagines her saying.

But as soon as she places the probe on her jelly-coated abdomen, the evidence is there on the screen for all to see, accompanied by the 'thwacking' sound of the heartbeat.

'He looks beautiful!' she cries, gripping James' hand as tears roll down her cheeks. She came so close to getting rid of this little life and now here it is in all its grainy, black and white glory. She now knows that she would never have forgiven herself.

'He?' laughs the sonographer. 'You sound very sure it's a boy.'

Clare looks at her in surprise. 'I do, don't I? Do you think that's significant?'

'Not particularly,' she smiles. 'Most people refer to the foetus as a "he" to begin with. One thing's for sure – it'll be either a girl or a boy!'

Clare looks at James shyly. He is staring goofily at the little shape on the screen. 'What do you think?' she asks him.

'I think he's ace,' he says, squeezing her hand and looking at her proudly.

Afterwards, they go to a café and sit gazing at the scan photos.

'Look at his little nose!' Clare murmurs.

'And his little thumb!' coos James.

They are smitten.

After that first scan, Clare finally allows herself to enjoy being pregnant. As her bump grows, so does her delight at the new life growing within her. James has moved in, which seems the logical thing to do, and Marco has now let out the room in his old flat anyway. Clare books in for her antenatal appointments, feeling a little thrill that she won't be doing all of this on her own.

'You really are glowing,' says Anna, looking at Clare admiringly one day as she gets ready for work. 'It's hard to believe how ill you were for the first three months.'

'I know,' laughs Clare. 'Probably a good job James wasn't

around. He'd have headed for Australia for good if he'd seen me then.'

'No, he wouldn't,' protests Anna. 'He would have said how beautiful you were and rubbed your back while you threw up.'

'Hmm. I wish I shared your confidence but thanks anyway.'

'So, how are you finding it? Living with James?' asks Anna, glancing at Clare in the mirror.

Clare thinks about it for a second while she applies her lipstick. 'Great,' she says cautiously.

'That's not the most ringing endorsement I've ever heard. What's up?'

'No, nothing's up – it really is great. But I suppose I'm still a bit scared that he'll freak out again and do a runner. I'm not sure I ever told you but his dad was a classic commitment-phobe, always doing a bunk and leaving his mum to cope with the kids on her own, then turning up out of the blue and expecting a hero's welcome. I suppose I'm worried that James could be just like his father. I still don't know how well he copes with responsibility.'

'None of us knows that,' says Anna wisely. 'Look at me and Toby. There's always the worry that he'll get cold feet and jilt me at the altar – he's done it once before after all.'

'Don't be daft!' cries Clare. 'Toby and you are the real thing. There's no way he'll jilt you. I'd put my life on it.'

'Well then, stop worrying about James. He's not going to run out on you either.'

Clare beams at herself in the mirror. Anna is right, of course. It was ridiculous to keep worrying about something that very probably wouldn't ever happen. And yet . . .

*

'We need to talk about getting a place together,' Clare says one evening as she and James are eating dinner.

James looks up in surprise. 'We've already got a place,' he says, looking around him.

'Yes, but we can't keep living with Toby and Anna forever, like four eternal students. Anyway, they'll no doubt want to get a place of their own too, now that they're getting married.'

'Don't see why we can't just stay as we are for now,' says James grumpily, piling a forkful of pasta into his mouth.

'Well, for a start there are only two bedrooms in this flat. Where would we put the baby?'

'Oh!' he says, putting down his fork and taking a sip of his water. 'I hadn't thought of that.'

'James!' chides Clare. 'And we'll have to start thinking about buying equipment and things pretty soon. I'm halfway through now. The other half will fly by and we need to be prepared.'

'What sort of equipment?' James looks at her suspiciously.

'Well, a cot, a pram, a car seat . . . that sort of equipment.'

'Oh, I hadn't really thought about that side of it,' he mutters.

'What, you just thought that the baby arrived and as if by magic, so did all the stuff they need?'

James laughs and looks sheepish. 'Yeah. I suppose that's exactly what I thought.'

Clare clears her throat, steeling herself for what she is about to say next. 'And you're going to have to get a job too, James.'

He nods. 'I know. I have been looking . . .'

'Not very hard,' Clare chips in. 'I want to take my full maternity leave, so we'll need all the money we can get.'

'Don't nag, Clare,' James groans, rubbing his forehead. 'I'll get a job, OK?'

'OK,' she says, frowning. She doesn't want to push him so she decides to keep her mouth shut.

The next day Clare decides to break the news of her pregnancy to her boss. She approaches his office nervously. 'Er, Martin, could I have a word?' she begins hesitantly.

'Sure,' he smiles, motioning her into the office. 'What's on your mind?'

'Well,' she says, sitting down opposite him. 'I'm not sure how you're going to feel about this but—'

'You're pregnant,' he cuts in, still smiling.

'How did you know?' Clare gasps, looking around her as if trying to spot the person who'd blabbed.

'I've got three children of my own, Clare,' he grins. 'I know the signs. And you've been showing pretty much all those signs for quite some time now.'

She laughs shyly. 'I'm sorry.'

He bats his hand in a dismissive gesture. 'No need to apologize at all. I'm pleased for you, if a little surprised.'

'Surprised?'

'I didn't know you even had a partner – that's if you do have one? It's quite an assumption these days . . .'

Clare laughs. 'Yes, I do have a partner, but only just. He got back from Australia a few weeks ago.'

'Well, that's good,' he says. 'It's hard enough having a child with two of you. How these single mothers cope is quite beyond me.'

'I know,' Clare agrees, thanking her lucky stars that she isn't going to be one of them. She had come very close. 'But

I fully intend to come back to work after I've had the baby,' she says, eager to reassure her understanding boss.

He nods. 'Good. I don't want to lose you. But I have to say that everyone says they'll come back and only a few of them actually do. I hope very much you'll be one of the ones who does.'

'I will be!' Clare insists, at that moment as certain as she has ever been that she will be returning to the job that she loves so much.

Being a lawyer wasn't everyone's idea of a dream job – for one thing it made you only marginally more popular than estate agents and tax inspectors. But it was all Clare had ever wanted to do. She found the intricacies of the legal system endlessly fascinating and felt that she was able to do some good by representing people who needed her help. She was paid well but she also felt that she was contributing to society at the same time.

Finally, to her great relief, James eventually secures work freelancing with the TV company he'd worked for before he left. He is a VT editor, which means he cuts programmes together and makes them fit for transmission. He is now back working with Marco, which pleases him because they had always got on very well together. And of course, he is also working with Rachel, who, according to James, is flying high and doing incredibly well. 'I bet she hates me,' Clare says to him one night when they are chatting about work.

He looks at her curiously. 'No, I don't think she does. Anyway, you didn't do anything wrong. But she seems very interested in your pregnancy. She's always asking me how you are.'

'Really? I reckon she was desperate for a baby herself with Toby,' Clare says, stroking her small bump contemplatively.

'What makes you think that? You didn't really know her.'

Clare shrugs. 'No, but I know the signs. She's at that dangerous age when she had invested too many of her child-bearing years in Toby.'

James goes quiet for a minute. 'God, maybe it's no wonder Toby freaked. I'd hate that.'

'Hate what?' she frowns. 'Hate someone to want to have a baby?'

'No! Yes. Oh, I don't know,' he stutters, his cheeks flushing. 'I'd just hate the pressure of knowing someone was desperate to have one.'

Clare looks at him, perplexed.

'All I'm saying ...' he continues, putting his hand over hers and rubbing her bump along with her, 'is that I'm glad ours was a surprise.'

She smiles and relaxes slightly. 'Me too,' she agrees.

A few days later, putting her make-up on in front of her dressing-table mirror, she tells James that she has lined up some houses for them to look at that evening. When he doesn't reply she turns round to see him sitting on the bed with his head in his hands. 'James?' she says. 'What's up?'

He shakes his head roughly. 'Nothing!' he barks.

'So ... you'll meet me at seven?' Clare persists. 'At Clapham Common tube?'

'Yes!' he sighs irritably, rubbing his face.

'For fuck's sake, James!' she snaps, feeling the irritation rising faster than her heartburn. 'You're acting like a teenager! This isn't just about me wanting to move on a whim, you know. We've got to find somewhere of our own before the baby's born.'

James stands up and comes over to her, wrapping his arms around her from behind. 'I'm sorry,' he whispers, kissing the top of her head. 'I'm really sorry.'

Clare knows, even before she has waited for an hour in the cold at Clapham Common tube station that evening, that he won't be turning up. He's gone. And this time it looks like it's for good.

Rachel

It is Marco who breaks the news to Rachel about Toby and Anna getting engaged. She almost has a sixth sense of what he is going to say before he speaks. 'I'm sorry,' he says, having blurted it out as quickly as he could. 'But I thought you would want to know.'

Rachel nods furiously. They are in a late-night coffee bar in Soho, having been to see the musical *Legally Blonde*, thanks to some free tickets Rachel got through work. The fluorescent lights are harsh on the Formica table tops, giving everything a greenish hue. She sips her latte which is surprisingly frothy and lovely, despite the chipped mug and ugly surroundings.

The noise and clatter of the coffee bar can't mask the silence which hangs in the air between them as Rachel tries to analyse how she is feeling. Hearing the words is like a punch to the stomach, but she has known that she would hear them sooner or later. Another part of her feels slightly comforted that Toby wasn't mucking about – he really did love Anna enough to marry her. For Rachel's part, she knows she will never, ever get married now – she just wouldn't be able to walk into a church and stand at an altar again – but Toby clearly feels differently.

'That's if he actually goes through with the wedding this time!' Marco adds bitterly.

Rachel laughs. 'Honestly, Marco, if I can forgive Toby, then you should too – Toby and I made our peace and he got back with Anna with my blessing. I know it's hard to understand, but I'm OK with it. Really!' she adds, seeing the look of disbelief in his eyes.

In many ways, life couldn't be better for Rachel. Having thrown herself back into work, she is doing fantastically well. The big entertainment show she is in charge of is at number one in the ratings, she is earning a good wage and is back in the bosom of her family.

And yet, when she returns to her flat – usually very late in the evenings due to the hellish hours she is working – she feels as if a cloud of loneliness is enveloping her. She misses Toby but only because she misses his presence. What she certainly doesn't miss is the constant worry that his heart really belongs to someone else and the nervousness that at any time she might come home to find that he had left her for Anna. But she craves having someone to cuddle up to in bed at night and someone to chat to as she gets ready for work in the mornings. Work fills some of the void but not enough of it.

Having grown so close to him after she and Toby split up, she now sees less and less of Marco outside of work, making her think that Becs' theory that Marco liked her as more than just a friend was wrong. Mind you, there are two reasons why she doesn't see so much of him. Firstly, she hardly ever gets away from the office in time to get to the pub for a drink like they used to. Plus, James has come back from Australia, much to Marco's delight, and the two of them now spend as much time as they can together, having missed each other's company in the time they'd been apart.

Rachel likes James – she always got on well with him – and is glad that he has come back from Australia to be with Clare. She has mixed feelings about Clare; she can't help being consumed by an overwhelming jealousy whenever she thinks about her having the baby that Rachel so desperately wants. But at the same time, she doesn't like the thought of her having to struggle on her own either. For reasons she can't understand, she finds herself taking an unusually in-depth interest in the minute details of how Clare is getting on and bombards James with endless questions. On more than one occasion, it occurs to her that maybe she is living out her own fantasy pregnancy through Clare.

James seems happy to be home and he is a great editor and popular with his colleagues so it suits her just fine to have him. Marco is like a dog with two tails now his old buddy is back in the building and the two of them scoot off together at every opportunity.

'Have you forgotten about me altogether?' she says sulkily as she pulls up a chair next to Marco in the canteen one morning.

Marco laughs. 'You can talk! You don't write, you don't phone . . .'

Rachel yawns. 'Do you know what? I never get a bloody minute. This job is great and I love it . . .'

'And you're doing really well,' he chips in cheerfully, stuffing the rest of a pain au chocolat into his mouth. 'Congrats on the ratings, by the way – I'm delighted for you to be getting three times the ratings for your celebrity froth than I get for my lovingly crafted masterpieces!'

'Clearly I know what the viewers want . . .' Rachel grins. 'Whereas you, my friend, only know what you want.'

Marco slurps his coffee and laughs. 'So, how are you doing?' he asks, looking at her carefully. 'You look knackered.'

'Thanks!' she replies, wishing she had had time to wash her hair and put on some make-up that morning. She really has let herself go. 'Actually, I'm a bit low,' she admits.

'Really? And why's that, do you think?'

'Apart from the obvious?' she says wryly.

Marco nods. 'Yeah, apart from the obvious. Obviously.'

'I dunno,' sighs Rachel. 'I think I'm still feeling jealous of Clare. Now that James has come home, everything's worked out really well for her. I just wish I was in her shoes, I guess.'

Marco pulls a face.

'What?' Rachel demands.

Marco takes a deep breath and looks around him conspiratorially. 'Well, I don't think everything's quite as rosy as you think in that particular garden.'

Rachel frowns. 'What do you mean?'

'Well, you know what James is like. I think he's finding the pressure a bit too much.'

Rachel feels a bubble of fury deep within her on Clare's behalf. She hardly knows the girl but she does know that she had been intending to have a termination before James reappeared like a knight in shining armour and persuaded her to go ahead with the pregnancy. 'He'd better not run out on her again!' she snaps, surprised by the vehemence of her reaction. 'He needs to grow up!'

Marco raises one eyebrow. 'Blimey, I'm surprised you're so

defensive of her. I thought you'd have been delighted at her misfortune.'

'Absolutely not!' Rachel storms. 'Why is it that men always think women will scratch each other's eyes out, given half a chance? I feel really sorry for her, if you must know. And as for bloody James – well, wait till I get hold of him!'

'Hey, steady on!' says Marco, looking worried. 'I'm not saying he is going to run out on her. I'm just saying that I think he's finding the pressure a bit too much.'

'Oh, diddums!' she snarls sarcastically. 'He ought to put himself in her shoes – then he'd know what pressure felt like!'

Marco smiles at her.

'What?' she shoots back at him.

'You're so funny when you're angry,' he laughs.

'Oooh!' she screeches in fury, standing up.

'Rachel!' Marco wheedles, trying to grab her hand as she snatches up her bag. 'Where are you going?'

'I'm going to find bloody James and give him a right good talking-to!' she cries, before turning on her heel and stalking off towards the company's edit suites.

James is in the fourth suite she looks in, along with one of her segment producers. 'Sorry to barge in, Trinny,' she says to the trendy-looking girl as she pulls up a chair. 'But could you give me and James a few moments alone?'

Trinny nods and scoops up her cigarettes and phone. 'No problem – I'm dying for a fag anyway,' she says as she scurries out of the room, letting the soundproofed door fall shut behind her with a satisfying thud.

James looks at Rachel in shock. 'What's going on?' he asks bemusedly.

'You might want to answer that question!' she says, scowling at him.

'Sorry, Rach, no idea what you're on about,' he says, running his hand through his scruffy blond hair.

'I've just been talking to Marco,' she begins, eyeing him suspiciously. 'He tells me you're getting cold feet.'

James blanches. 'What? What did he say?' he asks nervously, his eyes darting from side to side, clearly stalling for time.

'As I just said,' Rachel enunciates her words very slowly, trying and failing to disguise her white-hot anger. 'He says you're getting cold feet about this baby. Is he right?'

James doesn't say anything and looks away.

'Is he right?' she repeats, now feeling murderous towards him.

'Yes,' he says in a thin voice.

Rachel narrows her eyes but says nothing, waiting for James to continue.

'It just . . . well, it just all seems so real – having to get a place to live, buying all this stuff that babies apparently need and Clare's belly growing bigger by the day. I couldn't handle it.'

'What do you mean, you *couldn't* handle it? Shouldn't that be present tense?'

James flushes. 'I've left her,' he says. 'Last night.'

Before she even has time to think about what she is doing, Rachel has slapped him hard across the face. 'You fucking wanker!' she yells. 'How could you? How could you leave her when she's five months pregnant? And just before Christmas too!'

James' hand shoots up to his cheek and he looks at her in shock. 'You just hit me!' he says, in disbelief.

'I'll hit you again if you don't answer me,' Rachel cries,

shaking with rage. She feels as if he has walked out on *her*, rather than some girl she hardly knows.

To her stunned amazement, James bursts into noisy sobs. 'I just couldn't cope!' he wails. 'It all got too much and I felt like I was drowning.'

Rachel watches him for a second before she speaks. 'And how the hell do you think Clare feels? You stop her having a termination and then you run out on her when it's too late. She can't just run away! Get over yourself, James!'

James sniffs loudly and wipes his eyes roughly on his t-shirt. 'I don't know what to do,' he says gruffly. 'I've fucked it up again.'

Rachel feels herself softening slightly. 'Yes, you have. But you can still make it right. You can go back, apologize from the bottom of your heart and beg her to take you back.'

'She won't,' he says, shaking his head. 'I know her. She won't risk me hurting her again.'

'You stupid fucking idiot!' Rachel sighs. 'Why did you have to walk out on her? You would have been fine if you'd just hung on in there.'

He sniffs again. 'I know, I know ... What shall I do, Rachel?'

'Well, you can phone her for a start,' she says briskly, picking up his phone from the desk and handing it to him. 'You can tell her you had a funny five minutes but it's over now and you will make it up to her. Apologize. A lot.'

James takes the phone as if it is an unexploded bomb. 'What if she shouts at me?' he asks plaintively.

'You'd deserve it,' Rachel replies.

'OK ... well, can I have some privacy?' he says, his eyes filled with fear.

Rachel stands up reluctantly. 'OK . . . but I'm going to wait outside the door until you've done it.'

'Stop treating me like a little kid!' James snaps irritably.

'Then stop acting like one,' Rachel snaps back, walking towards the door. 'Make the call. Now.'

Rachel leans against the wall outside the edit suite, regretting that the room is totally soundproofed. Trinny rounds the corner, back from her cigarette break. 'Is it OK to go back in now?' she asks, her eyes darting towards the door.

'Not yet,' Rachel replies, shaking her head. 'Go and have another fag.'

Trinny raises her eyebrows and turns on her heel. 'You're the boss!' she laughs, already walking back the way she has come. 'Who am I to disagree?'

Just as she disappears from view, the door swings open and James' head appears.

'That was quick,' Rachel says, eyeing him suspiciously as she sits back down opposite him.

'It went to voicemail,' he replies wearily. 'But I left a message telling her that I was sorry and that I would make it up to her.'

'Well, I hope you did it with a bit more enthusiasm than that, but at least it's a start. So . . . where did you stay last night?' she asks, noting his dishevelled appearance.

'I booked into a hotel.'

'Why didn't you call Marco?'

'Too embarrassed, I guess,' he admits with a shrug.

'Well, you can't stay in a hotel indefinitely,' Rachel says. 'You can stay with me for a couple of nights but only if you do everything in your power to get Clare to take you back.'

'Really?' he says incredulously, perking up suddenly. 'God, that would be great. Thanks, Rach, you're a real pal.'

'A real mug more like,' she says grumpily, standing up. 'At least I'll be able to keep an eye on you.'

'So, I hear James is going to be staying with you,' says Marco, knocking on her office door and walking in without waiting.

'Yup,' Rachel replies distractedly, tapping away at her keyboard.

'How did that come about? I thought you were absolutely livid with him.'

'I am. But if he stays with me I can watch what he's up to and help him get Clare back.'

'And is that what he wants? He didn't seem so sure last time I spoke to him.'

'He's sure now,' she says, still tapping at the keys as she sends an e-mail. 'I gave him a good talking-to.'

Marco scowls. 'And how do you think Clare's going to feel when she hears James is living with you?'

Rachel shrugs. 'I don't suppose she'll care. And when James gets back with her he can tell her how much of a debt of gratitude she owes me.'

'Well, I don't think it's a good idea,' Marco says. 'Where will he sleep, for a start?'

'On the sofa bed, of course! Why don't you think it's a good idea?' Rachel says, looking up at Marco properly for the first time.

Marco scuffs his foot like a little boy. 'I dunno . . . it just seems a bit, well, weird. I think he should stay at my place instead.'

'But you've already got Dan. He's not going to want to

share with one of your reprobate mates who can't get himself together. Anyway, I could do with the company,' she says, turning back to her computer.

When Marco doesn't leave, Rachel looks up at him again, to find him looking at her peculiarly. 'What?' she cries, exasperated.

'Oh, nothing!' he snaps. 'Forget it!'

Rachel watches his retreating back as he stomps out of her office, and frowns. Either he was being possessive of her or he was being possessive of James – and she has no idea which.

That night, James travels home with her on the tube. 'So, how many times have you called her so far?' she demands bossily.

James looks up and pretends to count on his fingers. 'Er, one,' he says sheepishly. 'But I have left a message . . .'

'Big bloody deal. You'll need to show a lot more dedication than that. You need to call and leave a message for her at least ten times a day – for weeks, months if necessary,' she continues, mildly amused by the look of horror on his face. They sit in silence for a few moments.

'I don't think she's going to give me another chance,' he says gloomily as the tube train rattles through the tunnels. 'She told me enough times that she wouldn't.'

'Maybe not,' Rachel agrees. 'But you have got to do everything in your power to convince her. Maybe she will, maybe she won't – but at least you'll have done everything you could.'

The next morning, she takes him in a cup of tea to wake him up. She picks up his iPhone from the charger where it has been plugged in overnight and hands it to him. 'First call of the day,' she says. 'And you're to call her as soon as you wake up every single day from now on.'

James rubs his bleary eyes. 'Don't you think she'll find it pretty annoying me calling her this early?'

'Don't be ridiculous! She'll be up anyway and you have got to show her that she's on your mind all day, every day. Do it!' she orders as she leaves the room.

Rachel listens at the door while he makes the call. 'Hi, Clare, it's me,' she hears him say. 'Please call me back. I love you and I'm sorry for . . .' He pauses. 'For being pathetic. Anyway, call me. Love you.'

Outside the door, Rachel smiles to herself with satisfaction. How could Clare possibly resist when he sounded so sincere? She puts on some toast and wonders what would have happened if she hadn't got involved. He would probably have stayed away from her and she would have spent the rest of her pregnancy thinking he didn't care. Then she would have had the baby alone and it would have grown up without a dad and . . . Bloody hell, why does she always have to think about things so far ahead?

After work that day, Rachel manages to get away in time to join Marco and James for a drink. 'So, have you called her today?' she asks James as she sits down and takes off her jacket.

'Yup. Eight times – so far,' James replies proudly.

'That's my boy!' she laughs, toasting him with her white wine.

'Seems a bit ridiculous to me,' says Marco. 'If I were you I'd have stayed away from her.'

'Marco!' Rachel admonishes him. 'What a terrible thing to say.'

'Well, I'm only surprised it's not you saying it – after what she did to you.'

'It wasn't Clare's fault!' James and Rachel cry in unison.

Marco pulls a face. 'Whatever. But I still think you should come and stay with me, James. Dan won't mind you kipping on our sofa.'

'No – I'm better at Rachel's,' says James firmly. 'Not being rude or anything, Marco, but you don't bring me cups of tea in bed in the morning.'

Marco's cheeks redden instantly. He picks up his beer and drains it. 'Right, I'm off,' he says abruptly. 'Got an early start in the morning.'

'Jesus, what's up with him?' Rachel says, watching as Marco gives them a curt nod and leaves the pub.

'Dunno,' says James. 'He's like a bear with a sore head. Maybe he's jealous.'

'Jealous of what?'

'Me staying with you,' James replies casually. 'He seems very keen that I bunk down at his instead. He's very touchy where you're concerned.'

Now it is Rachel's turn to redden. 'Nah,' she says, noticing as she does so that her heart seems to be beating slightly faster. 'He's not interested in me like that and I'm not interested in him. We're just really good friends.'

'Uh huh,' laughs James, raising an eyebrow.

'Seriously!' she insists. 'I've known him such a long time and we don't think of each other in that way.'

'You might not think of him in that way but I wouldn't be so sure about how he feels . . .'

'Maybe it's you he's possessive of, rather than me?' Rachel grins, keen to move the conversation away from her. 'Have you considered that?'

'You're suggesting he's gay?' says James disbelievingly.

'No!' she laughs. 'I just mean that he's loved having you back – maybe he doesn't want to share you. Maybe that's why he was so narky about Clare – maybe he was jealous of her?'

James shakes his head. 'What is it with you women and your amateur psychology? He's probably just tired and grumpy and nothing more.'

Over the next couple of weeks, Rachel wakes James every day with tea in the morning, before travelling into work together. After a short break for Christmas, when they both head home to their respective parents, they settle back into the routine, with Rachel checking every day that he has made the calls to Clare. She doesn't just take his word for it either – she checks the recent calls list on his phone. True to his word, he was calling her ten times a day.

'I thought she'd have cracked by now,' Rachel mutters, scanning his phone one morning. 'It's been weeks.'

'Desperate to get rid of me, are you?' James laughs, rubbing his eyes. 'Seriously, Rach, I can always go and stay with Marco if I'm getting in your way.'

'No!' she insists, meaning it. The truth is she is loving having James there, even if they only ever see each other for a short while. It means she doesn't feel quite so empty when she comes home each evening.

'I knew she wouldn't have called me back by now,' he says solemnly. 'I'm not sure she'll ever trust me again.'

'She will!' Rachel assures him in a voice that sounds more confident than she feels. 'You just have to persevere. Show her you're serious. She'll come round eventually.'

Later that day Rachel goes to find Marco, who has been avoiding both her and James since that night in the pub.

'Hey!' she says brightly, poking her head around the corner of his office. 'Long time no see!'

'Oh, hi,' Marco mutters gruffly, looking up from the newspaper he is reading.

'Busy, are we?' she laughs, motioning towards the paper.

The corners of Marco's mouth turn upwards slightly.

'Ooh, careful, you nearly smiled there,' Rachel says, sitting down on his sofa. 'So, how're things?'

'Fine,' he shrugs. 'Not much to report. How about you? How's it going with you and James living together?'

'Marco!' Rachel cries indignantly. 'You make it sound like there's something going on between us. I barely see him, except when I check his phone to make sure he's called Clare every day.'

Marco smiles properly, finally. 'And has he?'

'Yup,' Rachel replies with a satisfied nod. 'Mind you, I'd have thought she'd have called him back by now. She's proving a tougher nut to crack than I thought.'

Marco looks away shiftily.

'What?' she demands. 'Why do you look so guilty?'

'Well . . .' he begins. 'It's just that I saw Toby for a drink the other night. I mentioned that James had moved in with you . . .'

Rachel feels an unwelcome fluttering in her stomach at the mention of Toby's name. 'And what did he say?' she asks carefully.

'Um, well, he seemed a bit shocked. I wonder if he might have got the wrong impression . . .'

'Oh, Marco!' she cries. 'Why did you have to tell him that? Now he'll tell Clare and she'll get the wrong impression too. Oh, you fucking idiot!' she storms, getting up and pacing around the office.

'Actually, I think that's out of order!' Marco shouts back. 'I explained that it was just until he had persuaded Clare to take him back. It's not my fault he didn't believe me. And you have to admit it looks a bit—'

'A bit what?' snaps Rachel, facing him, her hands on her hips.

'A bit suspicious!' he growls back. 'And I do think you seemed a bit bloody eager to get James to stay at yours instead of mine . . .'

'I WAS eager!' she shouts, aware that her voice is cracking. 'And so would you be if you had to come home to an empty flat every night, feeling so lonely and desperate that you wonder if it might be better to go to sleep and not wake up in the morning! So would you if you'd had your heart broken and been humiliated in the way I have in the past year. I just felt that by stopping Clare going through the same thing, it might help the way I feel about myself, which at the moment is more shit than you can possibly imagine. You have no right to question my motives, Marco. It's not fair!'

Marco looks at her in stunned silence. His mouth drops open to say something but no words come out and so he closes it again.

Rachel sits down on the sofa and starts to weep loudly into one of the cushions. Marco comes over and sits down beside her. He waits until she has calmed down slightly before he puts his arm around her shoulders and speaks. 'I'm sorry,' he says, giving her a squeeze. 'It's just . . . well, I was jealous.'

'Jealous of what?' she asks. 'Me taking James away from you?'

Marco's eyes soften and he laughs quietly. 'Er, no, not that!'

'Then what?' she asks, noticing as she looks at him how his dark eyes have almost turned black.

'I was jealous of James,' he says shyly. 'Staying with you.'

'Why?' sniffs Rachel.

'Oh, Rachel!' he laughs. 'I can't believe you don't know!'

She shakes her head and frowns. 'Know what?'

Marco takes Rachel's hand and looks at her searchingly. 'That I love you,' he says.

Clare

Toby and Anna's wedding is approaching fast. Clare is the only bridesmaid, with a stretchy, navy-blue dress that both flatters her and covers her bump at the same time. 'Just get me an enormous bouquet to hide it completely and I'll be good to go!' she laughed with Anna when she tried it on. Anna's dress is simple but stunning. Her mum and Clare had gone with her to buy it. Faced with a whole shop full of gorgeous creations, Clare wouldn't have known where to start but Anna, unusually for her, was absolutely certain about what she wanted.

They all rifled through the rails until Anna cried out: 'Here it is! This is the one!' pulling an ivory-coloured silk sheath from between a ghastly white meringue of a dress and a puffball-style peach monstrosity.

Cassie laughed. 'Shouldn't you try it on first, sweetheart?' she asked, raising her eyebrows.

Anna held the dress up against her body and looked down. 'Yes, yes, I'll try it on,' she said. 'But I know it's the right one.'

Cassie and Clare looked at each other and smiled. 'It's lovely to see her so happy,' said Clare as they perched on two velvet-covered chairs and waited for Anna to emerge from the changing room.

Cassie nodded. 'It is. I'm glad they managed to work it out. God knows what would have happened if they hadn't.'

Clare shuddered, not wanting to think about the bleak years that Toby and Anna had spent apart. 'She'd have been OK,' she said unconvincingly. 'She'd have met some rich banker and had lots of children.'

Cassie looked at Clare in surprise. 'No, we both know she wouldn't. We're both the same, Anna and me. We're like swans. We mate for life.'

Clare didn't say anything. Cassie's 'mate' had gone long ago, leaving her to bring up her two kids alone. 'Was it hard?' she asked. 'Doing it by yourself?'

Cassie looked at Clare's bump and bit her lip.

'Don't worry, you're not going to make me feel any worse. I'm expecting it to be hell,' Clare said quickly.

'Well,' said Cassie thoughtfully, 'I wouldn't describe it as hell. My children are my greatest achievement and I have absolutely no regrets. But even though Anna and Tim's dad left when they were still very young, he was at least there for the baby years. I wouldn't have wanted to go through that by myself. It's very hard, Clare, and you can feel quite lonely and isolated.'

'Luckily I've got Toby and Anna,' Clare reminded her.

Cassie nodded. 'Yes, and I know they'll look after you. But however good they are, there's nothing quite like having your partner to help you. He's the only other person in the world who totally understands that overwhelming feeling you get from a baby – in a good and bad way. Only the other parent will ever love that child as much as you.'

They sat in silence as Clare digested what Cassie had said. The truth was, she wanted James to be with her. But she had to prepare herself for the prospect of him not being able to cope and leaving her in the lurch yet again, repeating his feckless father's mistakes. She had built an emotional wall around her now that she wasn't sure anyone could ever get through again. Clare rubbed her bump affectionately. She felt as though she knew this baby so well already, maybe because she had come so close to not having it. She couldn't wait now to meet him or her properly and she knew exactly what Cassie meant about that overwhelming love a parent feels for their child.

A commotion in the changing room interrupted Clare's thoughts and Anna threw back the curtain and skipped into the room, twirling in her shimmering sheath. Cassie and Clare both gasped at the same time and Cassie burst into noisy sobs. 'Oh, sweetheart!' she gulped. 'You look so beautiful. That dress is perfect.'

Anna beamed. 'It is, isn't it? I knew it would be! What do you think, Clare?'

Clare raised her eyebrows and nodded to show that she liked it but she wasn't able to speak either. Anna looked so radiant that she felt choked – it had been such a long, hard road to get her here. Clare reached out and grasped Cassie's hand and they sat gazing at Anna as she spun around, looking at herself from every angle in the huge ornate mirror that almost covered one wall of the shop.

Clare stands on the tube, holding onto an overhead rail as the train lurches from side to side and hurtles through the tunnels, making her feel light-headed and queasy. All around her men occupy the seats, their heads buried in their free newspapers or their iPads, ostentatiously ignoring her pregnant belly so that they don't have to offer to let her sit down. In the past, she would have had no hesitation in demanding loudly that someone show some chivalry towards her but she is a different Clare now.

James' departure has knocked her confidence more than she could ever have imagined. She feels ugly, foolish and, most of all, scared. Toby and Anna are supportive and loving towards her but she knows that, in reality, she is on her own. Everyone had been happy to regale her with stories about how hard it would have been to be a single parent when they thought she was happily ensconced with James. Now, there is a deafening silence and a lot of sideways glances in her direction.

Her mother's reaction was the worst of all. Clare had avoided telling her for as long as possible but had had to tell her when she went to stay with her alone for Christmas. 'Well don't say I didn't warn you,' she said in a clipped tone. 'You should have gone through with the termination.'

'Wow, what a doting granny *you're* going to be!' replied Clare sarcastically.

Her mother didn't reply.

'I could really do with some support, you know, Mum,' Clare said, more softly this time.

'You mean financially? Listen, he might have run out on you but he'll have to bloody well pay for it. It's him you should be asking.'

Clare sighed. 'No, I didn't mean financially, actually. I meant emotionally. But clearly I'm looking in the wrong place. Forget it,' she said, bringing the subject to a close.

James has been calling her all day, every day, leaving message after message but Clare doesn't feel able to call him back. She knows she will need to deal with him once the baby is born, that's if he is bothered about having access to his child. But for now she needs to concentrate on herself and making sure she gets through her pregnancy in one piece. The changes to her body are becoming overwhelming. Her fingers and ankles are swollen and pink. The skin on her belly looks like it is straining to cover her growing bump and she has almost constant heartburn, causing her face to contort in pain.

In stark contrast to her own chaotic life, plans for Toby and Anna's wedding are well advanced now and there are only two months to go. They have booked the date for early April, just a couple of weeks before Clare's due date. They had offered to postpone it but Clare was insistent that they go ahead. 'We can't afford any more delays with you two!' she had said.

'But I want you to be my bridesmaid!' Anna had replied.

'I will be. Just make sure you get me a dress in stretchy material!' Clare had laughed, trying to share in her friend's happiness.

With only six weeks to go before her wedding, Anna takes Clare shopping for some much-needed baby stuff and to buy a few things for the big day. Clare had intended to get a flat on her own and try to manage by herself but luckily neither Anna nor Toby would hear of it. They were both determined to look after her as much as possible, to try to fill the void left by James. Rather than get on the tube and traipse around the city centre, Anna drives Clare's car to a big, out-of-town complex, where they can park easily and stop for regular coffee breaks whenever she needs to. At nearly seven months gone, she is starting to tire easily and the strain of the break-up with James is taking its toll on her mood.

'How are you feeling?' Anna asks her anxiously as they take their seats in a café, carefully distributing their shopping bags all around them.

'Like shit?' she laughs without mirth, concentrating as she carefully wedges her bump under the table.

'Well, at least there's not too long to go,' says Anna, pulling a sympathetic face as she pours out tea for both of them from a white china teapot.

Clare sighs loudly. 'No, I suppose not.' She takes a sip of her tea before she speaks again. 'In some ways I'm glad James isn't around to see me looking so awful.'

'You don't!' protests Anna indignantly. 'You look glowing.'

'Yeah, with sweat, which doesn't really count,' Clare pulls out her phone and glances at the screen.

'Any messages?' asks Anna, her voice hopeful.

Clare shakes her head. 'Nothing worth bothering about,' she says dismissively. 'Just the usual calls from James.'

Anna frowns back at her. 'The usual? You mean he's been calling you? I didn't know that.'

'He calls ten times a day, every day,' replies Clare matter-of-factly, pressing the delete button on her phone. 'I never listen to the messages, but they're always there.'

'Why didn't you tell me that?' Anna cries in disbelief. 'I had no idea. I thought there had been radio silence ever since you split up.'

'Well there has been – from my end,' says Clare wryly.

'Oh, Clare! Why won't you speak to him? Maybe you could work things out?'

'No way!' storms Clare furiously. She can't bear the

optimism in Anna's voice. 'He's let me down twice now – I'm not going to give him the chance to do it again.'

'But he's the father of your child. You're going to have to see him sometime.'

'He can see the baby once he's born. I just can't risk seeing him before or I might crumple.'

'Would that be such a bad thing?' Anna asks gently, still clearly shocked by the news that James has been calling her so often.

'As I said, he's done it to me twice now – he won't be getting another chance to hurt me.' Clare folds her arms defiantly over her bump as if to emphasize her point.

Anna sighs. 'Well, you seem pretty resolute . . .'

'I am,' says Clare, nodding.

Anna takes a deep breath. 'Well, I wasn't going to tell you this,' she begins awkwardly, looking embarrassed. 'But I don't want you to find out from anyone else . . .'

Clare scowls and leans as far forward as her bump will allow, resting her arms on the small table. 'Go on,' she says already knowing it will be something bad.

'Apparently James has moved in with Rachel. They've been living together for quite a while now.'

'What?' Clare gasps, her insides plummeting with shock. 'I don't believe it! And all this time he's been ringing me, leaving messages declaring his undying love and saying how sorry he is. Now I find out he's already moved on to the next one! God, that's unbelievable!' She feels a cloud of fury and hurt enveloping her and the tears threaten but stop short of falling.

'Did I do the right thing – telling you?' Anna asks, biting her lip nervously.

'Of course,' replies Clare crisply, still mentally reeling. For some reason she feels angry with Anna; she is confused, she doesn't know what to feel any more.

For the rest of the afternoon, they traipse miserably from shop to shop, buying bedding, Babygros, nappies and another five million different 'essentials'. When her phone beeps with yet another message from James, Clare looks at it in disgust and presses the delete button aggressively. 'Bloody two-faced bastard!' she spits furiously. Her heartburn has just got a million times worse.

Anna

As Anna and Clare arrive back at the flat, Toby is just coming in from a football match he has been to with Marco. 'How did you get on?' Anna asks, reaching up and kissing him as they shuffle into the hallway, their arms almost dropping off with the weight of the results of their shopping expedition.

'Good. But not as good as you I see,' he smiles, gesturing towards the piles of bags and reaching out to take some of them from Clare.

Anna begins to explain that she had no idea how much stuff babies need but Clare pushes past them and into her room, banging the door loudly behind her. Toby looks at Anna quizzically and, after depositing the rest of the shopping on the floor, she motions for him to follow her into the kitchen. 'I told her about James moving in with Rachel,' she whispers, nibbling nervously on her thumbnail. 'She hasn't taken it well.'

Toby rubs his face. 'Oh no . . .'

'Apparently he's been calling her all the time but she's refusing to speak to him. Now that she's found this out, there's no chance that they'll work it out.'

Toby looks shiftily in the direction of Clare's bedroom.

'Well, Marco told me today that James and Rachel's relationship is definitely platonic and is only "until James gets Clare back".'

'And do you believe that?'

Toby shrugs. 'I'm not sure.' He mooches towards the fridge and peers inside. 'Marco was acting really strangely though,' he continues, keeping his back to her. 'Kept going on about how great Rachel was, with this really stupid grin on his face. He's definitely got the hots for her.'

'And how do you—' Anna starts to say.

'I'm fine about it!' Toby barks, taking out a bottle of beer from the fridge. 'OK?'

'Well, you're clearly not fine about it!' Anna snaps back at him. 'Or you wouldn't be acting like this!' The distance across the kitchen seems cavernous as they stand looking at each other angrily.

'I'm not acting like anything!' he says irritably, before softening his tone slightly. 'Look, I'm with you, not Rachel, aren't I? So let's just forget about her . . .' He goes to the drawer and pulls out a bottle opener, before deftly removing the top.

'I'll forget about her when you do!' Anna hisses, unable to curb the anger that is inexplicably bubbling up inside her. 'I think it would be better if you didn't see Marco any more,' she continues. 'Every time you do, you come home acting differently towards me. He hates me and I think it rubs off on you.'

Toby takes a sip of his beer and shakes his head wearily. 'Anna, you don't own me. It's not up to you to decide who I can and can't be friends with.'

Anna's stomach tightens at Toby's tone. She takes a

deep breath and walks over to join him where he is leaning against the worktop, wanting to reduce the distance between them physically, if not emotionally. She doesn't want to row with Toby and it is so unlike her to feel this cross, but she is convinced that him seeing Marco is a bad idea. 'I'm sorry,' she says, grabbing the beer bottle off him and taking a sip. 'I just have the feeling that Marco would like nothing better than for me and you to break up, to get me back for what I did to Rachel.'

Toby blinks down at her. 'Men just aren't like that, Anna. Sure, Marco's loyal to Rachel, but he's also loyal to me and he knows how much I love you. Nothing can come between us, baby, so stop worrying. And get your own beer!' He pulls her towards his chest and wraps his arms around her. As she breathes in the smell of him that she loves so much, she prays that he is right and that they are indeed invincible.

Ella

The months pass by and Ella's life goes from bad to worse. She spends Christmas alone, unable to face anyone else's festive jollity and, true to his word, Jasper puts the house up for sale.

'You should bloody well fight it!' cries Monica angrily when Ella tells her. 'You were his wife! They wouldn't kick you out of your home.'

'I haven't got the energy,' Ella replies wearily.

'Are you OK, love?' Monica asks, her face creasing with concern. 'You haven't been yourself for a long while now. I know Max only died a few months ago but you seem to be getting worse, not better. And I hate to bring up the subject of work but you don't seem to be doing any writing either. The publishers have been understanding because of you losing Max but they're going to want the next book soon . . .'

Ella bites her lip, determined not to cry. She hasn't been able to bring herself to tell anyone what happened – not even Monica, even though she knows she would be supportive. She is too ashamed. They are sitting in a coffee bar in the heart of Piccadilly; Ella gazes out of the window at the people buzzing past, all with busy lives to lead, and feels, for about the millionth time, like she is looking in on the world from the outside. She just doesn't fit in and wonders if she ever will.

'Do you think you should talk to someone?' says Monica, cutting through Ella's thoughts.

Ella laughs bitterly. 'I've had more therapy than anyone else I know and it's done me fuck-all good. I'm a mess.'

'Maybe you're seeing the wrong therapist?' Monica suggests, taking a sip of cappuccino.

'I've seen so many and they're all the same,' says Ella gloomily.

Monica sighs and Ella wishes she could be more positive but she just isn't able to see any light through the blackness that seems to engulf her these days.

'You've got depression,' says Monica bluntly. 'It's nothing to be ashamed of, Ella. If you had tonsillitis you'd go to the doctor and get it treated. Depression is no different. Make an appointment today. There's no need to feel like this when you can do something about it.'

'You seem to know a lot about it,' Ella says flatly.

'I do. I've been there and I know how bad it feels. But, unlike you, I admitted I had a problem and got help.'

Ella looks at her agent in surprise. Monica always seemed so together and balanced. Ella suspects she is lying to make her feel better.

'It's true, Ella!' Monica insists, as if sensing what she was thinking.

Ella shrugs helplessly. She needs to see a doctor and quickly but not for the reasons Monica thinks. She has known almost since the night of the attack that she is pregnant but is unable to accept it, despite the numerous pregnancy tests she has done. Each time she perches on the edge of the bath, clutching the little white stick, praying that the result would be different this time. It is as if by blanking it out she could pretend it wasn't true.

Anna

It's a Sunday morning five weeks before their wedding and Anna and Toby are enjoying a long lie-in when the doorbell chimes loudly. Anna hauls her robe on and makes her way out into the hallway, squinting at the shadowy figure behind the opaque glass in the front door. She can't make out much except that it looks like a woman. She unhooks the chain and swings the door open, and finds herself face to face with Rachel.

'Oh!' Anna says, immediately conscious of her grubby dressing gown, greasy hair and unmade-up face. 'It's you.'

Rachel smiles nervously. She looks good. Her dark hair has grown to her shoulders and is glossy and thick. Her skin is glowing with good health and she is wearing a beautiful green vintage-style velvet coat that complements her complexion. 'I'm really sorry to disturb you . . . I thought you'd be up by now,' she stammers, looking embarrassed and flustered.

Anna pulls her robe more tightly around her and steps to one side. 'No, don't worry. We were just being lazy.' She stops abruptly as she realizes that Rachel won't want to hear about her and Toby in bed together. Come on in . . .' Anna frowns as she follows Rachel down the hallway, wondering what the hell she wants.

She is struck by how tall Rachel is; she towers over Anna in her bare feet. Even though they spent many years together, she still can't picture her and Toby as a couple. They look more like brother and sister. She leads her into the kitchen and automatically reaches for the kettle. 'Tea?' Anna asks her, pushing the hair back off her face. The atmosphere is strange and strained.

Rachel nods. 'Lovely, thanks. I'm actually here to see Clare. Is she in?' As she speaks, she glances around her, as if expecting Clare to materialize.

Anna nods. 'Yes, she's in her room. I'll go and get her in a minute. She's finding it very hard going, what with being so pregnant.' As she speaks, she watches Rachel's face carefully.

Rachel looks back at Anna evenly with unblinking eyes. 'I'm sure she is. It can't be easy doing it on her own.'

'Quite,' Anna agrees tartly. 'But she's taken the news about . . . well, about you and James quite badly. I'm not sure how she'll react towards you.'

'And what exactly is the news about me and James, Anna?'

Anna looks at her in surprise, taken aback by her acerbic tone. 'That you've moved in together. You *have* moved in together, haven't you?'

'Yes,' Rachel says calmly. 'But only until James gets Clare back. That's why I'm here. I wanted to explain to Clare that there's nothing going on.'

'Oh!' Anna feels foolish in the face of Rachel's calm maturity. 'OK, well I'll go and get—'

'Rachel!' exclaims Toby, interrupting Anna as he emerges into the kitchen, rubbing his hair sleepily. 'What are you doing here?'

'Hi, Tobes,' Rachel says shyly, making Anna's insides churn as she watches them both. 'I see you still look as crap in the mornings as ever.'

Toby laughs his acknowledgement and comes over to kiss her on the cheek. 'Unlike you,' he says. 'You always looked great and you still do.'

'Thanks,' Rachel smiles, her eyes shining up at him. Anna turns away quickly and busies herself making tea so that she doesn't have to watch them.

'So, how's the job going? I've heard good things about you – you won't forget it was me who gave you your big break when you're a squillionaire, will you?'

Toby laughs. 'How could I possibly forget?'

'And how're your mum and dad?'

'Great . . .' Toby trails off, as if remembering how well Rachel had got on with them.

'Send them my love,' Rachel says.

Anna drops the teaspoon with a clatter onto the stainless steel surface, hoping to interrupt their cosy conversation. Martha and Graham have been quick to accept Anna back into their family and they are always very welcoming towards her, but she has never been able to shake the feeling that they preferred Rachel, with her livelier personality and her brilliant career. Anna always feels like a bit of a failure in comparison.

'So,' Rachel says brightly, changing the subject quickly. 'Not long until the big day for you two.'

'Er, no,' Toby replies, sounding embarrassed.

'Listen, I'm fine about it,' she says firmly, looking from Toby to Anna. 'Really. So you don't need to feel awkward on my behalf.'

There is a long pause as Anna finishes making the tea and puts two mugs in front of Rachel and Toby.

'So, who's your best man?' Rachel asks, taking a sip.

There is another pause. 'Well,' Toby begins, 'I'd really like it to be Marco but . . .'

'But what?' Rachel asks, her eyes moving from Toby to Anna.

Toby looks down and says nothing.

'Toby feels that it would be a bit insensitive of him to ask Marco,' Anna speaks into the void. 'Seeing as he . . . well, he was already best man last time, when . . .' She stumbles over her words.

'When he didn't marry me?' Rachel says, her voice clear and unwavering.

Anna nods, her face flushing with shame.

'Well, we didn't get married, did we? So if you're holding back on my account, please don't. I'm sure Marco would love to be your best man, Tobes,' she says, and Anna feels a flash of irritation at her familiarity towards him.

'And you'd really be OK about it?' he asks earnestly.

'Uh huh,' she nods. 'More so now than ever,' she adds.

'What do you mean?' Toby frowns in confusion.

'I mean that Marco and I are together now. So he's happy, I'm happy and there's no need for you guys to feel any embarrassment. I'm pleased for you. Really, I am.'

Toby reaches across the table and takes her hand. 'Thanks, Rachel, that means so much,' he says.

Anna waits for him to drop Rachel's hand again and when he doesn't, she gets up and clears her throat, trying hard to keep her composure. 'Shall I go and get Clare then?' she says, more loudly than she intended.

They both look up at Anna in surprise, as if they'd

forgotten she was still there. 'Yes, why don't you?' says Rachel and Toby finally lets go of her hand.

Anna knocks on Clare's door.

Clare is in bed, lying on her side, staring into space.

'Clare,' Anna says quietly. 'You've got a visitor.'

Clare doesn't respond.

'It's Rachel.'

Clare rolls over so that she is facing away from Anna. 'Tell her to go away,' she says disconsolately. 'I don't want to see her.'

'No, Clare, you should see her,' Anna urges. 'I think we all got the wrong end of the stick about her and James . . .'

Clare lies still for a second, then rolls over again. 'Really?' she says cautiously.

'Yes, really. So come on, get your backside out of bed and come and talk to her.'

Clare groans with annoyance and hauls herself heavily out of bed, her pyjamas straining over her bump.

Anna registers the look of shock on Rachel's face as she and Clare walk back into the kitchen. 'Oh my God!' she half-laughs. 'Your bump is huge!'

'Tell me about it!' grimaces Clare.

'How are you feeling? My God, I just can't believe how . . . well, how pregnant you look!' Rachel babbles, staring at Clare's stomach.

Clare scowls. 'I'm not being funny, Rachel, but if you've just come round to gawp and comment on my size, I really could do without it.'

'Clare!' says Toby, looking embarrassed. 'Don't be so bloody rude.'

'No, honestly, it's fine,' laughs Rachel. 'I'm sorry, Clare. I think you look wonderful, it's just a shock, that's all.'

Clare shrugs irritably. 'OK, so why have you come round then?'

Toby, Clare and Anna all look at Rachel expectantly.

'Well,' Rachel says carefully, 'I'm mainly here because I heard that you were under the impression that I was living with James—'

'And are you?' demands Clare gruffly.

Anna glances at Toby to see him glaring in Clare's direction.

'Not exactly.' Rachel's voice is calm and measured. 'He is staying with me. But,' she adds, seeing the look on Clare's face, 'only until you two have sorted things out.'

'We'll never sort things out. I can't trust him any more,' says Clare flatly.

'I know it must be hard,' agrees Rachel, looking at Clare intently, 'but he is genuinely sorry and he wants you back. Surely you must know that from the messages he's been leaving you?'

Clare sticks her bottom lip out sulkily. 'I don't listen to them,' she says. 'I'm not letting him worm his way around me again.'

'But that's ridiculous!' Rachel's cheeks pinken as she speaks. 'It's the difference between doing this all by yourself or doing it with someone who loves you and wants to be with you.'

'If he wants to be with me he's got a funny way of showing it!' Clare shoots back. 'He'll be back and everything will be fine for a couple of weeks until the baby's born, then he'll get cold feet and do a runner again. I'm better off on my own – I don't need two babies to look after.'

Toby, Rachel and Anna look at her in helpless silence. Much as they all want her to get back with James, they also know that she might be right. None of them can guarantee that he won't leave her in the lurch again the minute the going gets tough.

'Look, Rachel, I appreciate you coming round,' says Clare, her tone more gentle now. 'But the only way I can get through this is to concentrate on the baby. I can't give him any room in my head. Do you understand?'

Rachel nods. 'I do. And I'm sorry. I just wanted to clear up any confusion.'

Watching Rachel carefully, Anna can see that her eyes keep lingering on Clare's bump and she can almost feel the desperation exuding from her. Anna can only imagine how unfair it must seem to her that Clare is pregnant and doesn't want to be.

'She's a really nice girl,' Anna says to Toby after they have said goodbye to Rachel.

'Yes, she is,' he replies. She watches him as he sits reading the papers and wonders what is going on in his mind. No matter how many times he has told her that he loves her, she is terrified that he will start to find her too clingy and needy, which she has to admit she is being at the moment. She feels so inadequate compared to Rachel, who is flying high in her glamorous career, while she is unlikely to ever progress from her lowly role as a primary school teacher.

'Stop it,' says Toby, without looking up.

'Stop what?'

'Thinking,' he says. 'It's dangerous.'

'You know me so well,' she laughs with relief, leaning over and kissing the top of his head.

Anna leaves Toby and goes to find Clare, who is on the phone to her mother. Anna lies down on the bed beside her and begins to leaf through a magazine while she talks.

Finally, Clare says her goodbyes and hangs up. 'Everything OK?' she asks, lowering herself down so that she is lying next to Anna.

'Uh huh. You?'

'Yeah – my mother doesn't even try to feign interest in my pregnancy. It's very strange. Regardless of what I thought, if I had a daughter, I'd make sure I was there for her, like your mum. My mum seems to take the view that I've made my bed and I can bloody well lie in it.'

Anna squeezes her hand and says nothing. She thinks about her own mum and how she is always there for her. She has been amazing helping her and Toby to organize the wedding, striking the tricky balance between being helpful and taking over completely. Anna knows that her mum would never, ever let her down and her heart constricts to think of Clare getting so little support at such a difficult time in her life.

'Anyway, what about Rachel turning up this morning, eh? Bit weird, wasn't it? To be sat there with Toby's ex-girlfriend, I mean,' Clare says, shaking herself slightly as she changes the subject.

'I know,' Anna agrees. 'And to make matters worse, she seems lovely. I mean, she didn't have to come round to explain the situation – it's no skin off her nose whether you and James get back together. She seemed to genuinely want to help.'

'Or to see Toby again?' Clare says, glancing slyly at her.

'Oh, don't!' Anna groans. 'I honestly don't think that was her motivation – I think she's OK now that she's with Marco.'

'Hmm . . . I bet Toby's not wild about that idea either. It's a bit close to home, isn't it?'

Anna doesn't reply. She is still trying to work out how she feels about it herself. Rachel being with Marco will mean a lifetime of being reminded that Toby came so close to marrying someone else and she will be a constant presence in Anna's life. Once again, Anna is struck by the irony that it is now Rachel who is the 'other woman' and she has to admit she doesn't like it much.

'So, now that you've cleared the air with Rachel, you can let yourself get excited about the wedding,' Clare interrupts Anna's thoughts. 'I think you've been holding back a bit.'

Anna nods. It's true; with Clare's awful situation and Rachel lurking in the background, feeding her guilty conscience, she hasn't felt able to behave like an excited bride-to-be. Or at least, she *thinks* that's why she's got such a feeling of foreboding about what lies ahead.

Ella

In the end, fate intervenes where Ella's courage fails her. She almost faints with relief as her body begins to reject the foetus. She thinks guiltily of all the other women who would despair at the same thing happening to them, but she can't feel anything except an overwhelming sense of release. This time she does call the doctor, who books her into the hospital.

Ella gathers up a few belongings in an overnight bag and hails a cab, feeling strangely calm as she settles herself on the back seat. The driver glances at her curiously in the mirror several times but she ignores him and gazes out of the window as the taxi lurches through the traffic. Finally, he is unable to help himself and nosiness gets the better of him. 'Visiting someone?' he asks in a strong cockney accent.

'No,' Ella replies as flatly as possible and turns away from him. He takes the hint and the journey progresses in blissful silence. As they pull up at the hospital, Ella pays the driver and steps out onto the kerb carefully, still reluctant to stand up straight and risk restarting the excruciating pains that have been crippling her all day.

'Is this cab free?' a voice behind her says and Ella turns her hunched frame around to find her face level with an enormous bump. 'Oh my God! Ella?' says the voice.

Wincing, Ella looks up to see who the owner of the bump is. Clare looks down at her in shock. 'Oh, hello, Clare,' Ella manages hoarsely.

'Are you OK?' Clare asks, looking at Ella with a concerned expression. 'You look terrible. What's happened?'

'Er, nothing,' stammers Ella. 'I'm fine.'

Clare frowns. 'You don't look fine. You look bloody awful. Let me help you into the hospital.'

Clare has never been one of Ella's favourite people. She dislikes her and knows that Clare can't stand her in return, so it feels strange to say the least when Clare hooks her arm through hers and leads her gently towards the reception area. They must make a comical-looking pair as they walk along, thinks Ella – Clare with her huge bump and Ella hunched over and shuffling.

When they arrive at reception, they stand awkwardly for a second as Ella wishes Clare would make her excuses and leave. She doesn't want Clare to hear what she is here for. 'Well, nice to see you,' Ella laughs an embarrassed laugh.

'I'm not leaving you like this, Ella,' says Clare briskly. 'Isn't there anyone with you?'

Ella shakes her head and bites her lip. 'No.'

'I was sorry to hear about your husband, Ella.' Clare looks down at her bump awkwardly.

'It's OK,' Ella says quickly. 'It's just a bit . . . difficult, at the moment.' They have reached the front of the queue. 'So, anyway, I'm fine. There's no need to hang around. Honestly. But thanks for your help!' Ella's voice is rising in panic with each word.

Clare hesitates before turning to go. 'OK, well, good luck,' she says quietly.

Ella smiles reassuringly and turns back to the receptionist. 'Hello, my name's Ella de Bourg,' she says as quietly as she can. 'I've had a miscarriage . . .'

The receptionist is kind and speaks in a gentle tone as she fills out Ella's paperwork. She feels like a fraud, knowing that she is glad that this has happened, instead of feeling bereft like most women in the same situation would feel.

She is given some forms to fill out and directed towards a line of chairs in a waiting room. As she sits down and focuses hard on the sheets of paper in her hand, Ella is aware of someone sitting down beside her. At first she ignores them, concentrating on what she is doing, until a beige-coloured plastic cup containing matching beige liquid is thrust under her nose.

'I brought you this,' says Clare. 'I've put sugar in it. I thought you might need it.'

Whether it is the stress of the situation finally hitting home or just someone being kind to her when she really doesn't feel like she deserves it, Ella doesn't know, but the floodgates open and she falls against Clare, weeping uncontrollably. Clare struggles to keep the tea she is clutching upright and leans forward to put it on the table in front of her before putting her arms around Ella and pulling her as close as her huge bump will allow. For the next ten minutes, she rocks Ella gently as she cries. The hospital staff, clearly used to this sort of distress, take little notice.

'If you want to talk about it, I'm happy to listen,' says Clare as Ella blows her nose and takes a deep, shuddery breath.

Ella looks at her. 'It's a long story,' she says glumly, her breath catching.

'Well, I'm not in a hurry,' says Clare with that brisk

manner that could be construed as being offhand but which Ella now knows to be the opposite.

When Ella doesn't say anything, Clare waits in silence for a while before patting her arm. 'Look, it's fine if you don't want to tell me,' she says.

'No!' retorts Ella quickly. 'No – it's not that I don't want to tell you. It's just that I don't know where to start. It's very complicated.'

'Well, why don't you work backwards?' Clare replies. 'I overheard why you're here. Is it . . . was it Max's baby?'

Ella shakes her head and swallows hard. 'No – Max died seven months ago now.'

Clare nods slightly. 'Of course. The day of the wedding . . . So where's your new partner? Why isn't he with you?'

'I don't have a new partner,' Ella says, feeling the hot tears forming behind her eyes once again.

Clare motions around her. 'How come you're here then?'

So Ella tells her. In a faltering voice, she tells her everything that has happened, making no attempt to make herself sound innocent in the whole sorry mess. She even tells Clare that she had been about to leave Max when he died because she was feeling trapped. She tells her how she had started to enjoy going out and flirting outrageously with other men, making up for all the fun she thought she had missed out on. Then she tells her about Charlie and what happened that awful night. To Ella's relief, Clare doesn't make any comment or start demanding that she must go to the police. She simply listens and nods. 'So that's why I'm here,' Ella finishes, glancing at Clare. 'And I feel so bad because I'm glad I lost the baby.'

When she stops speaking, Clare digests what Ella has told

her. 'You poor thing,' she says finally, taking Ella's hand and squeezing it. 'You poor girl.'

'I'm not a poor girl. I deserve everything I got,' Ella says miserably. 'And now Max's kids are selling the house from under my nose and I've got to get out. I think it's what's known as getting your comeuppance.'

Clare looks at her thoughtfully. 'I've been where you are, Ella,' she says quietly. 'I've wished that I would miscarry and felt all the guilt that you're feeling now. Yes, my circumstances are different but what happened wasn't your fault. You have to know that. And don't forget, I'm a lawyer. I deal with lots of women in your situation. If you want me to support you and get him arrested, I will.'

Ella shrugs helplessly. 'I just want it all to go away,' she replies.

Clare nods again and Ella feels a surge of relief. 'You've had a very tough time. I completely understand why you wouldn't want to relive it all.'

They sit for a few moments in companionable silence. 'So, what about you?' Ella asks, looking at Clare's bump. 'You must be due fairly soon.'

'Not as soon as I'd like!' laughs Clare. 'Still got almost eight weeks to go.'

Ella tries not to look surprised but fails miserably.

'I know, I know,' says Clare. 'I'm huge.'

'So, where's your partner?' says Ella, feeling comfortable enough now to be nosy.

Clare sighs. 'Oh God. My "partner",' she raises her fingers to indicate inverted commas, 'did a runner when it was too late. So I'm going to be a single mum and I'm absolutely terrified.'

'Haven't you got any support?' asks Ella, imagining how awful it must be to find yourself in that situation, knowing it could so easily have been her.

'Oh, yes. I've got Toby and Anna. They've been amazing,' says Clare, rubbing her bump affectionately.

'And . . . how are they? Toby and Anna?' Ella can feel herself reddening as she asks the question.

'They're so happy. They're getting married in a few weeks' time. I'm surprised you haven't heard through Toby's parents.'

'I might have done,' says Ella, her heart still skipping at the mention of Toby's name. She does have a vague recollection of her mother leaving a few messages on her answerphone. She has been so caught up in what was happening to her that she hasn't been able to face calling her back. 'God, I bet Anna still hates my guts – and who could blame her?'

Clare looks at Ella closely. 'I don't think Anna hates you any more. We were all young and stupid back then. She's really happy with Toby now, and being the sort of person she is, she would probably feel nothing but sympathy for you, if she knew what had happened.'

'You won't tell her – or Toby – what I've told you, will you?' Ella asks in alarm.

'No! No, of course I won't,' says Clare soothingly. 'I'm just saying that Anna isn't the sort of person to hold a grudge for all these years.'

'Who could blame her if she did? I fucked up her life,' Ella replies glumly.

'Ella, you need help,' says Clare. 'There are always reasons for the way we are. And while I absolutely hated your guts for what you did, even I can see that you've been damaged. Funnily enough, we're quite similar in that respect.'

'So why are you Miss Popularity and I'm Public Enemy Number One?' Ella asks with a smile.

Clare laughs. 'Well, because we respond to these things in different ways, I guess. Anyway, you should get help.'

'Ella de Bourg!' calls a nurse and Ella stands up. 'I'd better go,' she says, picking up her overnight bag.

'Well, I hope it works out OK for you,' says Clare.

'Thanks,' says Ella, already turning to go down the corridor. 'You too.'

Clare

Meeting Ella at the hospital has shaken Clare up more than she realized. She can't stop thinking about her and the awful situation she is in, and for the first time, Clare understands how lucky she is. Yes, she is going to have a baby on her own but she has a lot of love and support. Toby and Anna have been so good. They have nurtured and looked after her as if they were her parents – cooking, cleaning and helping her to prepare for the birth. Anna has come to antenatal appointments with her, while Toby has quietly sorted out the cot, the changing station and the buggy, as well as repainting her room to prepare for the new arrival. They seem more excited than she is. Even James – who still continues to leave messages every day – has started sending regular cheques 'to help buy anything you might need for the baby'.

'Do I detect a softening on your part?' asks Anna one morning after Clare has opened another note and cheque from him.

'What makes you say that?' says Clare carefully, playing for time. She folds the note and puts it back in the envelope.

'Oh I don't know . . . maybe the dopey smile on your face?' grins Anna mischievously.

Clare laughs. She has to admit that James has surprised

her. She had fully expected him to keep calling for a while, then get fed up and move on when she didn't respond. The fact that he has persisted and is now being thoughtful enough to send money too has impressed her. Clare suspects he is being guided by Rachel, but even so, she is starting to realize that he is serious about winning her back. The trouble is, the longer she goes without seeing him, the harder it gets. She feels fat and ugly. Her face and body have changed so much that Clare is worried that if he saw her now, he would be put off again. If he even recognized her.

'I bet he'd think you look beautiful,' says Anna when Clare tells her of her fears. 'I certainly do.'

But Clare isn't so sure. Her confidence has been knocked badly by his departure. So even though she misses him, she decides to go through with her plan not to see him until after the baby is born. That way she figures she will really test how genuine he is – if he can cope with a screaming baby and no sleep, she will know he is serious. Clare still can't shake the suspicion that faced with the reality, he'd panic and do another runner.

Hi,

Yes, me again. Go on, admit it, you're pleased to hear from me. I bet you waddle to the front door every morning in the hope of spotting my crappy handwriting. Did I say 'waddle'? Sorry, I meant glide. I love you and miss you. Isn't it about time you returned at least one of my calls? We must be into five figures by now. Spend the money on a phone call. RSVP!!!!

Jx

Clare lies on her bed and rereads the note James has sent her this morning. It is short but sweet.

She grins to herself and holds the note against her bump. He enclosed a cheque for £50 which she has put with all the others, uncashed. She doesn't know why but she doesn't want to spend the money he is sending – as if she is trying to prove that she doesn't need his help. But as she lies there thinking about him, she feels a twinge deep down in her stomach, a physical manifestation of the yearning she feels for him.

At that moment, Ella pops into Clare's mind. She has thought about her so much since the day she ran into her at the hospital. Having spent years hating her with a passion, when Clare saw how badly Ella's life had disintegrated, it was impossible to feel anything other than sympathy for her. Without an address, she can't contact her but she would like to get in touch, just to see if she is coping. She can hear Anna clattering about in the kitchen and goes out to see her.

'You don't have an address for Ella, do you?' she says quickly.

Anna frowns. 'Ella de Bourg? Blimey, where did that come from? No, I haven't got an address.' She pauses. 'But Toby could probably get one from his parents. Why do you want it? I thought you hated her.'

The wooden chair scrapes on the floor as Clare pulls it out and sits down heavily. 'No. I did hate her,' she begins, marvelling at how out of breath she feels. 'But did I tell you that I ran into her at the hospital when I went for my scan the other day?'

Anna drops the dishcloth she is holding and spins round, agog. 'No! What was she doing at the hospital?'

'She was pregnant,' Clare says quietly. Ella had specifically asked Clare not to tell Toby and Anna what Ella had told her, so she doesn't want to give too many details.

Anna nods knowingly. 'Oh, I see,' she says, turning back towards the sink.

'She had a miscarriage,' says Clare, aware that Anna was thinking Ella had had a termination.

'Oh, poor thing!' Anna's tone softens immediately. 'Who was the father? Her husband's been dead quite a while now.'

'I'm not sure,' says Clare, again not wanting to give too much away. 'But I don't think they were serious. She seemed in a bit of a bad way though. I felt sorry for her.'

'God, she must have been bad to make you feel sorry for her,' Anna says, sitting down opposite Clare.

'I was thinking of getting in touch with her,' says Clare, twiddling with a napkin that was lying on the table. 'Just to see if she's OK. I was also wondering if maybe I should call James . . .' she begins hesitantly.

'Oh, yes!' cries Anna, clasping Clare's hands in hers. 'Do, Clare, please. Life's too bloody short.'

Clare feels herself flush. 'I'm still not seeing him though!' she insists.

Anna nods. 'Yes, well, if that's what you want, fine. But you should definitely call him. Do it now!' she urges.

'God, you are so bossy sometimes!' laughs Clare, relieved to have voiced what she was thinking.

She almost runs back into her room and scoops up her phone before she can think about it for too long. Her hands are shaking as she searches through the address book for his name. She pauses for a long time before taking a deep breath and pressing 'call'. She listens nervously as his phone rings. 'Please answer,' she whispers to herself. 'Please pick up.'

After five rings, she is about to hang up when James' voice booms out: 'Hallelujah! She called! She finally called! About bloody time!'

Clare squeals with laughter and leans back against her pillows. It was so good to speak to him again. 'Are you drunk?' she laughs.

'Yes!' he shouts. 'Drunk on love! Can I come round and see you? I've missed you so much . . .'

'Whoa!' Clare shouts back. 'Hold your horses! No, you can't come round and see me.'

'Oh, Clare!' he groans. 'Don't do this! Please let me see you. I'm desperate.'

Clare feels a little tingle of excitement at the prospect of seeing him but she shakes her head firmly. 'No, we can talk on the phone, but I don't want to see you just yet.'

'But why?' He sounds dumbfounded.

'Just because,' she manages. 'I'll see you when I'm ready but it's too soon. Seriously, James, let's just take it very slowly. Tell me all about what you've been up to.'

'No!' he says gruffly, but she can tell by his voice that he is smiling. 'You go first. I want to know all about you and the bump. How's he doing?'

'It could be a girl!' Clare protests indignantly, even though she has a feeling it's a boy too. She has been offered the chance to find out the sex but wants it to be a surprise.

'It's not a girl, I just know it's not,' he replies firmly.

Clare laughs and they start to chat. Just like that, they pick up where they left off all those months ago. They talk about work, about the baby, how she is feeling and finally they talk about why he ran out like he did.

'God knows what I was thinking,' he sighs. 'I'm so sorry, Clare. I'm a prat.'

'You are,' she agrees.

'I know it's going to be hard for you to trust me again. But I promise you I'll never do it again.'

Clare shakes her head, even though James can't see her. 'You don't know that for sure, so don't go making empty promises.'

'I'm not!' he replies hotly. 'Honestly, Clare. If I could turn back the clock, I would.'

'I know that,' she concedes, more softly this time. 'But, James, if it freaked you out having to go and buy a few Babygros, how the hell are you going to cope with sleepless nights, a screaming baby and me looking like a deranged ape?'

James laughs. 'You make it sound so appealing!'

'But that's the point!' Clare says, trying to keep her voice serious. 'It's important that you don't just think about the romantic side of having a baby. Most of the time it'll be bloody hard work and we're going to have to really pull together. I can't be worrying about whether you're going to get bored and do a bunk again. I'll have to give the baby my full attention. And so will you.'

'Does that mean . . .?' he says, sounding excited.

Clare sighs and examines her nails which, she notes distractedly, have grown so much stronger during the pregnancy. 'It means that I'm thinking of giving you another chance.'

'Oh, Clare!' he cries. 'I won't let you down. I won't!'

'BUT,' she cuts in firmly, 'I don't want to see you until the baby's born.'

'But that's ridiculous!' he fumes. 'I could help you—'

'You can help me by staying away. I feel like shit and I don't want you to see me like this. But we can talk on the phone and obviously I'll let you know when I've had the baby.'

'And what then?' he asks sulkily. 'What if you decide you still don't want to see me then?'

Clare smiles. 'Believe me. I'll want to see you. I know it's a bit weird, James, but this is how I want to do it. It's the only way I think I can cope.'

There is a pause, followed by another sigh. 'OK, if that's how you want it to be . . .'

'It is,' Clare says firmly, smiling properly for the first time in months.

Rachel

Going to see Clare to explain why James was living with her wasn't the only reason Rachel had wanted to go round to her flat. She needed to see Toby again, to be absolutely sure that she wasn't still hung up on him. She was happy with Marco – he had made her smile again and she thought she loved him, but she knew that she couldn't be completely sure until she had seen Toby again.

When Anna opened the front door in her old towelling dressing gown, instead of feeling gleeful, Rachel's heart sank. She was so petite and fresh-faced. Even with no make-up and her hair unbrushed, she managed to look so flawless. Her hair was shiny and her skin looked pink and dewy. Beside her, Rachel felt like a lump, especially when she looked down at Anna's perfect, tiny feet, her toenails painted a pretty baby pink, in stark contrast with her own slightly deformed size eights. Rachel inwardly thanked the Lord that she had made an effort to look as good as possible as she made her way down the hallway and waited, her heart hammering against her chest, for Toby to appear.

When he did, Rachel's heart skipped and she waited for that overwhelming feeling that always overcame her at the sight of him. But although he was beaming at her, all she felt was a pleasurable delight at seeing someone she liked very much. Nothing more. She almost danced out of the flat, she was so relieved. Finally, she was over him.

She headed straight round to Marco's flat before going home. It was a Sunday morning so he too answered the door in his robe. His face lit up when he saw her. 'Well, hello!' he grinned, running his hand through his messy crop of dark hair. 'To what do I owe the pleasure?' He stood off to one side and gave her a small bow, to salute her into the hallway.

Rachel made her way in, then turned and wrapped her arms around his neck. 'Have I ever told you that I love you?' she asked, looking into his dark eyes, which flickered with confusion.

'Er, no. I'm not sure you have,' Marco replied cautiously.

Rachel kissed him on the lips. 'Well, I do!' she giggled, feeling giddy with relief, happiness and love. 'I love you, Marco!'

Marco frowned. 'Well, I love you too. But how come . . .?'

Rachel put her finger over his lips and shushed him. 'I just do.'

Later, they went for a walk in Hyde Park. The sun was shining, the sky was a powdery blue and it was one of those perfect early spring days. Daffodils were everywhere and the light reflecting off the water looked like a thousand dancing diamonds. 'I think this might be the best day of my life,' she told Marco as they ambled along, hand in hand.

He looked at her quizzically but didn't say anything, squeezing her hand tightly instead.

'I went to see Clare this morning,' Rachel said after a short pause.

'Uh huh . . .'

'To explain about James staying with me.'

Marco nodded and they carried on walking in a companionable silence for a bit longer. After a while they came to the water's edge, where they stopped and look down into the muddy depths. 'I saw Toby too,' Rachel said at last.

'Ah ha! Now I get it,' laughed Marco. 'That explains the weird behaviour.'

Rachel thumped him playfully on the arm. 'But seriously, Marco, it's helped me so much. Before today I wondered if I would ever get over him or whether he'd always be there in the background – the one that got away. Do you know what I mean?'

Marco met her eye. 'I wondered that too.'

'Well, it was nice to see him. But that's all it was – nice. It made me realize that what I've got with you is special. You're my best friend. When I'm not with you I miss you. It was different with Toby. We were never really friends – we dived straight into a relationship. Well, I suppose I probably forced him into one and he went along with it because he was on the rebound from Anna.'

'But you're still on the rebound from Toby . . .' Marco began, looking into the distance.

'I was, Marco. But not any more. That's what today's shown me. I can be happy for him and Anna because I'm happy – with you.' Suddenly Rachel felt shy and she could tell that she was blushing.

Marco put his arms around her and hugged her tightly. 'I'm happy with you too,' he said. 'But I know you don't feel a physical attraction for me the way you did for Toby. And there's not a lot I can do about that.'

Rachel looked at him in surprise. 'What makes you think that?'

'Well, we haven't . . . you know . . . yet. Which makes me think you don't want to.'

Rachel took his hand in hers and looked down at it. She had never noticed before how beautiful his fingers were. 'You know, being able to make someone laugh is the biggest aphrodisiac of all,' she said. 'And you make me laugh – a lot.'

'Which means?' he asked teasingly, his dark eyes twinkling.

'Which means that I think we should go home right now and see if the old adage holds true . . .'

Marco threw his head back and laughed loudly. 'Thank you, God! Thank you, Toby!' he yelled, scooping her up and swinging her around. 'Well come on then! What are we waiting for?'

The final weeks leading up to Anna and Toby's wedding should be a traumatic time for Rachel but instead she is the happiest she has ever been. Being with Marco truly makes her feel as though she has found her other half. Instead of worrying whether he is still yearning for some other, lost love like she did for most of her life with Toby, Marco leaves her in no doubt that she is his number one. He has restored her confidence and made her feel like the most beautiful girl in the world. Unlike Toby, who rarely told her that he loved her, Marco says it at least two or three times a day.

And she has found herself falling more and more deeply in love with him. He is so clever, funny and interesting that she never tires of his company. Soon they are spending every spare minute together and he stays over at her flat most nights, along with James, who is still squatting on the sofa bed.

'Why won't Clare let him move back in with her?' hisses Marco one evening as he and Rachel are lying in bed. 'It seems really daft.'

Rachel shrugs. Having seen her, she understands why Clare might not want James with her. On the phone she can be her usual witty, sparky self, but in person she is struggling physically. Rachel has to admit she was shocked by the size of Clare's bump and at the back of her mind she does wonder if it might freak James out, the way it had when he walked out on her before.

'Maybe it's for the best,' she whispers. 'I don't want anything to jeopardize them getting back together once the baby's born.'

'He's such a prat for leaving her,' says Marco.

'I think he knows that now,' Rachel says ruefully. 'If he could turn back the clock, he would. But at least he's won her back.'

'Thanks to you,' says Marco, squeezing her shoulder and kissing her cheek. 'She really owes you. They both do.'

'I know,' Rachel agrees. 'I just couldn't bear the thought of them being apart when there was a baby caught in the middle – and they are right for each other, I know they are.'

'Are you still jealous of her?' asks Marco after a long pause.

Rachel tenses. She had forgotten that in one of her lower moments she had confessed to him how desperately she wanted a baby and how much she envied Clare being pregnant. She wonders how he would react if she told him the truth.

'I'm not sure,' she replies, playing for time.

'Liar!' laughs Marco. 'I know you're still desperate for a baby, you don't have to pretend with me.'

Rachel exhales loudly and feels all the tension drain out of her body. Life with Marco just gets better and better. 'And my rampant baby hunger doesn't make you run for the hills screaming?' she teases, feeling like she knows the answer already.

'Yeah, it does actually, now I come to think of it,' he jokes, climbing out of bed and hauling on his jeans. 'I'll see myself out!'

Rachel laughs loudly and gazes up at him, feeling happier than she ever imagined possible. 'Thank you, Marco,' she grins.

'What for?' he asks, rolling back onto the bed and swinging his legs up onto the mattress.

Rachel strokes his forehead for a few seconds before answering. 'For bringing me back to life,' she says, laying her head on his chest.

The next morning, she wakes up early and looks over at Marco. 'What's wrong?' she asks, seeing that he is lying with his eyes open gazing at the ceiling.

He rolls onto his side and rests his head on his hand. 'I want to ask you something,' he says, looking at her intently. 'Something important.'

Oh God, thinks Rachel, *he's going to ask me to marry him*. Ever since her aborted wedding to Toby, she has resolved never to get married. 'Listen, Marco, if you're going to ask me what I think you're going to ask me, you should know that I could never, ever walk into a church again, or stand at an altar waiting for the groom to turn up. I am never getting married. Even to someone I love as much as I love you.'

Marco's eyes crinkle with amusement, and to Rachel's relief he doesn't look upset. 'No, that wasn't what I was going to ask you,' he grins.

'Oh,' she says, feeling deflated and slightly embarrassed at her speech. 'Well, what was it then?'

'Well, I wondered . . .' He hesitates and coughs slightly.

'Yes?' she prompts, wondering what the hell he is on about.

'I wondered if we should think about having a baby?'

Rachel gasps and claps her hand over her mouth. 'Oh my God!' she whispers. 'That is such a big decision.'

'I know,' Marco agrees, lying back down and cupping his hands behind his head. 'Much bigger than deciding to get married.'

Rachel doesn't say anything. In some ways this is the answer to her prayers but in reality, she and Marco are taking things so quickly that she needs time to think it through properly.

'Why don't you have a think about it?' says Marco gently, reading her thoughts. 'There's no rush – I'm not going anywhere. You're the only one I want to be with.'

'I do need some time,' Rachel admits. 'Not because I have any doubts about you – I don't. But just because . . . well, it's huge.'

'I know,' Marco says, taking her hand and rubbing his thumb gently over her palm, tickling it.

Rachel needs to talk to someone and the only person she knows she can rely on for total honesty is Becs. She calls her later that day from work. 'Can you meet me for lunch?' she asks as soon as Becs answers.

'Oh, hello, Rachel, nice to talk to you too. How have you been? Yes? Well, I'm great too, thanks for asking!' Becs waffles sarcastically.

'Yeah, sorry I've been a bit bad about keeping in touch,' says Rachel sheepishly. 'Work's been mad busy and—'

'And you and Marco have been mad busy too? And I'm not talking about work!'

Rachel laughs. Her sister is the bluntest person she knows. She was definitely the best person to speak to about Marco's proposal. They arrange to meet at a pizza place near Rachel's office. 'You're paying,' adds Becs before hanging up.

As usual, Rachel is there first. Becs dashes in several minutes later, flushed and out of breath, and flings herself into the chair opposite Rachel. 'I need wine!' she demands. 'Sorry I'm late, by the way. Tubes.'

Rachel smiles. They both know that even with no traffic on the roads and a chauffeur-driven limo, Becs would still be late.

'So, what's on your mind?' Becs asks, having secured her glass of red wine and taken several large gulps. 'Let me guess – Marco?'

Rachel nods and flushes. 'Look, Becs, I want to be absolutely sure that you're not put out by me being with him? I know you and he . . . well, you saw each other for a while.'

'Hardly!' laughs Becs. 'We spent the whole time talking about you and we never slept together. Didn't even kiss. It was obvious he was crazy about you, as I think I told you several times.'

'You did,' Rachel agrees. 'It took me by surprise. Falling for him, I mean.'

'Don't know why – he's so much more suited to you than Toby ever was.'

'Do you really think so?' Rachel can't help asking. 'What makes you say that?'

'Because you have the same sense of humour, he worships the ground you walk on and you know each other inside out. He's just about perfect for you. Honestly, Rach,' she continues, 'I love Marco to bits but he's not my type. And anyway, I've met someone myself!'

'Oh, Becs! That's fantastic! Tell me all about him.'

Without needing any encouragement, Becs starts to tell Rachel about her new boyfriend. He works in computers, is stinking rich and more importantly, she adds quickly, is a 'right laugh'. Rachel is thrilled for her little sister and can tell that she is genuinely smitten, as she talks on and on about his numerous qualities.

'He sounds great,' Rachel tells her, meaning it.

'So, what's on your mind?' Becs asks at last, draining her glass and motioning to the waiter for another.

'Marco's asked me if I want to have a baby with him,' Rachel blurts, unsure how to word it any more subtly.

Becs' mouth drops open. 'You're kidding!' she gasps.

Rachel shakes her head. 'Nope, deadly serious.'

'Wow.' For once Becs is lost for words.

They sit in silence for a while as their minds whir. 'The thing is,' Rachel begins, 'I'm so desperate for a baby . . .'

'So, what's the problem then?' Becs tears off a bit of bread and stuffs it into her mouth.

'I'm not sure if I'm diving into everything too quickly with Marco. We've only been together for a couple of months – isn't that a bit soon to be taking such a massive step?'

Becs chews on another piece of bread and shrugs. 'Not being rude or anything . . .' she begins.

Rachel laughs, knowing she is about to be just that.

'But you're not getting any younger. Sure, you could wait a bit longer but what difference would it make? You were with Toby for years and look where that got you. When you know, you know. So, the question you should be asking yourself is: do you know?'

A little thrill shoots through Rachel's body and she smiles at Becs. 'Yes, I know.'

'Then what are you waiting for?' Becs smiles back.

Rachel goes to find Marco the moment she gets back from lunch. 'Hey, gorgeous!' he smiles, shutting his office door and kissing her. 'What have you been doing?'

Rachel puts her arms around his neck and kisses him back. 'I've been wasting time, that's what I've been doing,' she says. 'But not any more. Can you get off work early tonight?'

Marco frowns as he thinks. 'Er, yes, I think so. Why, what are we doing?'

Rachel laughs as she speaks, feeling high with excitement. 'We're making a baby,' she says.

Anna

As the big day approaches, both Toby and Anna become more and more tense. They decide not to have a stag or hen weekend; in Anna's case, it's because Clare is in no fit state to accompany her anywhere and she doesn't want to do it if she isn't there. In Toby's case, he thought it would be insensitive as Marco is the best man and he doesn't want to 'rub Rachel's nose in it' as he put it.

Anna doesn't say anything but she is still not happy about Marco being the best man. She wishes that Toby had chosen someone else but even she can't think who that someone else might be. Even though Rachel has behaved with incredible dignity, Anna is still wary of her. She dreads her being at the church because she feels that she won't be able to enjoy her own wedding, knowing that many of the guests will also have been present at Rachel's non-wedding to Toby. She cringes on behalf of Toby's parents, who liked Rachel and were disgusted with him for what he did to her.

In the end, Rachel solves the problem by ringing Toby and telling him she won't be coming to the wedding. Anna overhears him on the phone to her and feels a wave of annoyance and jealousy when he starts pleading with her to change her mind. 'We'd really love you to be there,' he tells her.

Anna listens in and snorts to herself angrily. She thinks it will be a bloody good thing if she isn't there – why is he begging her to come? It would ruin the whole day.

'What's your problem?' demands Toby furiously after hanging up. 'Why were you getting so ratty when I was on the phone?'

'I wasn't,' she replies unconvincingly. 'Well, OK I was. But, for Christ's sake, Toby, it's much better if she stays away. She'll only ruin my day.'

'What – a bit like you ruined hers?' he shoots back, realizing as soon as he speaks that it is the wrong thing to say.

'Excuse me!' Anna storms back. 'I think you'll find *you* ruined her day just as much as I did!'

Toby reddens instantly. 'I'm sorry,' he stutters. 'It's just that she's a really lovely girl and . . .'

'If she's so lovely, why didn't you go ahead and marry her then?' Anna snaps, aware as she does so that she sounds like a sulky child.

Toby's face darkens with anger and she can tell he is struggling to keep his temper. Eventually he rubs his face and sighs. 'Yes, sometimes I wonder that myself.'

Anna gasps in shock. 'Toby! How could you say something like that?'

'Because you're driving me bloody mad, that's why!' he hisses, getting up and slamming out of the room.

Anna sits in stunned silence on the sofa. What is happening to them? Is she behaving badly? Is it her fault? She can't tell. Everything seems to be crowding in on them now that the wedding is getting so close. *Damn Rachel!* she thinks bitterly, knowing as she does that the only person who really can't be blamed for any of the problems Toby and she are having is Rachel. She has behaved incredibly well and even Anna has to admit she is a lovely person. She wants to hate her, to give her something to latch onto but it is impossible – there is simply nothing to hate.

Anna calls Clare on her mobile. She answers after a couple of rings. 'Hello?' she puffs, sounding out of breath.

'There was a time when I'd have assumed I'd interrupted a bout of energetic sex, hearing you answer the phone like that!' she laughs.

Clare harrumphs. 'Pah! Chance'd be a fine thing. The last time I had sex was when I got myself into this state in the first place!'

'I think you'll find it's physically impossible to "get yourself" into that state,' Anna corrects her and she laughs back. 'Where are you?'

'Er, I'm with an old friend,' Clare replies, sounding cagey.

'Really? Who?' Anna demands, wondering who she could possibly mean. She is the only one of Clare's friends who could be described as an old friend.

Clare clears her throat and for a minute Anna wonders if she is actually going to answer her. Finally, she speaks. 'Ella,' she says quietly.

'Ella who?' Anna asks, before realization dawns. 'Not Ella de Bourg?'

'Yes.' Clare drops her voice to a hushed whisper. 'Remember I told you she'd been having a bit of a bad time recently?'

Anna frowns, wracking her brains. To her shame, she has been so wrapped up in her and Clare's issues that she didn't really take in what Clare told her about Ella. Finally, she remembers. 'Oh, yes, didn't she have a miscarriage?' she recalls.

'Er, yes,' says Clare, still speaking in hushed tones. 'Anyway, I've seen her a few times since. She really needs some support.'

Anna feels a little prickle of unease. Something doesn't add up. Clare hated Ella and regardless of whether she suffered a miscarriage, Anna still can't understand why Clare would suddenly decide to be Ella's best buddy, having held such a grudge against her for all these years. If Anna's honest, she is also jealous that Clare might be striking up a friendship with someone else, especially when that someone else caused her such trauma. She shakes her head crossly, wondering what has come over her lately. Jealousy seems to be her stock emotion at the moment. 'Oh, OK,' she says glumly. 'Well, I'd better leave you to it then.'

'Did you call for anything in particular?' asks Clare.

'No, nothing important. Forget it,' she answers, her tone slightly piqued. 'I'll see you later.'

As Anna hangs up, her spirits slump further. Everything seems to be going wrong all of a sudden. She is getting married in a week's time to the man she loves and yet she has never felt more miserable in her life.

Ella

As Ella lets Clare out of the house, she marvels at the different directions life could take. If someone had told her even six months ago that Clare would turn out to be one of her most cherished friends, she would have laughed. Clare had never bothered to hide how much she hated Ella. But since their encounter at the hospital, she has been amazing. Despite her own, not inconsiderable problems, Clare has tracked Ella down and been persistent in keeping in touch with her, helping her to keep going, when all she wanted to do was end it all.

The first time Clare turned up at the house, Ella didn't want to let her in, worried that she would use Ella's vulnerability to get her revenge for what Ella had done to Anna. But Clare has never been a girl to take no for an answer and she seemed to know instinctively how bad Ella was feeling. At first, they just drank tea and made stilted conversation, punctuated by long, yet strangely comfortable silences. Gradually, however, Ella found herself opening up to Clare in a way that she hadn't been able to open up to anyone before, even her numerous therapists.

Clare encouraged her to get more counselling to deal with

what had happened and recommended a woman who specialized in victims of rape. As time went on, between Clare and the counsellor, they started to restore Ella's confidence and she felt that she could at least carry on, if not exactly live life to the full.

Very slowly, she started to write again and found that she could finally stop trying to hide behind someone else's character to help her escape from her own personality but could now draw more honestly on her own experiences. As a result her writing was better and more powerful and she was proud of what she produced.

She still didn't feel able to face reporting what had happened to the police but again, Clare made her see that she shouldn't blame herself for that. She said that, through her work, she saw lots of women who felt the same way and that it was entirely understandable.

If it was strange the way Clare and Ella had become friends, something even stranger was also happening. Max's son Jasper had put the house on the market and, thanks to the downturn in the market, there had been absolutely no interest at all, so Ella had decided to sit tight for as long as she possibly could without making any fuss. Max's family seemed surprised that she didn't fight them over it. The truth was, in the past she might have done, but now she just didn't have the heart.

Then, little by little and taking Ella completely by surprise, her relationship with Jasper started to thaw. He would call round to discuss the details of Max's will, or update her on the (lack of) progress on the house and instead of sitting stiffly upright on the sofa, rifling through papers he'd retrieved from his briefcase, as he had done before, he would relax a bit and even started to accept her offers of tea or, lately, something stronger.

To Ella's astonishment, she discovered that he had inherited his father's sense of humour and brilliant mind. They talked a lot about Max and began to laugh at shared memories. Ella tried hard to be as honest as possible about how she felt about Max, but despite all the counselling, it still didn't come easily to her. She talked about Max's good points and told Jasper truthfully that she had loved his father.

What she found more difficult to admit was that she had felt trapped and bored in the relationship and she certainly didn't mention that she had already told Max she was leaving him when he died. She couldn't bear for Jasper to think any worse of her than he already did. Or, more accurately, she couldn't bear for him to think of her as badly as she thought of herself.

After a couple of months, Ella noticed that Jasper would call in when he didn't have anything in particular to discuss with her. He would claim to have been 'just passing' and said he thought he would call in to see how she was doing. And as time passed, Ella grew to look forward to his visits and found that she was really enjoying his company. When Ella told Clare what was happening, Clare was typically blunt.

'You know what, Ella? You are weird sometimes! You can't possibly be contemplating having a relationship with Max's son! It's just too fucked up.'

'I'm not contemplating a relationship!' Ella had insisted furiously, but Clare had touched a nerve. Her feelings for Jasper were starting to deepen and Clare could sense it. Ella wondered if he could sense it too and, if so, what his reaction would be. She had never had a platonic relationship with a man, except Fabien but he didn't count on the grounds that he was gay, and it was a new and quite pleasurable experience to be with someone who seemed to be interested in her for who she was, rather than her face or body. She had changed so much since the attack and maybe this was the culmination of that change, that she was able to form a proper friendship with a man, without having to sleep with him.

The next time Jasper turns up, Ella offers to cook him something and he readily agrees. 'I'll go and get a bottle of wine,' he offers, shrugging his coat back on.

'No, it's OK,' Ella says quickly. 'There's plenty here in . . . in Max's, in your father's wine cellar.'

When he returns with the bottle he has selected, he opens it and puts a glass down beside Ella. As he is about to pour, she covers the top with her hand and shakes her head. 'No, not for me, thanks,' she says, quickly turning back to the stove.

'How come?' he says, looking bemused.

'I gave up drinking a couple of months ago,' she replies.

'Why?' The question hangs in the air between them. Ella almost laughs as she thinks about what the truthful answer would be: 'Because when I drank in the past, I seduced your father, who was married at the time, I took an overdose, slept with endless unsuitable men and finally ended up being raped, resulting in a miscarriage several weeks later, that's why.'

'Because I feel better when I don't drink,' she finds herself replying instead.

Jasper stands holding the bottle and looking at her, until she can't bear it any longer and spins round. 'What?'

she asks, laughing nervously. 'Why are you looking at me like that?'

Jasper grins and shakes his head. 'Because every time I see you or speak to you these days, you take me by surprise. I would have put money on you being a hard-drinking, hard-partying girl and here you are, this paragon of virtue. It's just not what I expected at all.'

Ella laughs and feels herself glow under his approving gaze. Men had looked at her that way before but only in a sexual way. Jasper was admiring her for who she was, not the way she looked. There is an awkward pause and she thinks for a moment that he might be about to kiss her but instead he turns away and pours himself a small glass of wine, which he sips thoughtfully as he walks over to the window and stares out over the garden.

'I always loved our garden,' he murmurs.

'Sorry?' Ella replies, turning away from the stove where she is stirring a sauce.

'Nothing,' he says quickly and Ella notices that his eyes are glistening with unshed tears. She can feel the ache coming from him across the room.

'I'm sorry,' she says quietly. It is the first time she has ever really meant an apology in her life.

Jasper nods. 'I know,' he says. 'I'm sorry too.'

Ella frowns in confusion. 'But you've got nothing to be sorry for.'

He laughs bitterly. 'Oh, yes I have! I have spent all these years hating you and now I discover that all along you were just someone who loved my father as much as I did. If I'm really honest with myself, I have to admit that I don't think my mother ever made him as happy as you did. We were a very happy family, that's not in dispute. But you made him really happy and I should have allowed him that, instead of letting my bitterness corrode our relationship. We were so close before . . .'

'Before me,' Ella finishes the sentence for him. 'Really, Jasper, your reaction to me is entirely understandable. I destroyed your family and even though you were all grown-up when it happened, I'm sure that didn't make it any easier, especially after losing your mother.'

Once again, the tears flash in his eyes and he looks away quickly. 'Yes,' he says gruffly, 'yes, you did destroy my family but so did he and he had more to lose than you.'

Ella can't meet his eye. She would have to live with the knowledge that she hadn't just destroyed his family, she had also destroyed Max. She had got what she wanted, only to find when she got it that she didn't want it any more. She would never know whether the stress of her leaving him had brought on Max's heart attack but she did know that it certainly couldn't have helped.

She walks over to Jasper and puts her hand on his firm, muscular shoulder. He stiffens for a second, before relaxing again as she pats gently, trying to take away his pain. Then suddenly he turns and is kissing her with an intensity she has never known before. But, instead of responding as she wants to, she is rigid with fright, as memories of the attack begin to flash to the front of her mind.

'No!' she cries, pushing him away, as she becomes overwhelmed with shame and fear. 'I . . . I can't.'

Jasper stares at her in shock. 'God, I'm so sorry, I don't know what came over me. You're right. This is just so, so wrong. I'm sorry. I'd better leave.'

He grabs his coat and almost runs out of the house, banging the front door hard behind him and leaving Ella shaking and crying for reasons that Jasper couldn't possibly know.

Clare

Clare's bump is so huge that she sometimes feels that if she simply leaned over to one side, she would roll all the way over and end up standing upright again. 'Weebles wobble but they don't fall down,' she sings to herself as she clears out the kitchen cupboards the weekend before the wedding.

'What the bloody hell are you doing?' laughs Anna, coming in from the shops and putting her bags on the kitchen table.

'Cleaning,' sighs Clare. 'I think it's called nesting. I've read about it in my pregnancy books. It's supposed to mean the birth's imminent.'

'God, I hope not!' Anna cries in horror, making Clare smile. 'I need you to hang on until after the wedding. Can't you just . . . stop nesting?'

Clare laughs as she scrubs the final shelf clean and wipes it down with a dry cloth. 'Too late,' she replies, admiring her efforts with satisfaction. 'I've cleaned everything there is to clean.'

Anna pulls up a chair and sits down, leaning her elbows on the table and running her hands through her hair.

'You OK?' asks Clare, wringing out the cloth she has been using. 'You don't look like an excited bride-to-be.'

Anna sighs. 'I am! Really I am,' she insists, somewhat unconvincingly. 'It's just last-minute nerves.'

Clare sits down opposite her, marvelling as she does so how far she has to sit from the table to accommodate her stomach. She picks up Anna's tiny hand with its pearly nails and rubs it gently between her own two hands. 'Anything you want to talk about?'

Anna meets her eye and Clare is shocked at what she sees there. Anna looks like a frightened rabbit. 'I'm scared,' she whispers, her voice quavering.

'Don't be daft!' laughs Clare. 'What have you got to be scared of?'

'I'm scared that Toby's not going to turn up.' Anna's bottom lip wobbles as she speaks and Clare realizes how distressed she is.

'Hey! What's brought this on?' she says in her most soothing voice. 'Toby loves you so much! Wild horses wouldn't keep him away.'

'We've been arguing so much though,' Anna cries, her forehead crinkling with worry. 'I really feel like I've been getting on his nerves lately.'

'No!' Clare insists. 'That can't be right. You're probably just in a heightened state of sensitivity because the wedding's so close. Honestly, Anna, I'm your best friend and I would warn you if I thought you had something to worry about, but I promise you I don't. I only see a couple who are so in love that I can even feel it when you're both in the flat, let alone when we're all in the same room. Then it's bloody unbearable! Especially for a sad old cow like me!'

Anna's frown softens. 'Really? You honestly don't think we've been a bit scratchier with each other than usual?'

Clare shakes her head, although even as she does so, she remembers several instances recently when there has been a frostiness between them that she has never seen before. 'No,' Clare assures her. 'It's just wedding nerves, that's all.'

Anna sighs. 'Thanks, Clare. You are such an amazing friend, you know.'

'And so are you,' Clare tells her. She gives Anna's hand a squeeze. 'Don't worry about anything. It's all going to be just fine. You must feel better knowing that Rachel's not going to be there now?'

Anna nods. 'Yes, I do. I just wish Toby wasn't so bloody keen to have her there. Don't you think it's odd that he tried to persuade her to come?'

Clare thinks about it for a moment and winces slightly as another Braxton Hicks contraction tightens her swollen belly. 'I think he probably wants to do the right thing by her. He'll always feel guilty about what happened and when you think about it, you wouldn't think much of him if he just forgot about it and moved on without so much as a backward glance, would you?'

Anna smiles. 'No, that's true. But I also wish Marco wasn't going to be the best man. It's making me feel really uncomfortable, the thought of him being there, looking daggers at me as I make my vows.'

'He won't be looking daggers at you. He'll be thanking God and all the choirs of angels that Toby didn't go through with the wedding to Rachel, or he wouldn't have landed her! He's probably eternally grateful to you, you daft thing!' Clare grins at Anna, knowing that she is right about this bit at least.

Anna lets out a deep breath. 'Oh God, I'm such a silly cow

sometimes. You're right, you're right. Of course you're right. He'd be sitting at home on his own tucking into a takeaway curry if it wasn't for me!'

'Exactly!' laughs Clare. 'Now stop worrying and show me what you've bought.'

Later that evening Clare is watching TV and suddenly feels an overwhelming urge to speak to James. She is starting to feel scared about the birth now that it is so close and she needs reassurance more than ever that he will still be around once it is over.

'Is that my missus?' he asks cheekily as he picks up the phone after two rings.

Clare feels a little glow of pleasure and grins stupidly to herself. 'Am I?' she laughs.

'Course you are! What's up?' he asks. 'It's not the baby, is it?'

'No!' Clare says quickly. 'No, it's squirming furiously but I think it's there for the duration.'

'Oh, I wish you'd let me see you,' he wails. 'This is torture!'

Clare's back is aching and she stands up, rubbing it as she paces up and down. She starts to waver. Having someone to hold her hand and rub her back for her would be so lovely right now. As the thought goes through her head she catches sight of herself in the mirror above the fireplace. Her hair looks as though she has stuck her finger in a plug socket and her skin has broken out in spots. 'No,' she says firmly, her resolve back in place. 'I don't want you to see me like this – I look like hell.'

James sighs. 'I don't believe you but if that's the way you want it.'

'It is,' Clare says, still firmly but in a softer voice.

'So, how are the blushing bride and gorgeous groom?' he asks, changing the subject after a short pause.

'They're . . . well, they're all right,' Clare says, still pacing up and down. She just can't get comfortable, whether she sits down or stands up. 'They're a bit irritable with one another, but I guess that's just last-minute nerves.'

'Yeah, probably. Christ, I hope he doesn't do another runner!' he says.

'James!' cries Clare, outraged but at the same time knowing that he has echoed her own worries. 'How could you even say such a thing?' she adds crossly.

'Sorry,' he replies, chastened. 'It's just after last time . . . well, it must be on Anna's mind.'

'OK, James! Enough,' snaps Clare. 'Let's talk about something else. Last time you and I argued over Anna and Toby, you buggered off to Australia!'

'Ouch!' he laughs. 'That hurts. Well, you can rest assured that I won't be doing that again. I've learnt my lesson. You've tamed the wild beast.'

Clare laughs, unable to resist his silly sense of humour.

'How's Rachel doing?' she says. 'I think it was pretty big of her to say she wasn't coming to the wedding.'

'Yeah, well she's that sort of person. And I don't think she's desperate to relive the whole bloody episode anyway. It would just be too close to home.'

'And what about her and Marco? Still love's young dream?'

James laughs. 'Yes – unfortunately. I'm beginning to feel like I've more than outstayed my welcome at her flat.'

'It's not for much longer. You've only got another couple of weeks to wait.'

'Actually, I've been thinking about that,' he says and Clare can tell that he is biting his lip as he speaks.

'Thinking about what?' she says, her voice hardening as the old familiar feeling of dread creeps over her.

'I think we should get a place of our own with the baby. It's going to be very crowded with Toby and Anna there.'

'I can't move out now!' cries Clare. 'They've gone to so much effort on my behalf. Toby's done up the room, built all the furniture and Anna's come to nearly all my appointments with me. I think they're almost as excited about the baby as I am.'

'I'm going to feel like a right spare part, aren't I?' James says sulkily. 'If Toby's so great, what the hell is there going to be left for me to do?'

'Oh, don't be so stupid!' Clare chides him. 'Isn't it obvious what there'll be for you to do? You'll be the baby's dad, getting up at night to do the feeds and giving me foot rubs on demand. Believe me, there'll be enough room for you to get involved. As long as you want to, that is, and don't let me down again at the last minute.'

'Do you really still think I would?' he says, sounding hurt. 'Haven't I done enough to convince you yet?'

Clare hesitates. 'Well, yes . . . but you can't blame me for feeling cautious, James, not after what happened. And I think that's the reason I can't contemplate moving out into a flat on our own just yet. I'm protecting myself, just in case.'

James sighs. 'God, I really fucked things up, didn't I?'

'Let's not dwell on that,' Clare says quickly. 'From now on, I'm not interested in the past. I want to concentrate on the future. Together.'

Ella

The morning after Jasper kissed her, Ella calls Clare. She is the only person Ella has confided in about the rape and the only person she feels she can talk to.

'What's up?' says Clare, sounding matter-of-fact.

'I think it might help me if I report the rape,' says Ella.

Ella can tell by the sounds of movement from Clare's end of the line that she is shifting position to get more comfortable.

'OK,' Clare replies slowly.

'Will you help me?' Ella asks, aware as she speaks how much she has come to depend on her former enemy.

'Yes, of course – you know I will. What's brought this on?'

Ella hesitates, unsure of whether or not to tell her about Jasper. She takes a deep breath and decides that from now on, honesty is her best policy. 'It's Jasper,' she says.

'Oh God, Ella!' Clare cuts in.

'No!' Ella stops her before she can continue. 'No, nothing's happened. It's just that, well, I really like him. And I think he likes me too. But while I've got this . . . this dirty secret, I just can't contemplate having any kind of relationship. I've spent my whole life lying, Clare. From now on I just want to be honest. If I report what happened, I feel that it will make it easier for me to come clean with Jasper about quite why I'm so fucked up. Do you understand?'

There is a long pause. 'I think so,' Clare replies at last. 'Have you spoken to your counsellor about this?'

'No,' Ella says. 'But I think she'd agree that it was the right thing to do if I felt ready.'

'And do you feel ready? I mean, really ready? It's not an easy thing to do, Ella. I will support you and point you in the right direction, but you need to be prepared that it will be very hard for you. And you also need to be prepared for the police never catching this guy. Although, I'd be willing to bet he's done it before and probably since . . .'

Ella nods, not wanting to even contemplate that by acting sooner, she might have been able to prevent it happening to someone else. 'I do feel ready,' she says, already feeling better for having spoken to Clare.

'Right then,' says Clare briskly, 'this is what you need to do . . .'

To Ella's amazement, the police are incredible. She had imagined having to go to a station to give a statement, where she would be regarded coldly as a woman of loose morals who had got everything she deserved. Instead, a young, sympathetic female officer comes to the house where, helped by Clare, Ella is able to tell her everything and give her as much information as she can piece together about her assailant. The officer doesn't say so, but Ella senses that she isn't the first woman to report him. Clare's legal expertise is useful but even more valuable is the fact that she holds Ella's hand and nods encouragingly, whenever she begins to struggle.

After the policewoman leaves, Ella lets herself cry. The

relief is totally overwhelming. For the first time in such a long time, she has the feeling that she has done the right thing. Clare makes endless cups of tea and hands Ella tissue after tissue, listening as she talks about the mistakes she has made in her life and how she is now going to put them right. Ella feels as though she has been reborn.

'So, what now?' says Clare, trying to stifle a yawn.

Ella looks out over the garden. 'I'm going to move out of this house and make a fresh start, with my own money in my own flat,' she replies. 'I've always relied on either Max or my parents for money and it's time I started to pay my own way.'

Clare nods approvingly. 'Yes, it is time for you to move on. There are too many memories in this house and it was never really yours anyway.'

Ella flinches slightly at Clare's words but she knows she is right. Ella has been like the cuckoo in the nest here, moving into Camilla's home, having stolen her husband. And more than that, she has never been happy here, even when Max was still alive. There is too much pain and anger tied up within these walls.

'And what about Jasper?' Clare asks, rhythmically stirring her tea and looking at Ella closely.

Ella feels herself redden slightly. 'I don't know. I think maybe I need to give myself some time alone, to be absolutely sure of how I feel about him.'

Clare stands up. 'Well, it looks like my work here is done!' she laughs. 'You should be very proud of yourself, Ella, it took a lot of guts to do what you did today,' she says, hugging Ella as tightly as her bump will allow. 'You can start to like yourself now.'

'Thank you,' says Ella. 'That's the nicest thing anyone's ever said to me, Clare.'

Clare smiles. 'I'd better go, I've got a big day tomorrow, waddling down the aisle behind Anna. You're definitely not going?'

'No, I think it's for the best,' says Ella. 'But I've sent them a card and I'll be thinking of them.'

'I honestly don't think either of them bears you any malice, you know,' Clare says over her shoulder as she makes her way down the wide hallway towards the front door.

'That may be true but I don't want anything to spoil their day. If there's the slightest chance that my presence would upset Anna, it's best if I stay away.'

Clare grins. 'You really have turned over a new leaf, haven't you? The old Ella would have been delighted to fuck things up for them!'

Ella grimaces. 'Please don't remind me. I'm embarrassed enough as it is. I was vile.'

'You don't need to be embarrassed any more, Ella. You've made a fresh start and you're a different person now. You can hold your head up high. Forget about your past and concentrate on your future.'

After Ella shows Clare out of the house, she stands at the top of the steps watching her as she drives off into the night and feels a twinge of excitement, wondering what the future might hold for her. She has a feeling that everything is going to work out just fine.

Rachel

As Toby and Anna's wedding approaches, Rachel feels a growing sense of sickness and dread. The memories of the humiliation she had felt that day seem to bubble up out of nowhere and she finds herself waking up in the middle of the night, sweating at the thought of it.

She doesn't feel that she can wake Marco and tell him what is wrong, so she lies awake night after night, staring at the ceiling and trying to calm her racing heart with deep breaths. On the nights he isn't with her, Rachel gets up and makes herself some tea, pacing around her room as she drinks it.

Rachel has taken the decision not to go to the wedding as much for herself as for Anna. She can't face the pitying stares of Toby's family, who she knows are still angry at what happened. She doesn't have feelings for Toby any longer, it is just that she can't cope with being talked about in hushed tones by them all as Toby stands at the altar and marries someone else.

As the day of the wedding dawns bright and sunny, somehow adding insult to injury, Rachel feels worse than ever. Sensitive to her mood, Marco looks at her apologetically as he starts to get dressed in his morning suit. 'I can still pull out, you know,' he offers as he sits on the bed and does up his tie.

Rachel shakes her head. 'No, you have to go. I'm happy for them. Really.'

Marco takes her hand in his. 'You're an amazing girl, Rachel. I can't believe how well you're handling this.'

Rachel almost laughs. On the surface she might appear to be coping well but inside she feels sick. She still reddens with embarrassment at the thought of that awful day. Strangely, as time goes on, it becomes worse as she remembers tiny extra details, like the look on her dad's face – his cheek twitching with anger as he realized what was happening and his eyes glistening with tears, something she had never, ever seen before. She hoped she would never have to see it again.

'What will you do today?' says Marco, leaning forward and checking his appearance in her dressing-table mirror.

Rachel shrugs. 'I think James and I will keep each other company. Maybe we'll go to the cinema.' Because Clare doesn't want to see James until after the baby is born, he hasn't been invited to the wedding. Rachel doesn't really understand why Clare is being so obstinate about it and feels that, in her shoes, she would have welcomed James back into her life months ago. But twice now he has hurt her badly and Rachel supposes that this is just Clare's way of protecting herself. 'James is finding it hard too,' she says, 'so we'll look after each other.'

Marco stands up and pulls on his morning coat, before doing a jokey twirl. 'So, how do I look?' he asks.

Rachel resists the urge to tell him he looks just as nice as he did on her wedding day and kisses him instead. 'Handsome, that's how you look,' she grins.

Marco's dark eyes dilate and he glows with pride. 'You have no idea how long I've waited to hear you say that,' he chokes. 'I love you.'

Rachel nods quickly, also struggling to keep her composure. 'You too.'

Once Marco has left, Rachel makes some fresh coffee and takes it in to James, who is still staying on the sofa bed in her sitting room. 'Are you asleep?' she whispers, peering into the gloom.

'No,' he whispers back and they both laugh. She hands him the coffee as he bunches a pillow behind his back and sits up. He slurps it noisily and gives a big sigh of satisfaction. 'Lovely! Thanks, Rachel,' he says. 'For everything.'

Rachel shrugs and perches on the sofa bed beside him. 'I hope it all works out.'

He takes another sip of his coffee and runs his thumb around the rim of the mug. 'Do you think it will?'

Rachel nods. 'Yes, I do.'

'You don't think it's a bit ominous that she won't see me before the baby's born?'

'Not ominous, no. Surprising, perhaps, but not ominous. I think it's her way of coping.'

They sit in silence for a few minutes, both deep in thought. 'Women are complicated,' he says finally. 'I'm not sure I'll ever understand them.'

Rachel laughs. 'And I'm not sure I'll ever understand you men!'

As she showers, Rachel thinks back to that day last summer when she had thought she would be marrying Toby. Although her main recollection is one of total embarrassment, she can also recall the feelings that she had had herself that morning. She remembers the gnawing doubt that had eaten away at her for months, even years. She hadn't appreciated just how stressed she'd felt until she didn't feel it any more. The worst had happened and she had survived. More than that, she felt light and freed from a life of worry and anxiety. Getting together with Marco was a bonus but Rachel realizes, as the water jets pound around her, she would have been OK on her own too. Toby, she decides, did her a huge favour.

James and Rachel travel to the cinema on James' motorbike, Rachel clinging onto him tightly, loving the sensation of the wind blowing through her hair as they speed through the sunny streets. Parking the bike close to Leicester Square, they head for the Empire, where they squabble furiously over what film to see. In the end, Rachel persuades him that her need is greater than his on this particular day and that he should let her choose. 'Oh, go on then,' he concedes grumpily. 'Just please God nothing by Richard Curtis.'

Rachel laughs. 'Strangely enough, I'm not keen on anything with a wedding theme today.'

'No, me neither. For very different reasons, obviously,' he adds hastily.

In the end Rachel picks a comedy, figuring that they could both do with a bit of cheering up. It turns out to be the right choice, as they both laugh through the mouthfuls of popcorn they keep shovelling in and she only looks at her watch twice to wonder if Toby and Anna would have made their vows by now.

Afterwards, they stumble out into the glaring sunshine and decide to head for the nearest bar. As they walk, Rachel rummages in her bag for her mobile phone to turn it back on, having switched it off for the film. While she is still scrabbling around, James has already located his in his pocket and switched it on. The continual beeping that follows suggests he has got lots of messages. 'Shit!' he cries, scanning the list of missed calls.

'What?' Rachel asks in alarm, immediately sensing that something is very wrong.

'I've got thirty-three missed calls,' he says. 'All from the same number. It must be Clare!'

Anna

On the eve of the wedding, all the angst and nerves that have been building up for so long suddenly evaporate and Anna feels as though she is literally floating on a cloud of excitement. She and her mum check into a lovely boutique hotel for the night, leaving Clare and Toby alone together in the flat. Toby had kissed her tenderly as she left, telling her that he wished they didn't have to be apart, even for one night and that he couldn't wait to marry her. Clare had hugged her tightly and told her jokily to 'make the most of your last night of freedom!'

She meets her mum in the lobby of the hotel. The minute Cassie sees Anna her eyes fill up. 'Oh God,' Anna grimaces, 'if you're like this now, how the hell are you going to be tomorrow?'

'A mess,' Cassie admits, blowing her nose. 'It's just such a big day in so many ways. Tim flew in last night with his new girlfriend, Jo – she's lovely, by the way – and it feels so good to have both my kids back with me. I miss you both so much.'

Anna's insides constrict with guilt. Her mum has devoted her life to bringing up Anna and her big brother and it must have hit her very hard when they left home, especially as

Tim had gone to live on the other side of the world. 'Well, you are just going to have to find a man yourself!' Anna tells her for the millionth time. 'It's such a waste a gorgeous woman like you being single.'

'Yes, I think maybe you're right about that,' Cassie says thoughtfully, taking Anna completely by surprise. Whenever the subject has cropped up before, she has always insisted that there was no one else for her but Anna's father.

Anna looks back at her in amazement as she wheels her suitcase into their room. 'Are you telling me you've met someone?' she asks, noticing as she does so that her mum is blushing furiously.

'Not quite,' Cassie mutters.

Anna lifts her case onto one of the beds and slumps down beside it. 'Then what?' she asks, looking at her curiously.

Cassie pushes the hair back off her face and sits down on the other bed, facing Anna. She leans forwards, taking Anna's hands in hers. 'I don't know how you're going to feel about it,' she says. 'How you or Tim are going to feel about it, actually.'

'Feel about what?' Anna's brow furrows in confusion.

'Well, it's your father,' Cassie says hesitantly.

'What about him?' A strange sense of unease is creeping over Anna.

'He got back in touch with me. A few weeks ago.'

'And you told him to drop dead, I presume?' Anna is struggling to comprehend what her mum is telling her.

Cassie laughs and squeezes her hands. 'Yes, of course I did.'

Anna feels herself relax slightly. 'Thank God for that.'

'But . . .' she continues, 'he has been very persistent.'

'So what?' Anna snaps.

'And, eventually, we started to talk,' Cassie continues. 'I've agreed to meet up with him.'

'No!' Anna cries. 'How can you? After what he did? To you, to all of us!'

Cassie sighs. 'I understand completely how you feel, darling, I really do. That's why I was nervous about telling you anything about it.'

Suddenly, a horrible thought occurs to Anna. 'You're not telling me on the night before my wedding so that he can waltz in and walk me down the aisle, are you?'

'No!' Cassie says quickly. 'No, of course not. My God, as if I would spring that bombshell on you.'

Anna heaves a sigh of relief. 'So, why have you told me now?'

'I wanted to let you know that he had been in touch. I suppose I thought it might prove to you that maybe I was right all along about you and me being like swans – we mate for life. You and Toby are so right for each other and I want you to walk down that aisle knowing you are marrying the only man you ever could.'

Anna nods, saying nothing.

'But, Anna, I'm not letting him back that easily, you know. If he is to have any part in my life – and it's still a very big if – it will be on my terms. I won't ever let him hurt me again.'

Anna sighs deeply. She doesn't know how to respond to this news. She can't imagine what her father would be like now and really has no desire to have anything to do with him after so many years. But she does want her mum to be happy and if this is what she wants . . . well, who was she to stop her doing anything?

Anna stands up and brushes herself down, both

metaphorically and physically. She doesn't want to think about this now. 'Well, as long as you don't allow yourself to get hurt again,' she says gently but firmly.

Cassie stands up and hugs her. 'I won't. I promise. Now, where do we start tonight? How about a massage?'

Anna grins and the butterflies of excitement and nerves begin to flutter again. 'Yes,' she says, 'that sounds perfect.'

The next morning, after a leisurely breakfast and with their nails manicured, their bodies massaged and their hair blow-dried, they are finally ready to get dressed. Cassie carefully takes Anna's wedding dress down from the doorframe and lays it on the bed. She unzips the cover and lifts it out with such loving care, it's as if she is holding a newborn baby. She helps Anna step into it and gingerly pulls up the zip which runs all the way from the bottom of her spine to the nape of her neck.

Anna spins around and looks at her. 'Well, what do you think?' she asks, looking down at the simple ivory sheath which falls in perfect folds down her body.

Cassie nods and swallows. She tries to speak but no words come out. She nods again and squeezes her hand instead. Anna laughs, feeling light with joy. For the first time, she allows herself to believe that this is going to be the best day of her life.

As they leave the hotel, several of the staff line up to give them a send-off. There are a satisfying number of sighs and oohs from the women, while the men grin broadly and clap as the two of them walk past, Anna clutching her bouquet and her mum clasping her hand, to stop herself from toppling off her delicate lilac heels.

The chauffeur holds the door to a white London taxi open, cream bridal ribbons jauntily decorating the front bonnet. Cassie and Anna climb in and they set off at a languorous pace, with shoppers and diners at pavement tables turning to give them curious glances as they pass. Anna looks up at the bright blue sky, the sun already warming the early April air and thanks her lucky stars that everything points to this being a perfect day.

The wedding car pulls up outside the church. It is a smallish church in Islington, with a grand set of steps, which is why Anna had chosen it. She would have liked to get married in the village in Suffolk where she grew up but she was worried that Clare wouldn't be able to make it, so decided to stay in London after all. Some guests are still standing outside looking out for the car. Anna immediately spots Marco, looking sweet in his morning suit. Beside him stands her brother, Tim, who will be giving her away. He is looking at his watch and glancing anxiously up the road. Anna waits for the chauffeur to open the door and takes his hand as she steps out of the car.

Tim comes running down the steps towards her and smiles. 'Anna! You look amazing,' he says, kissing her on the cheek and inviting her to put her arm through his. He then turns to their mother and proffers his other arm. 'Listen, there's been a bit of a hold-up . . .' he begins.

Anna whirls around to look at him. 'Oh my God!' she cries. 'He's not here, is he?'

Tim flushes and shakes his head. 'No. But don't panic! There's probably been a hold-up with the traffic. Let's just go for a walk in the grounds for a few minutes.'

Anna looks up to the top of the steps where Marco is frantically dialling on a mobile phone. He looks up and catches her eye. She knows immediately that Toby isn't coming. 'Oh my God!' she breathes, feeling faint with shock. Tim holds her up as her legs start to buckle underneath her.

'Let's get her back into the car!' he gasps at their mother.

The chauffeur, who had been about to drive off round the corner where he was looking forward to having a sneaky cigarette, yelps in alarm as the back door is wrenched open and his bridal cargo is deposited once again on the back seat. He has only ever had this happen to him once before, when the bride had a change of heart at the altar and literally did a runner from the church. 'What the hell's going on?' he asks in confusion as three people shuffle their way across the seat and slam the door shut.

'Sorry, mate,' says Tim. 'Can you just drive round the corner for a minute? There's been a bit of a hitch.'

The driver tries not to snort at the unintentional pun and thinks longingly of the cigarette he has been looking forward to as he puts the car into gear and moves off slowly. He glances curiously in his rear-view mirror. The would-be bride isn't in floods of tears as he might expect. She is taking deep breaths and fanning herself with her hand as she tries to stay calm.

'He'll be here – there must have been some kind of hold-up,' Tim says briskly, glancing back at the church, as if hoping that by some miracle Toby might suddenly appear.

'He won't,' replies Anna in a dull, emotionless voice. 'He won't be here and it serves me right.'

'Shhh! Don't say that!' says her mum, frowning with worry at her daughter. 'Tim's right, there must be some perfectly plausible explanation. Toby wouldn't do that to you.'

'Rachel's mum probably said the same thing to her when he did it before,' says Anna, in that alarmingly monotonous tone of voice. Suddenly, she seems to snap back into life. 'I bet Marco was loving it!' she hisses at Tim, who stares back at her in shock.

'No! No, he wasn't loving it at all. He seemed genuinely upset. He was ringing and ringing Toby but couldn't get an answer. I think he was worried that you would blame him.'

Anna's eyes cloud over again. 'Who could blame him for hating me? After what I did to Rachel.'

Tim and Cassie exchange glances over the top of Anna's head as the car draws to a halt around the corner from the church. The driver turns to Tim. 'Shall I just sit here for a while?' he asks, slightly nervously. 'Or would you like me to give you some privacy?' he adds hopefully.

Tim nods and the driver climbs out gratefully, already reaching for his cigarettes as he closes the door.

Silence descends in the car as the three of them are lost in their own thoughts. Tim is wondering how he can get hold of Toby and beat the living daylights out of him. Anna is wondering how she can ever face anyone again and her mum is wondering how she can help her daughter recover from such a horrible shock.

'I think we should just go home,' says Anna at last. 'I can't sit here any longer.'

'No! Let's give it just a few more minutes,' says Tim quickly, reaching for his mobile. 'I'll call Marco and see if there's any news.'

Anna takes the mobile from his hand. 'There won't be,' she says calmly. 'There won't be because he's not coming.'

Tim flushes with fury. 'God, the fucking . . . aah!' he cries, punching the door of the taxi in frustration.

'Let's just wait,' Cassie says quietly. 'He'll be here. I know he will.'

Once again, a thick silence fills the air as another ten minutes tick by. Anna stares straight ahead, her eyes dry and unblinking. Cassie and Tim both watch her with an increasing sense of alarm that maybe she is right: Toby isn't coming.

'Tim,' Cassie says finally, her voice shaking with unshed tears, 'why don't you go back to the church and tell everyone to go on ahead to the reception? I'll take Anna home.'

Tim nods and opens the car door. Just before he steps out onto the pavement, he puts his arm around Anna's shoulders and gives her a squeeze. 'I'm really sorry,' he says gruffly. Anna nods her thanks, unable to speak.

As the door clunks shut behind him, Anna seems to jerk into life. She grabs the handle and opens the door again. 'Tim!' she yells, shuffling across the seat and getting out. 'Wait for me!'

'Darling! Anna! What are you doing?' cries Cassie as Anna runs down the street after her brother, her train billowing out behind her.

As Tim and Anna round the corner, they almost collide with Marco, running towards them. 'I wondered where you were!' he gasps, puffing from the exertion of running.

Anna and Tim both screech to a halt. 'Is he here?' they cry in unison, Anna's heart soaring once more with hope.

'No, but . . .' Marco begins, but Anna isn't listening. She pushes past both men and runs towards the church like a woman possessed. On the steps, the congregation are beginning to emerge, looking confused and, in the case of Toby's parents, absolutely furious. Toby's father, Graham, runs down the stairs towards Anna. 'Oh, my dear girl!' he says, holding his arms open in a gesture of apology. 'I am so sorry. I promise you I will kill my son when I finally get my hands on him!'

Anna bursts into noisy sobs, finally giving in to the tears which have been brimming. 'Where's Clare?' she wails. 'I need Clare!'

There is an awkward cough from someone. Anna feels a hand on her back and turns in confusion. It is Marco. 'What's happening, Marco? Where's Clare?'

Marco's eyes soften as he looks at her with a sympathy that is worse than any of the anger or hatred he has directed at her in the past. 'She's not here,' he says quietly. 'She must be with Toby.'

Anna frowns. 'No! That's not possible,' she gulps in disbelief. It is all too much for her to take in. Had they been planning this all along? Were they always intending to go off together and play happy families? In which case, why didn't they just tell her? Why did they let her go through this humiliation?

Spinning on her heel, she turns through a haze of tears and pushes her way past the sympathetic faces and consolatory pats on the back. She is desperate to get back to the safety of the car and get home. Suddenly, she stops dead in her tracks.

'Where's home?' she says aloud, to no one in particular. Realizing that home is where the two people who have betrayed her are probably now cosied up on the sofa, congratulating themselves on having got rid of her, she slumps down into a sobbing heap on the ground. Through the fog of her misery, she is dimly aware of a motorbike pulling up beside her and someone getting off. Whoever it is bends down beside her and strokes her back.

'Anna!' says a voice.

Slowly, Anna raises her head and opens her eyes. It is Rachel. 'Oh God!' she moans, holding her head in her hands once more. 'I bet you're delighted by all this! He did it to you and now he's done it to me!' Anna begins to sob uncontrollably.

'No!' says Rachel, softly at first. Then, realizing that she isn't getting through to her, she raises her voice until she is shouting. 'No! Anna! It's not like that! Clare's gone into labour! James is on his way there – go with him!' she yells, motioning towards the motorbike, where James is revving the engine impatiently.

Anna raises her eyes again, sheepishly looking at Rachel. 'Really?' she whispers. 'But Toby? He's not here. He's jilted me – like he jilted you!' Fresh tears spring from her eyes as she speaks and she begins to hyperventilate.

Rachel looks around her helplessly, unable to get through to Anna, she is in such a state. Finally, she lifts her hand and slaps Anna's face. There is a loud gasp from the crowd that has assembled around them. 'Stop bloody crying and get on that bike!' shouts Rachel, helping a stunned Anna to her feet. 'Toby and Clare were on their way here when her waters broke – they both panicked and raced to the hospital, which is where they still are. Now, get on that bike and go with James.'

Rachel doesn't give Anna time to argue. She wrenches off her veil and ties it around Anna's waist, replacing it with the crash helmet she had been wearing herself. Then she holds Anna's train as Anna clambers on behind James and bundles it quickly into the box on the back of the bike. As soon as she is on, James roars off, narrowly missing a car.

The crowd mills around in shock as Marco wraps Rachel in a hug. 'Wow!' he breathes. 'You arrived just in the nick of time.'

Rachel grins and wipes a tear from her eye. 'Wow indeed,' she agrees.

Weaving through the traffic wearing a full wedding dress, Anna draws endless stares from bemused pedestrians, drivers and other motorcyclists. Several honk their appreciation, imagining that this is the bride and groom on their way from the church. James' scruffy jeans and Anna's tear-stained face may have given the game away to any who looked more closely.

Within ten minutes, they are pulling up in front of the hospital. James screeches to a halt and leaps off the bike. He is starting to run towards the entrance when a yelp from Anna reminds him that he isn't alone. Tutting with frustration, he runs back and yanks her train out of the pannier box, ripping the fabric as he does so. Without waiting to help her off, he darts once more for the door, Anna following as quickly as she can, given that she has lost one of her shoes and has a huge train fanning out behind her. 'Oh, fuck it!' she laughs, kicking off the other shoe and gathering up her dress, so that she can run that bit faster. She catches up with James just before the lift doors close and jumps in beside him.

'Oh God, please let me be in time!' James is muttering, over and over again.

Anna reaches out and takes his hand. 'You'll make it,' she says, saying a silent prayer that she is right. As the lift whirrs up to the fifth floor, Anna looks at James curiously. 'Hang on, I thought you were banned from seeing her until after the birth?'

James' eyes stay glued to the lift's LCD as it makes its way painfully slowly through the floors. 'I was. I think being in labour must have changed her mind. Rachel and I were in the cinema so I'd turned off my phone – only got the message when we got out. Jesus, I hope I'm in time, or she'll think I don't care.'

Anna wipes her face with the back of her hand, trying desperately to see herself in the dimly reflective walls of the lift. Her stomach starts to flutter as she realizes she will be coming face to face with Toby at any minute.

At last the lift arrives at the fifth floor with a jaunty ping. The doors judder open and James bursts out, with Anna following as closely as she can, her dress bundled unceremoniously under one arm. The midwives at the nurses' station look up curiously as the two strange visitors approach.

'Clare Stanton,' says James, trying hard not to raise his voice. 'She's in labour . . .'

'OK,' smiles a receptionist seated in front of a computer screen. 'And you are?'

'I'm the father,' says James quickly. The lady's eyes travel to Anna, standing barefoot beside James in her wedding dress, her make-up smudged and the tracks of recent tears still visible on her cheeks.

'Riiight . . .' she says slowly. 'Only there's a gentleman with her at the moment . . .'

'No, he's my husband – well, not quite my husband but

was about to be my husband, only Clare – she's my best friend, by the way – went into labour on the way to the church and they panicked and came here immediately . . .' Anna babbles, aware as she does so what a spectacle she must be making of herself.

The lady smiles and nods. 'Fine, well let me just check that it's OK and we'll show you to her room.'

James drums his fingers on the top of the desk while she makes a phone call, trying tactfully to describe the visitors. 'There's a gentleman who I believe is the father and a young lady in a wedding dress,' she whispers. Someone speaks at the other end of the line and the lady nods, then replaces the receiver. 'Yes, that's fine. Miss Stanton would like you both to go down,' she says. 'I'll tell you where to go.'

After getting directions to the delivery suite, James almost runs down the hall and bursts into the room, letting the door fall shut behind him. Anna can hear muffled voices from within and suddenly feels too shy to go in.

She is about to turn on her heel and walk back down the corridor when the door swings open again and Toby stands there. Anna gazes up at him in awe. He is wearing just a shirt and black trousers, with his morning jacket and tie discarded, but he looks like a film star. His skin has a light sheen of sweat and his hair is pushed back off his face to show off his chiselled cheekbones and grey-green eyes.

'I'm so sorry,' he whispers, coming out into the corridor and wrapping his arms around Anna, lifting her off her feet as he does so. Anna clutches her arms around his neck and buries her face in his shoulder, her tears soaking his shirt. They stand for several minutes without saying anything, Toby holding onto her as if his life depended on it.

Finally he puts her down and smiles. 'You've lost your shoes,' he says, motioning towards her bare feet.

Anna looks down, as if noticing for the first time. 'They were holding me back,' she laughs. 'Oh my God, Toby, you have no idea what I was thinking back there. I had convinced myself that you and Clare had run off together!'

Toby pulls her to his chest again. 'I would never do anything to hurt you. I'm so sorry, Anna. I just panicked and of course, we didn't have phones with us. I had to wait until we got here to call. Then your phone didn't answer . . .'

'Because I didn't have it with me!' Anna laughs, feeling almost giddy with relief. 'I didn't want it going off halfway through the service!'

'So then I was calling Marco and he was permanently on voicemail – obviously he was calling me. And then I had to try to get hold of James for Clare, who suddenly decided she couldn't get through it without him. Oh God, what a bloody mess!'

'Your parents are going to kill you!' Anna says. 'I thought your father might have a heart attack, he was so angry!'

Toby slumps against her. 'Oh God, you poor girl. It must have been so awful, you thinking I had stood you up. So, what's happening now? Has everyone gone home?'

Anna shrugs. 'I don't know. Rachel insisted I get on the bike and come here with James. I just left them all there.'

Toby looks at his watch, then back at Anna. 'You don't think . . . if we hurried . . . that we might still be able to make it?'

Anna's insides leap with excitement. 'Oh God! I don't know. Maybe. Let's call Marco and tell him to get them all back inside. We can take James' bike and we'll be back there in ten minutes! But . . . oh, Christ, what about Clare? We can't just leave her here!'

Toby turns and opens the door behind him. Anna can hear Clare groaning gently. 'Let's ask her,' Toby says, taking Anna by the hand and pulling her into the room.

Inside the dimly lit suite, Clare is sitting up on a bed, leaning forwards as James sits beside her holding her hand and rubbing her back. A midwife is checking monitors which are connected to some kind of probe attached to Clare's belly. Clare looks up as Toby and Anna walk in and immediately winces in pain. 'Yaaaargh!' she groans as a contraction wracks through her body. 'Oh, Anna!' she gasps once the contraction subsides. 'I'm so sorry!'

Anna immediately walks over and hugs her. 'It's OK! It's not your fault,' she whispers, stepping back for fear she might dislodge something.

'And it's not too late!' Toby cuts in quickly, looking at his watch. 'If we borrow James' bike, we can get back to the church and still get married . . .'

Clare looks at Anna in surprise. 'Really?' she cries. 'Well, what the hell are you waiting for? Go!' Her face crumples with pain again as another contraction hits.

'We can't leave you like this!' wails Anna.

Clare takes several quick, deep breaths before she can speak again. 'Of course you can! I've got James . . . .' She looks at him before continuing, 'I'll never forgive myself if you don't go through with it. Please, for me, go now!'

Anna grasps Clare's hand. 'Thank you! Thank you so much – breathe hard and stay strong,' she babbles before Toby, having scooped up his jacket, along with the keys and helmet from James, grabs her by the arm and yanks her towards the door. 'Let's go!' he says. 'Good luck, you two.'

'Good luck yourself!' shouts James as the door falls shut behind them.

For the second time in less than ten minutes, Anna is running barefoot down the hospital corridor, her ripped dress billowing behind her as she tries to clamp on her crash helmet. Once again, the lift is achingly slow and the two of them burst out onto the ground floor like two lions escaping from a cage.

They leap onto the motorbike, which is just about to be ticketed by a hospital security guard, who jumps back in shock at the sight which greets him. He stands scratching his head in amazement as the bike carrying the barefoot bride and the morning-suited groom takes off with a roar. 'Well I've seen some sights,' he mutters to himself with a grin, tearing up the ticket he had started writing out. Normally he is a stickler for rules and would never tear up a ticket but just this once wouldn't hurt.

Toby steers the bike through the traffic as fast as he can, travelling along the same route James had just taken. Passers-by who had seen Anna the first time round, now look on in puzzled amazement, as she speeds past with a different driver – this one looking much more suitably dressed for a wedding. Her poor dress is now oil-stained as well as ripped but Anna doesn't care. 'I'm getting married!' she yells to a startled taxi driver, who pulls up alongside them at traffic lights.

Toby punches the air and laughs as he revs the engine, willing the lights to change to green. They swerve around the corner to the church, just as the last stragglers are disappearing into the distance.

Rachel and Marco are helping an elderly aunt of Toby's down the steps when they hear the bike screech to a halt.

'What the fuck?' yells Marco, looking up in astonishment.

'Sorry, dear? What was that?' enquires the old lady kindly. 'I'm a bit deaf.'

Anna flings her helmet to one side and races towards the three of them. 'Wait!' she yells. 'Marco, get everyone back again – we're getting married after all!'

Marco shakes his head sadly. 'You're too late,' he sighs. 'The vicar's gone.'

Anna slumps down onto the ground in a dejected heap. 'Oh no!' she wails, fresh tears beginning to pour down her cheeks. Rachel kneels down beside her and puts an arm around her shoulders. 'Come on,' she soothes. 'It'll be OK.'

'No it won't!' sobs Anna, even in her distressed state registering the irony that it is Rachel who is comforting her at this precise moment.

'There's the vicar! Stop him!' shouts Toby, throwing himself in front of the vicar's car as he tries to pull out of the car park. 'Wait! We're here!' he cries, lying on the bonnet and talking to the startled vicar through the windscreen. 'Sorry we're late but please marry us!'

The vicar stops the car and opens the door. 'But everyone's gone,' he says, looking with concern towards Anna, who is still sobbing loudly on the ground.

'We don't care!' insists Toby. 'Please! You don't even have to get changed again – just do it in what you're wearing. Please?' he begs.

The vicar hesitates and looks at his watch. 'Well, it's most irregular,' he tuts, but Toby knows he has won. 'OK – I'll see you in there in five minutes.'

'Anna!' cries Toby, rushing over and helping her up. 'He'll do it! He's going to marry us!'

Anna's eyes widen and her tears stop in their tracks. 'Seriously?' she whispers. 'But everyone's gone . . .' She gestures around at the empty car park as she speaks.

'Marco and Rachel are here – and Great Aunt Kate!' laughs Toby. 'Kate'll be your bridesmaid, won't you, Kate?'

'What's that, dear?' replies Kate, who by now is seriously wondering if she has lost her marbles as well as her hearing. She is convinced she recognizes Rachel from Toby's first abortive wedding.

'Never mind,' smiles Toby, steering her back up the steps of the church. 'Just come with us.'

And so it is that Toby and Anna are finally married, with Marco fulfilling his duty as best man while an 80-year-old lady acts as bridesmaid and Rachel, wearing her jeans and a t-shirt, does a valiant job of playing the organ.

Anna takes her ripped veil from around her waist and places it on her head, trying not to notice the oil marks and holes in her dress as she makes her way barefoot down the aisle towards Toby who, despite the trauma of the morning, looks unruffled and handsome.

Toby smiles at Anna lovingly as she reaches him and lifts her veil, ignoring the trail of tears and mascara that cover her tiny face. 'You look beautiful,' he tells her, meaning it.

Afterwards, they walk out of the empty church and into the sunlight of a perfect spring afternoon. Anna looks up at her groom and smiles. They have finally made it.

Acknowledgements

First and foremost, I'd like to thank Amanda Ross for her friendship, encouragement and help with *RSVP* – I couldn't have done it without you!

Talking of friends ... thank you to the *London Tonight* girls: Rachel Bloomfield, Julia Dodd, Fiona Foster, Sofi Pasha, Yasmin Pasha, Clare Rewcastle, Stephanie Smith and Elke Tullett, for providing so much laughter (and inspiration!) over the past 18 years. Special mention too of Caron Keating and our 'honorary girlie' Stephen Gardner, who may be gone but will never be forgotten.

Grateful thanks to the brilliant Maxine Hitchcock and the whole team at Simon & Schuster for their excellent advice and suggestions for *RSVP*. It has been a pleasure from start to finish. Thanks also to my impossibly glamorous agent, Sheila Crowley and everyone at Curtis Brown.

Many thanks to Trinity College, Cambridge, for finally sending me an acceptance letter, 25 years after I got a rejection – shame it was just for research purposes!

Thank you Alex Bowley, Hanna Warren and all my friends and colleagues at Channel 4, which is possibly the best place in the world to work. And thank you to all the amazing producers who make my job such fun, particularly

David Sayer and the *Come Dine With Me* team, Glenn Hugill and the *Deal or No Deal* gang and Matt Walton and the *Coach Trip* crew. Thank you to Kevin Lygo and all the wonderful presenters I have worked with over the years – and those not-so-wonderful presenters who have at least helped me to lose weight through stress!

Finally, I would like to thank both the Duggan and Warner families for their love and support, especially my mum, Ann, and my mother-in-law, Daphne. And above all, extra special thanks go to my own gorgeous little family: Alice and Paddy, who are the best girl and boy ever, and Rob, who is my hero and makes everything possible. Love you!

If you enjoyed *The One That Got Away*, be sure to read more from Helen Warner . . .

With or Without You

What if everything you ever wanted was not enough?

Martha Lamont has it all: a passionate marriage, two well-adjusted children, a lovely home and a high-profile job as a showbiz interviewer for a major national newspaper. Her gorgeous husband, **Jamie**, is happy being a stay-at-home dad while she pursues her career.

But appearances are often deceiving. One day, Martha makes a discovery that rocks the very foundation of her world and she begins to question everything she thought she wanted.

Now, Martha must make the toughest decision of her life. Does she fight to keep the life she loves? Or are some betrayals just too big to forgive?

AVAILABLE NOW IN EBOOK

SIMON & SCHUSTER

Stay Close To Me

Amy enjoys a charmed life. That is until her husband's business collapses overnight, taking their house and savings with it. Will her marriage survive such an upheaval? Or is it a case of 'Till Debt Do Us Part'?

Kate has to juggle her job with two children and a husband, and wouldn't have it any other way. But her safe little world is rocked when she meets enigmatic Jack. Feeling increasingly estranged from husband Miles, Kate wonders if Jack can offer her a fresh start. But there's something about Jack that Kate doesn't know . . .

Jennifer is slowly recovering from the death of her husband. When she makes contact with old flame Hugh, she unlocks a dangerous Pandora's Box. She is desperate to find the answer to a question that has tormented her for decades. But will she be able to cope with the truth?

AVAILABLE NOW IN EBOOK

SIMON &
SCHUSTER